PROTECTING JUSTICE

JUSTICE TEAM SERIES

MISTY EVANS
ADRIENNE GIORDANO

ALG PUBLISHING

PROTECTING JUSTICE

As the premier political spin-doctor in the U.S., Fallyn Pasche can fix any problem--except her own. Her twin sister, Heather, a United States Senator, has been murdered, her father is barely speaking to her, and someone is after coded files Heather hid in a private safe. In order to decode the files and figure out what happened to her twin, Fallyn turns to the Justice Team. What she doesn't expect is the sexy bodyguard who shows up needing a little personal fixing of his own.

Tony Gerard sees failure every time he looks in the mirror. The former Supreme Court police officer lives with the knowledge that the Chief Justice—a man who was like a father to him—died on his watch. Now he's sure he can't protect anyone. When his first assignment for the Justice Team lands him in the media spotlight, working side-by-side with the country's foremost political fixer, Tony wants to run the other way. But Fallyn's devil-may-care attitude and tantalizing beauty bring out all of his protective instincts.

As Fallyn and Tony peel back the layers of a government scandal that threatens to bring down the most powerful man in the world, sparks fly along with the intoxicating danger. Desire and passion escalate with their perilous search for the truth as they find relief in each other's arms from their respective demons. When an unexpected enemy puts Fallyn's life on the line, Tony is forced to face his own failures in order to help her conquer hers. But will he once again fail to protect someone he loves?

To all those who keep us safe and protected.

1

The place smelled like Heather. Scents of lilac and vanilla. A cheap, but fragrant perfume her sister had loved since high school.

The doorbell rang for the twelfth time mixing with the drone of voices. People, food, a constant barrage of visitors. That's what happened when someone—particularly a United States senator—died. Friends and family gathered.

From her spot at the front window, Fallyn let her father have his moment greeting the newcomers in the foyer. All the while, out on the tiny front lawn, the press fought over a few feet of grass and badgered guests as they approached the front door.

Two hours earlier, Fallyn's plane had landed in DC and she'd gone into fixer mode, giving the press a statement, making sure her father had his meds, dealing with calls from the coroner and finding creative ways to fit the shitstorm of visitors into her sister's 900-squarefoot brownstone.

Jordan Lomax squeezed between Senator Morgan's staffer and a woman Fallyn didn't know. The young woman's Latino features were devoid of makeup, her hair in its normal braid. As Heather's trusted assistant and family friend, Jordan had been the one to find Heather's body. She'd also been the one to organize the casseroles and other food streaming through the door all morning.

"Fallyn," Jordan said, "there's someone who'd like to pay their respects to you personally."

All she wanted was for everyone to leave. To give her a moment to catch her breath and process.

The look on Jordan's face, though, told her it was someone important. Of course it was. Everyone in Washington had known Heather. "I'll be right there."

She took a moment to glance out the window. Damned press. After greeting whoever was looking for her, she'd have to deal with them. Call the cops or figure out some other way to clear them from the lawn. A lot of people in this town owed her favors. She needed to cash in and get rid of the vultures.

Staying close to the wall, she angled around an armchair and spotted a man in a black suit with an earpiece—Secret Service—waiting at the bottom of the steps.

Secret Service meant one thing. The president.

He must have come in the back way.

Taking a steadying breath, Fallyn entered the foyer. President Abraham Nicols was shaking her father's hand, Eric Pasche beaming as the packed house of visitors hovered close, listening in on the president's words.

"She'll be sorely missed," Nicols said to her father. Secret Service formed a circle around them, keeping the visitors at a respectful distance. "Her legacy won't be forgotten."

He'd been one of Heather's biggest fans.

Behind the president stood Ryan, the president's grown son, staring at her over his father's shoulder. His gaze connected with hers and froze for an instant.

She'd been getting looks like that since she'd been here—people struck by her identical appearance to her twin.

Ryan stood tall, broad shoulders filling out his Air Force dress uniform. The medals adorning his chest created an array of colors indicating they had a real-life hero in their presence.

He skirted his father and held out a hand. "You must be Fallyn."

She accepted his handshake and mustered a smile. He didn't know her, but she knew him. His father had asked for a favor concerning him not long ago. "And you're Ryan."

"Home for a few days leave and wanted to pay my respects." His sad smile seemed sincere. "My father thought a lot of your sister. I did too. She was a big supporter of the armed forces and everyone knew it. We're so sorry."

A lump formed in Fallyn's throat, as if she'd swallowed a peach pit, rough, and painful. "Thank you."

A pitiful, useless comment, but what else could he say?

The president moved over to them and reached out to embrace her. She flinched, then realized her faux pas. Abraham Nicols didn't go around offering hugs to just anyone and she'd have to suck it up or risk an embarrassing situation.

Reluctantly, she went into his embrace and gritted her teeth. She hated being touched, and she didn't have *that* kind of relationship with the president. If they'd been out in front of the reporters, she would have known it was nothing but a political move on his part. Knowing him, it still was.

But hugs were part of the process too. Everyone wanted to hug her right now.

"My condolences, Fallyn," Nicols said close to her ear. "Heather was special."

Fallen pushed aside the emotions his words stirred. The guilt. "Yes, she was."

If I'd only come to see her like I promised a hundred times. If I'd only picked up the phone.

The 'if onlys' were pointless, but their hovering presence, like the visitors hanging on every word by President Nicols, was a familiar weight. Fallyn had a lot of 'if onlys' in her past, especially where her identical twin was involved.

She tried to pull back, but Nicols wasn't done. "I'll be at the funeral. Send my office the details."

Jordan saved her, stepping up and offering the president and Ryan a drink. Always the hostess.

The two men begged off, and a moment later, hurried out the front door in a hail of goodbyes, the Secret Service clearing the way through the reporters.

That's what I need. A couple of big, burly guys to clear that lawn.

The media weren't going to be chased off, though. Just like the swamp of people inside Heather's house.

For a moment, Fallyn fought the urge to yell and tell them all to get out. Her heart hurt and her head was pounding. A part of her had been ripped away and she needed a moment—or maybe a billion moments—to figure out where she went from here.

Work the case. Stay focused.

It was her motto when Pasche & Associates' clients went spinning out of control. When you ran an elite consulting firm specializing in crisis management and media relations, every client—from the Bible-thumping politician coming out of the closet to the junkie actor returning to rehab—could make or break you. One wrong move and you could do irreparable damage to their careers, their lives, their families.

Jordan touched her back. "Can I get you something? A soda? Some green tea?"

From the time she was a kid and their mother had left them, Fallyn had been driven to fix other people's problems. She was good at it, too, the best. Her firm's multi-million dollar net income the past two years and its list of high profile clientele proved that.

Like her sister, power sped through her veins like a steam engine. Fallyn had even taken care of a few private messes the president had gotten caught in, making them disappear.

Talk about being in good with the most powerful man in the world. The paycheck had been sweet, but the fact the prez owed her a favor was even sweeter.

Yes, she was the best fixer in the country. Maybe even the world.

If only I could bring Heather back. "No, thanks, Jordan. I need to make some calls. I'm going upstairs."

Her father's voice cut through the room. "You're working at a time like this?"

Silence fell. All eyes swung her way.

Heather had been his golden child after their mother, Christina, had left him. With Heather gone—Fallyn still couldn't stomach the word *dead*—he'd taken to his bed and dumped all the funeral arrangements and other responsibilities on her. Carl and Jordan had managed to get him up and moving and over to Heather's place by the time Fallyn had arrived, but she hoped she wouldn't have to get him out of bed when the time came to bury his daughter.

"I need to make arrangements with the funeral home, the florist, and the caterer," Fallyn said, giving her father the stink eye. "You're welcome to help."

Dad turned up his nose, brushed past her on his way to the kitchen.

The front door opened—a guest leaving—and Fallyn heard a commotion on the lawn. She strode to the door and peeked out.

A fight had broken out between two of the cameramen. They traded insults along with fists, falling in a heap on the ground. Fallyn lost sight of them as the crowd closed in, ringside seats.

Oh my God. This is frickin' ridiculous.

Hustling upstairs to Heather's bedroom, she placed a call to an old college friend, Caroline Foster. Recently, Caroline had left her position with the FBI and now worked for Justice "Grey" Greystone.

Greystone ran a secret agency specializing in bringing certain criminals to justice. Specifically to people who thought they were above the law. One of Fallyn's clients had run afoul of Greystone's team last year, and after seeing the evidence on her client—and the confidence in the former FBI profiler's eyes—Fallyn had advised her client to get a lawyer rather than a spin doctor.

"Fallyn," Caroline said after she answered, "I'm so sorry about Heather. What can I do?"

This is what friends—real friends—did. They dropped everything to help. "The press is creating chaos on the lawn. Where do I get decent security guys in this town? Mean ones who aren't afraid to get their feathers ruffled?"

"Give me a few minutes and I'll have the best in the biz on your doorstep."

Had she been in New York, on her home turf, she'd have the situation rectified already. Here in DC things took longer. "Thank you. One more favor."

"Anything."

"Can I borrow your hacker? There are files on my sister's tablet I need help with."

"I'll see what I can do."

"Thank you. I owe you."

Fallyn disconnected, tossed her cell phone on the bed. Heather's bed. The one she'd died in.

Her breath became ragged, her vision tunneling to the intricate pattern of the comforter.

Five hours. It had only been five hours since Heather's body had been discovered.

The thought, mixed with the sensory overload, brought a flood of memories. Some good, a whole lot bad. She glanced around the bedroom. Small, conservatively decorated like the rest of the place, it drew Fallyn in. Her gaze landed on the framed 4x6 photo on her sister's nightstand. Fallyn's knees buckled and she lowered herself to the bed, her eyes still on that damned photo.

The two little girls, cheeks rosy from the heat of a summer day, stared back at her. Back then they were naive and blameless, Heather's curls tangled in the breeze with Fallyn's as they tipped their heads together. Arms around each other's necks, the girls in the picture seemed happy. The best of friends.

Identical twins, yet the two of them couldn't have been more opposite.

Heather was dressed in a cute sundress and matching sandals, Fallyn was barefoot. Her shorts and favorite ragged t-shirt were dirty and stained. In her eyes was the rebel already taking hold.

How could you leave me, sis?

A tear puddled at the corner of her eye and Fallyn brushed it away, setting the photo back on the nightstand. The doorbell downstairs rang again and her father's voice echoed over the din of the crowd downstairs.

I should go to him. Be by his side.

But Eric Pasche didn't want her comfort.

He wanted his favorite daughter back.

Jordan and her father, Carl, were by his side, sentries ready to do battle for him. They'd loved Heather too. Carl, Eric's longtime friend, and Jordan, personally knew everyone coming through the door. While Fallyn had built her career on fixing problems, this was one problem those two were better at.

Early indications were that Heather had suffered a myocardial infarction, but Fallyn's bullshit meter was pegged. What thirty-year-old woman in good health had a heart attack while sleeping? Sure, Heather had put on a few pounds since being elected to the Senate, but she was hardly overweight. She never smoked, rarely drank, and had never had so much as heartburn.

Maybe the stress got to her. Maybe if I'd been more supportive...if I hadn't moved to New York...

The words whispered through Fallyn's thoughts, an endless loop of guilt tormenting her. Her overactive brain circled back to those three little words. *It's my fault.*

She should have known Heather was stressed. Should have known she was on the verge of having a heart attack. They were twins, for God's sake.

Out on the lawn, the muffled sounds of arguing rose to the second floor. *Damn reporters.*

Part of her wanted to go off on the media for acting like children. A part of her—the fixer in her—wanted to walk out and use her skills to turn them into her allies. Give them the story they were chomping at the bit to run on the six o'clock news.

Heather Pasche: The Senate's 'It Girl.'

A strong proponent for women's healthcare and equal pay, Heather had also campaigned strongly for many of the economic issues American males held dear. She worked tirelessly on the Foreign Relations Subcommittee, and before that, the Ethics Committee, squaring off across the table from a couple of Fallyn's most elite clients.

Heather might have only been thirty, but she was going places, making a name for herself in the world of politics. Some said she'd be the first female president if Hillary didn't beat her to the West Wing.

Now, all that was gone. Heather wasn't going anywhere but into a box in the ground.

Enough.

Fallyn hopped off the bed, ran her hands over her forehead. None of this self-pity accomplished anything.

Work the problem. That's what she'd do. Tend to the details and give her sister the send-off she deserved. Starting with her appearance. Heather would want to be buried in something nice.

She strode to the closet, scanned the modest selection of her sister's suits. Dark blue, gunmetal grey, more blue. One black. Several skirts and a bevy of matching slacks. Two-inch heels in the same monotone colors.

How professional.

How boring.

Blouses offered a bit more color. Pink, purple, red. A dozen different white ones. Several black and blue. Fallyn was fingering a red blouse, holding the sleeve up to the gunmetal gray jacket, when she heard movement behind her.

"Thought I'd check on you," Jordan said, filling the closet doorway. She handed Fallyn a cup of tea and the scent of lemon drifted to her nose. "See if you needed help with anything for tonight. You're staying here, right? That's what your dad said."

The woman had been crying again, her red-rimmed eyes and the dark shadows under them a testament to her loyalty and devotion to Heather. While she might have landed the job with Heather because their fathers were friends, Jordan had proven to be a genuine ally.

"I was deciding on a suit," Fallyn said, kicking off her heels and sipping the tea. It was good. Refreshing. Just what she needed right now. "Maybe you can give me some direction. Which one was Heather's favorite?"

"The gray." Jordan reached down and lined Fallyn's Louboutins up alongside Heather's more conservative footwear. "She loved to wear the red blouse you were just looking at with it."

Well, at least there was something I had right. "I hate these suits. I want to remember her as the kid she was in that picture." Fallyn pointed to the framed photograph next to the bed.

Jordan studied the photograph. "That was her favorite photo. Maybe you should bury her with it."

Why hadn't she thought of that? "You're right. I should."

A soft silence engulfed them as they worked together to lay out Heather's burial clothes. Jordan attached a flag pin Heather always wore to the suit's lapel. Next came jewelry—a bracelet from Nepal, a pair of earrings from Brazil. Her sister had collected jewelry from every country she'd visited. Hose and shoes, and the outfit was complete.

Downstairs, she heard her father laugh. Carl's laughter joined his. It seemed disrespectful in a way, and yet, Fallyn knew Heather wouldn't want them moping. "How's your dad, Jordan?" Fallyn asked.

"He's not following the doctor's orders to slow down. He retired from State, but ends up 'consulting' all the time."

A text came in on Fallyn's phone from Caroline. Cavalry is on its way. His name is Tony Gerard. You'll like him.

One guy? That was it? The group of reporters outside would eat him alive.

Fallyn pocketed her cell phone and headed for the safe at the back of the closet. She wanted to finish up here and head downstairs for a front row seat when this Tony character arrived. "I was going to ask you about my sister's safe," she said to Jordan. "The funeral home said to bring the insurance papers and I..."

"Need the combination?" Jordan was always finishing her sentences. Had she done that with Heather too? "Sorry, I don't have it."

"Surprisingly, that is one thing she shared with me. It's not that.

When I was going through the items in the safe earlier looking for the insurance policy, I came across a computer tablet."

Fallyn retrieved it from the safe and held it up. "There's a passcode for the files. I tried a bunch of obvious ones, but none of them worked. Do you know it?"

Jordan stared at the tablet, reached out and touched the edge. "Funny, I never saw her use that. Are you sure it's hers?"

She'd asked her dad about it and he'd been clueless as well. "Who else's would it be? It was in her safe."

"It's just, she wasn't big on technology. A total throwback like my dad, but I could take it and try a few ideas with the passcode tonight after Dad goes to bed."

"Nah, don't worry about it. I'll figure something out."

They went downstairs and found the last of the crowd moving out the door. Carl helped Eric put his coat on. "Going to run your dad home," he said. "You need anything, call us."

Jordan reached to hug her and Fallyn automatically stepped back. "We'll talk tomorrow."

If the brush-off offended Jordan, she didn't show it. She knew Fallyn wasn't the touchy-feely type like Heather had been.

The woman stepped back, nodded. "I'd be glad to order the floral arrangements or line up the caterer if you need help."

While it was tempting, Fallyn needed to stay busy, keep her mind occupied. "I appreciate that. I can handle the flowers, but I'm not sure which caterer to use for the gathering at the church after the interment. Are you able to take care of that?"

Jordan's face lit up. "I'm on it. I'll get the one Heather liked."

No wonder Heather had hired Jordan as her assistant. She glanced between Carl and Jordan. "You two are welcome to ride with us to the funeral and the cemetery, if you like."

Carl nodded, all business. "Of course. Thank you. Let's go Eric. You've had a rough day."

They said their goodbyes, Fallyn accepting a brief hug from her father before the three of them tackled getting past the reporters. She withdrew, after a moment longer than she would have liked, and saw his face, the harsh lines, the sorrow. And now he had to deal with another crowd.

Those damned reporters. What she didn't need was Dad more upset. Time for a diversion. It was, after all, what she'd built her business on —statements that said a whole lot of nothing, but kept the reporters occupied while people slipped away.

"Hang on, Dad. Let me distract the reporters so you can get to the car." Throwing her shoulders back, she marched out the front door, headed down the sidewalk to give the media what they wanted—and maybe the full Fallyn Pasche brow-beating they deserved—when a big guy in a dark trench coat, wearing mirrored aviators and looking like a one-man army, emerged from the alley and every person on the lawn came to attention.

Well, hello, big boy.

Fallyn's pulse did a funny *thudthud* under her skin as she watched him close in on the reporters. A cameraman made a move toward her dad but the hunk in the aviators beelined, blocking his path and sticking his hand over the man's camera lens.

A female reporter next to him was courteously forced back several steps.

Fallyn returned to the house, where she watched, fascinated.

In under a minute, the hunk had every last one of the media backing away, herding them to the curb, several of them running for their news vans as fast as their footsteps would carry them.

Damn. Who was this guy?

After dealing with the press tearing up Senator Pasche's lawn, Tony rang the bell. Grey had called him less than an hour ago, told him to hot-foot it over to the Senator's place and bust up the collection of reporters turning the woman's death into public fodder.

The door opened and a woman answered.

It might as well have been Heather Pasche standing there. He'd known Heather. Not well, but he'd met her a couple of times when she'd interacted with the chief justice, and Tony, being assigned to the chief's protection detail at the time, had accompanied him.

Now, the good senator, as well as the chief, was gone and that same burn, that reminder of his failure, crawled up his throat like acid.

Don't go there.

He bit down, focused on the woman's high heels, her long legs, any goddamn thing that would take his mind off the chief. Any goddamn thing that would keep the panic, the absolute burning from inside out, at bay.

"Hello," she said, waving him in. "If I thought it was appropriate, I'd kiss you for chasing off those reporters."

"Appropriate?" he shot. "Who cares about that?"

He flashed a smile, a rarity these days, and entered the foyer, glancing at the immaculately tidy living room of the late Senator Heather Pasche.

"I'm Fallyn." She held her hand out. "You must be Tony Gerard. Caroline told me you'd be here."

He shook her hand, a brief clasp before letting go.

Her resemblance to her now deceased sister unnerved him. "Uh, Grey wanted me to let you know Teeg is on his way."

"Teeg?"

"Yeah. He's the Justice Team's techie nerd. Grey said something about a tablet you needed help with."

"Oh, that's great. Thank you."

Tony shrugged. "Don't thank me. I'm the messenger. As far as the press, I'll keep an eye on them, but I gave them the spiel about private property and they backed off. The cops at the corner helped."

"There are cops at the corner?"

"As of ten minutes ago, yeah."

Looking at this woman would never be torture. Her deep green eyes had a depth to them. Intense yet bright. Playful. Her light brown hair had lighter streaks and it accentuated her eyes, bringing out the green. Something told him she knew that. Knew that people, men particularly, would be drawn to them.

And the way she stared at him? The scrutiny. Hell, he could see the gears shifting. Like Grey, the Justice Team's leader, she didn't just look at you, she analyzed, mentally peeling back layers and figuring out how to extract what she needed. *Goddamn headshrinker.*

Last thing he needed now was a psychological exam. What she found inside his head would scare the crap out of her. Send her screaming from the fuckup and wondering why Grey even trusted him.

"So you work with Caroline?" she asked.

Small talk. Great. "Um...Sort of."

Three weeks ago Grey had approached him about full-time employment that entailed...well...whatever the hell they did in search of justice. At the time, it'd been a lifeline. A reason to leave the Supreme Court Police because without the chief, the man who'd been a father figure to Tony, the job was torment. Flat out horrendous. A daily bloodbath into the reminders of his failings.

But, of course, Tony's boss at the Court, fearing the resignation had been a rash decision, one born of grief over the loss of the chief justice—ya think?—wouldn't let him quit. Something Tony couldn't rationalize since they should have strung him up for blowing his assignment. His sole job that morning had been to keep the chief safe. Instead, the man bled out on a bridge.

All that crap about it not being Tony's fault? Who believed that?

Definitely not him. He'd lost control of the situation on the bridge, of the *chief*, and now the man was dead.

Period.

His boss though? He'd flat out refused his resignation. Made the argument that the chief's death was too fresh to make such a radical decision.

Instead, they'd reached a compromise. Tony would take his three weeks banked vacation, go to an island, get some rest, get laid, and at the end of that time, if he still wanted to resign, they'd throw him a great going away party.

Except Tony hated the beach and he hated being idle. The getting laid part he could live with. That was a plan he could get behind, but that first night, sitting alone in his apartment, even picking up the phone to call a woman was too much work. Even if female company could fill the void, she'd eventually have to leave and he'd be alone again.

Boredom and his own looping thoughts terrorized him. Sleeping didn't help. Between the dreams and his hyperactive brain, he'd relived the judge's death a thousand times.

By the third day of his vacation, he'd called Grey and damned near begged him for a temporary assignment until he figured out what the hell to do with his life.

And how to stay sane.

Justice Greystone to the rescue.

"Sort of?" Fallyn teased. "You don't sound too sure about that. You work for Mr. Greystone in what capacity?"

Still probing. But Tony had already diverted his eyes away from her and her analysis. *Nothing doing, lady.* He walked to the window, checked his peeps on the lawn. All good out there.

A cab pulled up and out hopped Teeg, the Justice Team's wunderkind of hackers.

Saved by Geek Boy.

He strode to the door. "Teeg is here. Mind if I let him in?"

"By all means. I'll get the tablet."

Three minutes later, introductions and the uber-polite can-I-get-you-anything formalities were complete and Teeg plugged the tablet into his computer.

"This'll take me a couple minutes," he said.

Fallyn's gaze came back to Tony. *More studying. Great.*

"So, Mr. Gerard, how long have you worked for Grey?"

Yeah. She wasn't gonna give up. He'd have to deal with her straight away. Tony looked back at her, made direct eye contact. "Not long. For the last five years I've been on a protection detail for the Supreme Court."

"You work for Grey *and* you're a bodyguard at the Court?"

Tony shrugged. He hated that term. But hell, if she'd shut up about his life, he'd let her call him anything she liked. "Yes, ma'am.

Consider me a contractor for the Justice Team." He smiled. "Moon-lighting. Caroline was worried about your...situation." He went back to Teeg who clicked a file, apparently making progress. "What have you got?"

"Not sure."

He typed in a passcode and the lock screen morphed into a back-ground of colors with a set of file folders lined up along the bottom.

"Neat and orderly," Fallyn said. "Just like Heather. Can I take a look?"

Teeg turned the tablet toward her and she scrolled through a couple of folders, brought up two images of what looked like receipts.

Then she hit a folder with multiple files. She clicked one. A spreadsheet with columns appeared.

"I'm not sure what this is." She angled the tablet back to Teeg. "It looks like dates and times, but this other column is a jumbled mess of letters, numbers, and special characters. Almost like passwords."

"Yeah," Teeg said. "But some have spaces in weird intervals, like a list of names, but the groupings don't make sense."

Tony had seen stuff like this. Classified documents. Hell, based on what Grey had told him, Fallyn probably dealt with shit like this on a daily basis. This was a woman who manipulated sensitive informa-tion for a living. Made it go her way.

Spin-doctor.

A job she was damned good at, from what he'd been able to find from his phone on the drive over.

She looked over Teeg's shoulder. "You can't figure it out?"

"I can figure out anything, just not in five minutes. The files are all coded with something I haven't seen before and I don't have a legend. It'll take me some time. Couple days maybe." He looked up at her. "I could take it with me."

"No," Fallyn said. "Absolutely not."

In the weeks since Tony had met Teeg, he'd learned a few things. The first being that Teeg had zero interpersonal skills. A nice kid, but there was a reason he sat huddled behind a computer all day. He simply did not want to deal with the bullshit that came with talking to people. Give him a computer, a keyboard, and some action figures and Teeg was a happy guy. Which was no doubt why Teeg swung back to him with that *help-me* stare.

Hell. Teeg wanted no part of this. Tony went back to Fallyn. "Ma'am—"

"Jesus," she said, "will the two of you stop calling me ma'am? I can't stand that."

Tony nodded. "Of course. Sorry. *Ms. Pasche—*"

She held up her hands. "Fallyn. Please."

"Okay. Fallyn, Teeg is good. The best in DC, but we're not talking about the Romper Room of hacking here. This tablet was locked in your sister's safe and my guess is a United States senator doesn't do that unless the device contains classified information. And classified information is hard to decode."

Fallyn rolled her eyes. "I get that. Believe me, I'm not stupid about classified government documents."

And, whoa, sister. What was up with the attitude? Forgive him for trying to be helpful.

Whatever. He'd cut her some slack. He understood the grief and irritability that came with the loss of a loved one. "Never said you were. Just not sure what you expect him to do in ten minutes. Because, no offense, if he could decode a senator's passcoded files that quickly, I want to move to Neverland and drink beer all day. At least there I'll be safe from terrorists who can hack our government's top secret files in three-point-five seconds."

Fallyn's head snapped up and those sharp eyes nearly took him apart. *Eeee-doggies.* Yeah, he'd been rude. Would probably get his butt chewed out for it, but miracle workers they weren't.

"Fine."

The word fine should have been obliterated from the English language. Fine never meant fine and it sure as fuck didn't mean fine right now.

Teeg swiveled his head to Fallyn then to Tony, eyes wide with panic. Clearly, the kid hated conflict.

Tony let out a mental sigh. If they were gonna get this tablet into

Teeg's possession, Tony would have to be the one to do it. A job he didn't much mind because he was stubborn enough to wear Fallyn down, to convince her to let them take the tablet.

Unlike Teeg, Tony wasn't afraid of conflict. He, in fact, thrived on it, hungered for it. Fallyn Pasche, he was quickly figuring out, would be a worthy opponent.

He faced her, met her gaze head on. "Fine what?"

"Fine you should move to Neverland because you are not taking this tablet anywhere."

Nice.

She grinned at him and that grin ignited a fire that got his junior brain—the one in his crotch—ready for all kinds of action.

Hello, Fallyn Pasche.

"Oh, crap," Teeg said.

Tony set his hand on the kid's shoulder, gave it a pat. "Take a break. Go have a smoke or something."

"I don't smoke."

"Then go outside and breathe. Give your lungs a treat so Fallyn and I can talk a minute."

The kid stared up at him with some kind of weird hero worship and Tony snorted again. Total pisser, this kid.

Teeg leaped from his chair and headed for the front door, closing it gently behind him. All the while, Fallyn kept her eyes on Tony, still analyzing.

Chess.

The two of them on opposite sides strategically maneuvering, trying to capture the other's king. And anything else that got in their way.

For him, checkmate meant walking out with that tablet.

Damned if it wasn't twisted, but for the first time in five weeks, he got off on the anticipation. The battle.

Time to get to work.

But Fallyn wouldn't be easy. He saw it in her rigid stance. Add to that the sharp curve of her cheekbones in contrast to her full, sexy lips and he might be done for. All that intensity mixed with feminine softness might just knock him to his knees. Again, something she was more than likely acutely aware of.

A burst of adrenalin roared into his brain and he breathed in. Enjoyed the high. Sick. That's what he was.

Oh.

Well.

"Talk to me," he said.

Her head dipped forward. "Talk to you?"

"Yep."

She laughed. "About what?"

"About why you don't trust us to take this tablet."

2

Tony Gerard was good. Really good. Alluring, focused eyes, wide shoulders, an almost military stance. A man who knew how to control a situation, as he'd proved by corralling the media.

He inched closer to her, crowding her a tad too much. "You know what the Justice Team does, right?"

"I...well...yes..."

She'd scanned the files on that tablet, finding nothing seemingly important at first. Receipts from a bed and breakfast in Virginia, a restaurant in the same town, and some ethics mumbo jumbo about previous cases the Supreme Court had ruled on involving military personnel.

After what she'd seen clients store on tablets, her sister's inventory was downright boring. One client was keeping a detailed diary of his multiple affairs on a tablet when he died. The diary, discovered when the tablet was retrieved from a secret safe deposit box, devastated his wife and three kids.

"I understand your apprehension," Tony said, "but you asked for help with the password and we came through. Decoding these files requires a little more time, but Teeg can do it, and anything on here is safe with the Justice Team. This is the team that exposed a crooked Attorney General and solved the murder of the Supreme Court Chief Justice. Grey has the highest security clearance possible."

"Heather wasn't just a senator. She's—she *was*—my sister."

"Even more reason to figure out why the tablet was in her safe."

"But..."

"What?"

Something about this code and the fact her sister had stored the tablet in the safe made the red flags in Fallyn's brain snap to attention. This was top-secret stuff, she'd bet her Louboutins on it.

But was it a diary or classified documents?

Her brain spun. She'd dealt with actors, playboys, spies, military leaders, political pundits, and even a few holy rollers over the years. Everybody had a secret. Everybody had something to hide.

Could Heather, her squeaky-clean sister and possible future president of the United States, have been hiding something too?

Never in a million years. Heather didn't keep secrets and if she'd ever made a mistake in her entirely perfect life, she would have shown it to the whole world. Thrown herself on her own sword.

So what's with the coded files? The secrecy?

Jordan hadn't even known about the tablet.

Could Heather have been a spy?

The thought made Fallyn chuckle and rub her eyes. She needed less tea and more vodka. A good night's sleep wouldn't hurt either.

A diary would give her insight into her sister's world, though. Maybe even insight into why the two of them had never acted like twins.

It could also be damning if it exposed some deep, dark secret, or classified information that should have never left the office.

She pressed her lips together before huffing out a breath. "Okay, look. Like you said, the fact that it was in her safe leads me to wonder why. I know my sister. She's the goody-two-shoes, always doing everything right. Everyone loved her."

"And?"

"And what's on that tablet could be bad. She's not here to explain it and that's not fair to her. My job right now is to protect her."

"You're worried you'll destroy her reputation by letting Teeg decode the information? You saw the kid. It's not like he's going to go on social media and broadcast it to the world."

"It's not that. It's just..." She paused to collect her thoughts. "I spend fourteen hours a day watching a morsel of information snowball and wreck people. I'm good at controlling a story, but I don't know what I'm controlling here and, frankly, I'm emotionally invested. I'm grieving. It's not a good combination. For all I know, this could be Heather's journal. Something extremely personal. So, the answer is no. Teeg is not taking that tablet. I need him to decode it, with me and only me present, so I can figure out what I'm dealing with. If it's bad, I'll figure out how to handle it. My sister's secrets will *not* be for public consumption."

There. If he didn't understand *that*, they had bigger problems than this tablet.

"I don't blame you for wanting privacy. I'd want the same. But if you want Teeg, he'll have to take the tablet."

Fallyn massaged her temples with shaky fingers. She needed someone to decode that file, ASAP. But with Dani, her tech girl in New York, and the potential shitstorm the tablet could unleash if it fell into the wrong hands, Fallyn's options were limited.

Work the case. Heather is no longer my sister. She's now a client. I have to figure out what's on this tablet and prepare for damage control.

"I have someone on my staff who can help me. She's in New York. I'll just take the tablet to New York and have her do it."

"Not advisable. Teeg is here. He's up to speed. Grey is up to speed." He stepped closer, touched her arm, let his fingers rest there. "Trust us. Please. We won't hurt you. Or your sister."

She glanced down and slowly drew away. "I'm sorry. I can't risk it."

He'd touched her.

A complete, overbearing, lughead of a stranger had touched her.

Sliding over to the front window, she brushed aside the lace curtain and watched him hail a cab.

Forget the fact fireworks had gone off when he'd rested his hand on her arm. Little pulses from her head to her toes went zinging through her body like she'd grabbed a live wire with her bare hands. Honest to God, she'd felt her ovaries damn near explode.

Tony Gerard was a no-go. A nonstarter.

Except from the moment he'd showed up on the front lawn, Fallyn had known she was in trouble. A woman would have to be dead not to feel that man's magnetism.

Captivated. That's what she'd felt. Drawn to him like no one she'd ever encountered.

At the curb, he hustled the tech geek into the backseat of the cab, said something to the driver, and shut the door.

Standing on the sidewalk in front of the brownstone, Gerard watched the cab drive off. He was tall, the streetlight spotlighting his dark hair. Dark hair, Fallyn noticed, that curled right behind his ears. Her fingers itched to touch those curls.

Sticking his hands in his coat pockets, he dipped his head and started walking. Was he parked nearby or did he live in walking distance of Heather's place?

Fallyn had to shift closer to the window and push the curtain farther aside to keep him in sight, his big strides eating up the sidewalk.

Don't look back. He'd catch her gawking if he did.

He moved with an uncanny grace for such a big guy. No, not grace. That was too feminine of a word for him. Finesse? Still not right. Fallyn wracked her brain. *Stealthiness.* That was closer.

At the corner of the block, he slowed, checking traffic before he crossed to the other side of the street. The lights of a dark SUV—an Explorer maybe—parked in a "no parking" zone flashed and then he paused at the driver's door.

Don't look back...don't look...

His chin came up. He glanced over his shoulder and...

Bam. Right. At. Her.

Fallyn jumped back, letting the curtain fall. *Dammit.*

She rubbed her arms, letting her fingers linger on the spot where he'd touched her. Scooting away from the window, she laughed at herself. *Too much stress.* Her brain and her emotions were on overload. That was the only explanation for the way he'd affected her. Pissing her off and making her horny all at the same time.

Heather had always been the affectionate one, hugging everyone, touching him or her on the arm or patting his or her back. While Fallyn loved social situations like parties, she never felt comfortable with any contact beyond a handshake. She used body language and words to convey intimacy, never a hug. It wasn't her style.

There was no underlying reason why she didn't like being touched. She'd never been hit or sexually molested—unless you counted the ass grabs Joey Polawski swiped whenever he passed her at the steam table at her father's restaurant. She'd worked there all through high school, chained to that damn steam table while Heather glided around out front as hostess, laughing and hugging the regulars and making damn healthy tips. Fallyn had begged her father to let her waitress. She'd been good with people even back then and Joey had been asking for a fat lip. Plus, she needed the tips, just like her twin, for college.

It wasn't until one of the normal waitresses ran away with a biker that Fallyn got her chance. She didn't ask her dad if she could work Tiffany's tables that night. She simply lifted Tiffany's apron from the back room, dug out the woman's order pad, and went to work, flipping off Joey on her way out of the kitchen. By the end of the night, she'd amassed more tips than anyone, including the tip jar at the hostess station.

Bonus, no one had grabbed her ass.

Back in Heather's small kitchen, she stared at the tablet on the table. If she hadn't needed to be at the top of her game tomorrow, she would jump in her car and drive to New York and put Dani, her tech guru, to work.

But dealing with the funeral preparations, her father, Heather's myriad of friends and political counterparts, as well as the press,

Fallyn needed to be rested and at her best come morning. After the funeral, she'd go home. Her home. Back to New York and Pasche & Associates. She had six open cases on her desk alone, never mind the dozens on Tabitha's and Niles's desks. Six clients who needed her there, personally managing their crises with her flare and expertise.

Dani she could trust to work on the tablet. The whole P&A team handled secret and damning information all the time. David Teeg and Tony Gerard? Well, no matter what Caroline said, no matter how much she vouched for the Justice Team members, Fallyn didn't trust anyone she hadn't vetted, and even out of those she did vet, she trusted few.

Upstairs, she drew a bath, and while the tub filled, she placed the tablet back in Heather's closet safe. She hoped she didn't end up blindsided tomorrow by whatever was in those coded files, but there was nothing more she could accomplish with it tonight.

After stripping down, she sank into the big clawfoot tub and rested her head on the edge. The warm water and bubbles loosened her tight muscles and she sighed. On the wall, an antique clock ticked off the seconds. *Tick-tick-tick.*

She didn't try to shut down her brain—a useless exercise—but let it meander where it wanted. Heather, the funeral, their father, the tablet...her mental list of to-dos grew with every item. The day's events spun in ever tightening circles until her brain landed on the last thing she wanted to think about.

Tony Gerard.

She preferred intellectuals. Men who engaged her brain and kept up with her quick wit and preponderance for logic. Not meatheads whose brain was smaller than their dick.

Professors, scientists, doctors and lawyers were all in her collection of past relationships. They'd provided mental stimulation even if they had, at times, left her lukewarm and indifferent in bed.

Intellectuals were safe bets. They were too wrapped up in their latest case, research, or discovery to want to dig into her psyche and figure out what made her tick. That was the way she liked it. She didn't need a soul mate. In fact, she wasn't sure she needed a man at all these days.

The more prominent and famous she grew with her business, the less time she had for anything else. She barely had time for a lunch date with friends once a month, much less a romantic relationship.

The men in her life wanted to cling to her or compete with her, those big brains accompanied by big egos. They tended to be too needy and demanding of her time and they were always trying to prove they were her equal. She often felt like she had an invisible dick between her legs they were constantly comparing theirs to.

Maybe that's why the bodyguard's touch, his very *maleness*, had affected her so much. She hadn't been touched by a lover in months. Hadn't been sexually satisfied in forever. Just thinking about Gerard and his long, muscular legs, broad shoulders, deep voice...

The way he'd dealt with those reporters.

Hot.

Hot.

Hot.

Fallyn shivered in the warm water. *And those hands.* Big, strong hands that could probably make her a very happy woman.

Damn. She glanced down, and yep, poking up through the bubbles, her nipples stood at full attention. The tightening in her lower belly confirmed her ovaries were once again awake too.

"Well, girls, this isn't the time or the place, so settle yourselves back down," she told them. "There is no Tony Gerard in your future."

Once she dried off and put on her nightgown, she slipped into Heather's bed. Her twin had a boatload of vitamins and supplements in her medicine cabinet, but nothing other than melatonin to help Fallyn asleep.

For half a second, Fallyn considered downing one of the natural supplements in order to help shut off her brain, but she knew better. She'd tried way harder stuff than that...sleeping pills, vodka, you name it. Nothing worked at calming her mind and they all left her hung over the next day. Not acceptable. She had to be on her game one hundred and ten percent all the time.

She pulled the framed photograph off the nightstand and hugged it to her chest. "I miss you, sis," she said as she closed her eyes.

The muffled sounds of traffic drifted through the window, lulling her along with the soft lilac and vanilla scent drifting up from the sheets. The bathroom clock ticked along, counting the seconds, the minutes, of her new life without her sister. The picture frame weighed heavy on her chest.

"You may not have always liked me much—and I know I never said it out loud—but I loved you fiercely," she whispered to the shadows.

3

Sometime later, Fallyn woke with a start, heart racing. She'd actually fallen asleep.

A noise—a soft rustle—came from downstairs, so faint, she wasn't sure she'd heard anything. Maybe she was confusing it with the traffic noise outside.

She rubbed her eyes and tried to blink away the fog in her brain. The clock read 2 a.m. Maybe she'd been dreaming. Imagined the noise.

She was about to get up and hit the bathroom to pee when she heard it again—the rustle. A stair tread groaned.

Shit! Someone was in the house, coming up the stairs.

Fallyn flew off the bed, a crash sounding at her feet. Pins and needles stabbed her big toe and ankle.

The picture frame. She'd fallen asleep with it, then sent it crashing to the floor.

At the noise, she froze, and so did whoever was coming up the stairs. Silence hung in the air, thick and suffocating. Not even a hint of traffic noise drifted up from the street.

Tick-tick-tick. Fallyn's heart thumped to the beat of the bathroom clock as she strained her ears toward the hall.

Reaching out, she felt for the nightstand. Where was her cell phone? Her fingers found a book Heather had been reading, the TV remote, the lamp.

No phone.

She'd left it downstairs.

Fight or flight?

Flight meant going out the second story window and down the fire escape. Smart, but no way she was running away.

Find a weapon.

The lamp. The base was fat, making the lamp heavy to hold, but it was all she had. She ripped the cord from the wall socket.

"Whoever you are, you better be prepared for a fight," she yelled as she wound the cord around the lamp base so it didn't trip her. Her voice sounded strong and sure even though she was shaking. "I'm armed and—"

She was in mid-turn, mid-sentence, when something struck the back of her head. She pitched forward, stepping in the broken glass, her body slamming into the chest of drawers and then ricocheting backward.

From the corner of her eye, she caught sight of a shadowy figure right before a fist connected with her ribs. Off balance, she still managed to throw the lamp and heard a grunt when it glanced off his body as she fell sideways.

Her triumph was short-lived. In the next second, he slammed the side of her head into the nightstand. Pain exploded behind her right ear and a buzzing filled her ears.

Then everything went black.

When she woke, the room had lightened. She was lying on the floor, broken glass scattered around her. The room spun as she pushed upright and she had to cling to the edge of the nightstand until her vision cleared.

Her tongue felt thick, her body moving in slow motion as she shifted her position. The drawers of the dresser had been yanked out, the contents sent flying. The closet door was open, her sister's conservative suits lying helter-skelter on the floor.

The safe.

Forcing herself up onto the bed, she focused on breathing and not passing out. She rubbed the back of her neck and concentrated on that damn ticking clock just so she wouldn't cry. After a minute, she felt strong enough to make her way to the closet.

Someone had tried to move the safe, she could see from the indentions in the carpeting now showing. But the steel fire safe weighed over three hundred pounds. It would take the Hulk or a small army to move it.

She was pretty sure there had only been one man.

One man who'd been searching for something.

Was he a common thief who'd heard about Heather's death and expected the place to be empty? Or was he someone far more sinister? Someone who wanted what was in that safe?

It took too long to get downstairs because she had to sit on her butt and scoot down each step one by one, but her stomach was rolling and her right eye refused to focus.

She didn't need 20/20 vision to see the mess the intruder had left in the living room. He'd been thorough after knocking her out, upending furniture, removing the pictures from the walls. The books on the bookcase—a collection of history and political biographies—lay scattered over the floor. Her sister's meager DVD collection of romantic comedies had joined them.

At least the front door was shut. Fallyn stumbled over and sent the deadbolt home. The locks still worked; the burglar hadn't damaged them. He'd disabled the security system—or had he? She couldn't remember if she'd set it before she'd gone to bed.

Leaning her forehead against the doorframe, she punched in the code.

By the time she made it to the kitchen and her cell phone, she was sweating, her hands shaking so badly she could barely hold the phone.

She had to call the police. Settling into a chair, she started to dial 9-1-1. That's when her eyes landed on the business card lying on the table.

Tony Gerard. He'd left it there "in case."

She rubbed her finger over the raised lettering. Whatever was going on with her sister and the tablet, Fallyn knew she was going to need professional help. The police had to be notified about the break-in, but she doubted there was much they could do for her except file reports and offer useless platitudes. She'd bet money on the fact the intruder had left no fingerprints, no DNA. And she certainly couldn't share her suspicions about the tablet with them.

It took three tries for her to dial the number correctly. When she finally heard Gerard's deep, powerful voice on the other end, she nearly wept with relief. Her head was pounding, her pulse racing. When she found her voice, it came out ragged and garbled.

She cleared her throat and tried again. "Mr. Gerard?"

"Who is this?"

"I know it's too early to be calling, but I have a situation—"

"Fallyn?"

He recognized her voice. "Yes, it's me. I..."

She heard bedsprings groan, and in her mind, she saw him sitting up. "Are you okay?"

No, she wasn't okay. She was scared, really scared.

Control. She just needed to exert some control. *Work the case.* "I think I may need your services."

She heard running water on his end. "What happened?"

"I'll explain when you get here."

There was a slight, telling pause. "I'll be there in ten. Are you safe?"

Was she? "I'll be fine until you arrive," she said, eyeing a set of butcher knives on the counter across the room. She didn't expect the intruder to come back so soon, even though it appeared he hadn't found what he was looking for. "But I could use some coffee. As strong and as black as you can get it."

"Coffee, huh? Okay, coffee is doable." Was that laughter lacing his voice? "Hang tight."

Coffee wasn't the only thing that was doable, Fallyn decided as she disconnected and stumbled to the counter to arm herself.

Any man who looked like Tony Gerard and would come running with coffee in hand at five in the morning was definitely going on her doable list.

Tony knocked on Heather Pasche's front door, a giant black coffee from his favorite Dunkin' Donuts at the ready. Yeah, he had a thing for donuts and coffee and the guys at the Court Police would rib him endlessly with cops and donuts jokes. He didn't have the fat gut though. Never would. He logged rigorous hours in the gym, damned near killing himself pumping loads most men couldn't budge. It wasn't about ego or being a gym lug. For him, the screaming endorphin release quieted the endless chatter in his brain, the obsessing over what was expected of him and what he should do, or be, or hope for. All those emotions—those fucking little bastards—buried inside him, picking at him. Waiting...

Forget it.

He knocked on the senator's door a second time and waited. Around him, the April morning mist gave off an eerie vibe and he glanced down the quiet street where DC traffic had yet to fully explode. He loved this time of day. Darkness hadn't surrendered and the chill in the air was enough to bring back thoughts of his father and their early morning fishing trips. They'd put on their gear and hats and hop into Dad's battered outboard fishing boat for a few hours. Always in the morning before Dad left for work and Tony for school.

At ten, he never minded getting up at oh-dark-hundred for fishing. School, yes. Fishing, no.

Footsteps from inside the house sounded and he turned back, waiting for Fallyn to let him in. *She'd better check that door before opening it.*

From the corner of his eye he spotted the curtain in the front window sway. *Good girl.*

"It's me," he said. "Tony."

Just in case she didn't recognize the guy on the doorstep who'd promised her strong coffee.

Numbnuts.

The door came open, but she stood behind it, peeping at him.

Hiding.

And, yeah, his shit-meter went bee-zerk. Still holding the coffee, he slid into the door opening and shut the door behind him. "You okay?"

"Yep. You bet. Good morning and all that."

Nothing in her voice made a believer out of him. The second he was clear of the door, she threw the bolt, her hands visibly trembling and—yeah—something had her rattled.

"Fallyn, what's wrong?"

She flipped the hallway light, illuminating the interior of the townhouse.

What the hell?

The sunken living room, the space that less than 24 hours ago had nearly given him hives with its neatness, was trashed. Whoever had ripped through there did it with gusto.

Cushions tossed, tables upended, photos knocked from walls. And the bookcase? That bastard had been cleared, its contents splashed across the gleaming hardwood floors. Books, DVDs, a few CDs, all of it merging into one hell of a mess.

He set the coffee on the foyer side table and whipped back to her. "Who did this?"

"I don't know. Someone broke in. A man."

"Did you see him?"

She shook her head. "Not really. Just shadows."

"What time was this?"

"Two-ish. I took a bath, fell asleep, and woke up to someone coming up the stairs."

Pig that he was, a vision of Fallyn, her perfect rack and trim hips lounging bare-assed in a tub shattered his mind. *Focus here, dummy.*

He stepped closer and she immediately inched back, reclaiming her personal space. She'd done that yesterday when he'd touched her, the whole thing a clear indication she did not like to be touched. Add that to his Fallyn checklist.

"Tell me what happened."

She pointed up the stairs. "The creaking stairs woke me up. He came up to the bedroom."

"Did you call 911?"

Slowly, she shook her head. "I left my phone downstairs to charge and Heather didn't keep a house phone in her bedroom. I grabbed the lamp so I'd have some kind of weapon."

Damned fool woman. He admired her spunk, but if the intruder were armed, she'd be riddled with bullet holes. And that would have left both twin sisters dead within 24 hours.

He shook his head, but bit down and forced himself to keep his trap shut. Any comment he'd make, most likely, wouldn't be a welcome one.

"Hey," she said, obviously cluing in to his disapproval. "I had to do something. I wasn't going to lay there and let some thief rob my sister's home."

"You could have gotten hurt."

She stared at him for a long second, but he'd be damned if he could read anything in her stony cheeks. She glanced away, took in the wall, the bannister, the steps before her gaze landed on the floor. Whatever caught her eye must have been fascinating because she stayed focused on it.

"Fallyn?"

"Yes?"

"Look at me."

Finally, she looked up and—*ah, dammit.*

Please, God, don't let him have...

His neck muscles coiled and locked. "Did he hurt you?"

"It's not bad."

"Crap."

She lifted her t-shirt revealing the start of a nasty blackish bruise.

Tony gawked, brought his hands up, and gently touched the undamaged skin around it. "Mother fucker. He hit you?"

When she drew back, he dropped his hands. "It's worse than it looks. I got one good lick in with the lamp before..."

If the bruise were the worst of it, they'd gotten lucky. Really lucky. "What happened? He didn't—" Tony waved one hand.

"Rape me? God no."

The tension in his neck blew apart and he ran one hand over his face, exhaled a couple of times to get his head straight.

"He slammed my head against the nightstand. Pow! Lights out. I didn't wake up until just a bit ago."

"Jesus!" Screw not touching her. She'd just gotten her ass kicked and he wasn't supposed to touch her? The guy could have killed her.

He closed in, put both hands on her head and gently turned her so he could take a look. She flinched and—bam—he let go. That fast. She didn't like his hands on her. Was it him or any man in general?

"It's a lump," she said. "That's all."

"Any double vision?"

"No."

"You sure? We should get it checked. Might be a concussion."

"No. I'm fine. It just...hurts. And I don't have time for that. My sister's funeral...my dad...I have things to do. I'm not letting this jerk get the best of me. Not when I intend to give my sister the service she deserves." She waved her arms. "I don't know who he is or what he wants, but the filth that did this will not take that from her. No way."

The woman had balls, an admirable sense of strength that wouldn't let her be pushed around. A scrapper.

He'd always been a fan of scrappy women. Ones who knew their power and how to get what they wanted, whatever that might be.

"I get that," he said. "But do you wanna crash in the middle of that service? You can make it perfect, but if you fall over, you'll be miserable."

She hesitated, just stood there staring at him like he was the antichrist. It'd be a miracle if she didn't toss him out on his ass. "I'm not going to the hospital."

"Didn't say you had to. I'll get someone to come here. While you're getting checked, we get crime scene techs in here to process the place. Multitasking."

She rolled her eyes and snickered. "My God, you're a pain in the ass, but I like it. Multitasking."

Another snicker.

Oh, honey. She didn't have a clue how true that 'pain-in-the-ass' label was.

He held out his hands. "I won't touch you. Just let me look at that bump again."

She dipped her head, let out a sigh. "Be gentle with me, big boy."

At that, he grunted. "Smartass."

"Can't help it. Just so you know, you startled me before, that's all. It's not that I'm afraid of you."

So, all right. Allowed to touch her. Progress made in less than three minutes. He ran his thumb gently over the spot, itching to drop a kiss there.

Uh, okay, *that* was weird. Since when did he want to kiss random Justice Team clients? This client though, something about her tugged at him. Her tough-as-nails persona and her grief inflicted vulnerability tapped into his protective instincts.

For her, the whole situation stunk.

Refusing to set her on edge with extended physical contact, he dropped his hands. "I'll get someone over here. Anything missing?"

"Not that I can tell. But Heather didn't keep cash or credit cards laying around. Or her good jewelry. It was all locked in the safe. He tried to move it while I was passed out."

"What? How do you know?"

"I checked it when I woke up. It's in the bedroom closet and it's heavy. Three hundred pounds at least and one of those stand-up floor models. There are dents in the carpet where he moved it."

Setting hands on his hips, Tony scanned the room, checking breach points, looking for damage, anything that would tell him how the guy got in. "Doors and locks all secure?"

"Yes."

He waved at the keypad near the front door. "Alarm?"

"I can't remember if I set it."

He raised his eyebrows. Seriously? She couldn't *remember*?

"I know," she said. "Believe me, I *know*. But, I'm going through something here. My sister, my *twin* just died and I'm not tracking right. So sue me because I forgot to set the goddamned alarm."

Yow. Consider him put in his place. "Hey, I'm a cop. I worry about shit like that." He picked up the coffee, handed it to her. "Peace offering."

She snatched the cup like it contained lifesaving drugs. "Thank you."

"Did you call the cops?"

"Not yet. I wasn't sure what to do."

"I'll call Grey. See what he thinks. Being she was a senator, this might be FBI jurisdiction. The guy could have been looking for anything. Trashing the place might have been a diversion or he didn't know where to look. Could be a random break-in. Heather's..." He stopped. Checked himself. She didn't necessarily need to hear the word death. "Heather has been in the news. Someone may have figured the house was empty and easy pickings."

Sick as it was, he'd seen it. People preying on the dead and robbing their homes immediately after their passing. Not only did loved ones struggle with grief, they had to figure out what was missing and file insurance claims.

"If it was random," she said, "someone has a solid set of brass ones to rob the home of a deceased U.S. senator."

She was right. Pulling this job would take the king of all idiots. Which, hey, it was DC. Plenty of candidates for the throne in this town. "Makes me think whoever this guy was, he knew what he was looking for. And it's valuable enough that he tried to move a 300-pound safe."

"And guess what was in that safe?"

"Heather's tablet?"

"Yep. Now do you see why I wouldn't let you take it yesterday? Whatever is on that thing is important to someone and they know it's here."

4

The cops and CSIs went through everything thoroughly and Fallyn hoped to hear back from them by the next day about fingerprints or DNA. Meanwhile, the house was a crime scene and she was being booted out.

While she'd originally planned to head back to New York after the funeral, that was looking like an impossibility. She had to pack up Heather's things and get as much in order as she could for her dad to handle, but now she couldn't get back into the townhouse until the police and investigators cleared it. They promised to do it quickly, but Fallyn knew how these things went. She'd be lucky to get back in here before the week was over.

Tony insisted on taking the tablet to Justice Team headquarters and turning it over to their computer geek. Tablet or no tablet, he was staying so close to her, she'd barely gotten her clothes on without him in the general vicinity. As she packed up her belongings, she could hear his low, deep voice from downstairs. It relaxed her.

Having Tony around wasn't exactly a hardship. Especially with her father, Jordan, and Carl all breathing down her neck. They'd been outraged when she'd informed them about the break-in and her injury, even though she'd insisted she was all right and perpetuated the idea that it was simply a burglar who'd seen the news about Heather's death and was looking for an easy score.

Never mind that the burglar didn't actually take anything that she could account for. The tablet had to stay a secret for now, although she wouldn't be surprised if Jordan had told Carl about the tablet in passing. The two were very close and shared everything.

She had calls to make and errands to run. And breakfast. She needed something besides coffee in her stomach.

As she went downstairs, she hauled her overnight bag in one hand and briefcase in the other. Tony spoke on his cell in the kitchen. As she entered the room, he turned his back on her, lowering his already quiet voice. "Yes, Amber, I know it's Mom's sixtieth birthday. I told you, I'll be at the party on Sunday." A pause. "I have a new client. Things may not be wrapped up by then, but I'll move heaven and earth to be there."

He lifted his gaze to the ceiling, rubbing his temples with his free hand. "Of course, it's important. I wouldn't miss Mom's birthday if it weren't. Look, I've got to go, okay? I'll call you tomorrow, and as things stand, I will be home on Sunday."

He disconnected, stowing the phone as he avoided her eyes. "Sorry. Family business."

"No apology necessary, Mr. Gerard." She set her bag down and tried to catch his eye. He stared out the window over the sink, scanning the area as if expecting a gang of bad guys to suddenly emerge. "I understand all about family."

"Tony."

"Huh?"

"It's Tony. When you say Mr. Gerard, I feel like my grandfather."

"Got it. Tony it is."

He picked up her bag and headed for the door. "I heard you tell the detective in charge that you had errands to run this morning. Where to first?"

"You're going with me?"

"I'm driving."

Well, well. How interesting. "You don't have to babysit me. I know my way around DC."

He retrieved her coat from the front closet and helped her put it on. "You're a public figure right now with your face all over the news. Best to have some security in place."

He was being polite but she heard the tone in his voice that told her she wasn't getting rid of him.

Good. She didn't want to. It was nice having someone to talk to. Someone whose personality and style matched her own.

Locking up, she followed him to his car at the curb. In the distance, a reporter snapped her picture. Tony saw it too. He was about to go into ass-kicking mode when she stopped him with a hand on his arm. "Let it be. I need breakfast."

He guided her into the seat of his Ford Explorer and she laid her head back on the headrest, closing her eyes as he made his way to the driver's side. It smelled like him in here. Musky with a hint of citrus.

"So I'm a client now?" she asked when he got in. "When did that happen?"

He buckled, checked his rearview. "Teeg's initial visit and clearing the reporters from the lawn were freebies. A favor for Caroline. As for me and my services? The minute you called me this morning and asked for help, I was on the clock. Grey will bill you."

Some kind of business Justice Greystone was running. "No forms to fill out? No down payment?"

Tony drove away from the brownstone, merging with traffic a minute later. "Boss man doesn't like to leave a paper trail. From what I understand, services rendered vary from client to client. No set fee. And, no, we don't require a down payment like Pasche & Associates. This gig is new to me, but apparently once Grey has decided to help you, we take you on good faith."

A government, off-the-books unit that operated on good faith? More like they didn't want anyone tracing them or their clientele. "Tell Caroline and Mr. Greystone thank you. I appreciate everything you've done for me, including the coffee service."

She was also impressed he'd done his homework on her business.

"Caroline sends her regrets that she couldn't make it to see you yet." He hooked a right. "Says she'll catch up with you as soon as she's back in town."

"No problem. Where are we headed?"

"Thought I'd get you settled at a hotel first. Grey suggested one." He looked over, shot her a grin. "They have excellent breakfast."

That grin made her think of a different kind of breakfast she wouldn't mind having. But he obviously had other commitments. Family ones. "Once you drop me at the hotel, you're free to go. I won't hold you up all weekend. You should be able to make your mother's party without issue. You can call Amber back and let her know."

They rolled down the road, fighting morning rush hour. Tony's driving skills were as impressive as everything else. "She's been cancer-free for three years, my mother. Every birthday is a milestone."

"Definitely. You should attend. You're lucky to have a mother. I'll be out of your hair, so there won't be an issue."

"Grey wants me to stay with you until we know what's on that tablet and that you're not in danger from it."

Until we decide?

Fallyn chose her words carefully. "Whatever is on the tablet, I'll be okay. I don't need a bodyguard." Need and want were two different things, of course. She might not *need* a bodyguard, but having one in her bed hit all of her *I want* buttons. "I've got your number. If I have trouble, I'll call you."

Tony didn't respond, continuing to drive in silence. He made a few more turns and they ended up in front of a 5-star hotel. "Teeg made reservations. You should probably avoid the restaurant and order room service, just to be on the safe side."

Efficient. She liked that. "I'm grateful for everything," she said, unlocking her seatbelt and grabbing her briefcase where the tablet nestled. "Thank you."

He didn't drop her off at the front where the bellman waited. No, he drove around to the back and parked.

"Did you see anyone out on the lawn yesterday that looked even remotely suspicious?" he asked as he undid his seatbelt and climbed out.

What was he doing? He came around and opened her door. "Why? You think my intruder was casing the place yesterday in all the commotion?"

He helped her out of the car and motioned her toward a back door. "Just a thought."

He took a keycard from his pocket and slid it through the security reader, ushering her inside after the door unlocked.

"Wait," she said, stopping him. "You have a key to the hotel?"

"Teeg dropped it off earlier while the cops were talking to you."

More efficiency. "And where do you presume you're going?"

"Upstairs with you."

"That's not necessary. I told you, I'm fine. You can leave."

"Afraid I can't. My orders are to stick with you until further notice."

Hardship there, but she didn't want him or anyone else to feel obligated. He had other people depending on him. "Well, if I'm your client, I say when the job is done. Your job is done, Mr. Gerard."

He smiled a patient smile like she was a toddler throwing a tantrum. "Like I said, it's Tony, and you, Ms. Pasche, have a bodyguard whether you want one or not."

The elevator doors opened to the concierge floor. In this case, a good upgrade from a regular room because guests needed a coded key to get off on this floor. Fallyn's briefcase in hand, Tony held his arm out, keeping her on the elevator until he checked the hallway.

Maybe the added security was overkill, but after the break-in at Heather's, why take a chance? If the chief's death had taught him anything it was that random situations weren't always random.

Now, in every event, he saw potential problems. Not necessarily a great way to live, but who the fuck cared about that? He needed to focus on a dead senator and keeping her sister safe until they determined what the intruder had been after.

Still on the elevator, Fallyn sighed. "Tony, it's a locked floor. Relax."

Never. When he relaxed, when he got distracted, people died. He'd learned that at twelve when he'd been outside shooting hoops while his father dropped dead of a heart attack in their kitchen. If Tony had been inside...

"No," he said. "Thanks for the advice, but I'd rather make sure you stayed in one piece. Kinda my job."

"Blah, blah, macho man."

He pointed left. "Your room is this way."

From his suit pocket, Grey's voice blared. Damned ringtone. Teeg, thinking he was funny, had randomly recorded Grey's conversations and then assigned team members clips of those conversations as ringtones. Tony's ringtone? *Dumbass, drop whatever the fuck you're doing and call me back.*

In Tony's mind, that should have been smartass Justice Team member Mitch Monroe's ringtone.

"Crap," he said, digging the phone out. "Hey, boss."

Fallyn's mouth hung open, her face stretched wide and clearly entertained. Not exactly the ringtone he wanted going off in public.

"Where are you?" Grey asked.

"Just got to the hotel. Heading to her room. What's up?"

"I'm here. At the hotel. I need access to her floor. We gave you the keys."

Ho-kay. If Grey hauled his ass over here, he had news.

Or an issue.

"Problem?"

"Heather Pasche's autopsy report."

Grey always sounded serious, oftentimes irritated. Tony was learning the subtle differences in those tones. This one said there something bad in that autopsy report. *Shit.* "Let me get Fallyn squared away and I'll come down. Two minutes."

Fallyn stopped in front of suite 845, pointed to the number posted on the wall. "Home, sweet, home. What was that about?"

"It's Grey. He's downstairs."

"I gathered that. Why?"

Tony popped the key into the door and pushed through, letting Fallyn step in behind him. The door swung closed and he set her bag down, again holding his arm out to block her. "Stay by the door a second. Let me clear the place."

She rolled her eyes, but stayed put. The nice thing about hotel suites was the time it took to clear them. Inside of a minute, he checked the closet and bathroom. Shower curtain. Check. Miniscule linen closet. Check. But hell, it'd be some kind of miracle if anyone could fit inside that bastard. Bathroom cleared, he strode to the window, shoved the curtains back. No locks. Windows inoperable.

Satisfied there were no breach points, he turned back. "You're good."

"Thank you. You didn't answer my question about Grey."

"Caught that, did you?"

"I did indeed. Now spill."

He met her gaze, held it for a second. He could say he didn't know, throw his boss under the bus and get himself out of a potentially awkward conversation. But, nah. When had he ever run from conflict?

Twisted bastard that he was, he got off on it. "He needs to talk to you. Your sister's autopsy report came back."

"Mr. Greystone has my sister's autopsy report? Is there a problem?"

"I don't know. All he said was he had it and wants to talk to you."

"But he came here rather than calling."

"Yes, ma'am."

"Alright then. I guess you'd better get down there so we can see what the problem is."

She bent to pick up her bag and he strode toward her. "I got it."

"Tony, I can lift a Rollaboard suitcase."

"I know you can. Doesn't mean you should."

"And who said chivalry was dead?"

"Not my uncle. He'd whip my butt if he saw me letting you pick anything up."

And, dammit, the second it left his mouth, he knew it was a mistake. If he'd learned anything in the last day about Fallyn and her ability to analyze a situation, she'd ask him about it, about his uncle, which would lead to his father not being around and they didn't have time. Not with Grey waiting on him.

"Your uncle?"

Bingo. If only he could predict the stock market that well.

He headed toward the door. "My dad died when I was twelve. My uncle took over the how-to-be-a-man lessons. Stay here. Throw the safety when I leave."

Tony found Grey standing at the entrance to the private elevator bank, as usual messing with his phone. He wore his typical federal agent uniform of a dark suit and white shirt, but his tie? That baby had some flair to it. According to Brice Brennan, another member of the Justice Team, Grey's fiancé had been systematically upgrading his ties.

Without his knowledge.

"Hey," Tony said. "Nice tie."

Grey grunted. "Swear to God, she's gonna kill me. Between this wedding crap and throwing out my ties, it's a war every night." He held up a manila envelope, waited for a couple to pass and leaned in. "Autopsy report. After the break-in at the senator's I got curious. Media reported she had a heart attack, but figured I'd check if there was anything suspicious."

"And?"

"Heart failure, for sure, but she was on medications to prevent that. However, she had prescription drugs in her system that don't mix well. A new drug called Perisoladol was one of them."

Tony rolled his bottom lip out. "Never heard of it."

"Me neither. The ME gave me the basics about the drug, but it looks suspicious. Figured I'd ask Fallyn about it."

Tony gestured to the elevator. "Then let's roll."

. . .

Grey pulled the autopsy report out of the envelope, slid it across the coffee table and spun it so Fallyn could read it. In an effort to not crowd her, to give her space while she read a report containing the details of her sister's death, Tony watched from his spot near the windowsill. Considering Fallyn and Grey had just met, they'd gotten right to the extremely personal business of Heather's autopsy report.

"I've worked with the ME on several cases," Grey said. "Told her you were my client and she released a copy of the autopsy to me. I hope you don't take offense at me overstepping boundaries, but I felt it was important."

For whatever reason, Fallyn looked up at Tony, still leaning on the windowsill, hands resting at his sides. He held her gaze a second, felt the energy in the room shift. He just wasn't sure what it had shifted to. The woman was a total puzzle. What did she need? Support? Reassurances? Privacy?

Hell if he knew. She just sat there, looking at him, her facial expression blank. Zippo.

A long few seconds ticked by and nobody moved. Having seen and sensed enough, Tony boosted off the windowsill, took three steps closer and held out his hands. "What do you need right now? You want us to go? Give you a minute?"

She shook her head and pointed to the open spot next to her. "Sit. Please. I need to read this and I'm guessing Grey is about to tell me things that may or may not surprise me. Since I'm not sure, I'd like another neutral person to read this with me. Will you do that?"

He nodded and sat down beside her.

She glanced back at Grey. "Give me the summary version."

"She had a heart attack."

Fallyn's shoulders dropped half an inch. Relief maybe. Hard to tell with her total freaking lack of facial expression.

"Okay," she said. "We knew that. Why are you here showing this to me as if there's more?"

"Were you aware she had a heart condition?"

"A heart condition?"

Tony met Grey's eyes—*tread carefully, my friend*—and his boss scratched the side of his face.

"It's in the report, but it's called Long QT Syndrome. It's a rare heart disorder that causes arrhythmias. Usually brought on by exercise or stress. Your sister was on medications for it, so she must have known she had it."

"Oh my God, she never told me that." She dipped her head, scanned the report. "And this QT thing caused a heart attack?"

"I'm not sure. I have a call into the ME because there were high amounts of Perisoladol found in her system. I was hoping you might know if she was taking it for her heart condition or not?"

Fallyn shook her head. "I had no idea my sister even had a heart problem."

5

----

*F*allyn had always excelled at processing bad news and finding a way to spin it into something positive.

Always. Until this moment.

Heather had suffered from a rare heart condition? Since when?

Why hadn't Heather told her? How did she not know on some deep, sisterly level that her twin had health problems?

Fallyn's own heart bounced around in her chest like a Mexican jumping bean. She put her hand over it for a moment, wondering if that's what Heather's had felt like before it stopped beating forever.

The words on the autopsy report blurred. Grey pointed at a section with various drugs listed in it. "With her condition, Heather should never have taken Perisoladol. And definitely not with the other drugs she was on. The ME has referred the case to Metro, so be expecting a call from a detective. The Capitol Police will get involved, too, since she was a Congresswoman. They'll be looking into it to see if the prescribing doctor was negligent or perhaps the pharmacy that filled the prescription got something mixed up. However, the ME pulled her medical records and there are no notations from her heart physician about giving her a prescription for this. Do you know if she had more than one physician?"

"I think she was still seeing our family doctor, Allan Thymes, but that's all I knew about. I had no idea she was seeing a specialist. Jordan, her assistant, might be able to tell us."

"You should talk to her, find out if she can shed some light on this because Heather either went to a second doctor and got the prescription, or she got it by some other, less traceable, means. Even for someone who *should* have been taking that drug, the amount found in her system was way more than normally prescribed."

"Less traceable means." Fallyn sat back. "You mean like a drug dealer?"

"Perisoladol is prescribed for some cardiac patients and has a side effect that stimulates food to move through the digestive tract, thus making things easier on the heart. That side effect is attractive to dieters. They've hailed it as a diet pill and there's a growing black market for the drug."

"My sister didn't need to diet." But even as she said the words, she remembered how depressed Heather was about the weight she'd gained while on the campaign trail. It was hard to eat right and exercise when you were making speeches and shaking hands sixteen hours a day. Heather had turned into a health nut. Vitamins, supplements, protein powder—she tried anything and everything if it would improve her health.

Grey's cell phone rang, blaring in the quiet room and making her jump. Tony touched her shoulder as Grey, seeing the caller ID, stood and walked into the bedroom to answer it.

Tony's presence next to her felt solid and reassuring, yet she shifted away from his hand and stood. This time it wasn't because she didn't like being touched, she simply couldn't sit still.

Did her dad know? Had he and Heather kept the heart problem from her for some bizarre reason? Since it was genetic, wouldn't they tell Fallyn so she could be checked for it, too?

"You would think twin sisters would share everything," she said, marching over to the window and staring out at the sky. "Especially something like a heart problem."

"I don't know anything about twins," Tony said, kicking back in his chair as if this were an everyday, routine event for him. "But I got a passel of sisters and, yes, ma'am, they share everything. Hell, they'll send five-hundred texts to each other over what color outfit to wear to our mother's birthday."

Was that supposed to make her feel better? "Heather never texted. She never called. If I wanted to check on her or even just chat about Dad or something in the news, I did the texting and calling. It wasn't as if she wouldn't talk to me, she simply never initiated communication. If I got her on the phone, we'd talk until our cell batteries were dead, but I guess calling me up and saying, 'Hey, sis, guess what? I have a heart condition' probably wasn't at the top of her list."

Tony gathered up his long, muscular body and joined her at the window. "The thing about my sisters, is they'll talk for an hour about what color to wear, but they won't even mention having a cold. Amber had a fender bender last month and never bothered to tell us. She didn't want to worry us. I'm guessing Heather felt the same. Unless they're butting into my business, my sisters don't tell me squat. Probably because I go apeshit when one of them gets sick or hurt. I'm guessing you have a protective streak like that."

How right he was. "I'm younger by a minute, but I've always felt like I had to protect her. I can't stand to read criticism about her as a senator. I couldn't even be there the night she was elected because I was freaking out that she might lose. After she *was* elected, whenever there was the slightest drop in her popularity polls, I felt like tearing someone up."

He smiled at that. "She didn't want to worry you."

Grey emerged from the bedroom, sticking his phone in his inside jacket pocket. "Gotta run. Brennan needs backup and Monroe is still out of town with Caroline."

He turned to Fallyn. "As soon as I get more info from the ME, I'll be in touch. Tony will stay with you tonight to be on the safe side. You need anything, have him call me. Got it?"

Intense. Like many of her powerful clients, Justice Greystone had a way about him that projected authority and control. Fallyn decided right then, with his dark eyes tunneling into hers, that she preferred to be on his good side. "Got it."

"The ME already contacted Metro PD with the information about the drug interaction, so be expecting a call from them."

"I will. Thanks."

He nodded, threw a wave at Tony, and left.

She turned and found Tony staring at her. She stared back, sizing him up.

"What?" he finally said. "Do I have something on my face?"

He reached up, ran his hand over his mouth and his jacket flapped open again, showing off his broad chest and flat stomach. There was a gun hanging in a holster under his right arm.

Power, authority, control. Just like Grey. "Do you get along with your boss?" she asked.

His brows lowered a fraction. "I haven't been with the team long. Still feeling my way around. Why?"

It was easier to analyze him than think about the fact Heather hadn't shared her health issue. "Just curious. You both exude testosterone like bulls. Usually makes for a lot of ill will when you work together."

All Tony did was grunt, but she saw the slightest quirk of his lips.

"I'd like to know more about the drugs in my sister's system," Fallyn said. "Especially before I have to talk to the cops. I'm going to huddle up and do some research. You game?"

"Absolutely. How about some breakfast? I'll order it."

Her stomach flipped. "Honestly, I'm not hungry anymore."

Frustration passed over Tony's face. Brief, but it was there. "Understandable, but you need to keep your strength. Some toast, at least?"

For some reason, she wanted to make him happy. Toast was a small concession. "I can probably do toast. Jelly too."

He smiled and snatched up the hotel phone while she grabbed up the autopsy report and marched into the suite's bedroom.

He followed a minute later, shrugging off his suit jacket as Fallyn fired up her laptop at the desk. He took out his phone, and plunked down on the edge of the bed, holding up the phone so she could see he was connected to the Internet. "What do you want me to search for?"

"I'm going to Google Long QT syndrome. Could you look up that drug Grey was talking about?" She leaned over and spelled it from the autopsy report. "P-e-r-i-s-o-l-a-d-o-l."

"Got it."

Fallyn read article after article, most of them serious medical papers that were way over her head. Room service arrived with toast, bagels, tea, and coffee.

Munching on a piece of toast with strawberry jelly, she finally found an article she could understand. "Get this," she said to Tony. He was downing more coffee. "Long QT syndrome is a disorder of the heart's electrical activity in which delayed repolarization of the heart following a heartbeat increases the risk of episodes of irregular heart-beat. These episodes may be brought on by a variety of reasons, including exercise and stress, and may lead to palpitations, fainting, and sudden death due to ventricular fibrillation."

Exercise, stress—Grey had mentioned both were triggers and the article confirmed he was correct. "I wonder if she started taking all those supplements and vitamins after she found about her heart problem," Fallyn said. "Her medicine cabinet at home is full of them."

"Herbs and supplements can be dangerous to take while on other heart medications." Tony swiped at a screen on his phone. "Some can cause excessive bleeding, lowered blood pressure, and a host of other complications."

Finishing off her toast and brushing crumbs off her hands, Fallyn closed her laptop. "I don't remember seeing any prescription meds at Heather's place. I need to go have a look at her medicine cabinet."

Tony was leaning back on the bed with one hand, his phone still in the other. He'd run his fingers through his hair, disheveling it. It was a good look, mussed hair. The rolled up sleeves of his button-down revealed a muscled—like the rest of him—forearm covered in an intricate tattoo. A compass woven with a sunburst and flowers that wrapped completely around from wrist to elbow. And, ooh, she wanted to know about that tattoo.

"You want to go back to the townhouse? Right now?"

"The police kicked me out, but they should be done collecting evidence by now, right? Even if they're back for more, I'm going in."

One side of his mouth lifted in a half smile and he hauled himself off the bed. "It's not a bad idea. We could get a jump on this thing before the cops. Control the story."

"I like the way you think, Tony Gerard."

Midday traffic was much lighter than the morning rush. On the way to the townhouse, Fallyn pulled out her cell. Over a dozen calls and almost as many voice mails.

Crazy ass day.

But the voice mails had to wait. First, she scrolled through her contacts and found Allan Thymes's number. There was no answer, so she left a message, asking him to call her back. She placed her next call to Jordan.

"Did you know Heather had a heart condition?" Fallyn asked.

Jordan hesitated. "A heart condition? What kind of heart condition?"

"One she was seeing a specialist for. You never made any appointments to a heart doctor for her? Or any other specialist?"

"She saw a nutritionist a couple of times. I didn't think anything about it because it was right around the time she started her new diet and exercise routine."

So Heather had been keeping secrets from Jordan too. "Was Heather obsessing about her weight?"

"Fallyn," Jordan sounded perplexed and a little exasperated, "where is all this coming from?"

"Sorry, Jordan, I'm just trying to figure a couple of things out. Was she taking diet pills or obsessed with exercising?"

"Of course not. She had a full schedule and could barely squeeze in her weekly Pilates class, but she did. She ate well and took lots of vitamins."

And yet, something had backfired.

Fallyn ended the conversation and tipped her head back against the headrest. First the tablet and now this revelation about Heather's death.

When they arrived at the townhouse, anxiety pumped through her veins. She was out of the car before Tony put it in park.

"Dammit, Fallyn!" he bellowed. "I need to clear the place and make sure no one's in there!"

She didn't wait, hustling across the road. Yellow crime scene tape fluttered in the breeze.

Ripping it down, she flung the door open and grabbed a heavy, bronze candlestick holder Heather had loved as she passed the table in the foyer.

"Fallyn!" Tony stormed through the door, grabbing her elbow and whirling her around. "What the hell do you think you're doing?"

The place was still an utter mess but absolutely quiet. She could hear her breath whizzing in and out of her mouth, her pulse pounding in her ears. No cops or anyone else.

She raised the candlestick to show him. "It's okay. I'm armed."

Tony rolled his eyes and maneuvered her to the side. "Stay here and let me do a sweep."

God, she hated bossy men. She jerked her elbow out of his grip. "Bullshit. I'm not staying here. I'm going upstairs to the bathroom."

He was breathing slightly hard, too, having run across the road to catch up. Or maybe he was pissed because, my oh my, he had a look about him. "Listen up," he said. "I get what you're doing right now and that you need answers. I've been there. You getting killed because you've busted in on someone searching the place won't help you protect your sister's privacy. You have a job to do. So do I. My job puts you first. If you're safe, you can do your job. So, right now, you're going to plant your ass where I tell you so I can clear this house. And maybe keep you alive. Got it?"

Something released in her. A subtle click in her chest. Her shoulders dropped an inch, tension falling out of them like a balloon bursting. Her lips turned up. "Okay. So that was kinda hot."

He rolled his eyes. "Stay put or we're gonna go at it."

She might welcome that. A couple rounds with Tony Gerard would do her good. "Do you threaten all of your clients?"

Light from the wall sconce glittered in his eyes as he moved into her personal space and stared down at her. "So far, just you."

Intimidating, much? She stood her ground, took a deep breath as he held his hand out, grabbing hers and squeezing.

"I'm here to help you," he said. "Please believe that."

"Can we compromise?"

"How?"

"I'll follow behind you while you do your sweep."

He didn't like it, she could see it on his face. "Besides," she said, "I'm safer with you."

Ha. That got him.

He smiled, shook his head. "Unbelievable."

"You know I'm right."

Still holding her hand, he pulled her behind him, then let go as he started the sweep and it was all she could do not to be freaked out.

Not because she didn't like his touch.

Because she *did*.

By the time they got upstairs to the bathroom medicine cabinet, perspiration had broken out along her hairline. She unbuttoned her coat and Tony helped her off with it. Avoiding his steely eyes and ignoring the sensations zinging through her from his touch, she avoided the broken glass from the picture frame still on the floor and went into the bathroom. There, she grabbed all of the bottles from the cabinet and came back to dump them on the bed.

Together, she and Tony sat on the bed and started going through the vitamins and supplement bottles. Sure enough, there were two small prescription bottles mixed in with them.

Neither sported the name Perisoladol.

Her phone buzzed in her coat pocket. She dug it out and let go of an annoyed sigh. Metro PD. A detective had left her a message earlier that he wanted to talk to her about her sister's death. He was apparently persistent.

She clicked on the ignore button and sent it to voicemail. Until she understood exactly how and why her sister had died, she wasn't going to talk to the detective. For God's sakes, her sister had barely been gone twenty-four hours. *Give me a couple of fucking hours to grieve.*

She'd just put the phone down when it rang again. This time it was Dr. Thymes. "Fallyn, my dear," he said. "My answering service told me you called. I'm so sorry about Heather."

Dr. Thymes was at least 70 if not older. He'd been their doctor since they were kids. "Thanks for calling me back, Doc. I have a question for you. I assume you knew about Heather's heart condition. Did you refer her to a specialist?"

"Indeed I did. Dr. Chen."

Both prescription bottles listed Chen as the prescribing doctor. "Was Dr. Chen the only specialist Heather was seeing?"

"Fallyn, you know with the HIPAA laws and all, I'm not supposed to share information."

"My sister is dead, Dr. Thymes." There. She'd said it. Finally uttered the hateful word. Fallyn fought the wave of panic, shook her head. "At this point, Heather doesn't care."

Thymes cleared his throat as if he didn't like her tone or the fact she was asking him to violate his deceased patient's confidentiality. He complied anyway, probably because he was an old friend as well as their doctor. "Dr. Monica Chen is the best cardiac doctor on the East Coast. If anyone could help Heather, it was her."

"So you didn't refer Heather to anyone else?"

"As far as I know, Dr. Chen was her only other doctor."

"Do you know if Heather might have been taking a drug called Perisoladol?"

The doctor repeated the drug name. "Definitely not with her type of heart condition."

Then how did it end up in her system? "Thank you, Doc. Give Helen my love."

"I will. Say hello to your father for me. He's due for a checkup, you know. Especially after this."

She didn't know, but she added it to her growing to-do list.

Once they'd disconnected, she sat staring at the dozen or so bottles on the bed. "There's no Perisoladol here, and our family doctor said that no competent doctor would prescribe that for her."

"So maybe she got it off the street," Tony said. "Kept it at her office or something."

"Heather wouldn't buy shoestrings from a drug dealer, much less a prescription medication. Besides, she was too smart to mix medications without doing research on them, and as you and I found, there's plenty out there about Perisoladol and QT syndrome." She waved a hand over the vitamin and supplements bottles. "Heather was so thorough, she probably knew the Latin names, uses, and side effects of every herb and concoction here."

"Could your sister have been suicidal?"

Fallyn blanched. "Suicidal?"

"Sorry, that was tactless." He raised his hands. "Just throwing it out there. Maybe she got her hands on one big dose knowing it would end it for her."

"Never. I may not have known everything going on in her life, but she wouldn't have done that. She wanted people to think she was perfect and she was pretty damn close. Her ego alone would have kept her from killing herself. She believed she could actually change the world, make it a better place. She had a mission. A calling. A purpose." She shook her head. "No suicide. Definitely not. Why take all these health supplements if she *didn't* want to live? Why bother taking the heart medications in the first place if she wanted to end her life? There's no way she would have put her life in danger."

"And no doctor would have either."

Fallyn glanced at him. "Which means?"

Tony scrubbed his face with a hand. "Pure speculation, but maybe someone intentionally gave her that big dose of Perisoladol."

Her blood ran cold. The implication was staggering. She couldn't believe it, even as the words left her mouth. "My sister might have been murdered."

6

Fallyn led the charge down the long hallway of the Hart Senate Office building after they made it through several layers of security. Her quick strides scorched the floor. She could get those long legs moving when she put her mind to it, even in those damn heels.

She swung a left at the end of the corridor. Two doors down she stopped, gave the doorknob a flick and marched into an office. Bam. She was in. Tony followed her, shutting the door behind him.

A young woman, probably not even of drinking age, with short dark hair and a cute face sat at the reception desk, phone to her ear. As she spoke, a series of beeps and rings from the other lines echoed in the office. The young woman pressed two fingers into her forehead.

Busy day. Not unusual, Tony supposed, since they'd just lost the woman who ran this office.

He glanced around at the muted gray walls and oiled white trim. The place had a beachy feel. Kinda struck him as odd for a senator's office, yet the Heather Pasche neatness and tidiness were present.

"Yes, ma'am." the girl said into the phone while Fallyn hovered. "Thank you. I will have Jordan call you as soon as she's back."

She hung up. "I'm so sorry."

She tapped buttons on the phone, silencing the other two ringing lines and looked up, her gaze landing on Fallyn, her dead boss's twin.

If this girl didn't know Heather had a twin, well, she might be thinking a ghost just wandered in because her mouth slid open and hung for a few seconds.

"Oh my God," she said.

Fallyn stuck her hand out. "Fallyn Pasche. Heather's sister. We haven't met. You must be the intern."

The young woman stared at Fallyn, her eyes glued to her face, mesmerized. With Fallyn's hand hanging in midair, the intern's gawking stare would have them sticking the landing in awkward territory.

Tony stepped up, gently pressed his hand against Fallyn's wrist while he cleared his throat. The intern dragged her gaze to Tony.

"I'm Tony Gerard. Supreme Court security and a friend of Fallyn's. She needs access to Heather's office."

"Oh, um..."

"Yes," Fallyn said, not missing a beat at him throwing his job title in there. "Heather has personal items that are missing. I think they're probably in her desk."

"I, uh." The intern pinched her nose. Her badge ID read Emily. "Wow. I'm sorry, I can't do that."

Fallyn's tone was downright frosty. "Excuse me?"

The intern winced, obviously realizing she'd just shot down a grieving sister. "Ooh, that was bad. I'm sorry."

If Tony were a sighing man, he'd offer up the mother of all sighs. This kid? Way out of her league. What the hell were these people doing leaving a college kid alone after the death of a United States senator. One more time, he glanced around the small office, hoping someone might pop out of one of the closed doors—most likely offices—and rescue the intern.

Nope. No one popping. Unless he considered Fallyn's red face and her head about to blow off. He held up a hand. "Is Jordan available?"

The intern snatched up the phone. "Jordan. *Yes*. She's in the cafeteria, having lunch with her dad. Let me call her."

Repressed energy flew off Fallyn, lacing the air, filling the small space with all that impatience, and nearly knocked Tony on his ass. He'd give her credit because she wanted to push by, get on with her search, but she stood still, her body stiff—controlled—as she absorbed the fact that a college kid had just refused her access to her dead sister's office.

The intern cast her eyes downward, her gaze shooting to the phone, the desk pad, the stack of folders, everywhere but at them.

Yeah, *way* out of her league.

"Hi," she said into the phone. "Ms. Pasche—uh, Fallyn—is here and needs to get into the Senator's office. Would you please call me back?"

She disconnected and finally looked up at them, her lips forming a shaky smile. "She didn't answer."

"Well," Fallyn said, "as you can imagine, I have a lot to do. Unfortunately, I can't wait for Jordan. Here's an idea I'm sure we can agree on. I'll go into Heather's office, start gathering what I need and you can go fetch Jordan. Then, if Jordan has a problem with me being in there, which, given the circumstances she won't, she and I can discuss it. That gets you out of the middle."

Fallyn didn't wait for a response and headed for one of the closed doors.

"Wait! I'm not supposed to let anyone in there unless Jordan is with them."

Waving her off, Fallyn pushed open the door and disappeared inside the office.

Again, Tony the un-sigher went into maintenance mode. "Where's the cafeteria?"

"The cafeteria?"

"Yes." He waggled a finger. "Go find Jordan."

Clearly thankful for the reprieve, the intern hopped up. "Yes. Absolutely. I can do that. It'll only take a minute. I'll be right back."

The intern rounded the desk, hustling out and Tony moved to the doorway of Heather's office.

"You know," he said, "you could have given the kid a break and waited for her to find Jordan. She's crapping her pants. Let's not get her fired to boot."

Fallyn had already tossed her purse on the giant desk and started in on the drawers. "Jordan knows I'm a pain in the ass, and she won't care. I'm family and I'll tell her I promised Emily I'd stay out until they got back, but oops...I couldn't wait any longer."

"And you called me a pain in the ass. Who'd a thunk you were even worse?"

"Shocking, I know." She shoved the drawer closed, moved to the next one. "Do me a favor, start on the bookcase. See if she's got anything hidden behind the books. That was a favorite hiding spot for her when we were kids."

To his left, along the wall, sat a sofa with a bookcase anchoring the other side. Before he could move, voices from the outer office erupted. A brunette, not much older than the intern, and an older man filed in from the hallway. He'd seen them the previous night when he'd chased off the reporters.

Tony swung his thumb. "We got company."

The brunette pushed by him, followed by the man. "Fallyn!" she said. "What are you doing? You can't just rummage in Heather's desk. You shouldn't even be in here. There could be sensitive information in there."

The intern scurried in and Tony saluted. "That didn't take long."

"They were already on their way back."

Still at Heather's desk, Fallyn continued her search. "I'm not interested in the secrets of our U.S. government, Jordan. I know most of them anyway."

"What are you looking for?"

"I can't say."

The older man stepped closer. "Fallyn," he said, "you *really* need to calm down and take a step back."

And, yeah, Tony's shit-meter went ballistic. Fallyn had mentioned

Jordan's father was an old family friend, but even still, his tone sucked. And with all of them facing Fallyn, it looked like a damned firing squad. Jordan spun back and angled around him on her way to the outer office. He took over her spot next to the desk.

Fallyn opened another drawer. "Carl, the last thing I need to do is calm down. I'm sure Jordan told you, if you didn't already know, but Heather had a heart condition."

"I just found out."

"Then I don't need to bring you up to speed. Aha." She held up two vitamin bottles and shoved them at Tony. "We're taking these."

"Okay," Tony said.

Being a smart man who'd grown up with five women, he knew when not to argue. Not that he would have anyway. The woman had a right to figure out what happened to her sister.

Carl poked a finger at Tony. "Who are you?"

"Tony Gerard. I got the press out of your face last night. Point at me again and I'll take that finger off."

Clearly entertained, Fallyn gave him a thumbs up. "I should hire you." She tucked her hair behind her ears and reached for the last desk drawer. "Tony is a friend, Carl. He's helping me sort through Heather's things. Now, if the rest of you are not going to help me, please leave."

Carl held two hands up. "Fallyn, dear, I know you're upset. Heather's death—"

"Upset?" She rummaged through the drawer, tossing folders, notepads, a makeup bag, on the desk as she went. "I'm beyond upset. My sister just died. If that weren't enough, she had a heart problem she chose not to share with me. One that's apparently genetic and—oh, gee—maybe Fallyn should be tested too? But that's another issue. I'll have to live with the fact she kept it from me. And that hurts. I think I have a right to be just *slightly* upset about that. Because,"—she threw her hands out—"guess what, kids, my sister's body is loaded with Perisoladol, a drug that causes arrhythmias. Which, as you can imagine, is not good for someone with a heart condition. I might be having a goddamn arrhythmia right now myself. So, yeah, I think I'm allowed to be *upset*."

She slammed the drawer, stood tall, set her hands on her hips and looked at Tony. "Am I right or am I wrong?"

Crazy woman. But, sick fuck that he was, he loved it. "You have the right to feel however you want."

"Good man. Thank you."

Her cell phone rang and she dug it out of her purse. "Lovely. My Dad. Let's all pile on." She punched the button. "Hi, Dad...Well, I'm going through Heather's office. There are some things we should talk about... No, Dad, I'm not causing trouble." Jordan entered the room and Fallyn glared at her. "I don't care what Jordan said. I'm not hysterical."

This was dirty pool. That snitch Jordan had called Fallyn's father. And now she stood behind her own father, her face a mix of concern and smug.

Sneaky witch.

Through the phone, Fallyn's Dad unloaded on her. The words weren't clear, but the yelling came through and Jordan and her father stood, nodding their approval.

These people? Seriously wacked.

"Dad, I'm looking for something. I'm trying to help...Why are you screaming at me? ... I know you lost a daughter, believe me... No...I'm not trying to aggravate you."

She looked up at the ceiling and closed her eyes while Jordan and her father watched the show and Tony's shit-meter finally exploded.

Not letting this happen.

He smacked his hands together. "You know what? I think we'll give Fallyn the room. Family privacy. Everyone out."

"We are family," Carl said. "I'm not leaving,

"Yeah, you are. When Fallyn is ready to talk to you, she'll let you know."

After a three second stare down, the man got the full brunt of Tony's don't-make-me-kick-your-ass stare and spun toward the door.

"Thank you," Fallyn said, covering the mouthpiece of the phone with one hand.

He paused a second, meeting her gaze and—bam—like a punch to the chest, his air locked up. Fallyn, in her designer suit and killer heels, those green eyes so intense and...hot...rattled something inside him. In a big way.

Focus here, pal. He followed Jordan and her father out the door, closing it behind him. Blocking the doorway, he crossed his arms, and forced air into this lungs.

"Look," Carl said, "I'm not sure who you are, but I've known this family for years, and you're not helping."

I'm not helping? Really? "Actually, sir, I don't think I'm the problem."

"What does that mean?"

Tony shrugged. "She's grieving. Maybe you could give her a little space." He looked over at Jordan, once again hiding behind her father, her lips pinched. "Fallyn is looking for Heather's medications. Have you been through her desk? Did she keep any here?"

When she remained silent, Tony shook his head. "You people are ridiculous."

Carl nudged closer. Any other time, Tony would have found it humorous since he had a least eight inches on the man and outweighed him by a good fifty pounds. Talk about a Napoleon complex.

"I want to know who the hell you are. If you're suddenly so close to Fallyn, why have I never met you?"

"Sir, all due respect, my relationship with Fallyn isn't your business. When she gets off the phone, she'll decide what she wants to tell you."

"Do you know who I am?"

Sure he knew. He was a retired State Department employee turned contractor. Once an assistant to the Secretary of State, Carl Lomax had all sorts of connections in DC and elsewhere. Rumor had it, he was the guy to call when a deal between two countries needed to be made. The ultimate power broker. "I do. I also don't care. Fallyn is my concern."

Behind him, the door swung open and he slid to the side. He took in Fallyn's puffy eyes and downturned lips and a chunk of him broke away. He knew grief and it sucked. On all levels. But if she'd been crying, she'd hid it well.

He grabbed her forearm. "You good?"

"I'm fine. Come in." She motioned him in, but held her arm up before baby Napoleon and Jordan could enter. "Just Tony. I need a minute."

She closed the door behind him, plastered on a cheery smile. "Welcome to my madness."

"Tough crowd."

"Thank you for clearing them out of here. My dad is—" She hesitated, looked up at the ceiling then met his eyes again. "Having a slight breakdown."

"Understandable."

"Heather was the good one. His favorite. The daughter he was proud of."

Un-hunh. What the hell was he supposed to do with that one? Because seriously, he didn't get it. He had four sisters and sure there were times when his mother liked one of all five of her children better than the other. None of them were perfect, but each of them, in their own twisted way had moments of perfect.

His mother saw all of those moments.

"You know," he said, "I gotta say, I don't get that. You've built a business, a *tough* business in a town that will eat someone alive if they screw up."

"She was a senator."

"Oh, right, because senators are the epitome of perfection. They own the high moral ground. Please. Honey, you wouldn't have a job if senators didn't fuck up. From where I'm standing, it sucks that the people around you—people who are supposed to love you—get in your face about crap they shouldn't be getting in your face about. You're going through something here and all they can do is yell at you? I don't get that. But hey, that's probably just me."

"Oh, snap."

"What?"

She grabbed the front of his jacket and yanked him forward, her gaze glued to his lips and—hell—his boss wouldn't like this much.

She kissed him.

An all-out assault of lips and tongue that instantly made him hard. Because, yes, folks, he was a man and when a beautiful, accomplished woman damn near climbed on him, he responded.

Sue me.

He wrapped his arms around her, hauled her up on her toes and gave as good as he got, matching her, stroke for stroke, with his tongue. She looped her arms around his neck and arched into him, her toned body curving into his. Damn, that felt good.

No, sir, Grey would not like this. At all. He'd never been one to mix business with pleasure, but right now, pleasure was sure outmanning the business part.

Oops.

Once again, his uncle's voice was in his ear, lecturing him on the principles of being a gentleman.

Being a man.

Fallyn was hurting. Vulnerable. He shouldn't be using that for his own pleasure, but he also wouldn't be the one to back away and risk her thinking it a rejection. No. He'd enjoy this crazy effing moment and chalk it up to her blowing off some steam.

He pulled her in tighter, let his lips wander along her jaw and worked a soft moan from her.

"This is so not good," she said.

He laughed. "Was just thinking the same thing."

"We should stop."

"Sure should."

"Is it bad that I don't want to?"

"You're asking a guy with an erection the size of Texas?"

Fallyn burst out laughing and the sound ricocheted against the walls of her dead sister's office and that fast, it was over, the supremely excellent energy of that kiss, gone. Still laughing, she rested her forehead against his shoulder. "Thank you."

"No," he said. "Thank *you*." Time for a little levity. "Because now I get to walk out of a senate office building at full salute."

Again she laughed. "Oh, my God. You're such a pig. But, truly, you saved me from a major meltdown."

"Glad I could help."

"You did more than that. No one ever takes my side. Everyone piles on. Normally, I can handle it. It's like some weird form of entertainment to them and they love to watch me struggle. I don't like to give them that satisfaction, but today...Well, today, you gave me exactly what I needed. Support."

"Well, sweetheart, I think it's time they stop piling all their shit on you."

She stared up at him, her sad eyes a little brighter. "Yes. I think you're right." She tugged on the lapels of his jacket and stepped back. "Now, before the cops catch up with me to relieve me of Heather's meds, we need to send a few of those pills to a lab for testing. I want to get ahead of this before the press gets hold of it."

Fallyn felt like her world was spinning off its axis. She'd lost her twin, and now she suspected Heather might have been murdered.

The panic started low in her stomach the moment her dad had called. Carl and Jordan had been yelling at her, her father had been yelling at her, and all she wanted to do was put down the phone, lock the doors, and cry.

Fallyn Pasche did not cry, by God. Ever.

Thank the universe, the feeling passed quickly. She was back in fighting form within seconds because of Tony Gerard.

Tony had been there, ushering Carl and Jordan out, giving her a moment to speak to her father in private. A familiar calm had settled over her. Work the case, she'd reminded herself, even while her father was reading her the riot act.

Heather is my client. Everyone else can go to hell.

Tony's encouragement, his resolute support when she'd been close to a meltdown, had brought the fragmented pieces of her brain and emotions back to center. She'd been so relieved, so surprised at his unwavering help, that she'd lost her mind and kissed him.

So not the proper response to finding out my twin may have been murdered.

Which brought her back to the gnawing panic under her skin. There was more in Heather's office she needed to look through, but Detective Hollister had called for the third time and she couldn't blow him off much longer. The U.S. Capitol Police had called him and were now working with him. She should expect a call from them as well.

So far, the CSI techs had found no fingerprints that didn't belong in Heather's townhouse. Heather's, Eric's, Fallyn's, Jordan's, and Carl's. A bunch of others', but duh, there had been dozens of people at the townhouse the previous day. Dozens, including other Congressmen and women. Even the president.

Hollister had spoken to Heather's doctors and the pharmacy tech where the prescriptions on record had been filled. Nothing seemed remiss. The next step, he'd told her was to send the prescription bottles from Heather's place to a lab for analysis.

Fallyn had the bottles in her purse. As Tony drove across town to the Metro precinct, she snuck one pill out of each bottle and snapped a picture of the pill and the prescription label on the outside before dropping the pill bottles into a plastic baggie. The detective hadn't mentioned vitamins and supplements and Fallyn hadn't volunteered that information. Once Det. Hollister spoke to Jordan, he'd no doubt find out about Heather's health nut status, but by then, the vitamins would all be at a private lab Grey had on speed dial.

"You're quiet," Tony said as he hooked a left and dodged the insanity known as DC traffic.

"Are you complaining?"

He smirked, his mouth lifting into a sexy little tilt. Oh, the man had a way about him.

"Nope. But when a woman like you is quiet, it's not necessarily safe for the rest of us."

"Ha!"

"What's up? What are you gnawing on?"

"Aside from my dead sister?"

Tony jerked one shoulder. "We'll figure it out. There has to be something somewhere that'll give us a lead. I know everyone thought she was perfect, but you know as well as I do, the perfect ones have the biggest secrets."

Fallyn sat a little straighter, swiveled her head to Tony. Sensing the energy change, he glanced over. "What?"

"Miss Perfect."

"What about her?"

Fallyn waggled her hand. "Oh, my God. I can't believe I didn't think about this. Last year there was a bill. It was approved by the House and sent to the Senate. Big brouhaha."

"Which bill?"

"The one about the military pay scales."

Eyes still on the road, Tony pursed his lips. "Yeah. Got it. Didn't pass, right?"

"Correct. My sister was the swing vote."

He glanced at her, his dark eyes hidden behind his sunglasses, but his eyebrows had hitched up before he turned back to the road. "No shit?"

"No, shit, big guy. She voted no and the military families nearly lynched her."

"I can see why."

"What the media failed to report was why she voted against it. The buried language in that bill allowed for billions to be sent to troops in foreign countries. Oh, Pakistan, you need a tank? We'll give you five million dollars, compliments of the United States taxpayers. She got slaughtered in the press and time and time again she argued that she wanted that language removed. She wanted the bill to be about supporting *our* military. Not someone else's."

"Let me guess, nobody heard that part."

"Hell no. Not at first. It was a perfect storm. The squeaky clean junior senator from Maryland disses US military families. The pundits chewed the flesh off her bones. I begged her to let me help, but she wouldn't do it. As she put it, she didn't want to go negative. *Please.*"

Even now, months later, the frustration bubbled up, clawed at Fallyn. That fiasco could have been nipped so easily. One expertly placed sound bite on a radio show where the host owed her a favor and—boom—problem solved. But, no. Heather wanted to let it die down on it's own. As if.

"I remember it now. The Chief Justice griped about it one day."

"Everyone was griping." Fallyn twisted in her seat, poked a finger. "She got death threats from that cluster. I mean think about all the struggling veterans in this country. And, my cute sister in her cushy townhouse and sixty-thousand dollar car rejects a bill that'll help military families. Eventually, the roar faded, and the sane people who did listen to her trumped the rest, but who knows? There are lunatics out there." She dug in her purse, pulled out her notepad. "We need to check her emails and ask Jordan if there've been any other death threats."

"It's worth checking out."

"Bet your butt it is." She twirled her pen. "Let's get Grey on this. And David Teeg. See what they come up with."

Was she impeding an investigation? Since nothing formal had been declared yet, she was running with her gut. Metro assured her that they and Capitol Police were only "looking into" the preponderance of the drug in Heather's system and that bought Fallyn time. Time to find out what was on that tablet and what role it played in all of this. Was the person who'd broken into the townhouse looking for the tablet or something like the Perisoladol? Had they planted it there and came back to retrieve it? If so, they'd have had plenty of time to take it after Fallyn had been knocked out.

Which meant there might not be any evidence in the bottles she had in a giant Ziplock in the backseat, but she didn't care. She'd even swiped the protein powder and breakfast nutrition bars from the cabinet. She was sending them all to Grey's lab right after she 'complied' with Det. Hollister's wishes.

When they arrived to talk to Hollister, Metro PD was the epitome of chaos. There had been a major accident on the 395 and a gunman with a hostage at some convenience store clear across town still hadn't given up. Phones were ringing, people were yelling, perps and witnesses were piling up everywhere Fallyn looked.

And I thought Pasche & Associates got crazy sometimes.

With a flash of his Supreme Court badge, Tony guided her through the main reception area, thick with fluorescent lighting and grimy floors. They passed through the metal detector, went down a hallway, and took an elevator to the third floor where Tony navigated her toward a sign that read Homicide.

He seemed to know his way around the precinct well, deftly maneuvering her around a drunk shouting about his right to a phone call.

The whole place smelled like body odor and pepperoni pizza, which was not a charming scent when her stomach was so empty and churning.

At the detective unit, Tony knew the man behind the desk. He asked for Det. Hollister but Hollister had been called out on a homicide.

Homicide. Fallyn wondered if Heather's death would soon be labeled with the same cold term.

Tony noticed her swaying slightly—did anything escape his eagle eyes?—and took the bag with the prescription bottles from her hand. "Hollister needs this," he told the desk sergeant. "We can't wait for him to get back."

The man gave Tony some papers to fill out, then said to her, "Hey, ain't you the senator's twin? The one who died? I seen you on TV. Real sorry about your sister."

"Thank you," Fallyn said, pasting on a fake smile. Even after all the condolences, she still didn't know what to say.

The fake smile lasted until she and Tony were back in his Explorer, heading for parts unknown.

"You need to eat," he said, and she was too tired, too wrung out to argue.

A few minutes later, she was surprised to find her stomach actually appreciated the double cheeseburger and fries that Tony placed in her lap from a drive-thru. He didn't talk as they sped out of the city and she stuffed her face with greasy, but delicious food. During her meal on the run, a detective from the Capitol Police finally caught up with her, asking the same questions and spewing the same rhetoric as Detective Hollister.

Eventually, the CP ran out of blanket statements and Fallyn came up for air. "What an extreme waste of time and resources," she said to Tony, putting her phone on silent. She didn't want to rehash her sister's health or her sudden death with anyone else for today. "The duplication is unreal."

"Our government at work," he said.

They were on a back road with a sign that declared they were entering an old army base that looked deserted.

Yep, straight out of a horror flick. "Where exactly are we?" she asked around her last French fry.

"Top secret. Close your eyes and pretend I blindfolded you 'cuz this place is strictly off the map. If you ever say you were here, you might end up 'disappeared', as one of my fellow Justice Team squad members likes to call it."

Blindfolded. With Tony calling the shots. Oh, the images that conjured. "I'm closing my eyes. If there's one thing I've learned in my job as a fixer, there are some things you don't want to ever see or hear."

"So you can deny you knew about them?"

"So I can sleep at night."

"Why do you do the job if it bothers you so much?"

That was always the question people wanted to know. "Everyone screws up. Every, single one of us. I did when I was a teen. We deserve a second chance sometimes, or we need to air a secret, and my team is there to help. That's how I sleep. Yes, there are things I don't need to know, but overall, what I do for people helps them deal with shit and survive. We don't take on killers or rapists or abusers. But there are a lot of others out there walking a fine line and paying an awful price for mistakes no one would pay attention to if they weren't already in the limelight."

The Explorer bounced to a stop. Tony lowered his window and she heard the sound of a buzzer. A gate opening.

"Can I open my eyes yet?"

"Nope," he said. "Just remember, if Grey asks, you were blindfolded. It was the only way to get him to agree to let you come here."

She made the 'OK' sign with her fingers.

She had to let Tony touch her as he helped her from the SUV, across some pavement, and in through a door. "You can open your eyes now," he whispered, his hand staying protectively on the base of her spine as she stepped into a large, open room.

Fluorescent lights, concrete floors, a random desk or two. The smell of strong coffee teased her nostrils and overrode the scent of abandonment just under the surface. Total opposite of the police station, and yet, Fallyn had the sneaking suspicion more got accomplished in this room on a daily basis than the cops down at the precinct accomplished in months.

David Teeg occupied one corner of the room with a large desk and multiple screens that resembled the cockpit of the Starship Enterprise. Even his chair was a high-tech looking thing with an integrated keyboard and ergonomic design. *Dani would be jealous.*

From behind a cheap room divider, Justice Greystone emerged. "Ms. Pasche. Welcome to team headquarters."

"Don't you think you should call me Fallyn?" She crossed the room to take his outstretched hand and shake it. "You *are* showing me your war room, after all."

"It's not much," he said with the politest of smiles. "Nothing, I'm sure, like Pasche & Associates."

Boy, he had that right. Because of their clientele, P&A had to project a certain air of upscale everything: competence, power, prestige. The office space Fallyn rented cost a fortune, but looked like a spread in Interior Design Magazine. At least the reception room and private consultation rooms did. The back room where the group did their nitty-gritty brainstorming lacked the same finesse and polish. It was, however, soundproofed and had top-notch security features, just in case someone might be listening in.

It appeared Grey took privacy and security seriously, too, even though the Justice Team's "clients" were from the other end of the spectrum. She noted Mr. Teeg's screens showed a variety of security footage from cameras no doubt mounted around the premises. If she were a betting woman—and she was—she'd lay odds on infrared wires and an electrified fence to round out the system.

Fallyn returned Grey's smile. "I don't let strangers into my war room, so I imagine this goes against everything in your nature."

The corner of Grey's lips twitched, a movement Fallyn was beginning to realize was his version of a real smile.

"We dropped the prescription bottles off at the precinct," Tony told him. "Fallyn kept a pill from each of the bottles to do our own analysis, and we brought all the nonprescription vitamins and supplements."

Fallyn produced the bag of vitamins she'd kept from Hollister from her briefcase and Grey took them. "I'll get these off to the private lab we use *ASAP*."

He must have seen her slight hesitation, because he followed up with a reassurance. "They run a lot of classified, off-the-books stuff for us. Privacy is paramount with them. You don't have to worry about leaks."

Exactly what could be leaked that would hurt her sister, she wasn't sure, but at this point, she had to cover all her bases. Make sure this stayed quiet until she figured what the hell was going on. "Thank you," she told Grey. "I thought of something else earlier."

"What's that?"

"My sister took a lot of heat a few months back over a bill she voted against concerning raising military pay."

That got Grey's attention. "What kind of heat?"

"The kind none of us want. Hate mail, *death* threats, the whole gamut. Can you help me look into that? See if the FBI got involved at all? She never told me, but..."

Well, she didn't need to go into details about her lack of communication with her twin. Apparently Grey got the message as he was already in motion, jotting himself a note.

"I'll see what pops up. If there were death threats, the FBI will have a file."

It was hard giving control of a potential landmine over to these people, but on the flip side, they handled matters like this on a daily basis, just like Tony had told her that first night. They were experts. For once, it was a relief not to be the only one trying to defuse a bomb, especially since she didn't have her own team there working with her.

If that's what this was...a bomb.

Grey set the bag on the nearby desk and motioned her and Tony over to Teeg's "office." He pointed at a screen on the far right. "Teeg managed to break the code on one section of the file you found on your sister's tablet. It appears to be a list of names. Last, first, middle initial."

Teeg grunted. "It was a simple code, like a spy cipher wheel kids make at summer camp with a couple of paper plates. Totally bogus."

Interesting. David Teeg didn't seem the type to do summer camp. "We went to Camp Sawpepper together every summer for two weeks. Heather loved those stupid spy codes and message games."

"Took Teeg hours to figure it out," Tony pseudo-whispered, his dig garnering a glare from the computer whiz.

"So sue me." Teeg tossed a paperclip he'd been twiddling onto the desk. "I thought it would be legit, you know, a coded top-secret file on a senator's tablet. Something complicated, modern, probably military. A code like that, you'd need my high-tech decoding software for." He started rambling about codes from WWII all the way up to "that China thing" which Fallyn ignored.

Finally, Grey held up a hand and Tony whistled at the same time, stopping the computer whiz in mid-sentence. Teeg got up from his futuristic looking chair, gave them all a dirty look, and walked away. "I need a break."

Grey and Tony exchanged a look that included an eye roll from

Tony and a temple rub from Grey. Fallyn understood completely. She'd had plenty of eye-roll moments with Dani.

"Anyway, as I was saying." Grey indicated a column in the middle. "We're not sure about this. It doesn't seem to be a code, per se, but more like a designation."

For each entry, there was a letter and one or two numbers. For a long minute, they all stared at the screen.

13A, 7C, 9E — Fallyn mentally went down the list. Apartment numbers? Parking garage slots?

Grey pointed to the next column. "Over here are country abbreviations. GB equals Great Britain. CH, China. CA, Canada, etc."

People from around the world. There had to be a hundred or more.

Fallyn unbuttoned her coat but left it on. The building was chilly even if it was in the fifties outside.

"So what do you think those are?" Tony pointed at the middle column of letters and numbers again. The puzzle seemed to be bugging him as much as her. "They look like seat numbers. You know, like for a basketball game or a concert."

"That's it!" Teeg burst back into the room, running toward them, the door he'd come through banging against the wall.

"What is?" Tony said.

The computer whiz bombed around them, dropped into his chair, and started typing. "Seat numbers! We need to cross reference databases with those names and seat numbers."

They all watched as the middle screen went blank, then Teeg's typing appeared in lines and lines of computer code Fallyn had no way of understanding.

While the computer scrolled and Teeg typed, a new screen came to life with an internet search. Tony, who was standing entirely too close to her, touched her back again.

He could feel it too. The electricity. The adrenaline.

His touch was light, easy, no hidden message, although if his touch *had* suggested he wanted to kiss her, she wouldn't have minded.

She liked the closeness. The touch didn't freak her out. In fact, she almost grabbed his hand and anchored it to her hip. Go figure.

But then the large screen showing the internet search results came to a standstill. "Got it," Teeg said. "The letter-number combos *are* for seats. Tony, you're a genius."

He did some finger action again on his keyboard and a copy of the tablet spreadsheet merged onto the large screen in front of them, nestling side-by-side with the search page results.

"What is that?" Fallyn pointed at the search engine screen. "It looks like a newspaper article."

"It is," Grey said.

Tony slid forward to eyeball both items, releasing her and putting his hands on the desk as he read. "Holy shit."

"Holy shit, what?" Fallyn said. Her skin crawled but she didn't know why.

He looked over his shoulder at her, his face grim. "The list on your sister's tablet corresponds exactly to the names of the people who disappeared on CanAir 702 two months ago."

The CanAir disappearance had rocked the news. One hundred and twenty-eight people had disappeared over the Gulf of Mexico. No plane had been found, no bodies, no wreckage washed up on shore. Some speculated aliens had stolen the plane and its passengers. Some said it was the Bermuda Triangle effect, even though the plane's last known coordinates were nowhere near that area. Others claimed the plane went off track and ended up on a deserted island. The fact was, no one knew, but experts speculated the plane had crashed into the ocean.

On top of that, the CIA had verified that a known terrorist leader had been on board under a bogus identity. While there was no evidence Abdul-Nasser Nazari was responsible, most people believed he'd taken the plane down as an act of terrorism.

"Those names are hardly a secret," Fallyn said. "I don't know why Heather would have had a coded file of them, but..."

A flicker of doubt crossed her mind. She took a step back. There was something here. Something about her sister, the information on the tablet, and a missing plane full of innocent people. Had Heather been suspicious of the plane's disappearance and been investigating it?

Had that investigation gotten her killed?

Jesus.

Why? Who? Fallyn's brain spun with questions.

"We need to decode the rest of the file," Grey said, a few questions showing in his own eyes. "Heather used a different code for each file in the folder. Any chance she learned more than one code at camp?"

Fallyn sighed. "Can you believe sixteen?"

All three men looked at her like she was nuts.

Her sister had hated bugs and weeds, but she loved geeky games. "She was head of arts and crafts time every year and one of her favorite things to do with the younger campers was play spy games."

"Sixteen. Wow. Okay," Grey said. He handed her a paper and pencil. "Write them down and Teeg will work on it."

Tony touched her cheek. "Then we better head to the hotel so you can get some rest. It's been a rough day."

Rough was an understatement. She nodded and wrote down the codes she could remember—it had been such a long time—and then buttoned her coat. Thinking about camp, good memories and some not-so-good flashed through her mind.

Not now. There was no going back in time and fixing the past. All she could do was concentrate on the here and now.

Seeing she was ready to go, Tony left the desk he'd been waiting at and held out a hand to her.

She hesitated for half a second, then gave in and reached for him. He drew her to the door and stopped. "Close your eyes, sweetheart, remember?"

"What, no blindfold?" she teased, but did as instructed, trusting him to lead her safely back to his Explorer.

He smacked her playfully on her backside as they crossed into the parking lot, then leaned down close to her ear. "Maybe later," he said soft and low and Fallyn's pulse went into overdrive.

7

The next day, Fallyn felt like it was her own funeral.

Organ music rose in the air. Seeing Heather in the casket was too much. Her sister—the other half of her—was...was...

Dead.

The hollowness ate at her. She'd never been without her sister, even when they were kinda, sorta, estranged.

That connection, that undeniable blood bond, was now broken. Seeing her twin in the casket, with too much makeup and the awful pallor underneath that no amount of foundation or blush could compensate for, made Fallyn's already churning stomach and pounding head intensify their one-two punch.

Breathe.

Thank God the casket was closed now. She never thought she'd outlive Heather. Never thought she'd be sitting in a church pew, jaw clenched, eyes straight ahead as the young priest droned on with Heather's eulogy, their stoic father clenching his hands and staring at the wooden floor.

The bitch of it was, even with the makeup, the face in the casket had looked a little too much like her own. Talk about seeing her life flash before her eyes...it had so unnerved Fallyn during the visitation, she'd barely made it to the ladies' room before losing the breakfast Tony had made sure she'd eaten that morning.

Of course, her mother's appearance, though brief, hadn't done much for her either.

It took guts for Christina to show up and pretend to be in pain over a daughter she hadn't seen in years. Guts to walk through that visitation line and hug Eric.

She'd tried to hug Fallyn, too. No way in hell that was happening.

No fucking way.

Not after the mess she'd so easily left behind, wrecking two young girls' lives and ripping out their father's heart to go live with another man.

Their *mother*—Fallyn couldn't bring herself to call that woman Mom—had said her goodbyes and slipped out without another word, and even though Fallyn was relieved that her mother had left without a scene, her heart felt shredded. There had been no apologies from Christina. No remorse that she'd left her daughters behind and now one of them was dead.

Stop thinking about her. The woman didn't deserve the time. Think about something else. Something besides death and abandonment.

Tony Gerard. She stopped herself from turning in the pew and looking for him. He was behind her somewhere in the church. Keeping an eye on her. Keeping her safe.

She had to admit, as crass as it seemed at her sister's funeral, having a competent, if slightly uptight, good-looking man around wasn't the worst thing. He'd been a rock for her, helping her with everything. After her visit to Heather's office, Eric had pulled a number on her, insisting they move up the timeline of the funeral. Hence, Fallyn had needed to shift gears the moment they left the old army base and throw herself full-throttle into funeral arrangements.

The priest turned the pulpit over to one of Heather's contemporaries, a fellow senator who'd sat on the Ethics Committee with her before Heather had moved to Foreign Relations. Fallyn fidgeted, listening to the glowing praise the man rained down on her dead sister. Behind him, solemn, graceful angels stared down at those gathered, their white plaster bodies in direct contrast to the dark clothes of the mourners. Sunlight filtered through the stained glass windows as the words echoed off the high ceilings.

As the congressman spoke about Heather's commitment to justice and her snarky sense of humor, Eric Pasche raised his head, and soft rays from a nearby window caught the grey in his hair. His lips trembled with a slight smile. He reached over and grasped Fallyn's hand.

She gripped the big, rough hand, tears threatening to spill out the corners of her eyes. She never flinched from his touch...in fact, she craved it, but her father's touch was a rarity. He was proud of Heather; happy at the turnout of so many powerful people to pay homage to his favorite daughter.

Fallyn didn't blame him. Heather had been a good person, always fighting the good fight. She deserved this. Their father deserved this.

She hoped President Nicols kept his word and showed up. That would really make her father's day.

But what if...

Fallyn's head throbbed without mercy. Thoughts scratched and clawed at her brain. Heather had a tablet in her safe with coded—probably classified—information on it. She'd had a heart problem and ended up with some funky drug in her system. Someone was after that tablet.

On the other side of her, Carl patted her arm. Jordan's father had a knowing smile on his lips that matched her father's. The two men had grown up together on the south side of DC. Fallyn knew her father had turned to Carl at least once for financial help with his restaurants during the last recession. Carl was the reason Heather had gone into politics. The reason Jordan had worked for her.

His pat was brief, just a quick touch and a wink when she glanced at him. He knew how awful this was for her—for all of them—but he'd always encouraged Fallyn as much as he had Heather. Fallyn had confided in him on occasion through the years and was grateful for his help today, getting her father ready for the visitation and funeral, being her support when she had none.

It was good to have him and Jordan surrounding her. A makeshift family, but one that worked right here, right now.

The forlorn notes of *Amazing Grace* brought her out of her reverie. She'd completely missed the end of the senator's speech. As the congregation rose to sing, two men approached the pulpit in dark suits. The organist stalled and everyone turned toward the back door.

Fallyn, in her heels, turned too, and looked over the heads of the people near her. More men in suits and sunglasses came down the aisle, followed by the President of the United States. Fallyn felt eyes on her. She glanced around and saw Tony near the rear of the church watching her instead of the leader of the free world.

Her pulse quickened. From Tony's look or the president's arrival? She wasn't sure. Quickly, she diverted her attention back to the president and his cavalcade. Even though she'd personally spent time with President Nicols, the power that radiated from the man still sent chills over her skin.

Her bodyguard did a fine job of that too.

President Nicols approached the front of the church, surrounded by Secret Service, and took a moment to veer over to her and her father. He shook her father's hand, said a few soft words, and Eric Pasche came alive for the first time in days. He smiled a real smile, his eyes lit up, and he returned the president's handshake with gusto.

Nicols then turned to her, sadness and sympathy showing in his eyes. A lump formed in her throat as she shook his hand.

"Fallyn, my dear," he said warmly, "we all felt as though Heather was part of our extended family and we're devastated at her passing. I can't imagine what it must be like for you, her twin sister."

He pulled her into one of those unexpected embraces that left Fallyn gasping for air. When he let go of her, he squeezed both of her arms and she gritted her teeth to keep from jerking away. "If there's anything you or your father need, please call me."

She nodded, forcing a smile. "Thank you, Mr. President. I will."

He proceeded to the casket which was draped with red roses, white lilies, and beautiful purple lilacs. As he laid a hand on the flowers and bowed his head, Fallyn caught the scent of the lilacs drifting across the room. For a moment, the president closed his eyes as if offering up a private prayer for her sister, then raised his head and motioned everyone to take their seats.

He didn't stand at the pulpit, instead using his booming voice to speak to the crowd from behind the casket.

As the president told a funny story about Heather, her father beamed. So did Carl. Too bad her mother had missed this part. *We turned out pretty good, despite you, Mom.*

The moment was over too fast and the tones of *Amazing Grace* once more rose into the air as the president made a swift departure. The congregation sang, the casket was wheeled out, and Fallyn and her father were escorted through the back of the church to a limo waiting outside that would take them to the private graveside service.

Fallyn felt Tony's eyes on her the whole time.

After the graveside service, Carl offered to take Eric home. The sun was setting, Fallyn was desperate to get out of her heels, and she was anxious to catch up with Tony who was talking on his phone as he waited for her at the bottom of the cemetery hill. The whole time, she'd scanned the area, watching for her mother. The woman had never shown up, but Fallyn's nerves were still on high alert.

She waved at her father, Jordan, and Carl as the limo drove off. She needed to get back to the hotel and freshen up before she gave the hounding press a statement. No doubt some of them were waiting outside the gates to pounce the moment she showed her face. A face they seemed to like because it had shock value. People continued to look at her as if she were a ghost.

All she could hope, as she walked slowly down the hill, was that the media had assumed she was in the limo and leave to follow it back to the church.

Not that she wanted her dad subjected to their questions, but Carl and Jordan would protect him and chase off the reporters. If he'd given her more time, she could have lined up some security for him, but no. He'd been adamant to get this over with, so he had to deal with a little fallout.

The sun was setting. One long, hard day over. Grief seized Fallyn's heart and she had to stop for a moment and catch her breath.

One foot in front of the other, Fallyn. Keep moving.

Her feet obeyed. As Tony ended his phone call, his dark eyes watched her all the way to his Explorer. He helped her into the seat without a word, squeezing her hand before he pulled out and took off for the hotel without her even asking.

8

*T*ony sat on the sofa in Fallyn's suite checking his emails on his laptop while his client slept in the bedroom.

All night he'd sat in that living room, his mind ping-ponging between Heather Pasche, an airline manifest, and Fallyn.

In a bed.

Feet away.

He shook it off, checked the time on his laptop screen. 7:50. He glanced at the closed bedroom door again. Maybe he should check on her? Make sure she was okay.

But what could be wrong? Aside from a couple of fitful naps, he'd been on watch most of the night and all had been quiet. Not even anyone in the hallway in the middle of the night.

"She's tired, idiot," he said.

After the last few days, she had a right to that. Plus, it had been after midnight by the time they'd gotten back last night and she'd dropped like a stone into bed.

His e-mail dinged and he glanced at it. Sister number two making sure he knew what time Mom's party was.

Man, these girls ran herd on him. He zapped back a quick "Got it," and hit send.

Two down, two to go.

"Morning," Fallyn said.

He glanced up, found her standing in the bedroom doorway, her hair piled in a messy knot on top of her head. She wore one of the hotel bathrobes that hit her just above the knees of her bare legs. She'd cinched it tight at the waist, covering most of her torso but leaving just enough of a V at the neck where more bare skin peeked out.

And, man-oh-man, his mind went all kinds of places wondering what, exactly, she wore under that bathrobe.

He cleared his throat. "Morning. Sleep okay?"

She nodded. "Yep. Yepper. Just gonna hop in the shower and we can get rolling." She pointed at the laptop. "You're a busy boy already."

"I was up. Figured I'd make use of the time. Clearing emails."

His laptop dinged and he glanced at it, shaking his head. "Never frickin' fails."

"Something wrong?"

"No. My sister." He fired off another "Got it" and went back to Fallyn. "Three down so far. All highly concerned that I will forget to attend my mother's birthday party."

Fallyn laughed. "You have a history of that?"

"No. Which is why it's funny. So far, one has called, two have e-mailed and sometime in the next twelve hours number four will text. They are nothing if not predictable."

Fallyn met his gaze and held it for a long second, a small smile that fell short of the full load one.

Dumbass.

Whining about his sisters when Fallyn had just buried hers. "Damn," he said. "I shouldn't...I'm sorry."

"For what?"

"My sisters. That was insensitive."

"Oh, please. Just because my sister is..." She paused, squeezed her eyes closed, tilted her back a second before looking at him again. "Well...it doesn't mean you can't moan about yours.

85

It's fine. It's nice that they stay in touch. You said your dad passed?"

"Yeah. Since then, I'm the token male."

"I'm sorry."

"I'm used to it."

"It explains a lot." She rolled her hand. "You have that fierce protective streak. I can see why they have you guarding Supreme Court Justices."

"Oh, Christ," he said. "Honey, you have no idea."

"Oh, yes I do. Tony Gerard, think about what I do. I'm not about to let you into my private life, let you stay in my hotel room, while I sleep, without checking you out. I know about the judge."

Shit. He sat back, propped his feet up on the coffee table. Mr. Casual. "Yeah. My protective streak failed—in a big way—that time."

"He got out of the car after you told him not to. How is that a failure?"

"How do you know that?"

She shoved her hands in the pockets of the robe. "The Justice Team doesn't have the only hacker in this country. One of my staff plucked some reports from the Supreme Court Police files."

"Well, shit. You know it all?"

"I do. I know you tried to quit and they wouldn't let you. I think that says something about you, no?"

Pity he didn't need. Or want. He set his feet on the floor, straightened his laptop. "I don't know what it says about me. All I know is a man I cared about is dead." He looked over at her. "And I don't want to talk about this."

"It's not your fault."

"So, listen," he said. "While you were getting your beauty sleep, I did some research."

She wandered over to the sofa, sat down next to him and the faded scent of her perfume—something clean and airy—lingered. "Okay," she said. "You don't want to talk about it. I get it. But you saw my emotional nonsense yesterday so I owe you one."

"Thank you," he said. "I appreciate it. That you care. But I'm good."

"Sure you are. Just like me."

Two hot messes.

"Did you know your sister was on the Foreign Relations committee?"

"Actually, she was on a subcommittee. The subcommittee on Western Hemisphere, Transnational Crime, Civilian Security, Democracy, Human Rights, and Global Women's Issues."

"Wow. You remember all that?"

She bumped him with her shoulder. "When you're reminded daily, by multiple people, you do. She was Miss Perfect, remember?"

"Jeez."

"Ach." She smacked herself on the head. "Did that sound as bad as I think it did? I swear, Tony Gerard, there's something about you that makes me forget to filter."

"And that's a bad thing?"

"For someone who makes a career filtering messages? You bet it is."

"Maybe you should give yourself a break once in a while. Me? I could give a shit about your lack of filter. I'd rather see you ditch the filter. You're entitled. Especially now." He turned sideways, tugged on a loose strand of her hair. "Shoving all that anger and hurt away will eat you alive."

When did he become a shrink? God knew he had his own issues in that department, but this? No way should he be lecturing her on dealing with grief.

Her gaze was steady on his, her green eyes drilling into him and if he knew females at all, she was thinking. Analyzing him again like she'd done that first night. About something he'd said, dissecting it, breaking it down into smaller components she could arrange and rearrange.

All so she could pounce on it.

"What was it like losing your dad so young?"

Bingo.

He snorted. Women. "The usual." She gave him a look like he'd opened his skull and dropped its contents in her lap. "I was a kid, Fallyn. What did I know about grieving? We buried him and we went back to school and sports and anything else my mom could think of. She kept us moving."

"Which is why you know about shoving away anger and hurt. And now we add the judge to that."

"We're not talking about me."

"What if I want to talk about you?"

"Oh, good luck with that," he grinned at her and made a show of poking the mouse pad on his laptop. "Back to this. Your sister was on a Foreign Relations subcommittee. I find that interesting."

"Why?"

"Not so much that she was on the committee, but the *Foreign Relations* committee—or a subcommittee of Foreign Relations. And then we find coded files regarding an international incident on her tablet. And, hello? Foreign Relations helps develop foreign policy. You don't think a terrorist leader who died in a suspicious plane crash, and oh by the way, that plane was carrying passengers from six different countries, has anything to do with foreign policy? If you don't think so, come join me in Neverland again where we can pontificate on what a peaceful world we're living in."

Fallyn stood, set her hands on her hips, and paced in front of him. "I see your point, but maybe her committee was quietly looking into it, trying to determine if it was an accident or terrorism? I'd expect that."

"As would I. Except we think your sister was mur—" He stopped. Caught himself and sat back.

"My sister was murdered. You can say it. We're trying to figure this out. Mincing words won't help. My sister was murdered and someone tried to steal her tablet."

"Yes. The data on the plane crash can't be a coincidence. Can't be. What I don't know is how we find out. That's your area. Who do we ask?"

She stopped pacing and bit her bottom lip. "Jordan. Or Carl.

Between them, Heather may have confided in them. Or Carl, with his State Department contacts might have heard something."

The blueberry scone Tony bought her at the food truck three blocks from the townhouse was quite seriously the best one she'd ever had. The coffee was a smoky dark roast she loved too. Who knew that little hidden gem of a food truck could give her favorite NYC coffee shop a run for its money any day?

She was laughing at a story he was telling about his sisters as he unlocked the townhouse door—he always had to go first and 'clear' the place—and stepped across the threshold.

"You've got a little..." Tony said, pointing to the corner of her bottom lip. "Blueberry right there."

She licked her lips, his gaze tracking her tongue, and she felt a pulse of heat erupt between her legs. "Did I get it?"

"No." Their eyes locked, and a second later, he touched her, gently rubbing his thumb across her lip. His fingers grazed her jawbone and he let them linger on her skin. "There. All gone. Stay put so I can make sure we're alone."

But he didn't take his hand away. Didn't move to clear the townhouse.

Fallyn didn't pull back. What was this man doing to her? He was brassy and pushy and always touching her.

She should run. Now.

He was also smart and funny and drop dead sexy. If she weren't feeling so downright horny every time he looked at her, she'd definitely make him a job offer.

She *was* feeling horny, however, and on the heels of that thought came a wash of guilt. Here she was, standing in her dead sister's house and thinking about jumping this man's bones.

Disgusting. Get a grip, Fal.

She couldn't look away, though. His eyes held her in their grip. His fingers caressed her cheekbone.

"Oh, hey, guys!"

The woman's voice made them jump apart and Fallyn whirled to find Jordan coming down the stairs. "Jordan. What are you doing here?"

"Cleaning up." She hit the bottom stair and waved a cleaning rag around at the living room. "It was a disaster and I knew you were having a hard time dealing with all of this, so I thought I'd help out and get the place back in order. I cleared my calendar this morning and had hoped to be done before you came back to sort through the rest of Heather's things. I was just about to start upstairs. It was going to be a surprise."

She gave Fallyn a sad face, but then smiled, her gaze bopping over to Tony, then back to Fallyn. "Are you feeling better?" she asked, voice switching from *shoot, you caught me* to a concerned mother hen. "The other day you were a little...you know...?"

"Crazy?" Fallyn said as Tony closed the door behind them.

Jordan smiled. "I was going to say *overwhelmed*."

Fallyn had not felt overwhelmed. Pissed off, yes. Freaked out a bit, definitely. Sad as hell, you bet. But not overwhelmed. Finding out Heather had a heart problem, and then discovering she had a large amount of a drug in her system that could cause a heart attack had sent her reeling, but she handled crises on a daily basis in her career. The more the better because she thrived on it. It made the blood in her veins sing. She didn't do 'overwhelmed.'

"I'm fine. Thanks for asking. How about you? Did you get any sleep last night?"

Jordan went on about her workload and all the reporters calling her. Fallyn let her talk and nodded at the appropriate moments, but her mind kept wandering back to Tony.

He took the plastic coffee cup from her hand and helped her off with her coat while Jordan talked. Such a gentleman. She didn't get that in New York. Not that she'd ever really wanted it. Any guy who acted like she needed him was shown the door. With Tony, it felt different. He respected her and his show of manners wasn't about making her feel inferior.

The couch and chairs were back in their rightful places; the bookshelves were once more neat and tidy.

"The place looks picture perfect, Jordan. Just the way Heather liked it."

Jordan's smile showed a lot of teeth and a certain pride. Her thoughtfulness, at least in regard to Heather, was another thing you didn't find much in the hustle and bustle of New York City. "I've terminated Heather's cell phone contract and caught up on the bills. Did you figure out the passcode for that tablet? I have some ideas about what Heather might have used."

"I figured it out, thanks. There was nothing on it but some copies of receipts and stuff." Fallyn accepted her cup back from Tony and took a sip. "Actually, Jordan, I'm glad you're here for another reason. I was going to call you this morning with some questions about the subcommittee Heather was on."

"The Senate Foreign Relations?"

Fallyn nodded. "Do you know what they were investigating when Heather died?"

Jordan gave her a funny look and wadded the cleaning cloth in her hands. *Code Red, everybody. Fallyn's riding the crazy train again.*

"What *weren't* they investigating?" the young woman asked with a chuckle. "The Foreign Relations subcommittee deals with transnational crime, human trafficking, global narcotics, human rights, you name it. Heather loved it because they worked on global women's health issues. My dad said they're really going to miss her."

"They also investigate terrorism, correct?"

"They oversee matters relating to terrorism in the Western Hemisphere, yes. Why?"

"Were they investigating the CanAir disappearance by chance?"

A frown crossed Jordan's face. Tony leaned on the doorframe—did the man ever stand up?—and Jordan glanced at him with that funny look on her face. *Help me*, it said. *She's gone round the bend.*

"Of course they looked into it," Jordan said. "It's standard protocol since it fell in their jurisdiction, but all they did was an overview. The president and the CIA ruled it as an act of terrorism by Abdul-Nasser Nazari three weeks ago."

"So there was no real investigation by the subcommittee?"

"Why would there be?"

Fallyn mentally sighed and reached for the never-ending supply of patience she used with clients. "The plane went down near the Gulf of Mexico with a terrorist on board that carried people from half a dozen different countries. I'd say that falls in the Foreign Relations subcommittee's wheelhouse."

"The plane didn't originate in the U.S."

"It was carrying five U.S. citizens and Nazari is on Homeland's most wanted list."

Jordan shrugged. "They reviewed the case, that's all I can tell you. I type up Heather's notes from the subcommittee meetings—you know how she did everything in longhand—and I remember a notation that the committee reviewed the case and agreed with the CIA findings. Case closed. There was nothing to investigate. No plane, no eyewitnesses, no nothing. Why is this so important to you?"

Because I am, indeed, a little crazy. "Just something I was thinking about. The CanAir disappearance was such a big deal there for a while, and I never got to ask Heather about it. You know, if she had any thoughts about what might have really happened to that plane."

"A terrorist took it over and killed a bunch of people." Jordan glanced at her watch and tossed the cleaning cloth onto the coffee table. "Jeez, time has gotten away from me. I better get going. There are a lot of details to wrap up at the office."

So the cleared calendar had suddenly filled up? Fallyn smiled at her. "I also need to ask about that bill she vetoed last year. The one that brought on all the bad press. She received death threats from that, didn't she?"

"The FBI investigated all of them and none were credible." Jordan brushed by her and grabbed her coat from the tiny coat closet. "And by the way, I got into quite a bit of trouble over you two barging into her office the other day. Heather, like every senator, dealt with sensitive government and military information."

Behind her back, Tony rolled his eyes. Fallyn fought hard not to grin. "Sorry about that, but I needed to see what she had for prescriptions."

"Did you find that drug you were talking about in any of her things?"

"No," Fallyn admitted. "But someone gave it to her. I just have to find out who."

"Detective Hollister came by and asked me a bunch of questions. He seems very competent, Fallyn. Maybe you should leave this in his hands."

Not likely. Fallyn went to the door and opened it. "I'll check in with you later."

Jordan didn't try for a hug this time, but she did pat Fallyn on the arm. "Don't forget to get her suits ready for Fresh Start. Sydney Banfield, the director, is doing her annual career day at the shelter. Heather always donated suits to it for the women. Ms. Banfield will be stopping by to pick them up. I gave her your number so she can work out details with you."

Once she was gone, Fallyn crossed her arms and tapped the bottom of her coffee cup against her elbow. "So that was a dead end."

Tony boosted off the doorframe and grabbed his cup from the foyer table. "Why do you say that?"

He took hers from her hand and headed into the kitchen.

Fallyn trailed behind him. "You heard her, the subcommittee reviewed the case and were satisfied with the CIA's findings. Case closed. The FBI investigated all of the death threats and none were deemed credible."

He poured the contents of each cup into a ceramic mug and stuck both of them in the microwave. "And you don't think Heather might have been doing her own investigation into CanAir?"

"That's exactly what I think, but Jordan obviously doesn't know anything about it. I'm going to have to dig deeper."

"Is there anyone else you can ask without throwing up red flags and bringing unwanted attention to yourself?"

"Maybe. For now, I need to go get those suits ready for this Fresh Start gal."

"You'll like Sydney. She does good work at the shelter."

"You know her?"

The microwave dinged. Tony handed her the mug with her coffee in it. "She's Grey's fiancée."

"No way."

He grinned. "Tough as nails. Like you. She's got him wrapped around her pinky."

The thought of a woman bringing Justice Greystone to his knees made Fallyn smile. Every one of them—the male species—had an Achilles heel and the right woman could use that to her advantage. She looked forward to meeting this Sydney Banfield. "I like her already."

"So you want to head upstairs?"

There was something flirty in his voice. His eyes held hers with that smoldering look in them.

Fallyn's throat suddenly went dry. She took a swig of her coffee and realized, too late, it was too hot to chug.

Coffee spewed from her mouth and she vaulted for the sink. "Oh, God, I'm so sorry," she said, hiding her face with her hand. She tore a paper towel from the holder and wiped her mouth, coughed and sputtered, and tried to breathe.

A glass of water came into her view with a big, strong hand wrapped around it. Tony chuckled as she gladly accepted it from him and got her coughing under control.

"That coffee," she sputtered. "Too hot."

"Funny," he said, sipping from his mug and grinning at her. "Mine's just right."

Bastard. She drew a deep breath, set down the water glass and rubbed her hands together. "So you were saying?"

"The suits? They're upstairs in the closet?"

That's not what he'd meant when he'd flashed those sexy eyes at her. "Of course,"—*you tease*—"I'll get started on those, but you really don't have to stay. I mean, Grey has the tablet and no one's taken another run at me, so I guess I'm safe here. You must have other things to do."

"You let me worry about that," he said. "Now let's get those suits together."

An hour later, the suits were ready and the bedroom was looking as clean and neat as it had before the break-in. Fallyn was going through a bunch of Heather's bills at the kitchen table, Tony working on a laptop and occasionally answering texts and emails, when the door-bell rang.

Fallyn started for the door. Tony grabbed her from behind and stopped her, going to the door himself. "It's Jordan's father," he said, looking out the peephole.

"Well, let him in."

"You sure you're up for round two with him?"

She waved off his serious look. "He's a good friend of our family and was Heather's biggest supporter outside of my dad. I'm sure he's just here to check on me. I *was* a little crazy the other day."

Tony's serious face morphed into a grin. "I like your brand of crazy."

She batted his arm. "Let the poor man in."

"Sir," Tony said, opening the door but standing in the way. "What brings you here?"

"Me? What are *you* doing here?" Carl asked.

Fallyn shoved Tony out of the way. "I'm sorry, Carl. My...Tony...is a little overprotective. Come in."

Carl stepped inside, fidgeting with a cardboard box in his hand. "Jordan gave me this the other day. A few of Heather's personal items. I meant to bring them by sooner, but you know how it is."

"You didn't have to do that." Fallyn accepted the box, but found it lifted from her hands by Tony. He took it into the kitchen and stayed there, out of sight, but eavesdropping, no doubt. "I would have picked it up."

"I wanted to check on you, anyway." Carl glanced around. "Jordan said you didn't find the pills you were looking for."

Word traveled fast. "No, we didn't, but I believe Detective Hollister sent the prescriptions to a lab to have them analyzed. Maybe one of the bottles was mislabeled or had the wrong drugs in it."

He removed the hat from his head and frowned. "This is a serious accusation, Fallyn, that your sister was given—or purposely took—a drug that caused her heart failure."

And what? Now he thought Heather committed suicide? Fallyn nearly gawked. The balls. "What are you insinuating, Carl?"

Carl's eyes turned hard. "Nothing, Fallyn. Whatever you're thinking, get it out of your head."

"The autopsy report doesn't lie. She had high amounts of Perisoladol in her system. There is no prescription for the stuff. We need to know how it got there."

A sigh. He fingered his hat, working it in circles. "Jordan said you're asking questions about Heather's investigations now. What are you trying to do, here, Fallyn?"

Good God—was he accusing her? "I'm trying to get answers to my sister's death. It's not out of the question that someone purposely gave her a drug that killed her."

Carl blanched. "You don't know that."

"I *do* know that, and I'm going to dig into every corner and every crease until I figure out who did this to her and why. Was it someone still pissed about her vetoing that bill or something else? Do you know anything about her investigating the CanAir disappearance?"

Another round of the hat through his bony fingers. "I do not, but if I promise to look into it, will you stand down for now?" He lowered his voice, his eyes softening once more with pain and something else. Something that reminded her of her father when he was going to give her a warning. "You're going to piss off the wrong people in Washington, Fallyn, and for what? Possibly nothing. Let me handle the political side of this thing. I can do it without bringing attention to myself or getting you in hot water."

His continued contracting at the State Department afforded him a lot of leverage. He had access to files and information Fallyn could only dream of. "You're right." A statement everyone loved to hear and one that usually put them at ease. "Do what you can and let me know what you find out. I appreciate your help."

Which didn't mean she was going to stand down, but appeasing Carl and getting him off her ass was her first goal.

"Good." He returned the hat to his head, everything settled. At least in his mind. "I'm taking your father to dinner tonight. You're welcome to join us."

Oh, boy. Dinner with her dad and Carl. *Shoot me now.* "I think a boys' night is in order for Dad without me tagging along."

Carl nodded and left. Fallyn shut the door and leaned against it, blowing out a long breath.

Tony emerged from the kitchen. "You backed down on that one."

"Funny thing is," Fallyn said, reaching for her cell phone, "the more people tell me to lay off, the more bullheaded I become about forging full steam ahead."

"Who are you calling?" Tony asked.

"A guy who owes me a really big favor." She listened to the phone ring on the other end. "It's time to cash it in."

Tony opened the door to the dive burger joint and even from his spot on the threshold he inhaled the aroma of searing meat. The place didn't look like much, but it smelled pretty damned good. He waved Fallyn inside, giving her a skeptical look in the process. Between her and the guy they were meeting, they couldn't come up with a better locale? Perhaps one where someone wouldn't get shot?

And, maybe, Fallyn could have left her designer suit and shoes in the closet for this field trip? Jesus, they'd be lucky if a bunch of gang-bangers didn't file in carrying semi-automatics and force her to strip.

Which, of course, would compel him to do some serious ass-kicking and potentially wind up with a few bullet holes himself.

Definitely should have put her in sweat pants.

"Hey," she said, seeming to read his mind, "he chose the place. Not me."

"Well, that makes me feel marginally better considering your shoes probably cost more than the entire building. You could have gone for a look that didn't scream I-have-money."

At that, she burst out laughing and the sound of it, despite the fact that he should be royally pissed that she took her own safety for granted, made him smile. Fallyn wasn't exactly easy. This was a woman who'd take a man's leg—or possibly other body parts—off if he crossed her. But underneath all the toughness he sensed compassion and a willingness to do whatever it took to protect her loved ones.

And on that, they were of the same mind.

So he'd give her a pass for laughing at him.

This time.

"There he is," she said, marching toward a booth on the far side of the restaurant.

"You want me to stay scarce?"

"Nah. He knows if I'm with someone, he can trust them. I built a reputation on discretion."

As they approached, the man met Fallyn's gaze then sized up Tony. *Yeah, dude, I'm staying.*

On the table in front of him was a half-eaten burger and some fries. Obviously, the guy had opted for an early lunch. His attempt at covert action. His *attempt* to look like he wasn't a government employee having a clandestine meeting about a potential cover-up.

Without stopping to exchange pleasantries, Fallyn slid into the booth, Tony beside her.

"Hey, Fallyn," the guy said.

"Hi, Blake. Thanks for meeting us. This is Tony."

Blake nodded but didn't bother with a handshake. All part of the effort to appear they hadn't just met, Tony supposed.

Whatever. As long as they all got out without Fallyn's shoes getting boosted. Tony glanced around the mostly empty restaurant, made brief eye contact with an older man sitting three tables over reading a newspaper. The guy quickly averted his eyes and went back to his paper.

Outside of that, the place was quiet for 10:30 on a Friday morning.

"So, what's up?" Blake said. "I need to get back."

Fallyn clasped her hands together on top of the scarred Formica table. "I need to know what's up with the Foreign Relations committee's investigation on the CanAir flight."

"Which one?"

Tony rolled his eyes.

"Blake," Fallyn said, "don't be an asshole. We're both too busy and my sister is dead. I'm well aware that your boss..." she turned to Tony and nodded toward Blake, "...*his* boss is Senator Dolan, a member of the Armed Services committee. He and Senator Margaret Oren, the chair of Foreign Relations, have a standing meeting every Wednesday at noon in a room on the fourth floor at the InterContinental." She looked back at Blake, "I think you should stop screwing with me."

Jeez, the woman was hell on wheels.

A seriously pale Blake held his hands out. "How am I screwing with you?"

She leaned in. "In the next ten seconds, you're going to tell me you don't know what I'm talking about. Which, we both know, is a lie because your boss, a married man, is having an affair with a colleague, a married woman, and my guess is there's a lot of pillow talk that goes on between two senators. Pillow talk that most likely starts to leak into each respective senator's office. And since one of the senators we're talking about chairs the committee investigating a highly suspicious plane crash involving the most wanted terrorist in the world, I think there's a high propensity for leakage. So, please, Blake, cut the shit and remember that you owe me your career after I bailed you out of that little DUI problem last year."

And...wow. That right there? Smoking hot. Total turn on. No prisoners. Bam. Right to the jugular. Damn, he loved that. Watching her work, watching her plow through the bullcrap to get to what she needed. The only thing missing in the I-want-to-do-her department was an erection.

And if she kept this up, his body would definitely pony up one of those.

Blake shifted his gaze to Tony, again sizing him up. If Blake expected a reaction from Tony, he'd be waiting a while. Tony had worked for the Chief Justice of the Supreme Court long enough to become an expert at the nothing-face. Right now, he was all about the nothing-face.

After a few seconds, Blake faced Fallyn. "You want to keep your voice down?"

Ha. Classic stall tactic.

"Don't test me," she said. "My voice is down. Now, what's up with this investigation? There's no way Foreign Relations believes this guy blew himself up. His ego was too big." She nodded toward Tony. "Abdul-Nasser Nazari wouldn't put himself on a plane he wanted to blow up. He'd want to see the fallout. Watch the carnage. And if your boss doesn't want the grieving sister of one of his committee members mouthing off about a cover-up, not to mention his little weekly trysts, you'd better come clean." She dug one finger into the table. "My sister is dead. I want to know why."

"I thought she had a heart attack."

"She did. A medicinally-induced one. A drug called Perisoladol. And golly gee, we can't find a prescription for that anywhere. And, double golly gee, my sister has a load of encrypted files about this plane crash on a tablet. And, triple golly gee, someone broke into her house the other night and knocked me on my ass looking for something. You're a smart guy, Blake. You can figure this out."

Blake sat back and stared out the grimy window to the traffic on the street. Fallyn kept her focus and the enormous pressure on him. Eventually, someone would have to give. Chances were, it wouldn't be Fallyn.

No wonder she excelled at her job. Grey should hire her to round out his merry band of operatives. She'd break anyone's balls.

A solid minute passed before Blake gave up on the window and faced Fallyn. "You didn't hear this from me."

"You know I'll protect you. And Tony will do the same. All we want is the truth."

He nodded. "Word around the office is that Foreign Relations said they were done investigating. That's bull. They're all over this. They're *saying* Abdul-Nasser Nazari blew up the plane as an act of rebellion, but they don't believe that."

Why?

Tony wanted to ask the question, but wouldn't. This was Fallyn's show and she had a plan. His getting in the middle of it wouldn't help her.

"Why?"

Atta, girl.

Blake pressed his lips together and broke eye contact. He stared out the window again, his head inching back and forth, the movement so slight it was barely there. Whatever he wrestled with, it had teeth.

Fallyn sat forward, touched his hand and drew his attention. "Blake, I need this. Please. You can trust me. You know you can. Besides, we both signed a confidentiality agreement last year. Your secrets are my secrets."

"I don't know everything and I sure as hell don't have a direct line to Foreign Relations. All I know is what I hear from my boss."

Here we go...

Adrenaline ravaged Tony's veins and he battled to sit still. Stoic. Following Fallyn's lead because she hadn't budged a millimeter. For her, meetings like this were a daily occurrence. Before this meeting, he didn't get it. Why she'd want control of people's secrets. Now? Feeling the rush of whatever Blake was about to say, he got it. Understood it on a primal level.

Fallyn was an adrenaline junkie.

And he wanted her.

"I don't care," Fallyn said. "Tell me what you do know. I'll figure out the rest."

"The day after the crash, I was in a meeting with the senator—"

"Dolan?"

"Yes. He got a call from Senator Oren. Dolan asked me to step out of the room. Which I did. I stood outside the office while he took the call."

"You didn't hear anything?"

He shook his head. "No, but his wife called on another line and one of the staffers told me she was holding."

"Well, that's a pickle," Fallyn said, totally deadpan.

Blake snorted. "Yeah. I cracked the door just to let him know his wife was holding and he didn't put Oren on hold, just looked up at me like WTF? I informed him his wife was on hold and he went back to his conversation."

Again, he glanced out the window and Tony felt for the guy. Clearly, he wanted to be loyal to his boss, something Tony respected, but Fallyn, she'd played that dead sister card and nothing would keep her from badgering this guy until he caved—something they all knew.

"What'd you hear?" Fallyn asked.

Blake met her eyes. "As I closed the door, I heard Senator Dolan say something about Ryan Nicols."

Whoa. Ryan Nicols. The President's son, who they'd just seen at Heather's funeral in his Air Force dress uniform with the medals that could cover a city block. Lieutenant Ryan Nicols was one of the best fighter pilots the United States military had ever seen.

"What about him?"

Blake held his hands out. "I don't know. I swear to you I don't. But, I'll tell you this, the next day, I was out for drinks and saw one of Oren's staffers. He was bragging about his boss getting called to the Oval the day before." He waved his hand. "We're a competitive bunch. The Oval office? That's major. And that would have been the same day Oren called Dolan and they talked about Ryan Nicols."

Fallyn sat back, looked at Tony with squinty eyes. "You tracking this?"

"Yeah," he said. "My guess? The chair of Foreign Relations calls to tell her lover that she's been summoned to the White House. And for whatever reason, the president's son is involved."

9

*R*yan Nicols. The president's son.

Senator Oren. The chairman of the Foreign Relations Committee.

Fallyn paced the suite's living room, her brain making a lot of connections she didn't particularly like. Ones that seemed completely logical if also completely immoral and unethical.

Of course, this was the nation's capitol. Immoral and unethical went hand in hand.

"Why is there so little about this kid in the news?" Tony said from the couch.

Hates desks. *Check.* They were probably too confining or something for the big guy. If only she could take him to her P&A office and show him the fun things one could do on a desk.

Focus, Fallyn.

Currently, Tony was deep couch sitting with his feet on the coffee table and his legs sprawled as he surfed the Net for articles on the First Son.

"You'd think with his family in the White House, and Ryan an accomplished Air Force pilot, he'd have a little more screen time. Hell, he doesn't even have a Facebook or Snapchat account."

"He was voted one of the military's most eligible bachelors last year," Fallyn said. "The president blew a gasket. Ryan's on a Special Forces team that very few people know about. Very few. It's called Redwing, and those guys are so elite and perform such secret missions, they can't afford to have the public know anything about them. Not even within the other U.S. military branches that they live and work in on a daily basis. Their wives, their best friends, their moms and dads... none of them can know that they're involved in this Redwing team. The secrecy of the team is of vital importance, so I'm told, because of national security, blah, blah, blah. Just knowing about it can put you in serious danger. Lucky me, I had to make that little 'most eligible bachelor' notoriety go away and go away fast. I couldn't even bring my team in on it. Just me as a personal favor to the president."

Tony shot her a tilted, mischievous grin that gave his dark eyes a slight edge. "So now that you've shared that tidbit of trivia with me, do you have to kill me?"

Only if he wanted her to kiss him to death. "I was sworn to secrecy, and normally, no, I do not take that kind of thing lightly and blab it to the first good looking bodyguard who comes along, but in this case, I know you deal with top-secret stuff all the time and know, like me, how to keep your trap shut. I need someone to bounce ideas off of, and since my team is back in New York, you'll have to too."

She smiled back at him and, for a second, saw that smoldering look replace the mischievousness. Before he could say anything, or grab her up for one of his power kisses, his phone went off.

Damn it. She was looking forward to that kiss.

"It's Teeg," he told her as he answered the phone. "Yeah, Geek Boy. What's up?"

At the same time, her phone rang. Blocked number. Hmm. She let it go to voicemail and listened to Tony talk to his tech guru.

Poor Teeg. She felt sorry for him being surrounded by all the government agents who teased and made fun of his skills while totally relying on those same skills to make their jobs easier. She really should fix him and Tabitha, one of her employees, up one of these days. The little tingle she got behind her ears when she saw an opportunity to fix someone was nagging her. She had that when she thought of David Teeg.

Even more so when she looked at Tony Gerard who was now bent forward, feet on the floor.

Her phone dinged that the caller had left a message. She punched in her passcode and listened while she stared at Tony.

When was the last time she'd felt this way over a man? The tingle that said he needed fixing but the fixing he needed was found between her legs and in her arms.

A man's voice broke into her thoughts. "Ms. Pasche, this is Special Agent Allan Bronco. I've been alerted by the U.S. Capitol Police that there is an investigation into your sister's death. I need to interview you and would like you to come to my office today at 3 p.m. Please confirm this will work for you. See you then."

Great. Now the FBI wanted to interrogate her.

"You sure?" Tony was saying, bringing Fallyn's mind back to the moment. "Interesting. We were just discussing him. Yeah...send me a screenshot and I'll show it to Fallyn and get back to you."

"What is it?" she whispered.

Tony held up a finger. "Hey, Geek Boy?" There was a pause. "Good work."

She liked a guy who complimented co-workers on a job well done. Tony disconnected and tapped a couple buttons on his phone. "You're gonna love this."

He turned the screen around and Fallyn leaned forward to look at it, but it seemed too small to read so she hustled over to the couch to sit next to him.

He made room for her, tucking her close to his body and holding the phone for her. He smelled good and the body heat radiating off of him enveloped her.

She squinted, still couldn't make out the words. She needed her readers on for this small shit. "Can you enlarge the page? I'd swear that's a curriculum vitae of Ryan Nicols."

Tony tapped the screen, enlarging the words at the top of the page. "You wouldn't be wrong."

Fallyn snatched the phone from him, scrolling past the name, age, and multiple bulleted paragraphs. Sure enough, the screen shot Teeg had sent was a fairly in-depth and completely classified, top-secret document of Ryan Nicols' education and military training. "This was on my sister's tablet?"

"Yep."

Fallyn scrolled some more. There was no mention of Ryan's Special Forces team, but that was no surprise. She handed Tony the phone. "Okay, so here's what we know. Senator Oren, the head of the Foreign Relations committee launches an investigation into the plane's disappearance. Then she gets called to the president's office and is presumably told to drop it. It's an act of terrorism, end of story. She's confused, befuddled, but goes along with it. What else can she do? However, she's a smart woman and wonders why the president wants her off of it. If the disappearance of CanAir 702 wasn't an act of terrorism, something else happened to it." She slowly circled one hand. "So, let's kick tires here. Throw around some ideas."

"Mechanical failure," Tony said. "Or, if we're being dramatic, one of the pilots wigged out."

"Or a passenger on board went crazy and took it down."

Tony shrugged.

"But why would the prez care about any of that? Mechanical failure, crazy pilot or psycho passengers. If any of those options were viable and he got involved at all, he'd make a statement and move on. Leave it to the NTSB to figure out."

"Okay," Tony said. "So why didn't he do that?"

"I don't know. If we're going for the drama again I'd say the only reason he wants that investigation canned is because he doesn't want the public to know what happened to CanAir 702."

"So, Senator Oren gets nervous. The president has shut her down and she doesn't know why. She wants to talk it out with someone. Calls her boyfriend, Senator Dolan."

Fallyn nodded. "And somehow Ryan Nicols' name comes up and

that's when Blake overhears it. He's an expert pilot. Maybe they do believe the pilots on board had something to do with the plane going down and he offered some insight?"

"How does your sister play into all of this?"

"I don't know, but I bet Senator Oren asked her to secretly look into it while she played along with the president. Let him think the investigation was closed. Meanwhile, Heather was looking into Ryan Nicols and that plane manifest. Did Teeg decode anything else?"

Tony shook his head. "Caroline and Mitch are working an assignment and needed Teeg's assistance. That one had to take precedence over this for a few hours. He's back on it now."

One tech specialist for a whole group of agents wasn't ideal, yet Fallyn understood the skeleton crew. She ran her team the same way. It had to be people with certain personalities and those who understood the intangible side of the cases they dealt with. A rare breed.

Tony's phone buzzed with an incoming call. He saw the ID, clicked the call over to voicemail without missing a beat.

"Sister?" Fallyn asked.

Tony shook his head. "My supervisor at the Court. He probably wants to remind me my vacation time ends soon."

"And?"

"What?"

"Are you going back?"

He zipped his lips and sat up, making a lot of work out of putting his phone away. He stood, the couch jostling her as his weight disappeared. "I assume you want to talk to Senator Oren?"

"Oren won't talk to me. Not if I so much as mention the CanAir disappearance and my sister's research. I mean so far, no one but us and the cops even know Heather's death is suspicious. If I do mention that the CanAir disappearance and Heather's death might be connected, no way Oren will put her neck out. After all, she could be next."

She reached up and touched Tony's hand. Didn't grab it, just lightly caressed those long fingers. "Tony, what happened to the chief justice wasn't your fault. I know everyone tells you that, and you probably disagree, but it's the truth."

A slight shudder went through him at her touch. He cleared his throat, looked away. "I was his protection detail and I screwed up. Now the man is dead. How is that not my fault, Fallyn?"

Her heart went out to him. "I read the reports, saw the video. Neither you nor the chief had any idea that man on the bridge was staging the road rage fight in order to get at the chief. Justice Turner bailed out of the car before you could do anything. I know from a lot of reports that he was a tough cookie and did whatever he wanted. You couldn't have stopped him from jumping out of the car to play peacemaker anymore than I could have."

"I *did* try to stop him and he didn't listen, but that's not the point. Don't spin this like you would one of your client's problems."

Okay, that stung. But she didn't stop touching him. She wasn't backing down.

Standing to her full height, she was glad she still had her heels on. He towered over her by a few inches but she was close enough to nearly meet him nose for nose. This would have to do.

She held tight to his hand, even when he tried to pull away. "I know what you're going through. I've been there, believe me, with a similar situation and it killed me for years. I know that there are some things you can't forget, you can't take back. No matter how much you wish things were different and you flagellate yourself over them, they are still there. Little demons waiting to rip at your heart and eat your soul every time you start thinking about the what-ifs. You blame yourself and those demons love that shit. That's what keeps them strong."

His gaze bounced around her face, her hair, anywhere but her eyes. "Tony, you can't give into them," she said, forcing him to look at her. "One way or another, you learn to move around those demons when they pop up. You tell them to get lost because what you do today matters, not yesterday. What happened yesterday is in the past and the only person dwelling on it is you. You can't change it, but you can make a difference *today*. Learn from the past and all that cliché stuff and forgive yourself. You go over, under, or around those demons, but you get through them one way or another and keep helping the people who need you. Keep loving the people who love you."

He started to move away. "I appreciate the pep talk, but—"

She clamped onto his hand and jerked him back. His chest crashed into hers. "Shut up," she said. "I'm not done."

The corner of his mouth twitched and he let out a long-suffering sigh as if he were merely tolerating her, but she didn't care. She had something to say and he was damn well going to listen to her.

"I didn't know the judge personally, but I do know from all accounts that he was a man who lived his life the way he wanted. No regrets. He wouldn't want you struggling with this, Tony, and making yourself miserable. He would want you to move on and live with no regrets like he did."

A muscle in his jaw moved but he didn't look at her. At least not for a long minute. When he did drop those sexy dark eyes down and meet her gaze, she saw a hint of challenge, but also of acceptance. She'd hit the nail on the head.

"He was like a father to me."

The judge. His uncle. Both father figures. "I get that. And now you honor his importance in your life by living the way he showed you—by his example."

That muscle in his jaw went a little crazy again, as if he were grinding his teeth to keep from spewing something. His gaze dropped to the floor, long, dark lashes obscuring her view of his eyes.

For the first time in a long time, she wanted to wrap her arms around someone. Hug them. God help her, she wanted to fix him, even if it meant nothing but hard, fast sex to make him forget the pain for a few minutes.

Or a few hours. She was good with either.

Gently, she brought her other hand up to caress his face, lingering on that muscle in his jaw. It would be so easy to kiss him, to lean in and close that last little bit of distance between them...

Tony grabbed her wrist and jerked her hand away from his cheek.

His other hand went around her waist and he tugged her forward, her breasts smooshing up against his chest once more as he drew her up those last few inches and put his face right in front of hers. The edge was back in his eyes. A boatload of pain too. "Don't do that, Fallyn, unless you want trouble."

She knew that pain. Had felt it a time or two herself. "Let me help you."

"I'm not one of your clients."

"I never said you were."

His dark eyes held hers, scanning, searching. For what she wasn't sure. Permission to let their hot, hot chemistry out of its cage? To shut off their client/bodyguard relationship for a little while and just be a man and a woman who wanted each other?

"I don't need to be psychoanalyzed," he ground out. "I don't need fixing."

"Good. I'm not a therapist. Doesn't mean I don't understand what you're going through or that I can't tell you to stop beating yourself up over what happened to the judge."

"Are you going to shut up and kiss me or talk me to death?"

Well, when he put it that way. She tipped her lips up, an open invitation. "Do you really need to—?"

Message received. His lips crashed down on hers, sucking the breath out of her. She couldn't move, his arm holding her against his body, his hand locked around her wrist as he bent her backward from the force of his kiss.

But she didn't want to move away. She wanted to be his. Wanted that deep satisfaction of making him forget everything for a few mind-blowing minutes. Lifting her free hand to the back of his neck, she ran her fingers through his soft hair, tugged a little.

He broke the kiss, his eyes downcast again. "Wait."

Fallyn's heart sank as they both panted like runners for a moment in silence. She knew what was coming even before he said it. She wasn't his type. He never mixed work and pleasure. Any excuse he could come up with to make her back off.

She scared men, plain and simple. The harder and stronger they were, the more she scared them. "What's wrong, Tony?"

He completely let go of her, stepping back with his hands in the air. "This is a bad idea."

The sudden loss of his presence left Fallyn off balance in more ways than one. His touch, his heat, his very power gone, creating an ache between her legs and in her chest. "I want you," she said. "You want me. Why is that a bad idea?"

His eyes finally met hers. "Tell me why you don't like to be touched."

What? Where had that come from? "I was just touching you. Obviously, I *do* like being touched. By the right person."

His eyes narrowed, causing little crinkles at the corners. "Right person?" He shook his head and laughed under his breath. A derisive laugh. "I'm *not* the right person for you."

She kissed him lightly on the jaw where his muscle was going crazy. "Sorry, but I get to decide who's right for me, not you."

He took a step back, still keeping his hands in the air but grinding his teeth again as if willing himself not to touch her. "Neither one of us in a good spot right now. Sex only complicates things. I won't take advantage of you."

She couldn't help it, she burst out laughing. "You really think any man could take advantage of me? Ever?"

"You're still processing your sister's death. I get it, you want to blow off steam and have some fun. Get away from murder and conspiracies and the shit in your head. I could use a little of that myself, and honestly, I may self-implode if I don't get inside of you soon, but that would be a huge mistake, and I don't need anymore mistakes of that magnitude."

"Having sex with me would be a huge mistake? Boy, you really know how to charm a girl."

"I'm being realistic."

"You're being stupid." She stepped forward and trailed her hand down the buttons of his shirt to his waist, tugged the white shirt free from his pants. "I'm not some helpless girl you, or anyone else, can take advantage of because I'm grieving for my sister, and you know it.

I think you're scared and you're using that as an excuse not to follow wherever this leads."

"Is that a challenge?"

She shrugged, unclasping the top of his pants. Her self-control had seen it limits. If he didn't take her in the next thirty seconds, she was going to implode right there along with him. And where was the fun in that? "Take it however you want to, but let's do this."

He grabbed her around the waist, lifting her off the floor with one arm as he backed her against the wall. She hit so hard, the picture hanging three feet over, bounced and nearly fell off. "I'm going to make your world spin."

Pinned to the wall, she wrapped her legs around him and tilted her head back as his lips went to her neck. *Finally.* If her instincts were right, and they always were, Tony knew how to make a woman very, very happy.

He licked her skin, bit her earlobe. The sharp sensation went straight to that spot between her legs and made her throb with need. He was strong, holding her up with no problem as his hands worked under her silk shirt and cupped her breasts through her lace bra.

"Hell, yes," she breathed as he tweaked her nipples, his erection straining between her legs. She clasped her legs tighter around him. "I want you, Tony. All of you. Don't hold back. I won't break."

He stopped for a moment, nestling his face against her neck, his big body tense with unspent desire, warm breath raising gooseflesh on her skin. "I don't want to hurt you."

"You won't."

She wrapped her arms around his neck, ran her fingers through his short hair. His fingers dropped to the hem of her skirt and he shimmied up the material, hands brushing her thighs and pausing for a moment on the top her stockings.

"Jesus." He let out a string of curses. "If I'd known you were wearing this,"—his fingers traced her garter—"I would have imploded for sure before I got my hands on you."

Ah, a lingerie man. She'd seen him staring at her heels earlier, gaze following the contours of her calves. "If I'd known that's all it would take to get you inside me, I'd have skipped the talk and went right for the strip show."

He moaned and released her, setting her feet on the floor. Before she could protest, he reached behind her, unzipped her skirt and let it fall.

His gaze dropped with it, taking a long, slow, agonizing stroll up her legs and stopping at her panties. He touched her thigh, letting his fingers caress the nylon before heading for the silk. She was wet and ready and sucked in her breath when he parted her folds with his expert touch.

He kissed her, teasing her with his tongue. His thumb found that sensitive bundle of nerves between her legs and did the same thing there. Teasing, stroking, building a fire inside her. Fallyn parted her legs, giving him better access.

His lips, his tongue, this fingers...they all led her to the edge of her climax, his strokes between her legs becoming harder, faster. She moved with the rhythm, grabbing onto his upper arms and arching her back as he took her over the edge.

Her vision blurred, whited out, tremors racking her body. He caught her as her knees gave out. Held her. When the orgasm receded, he carried her to the couch.

She was still shaking from head to toe. Tony kissed her deep, running his hands up and down her legs.

A blaring came from the coffee table—her phone. The tone was a familiar one that she hadn't heard in a while, interrupting her bliss as Tony drew back.

Cracking an eye open, she cut her gaze to the side. All her muscles tensed when she saw the caller ID on her screen.

White House.

Tony saw it too, his face going stormy as he handed it to her. "Guess you probably want to take this."

She could barely sit up, but she managed to cling to him as she answered and tried not to sound out of breath. "Fallyn Pasche."

"Ms. Pasche," the woman on the other end said. "Please hold for the president."

10

$\mathscr{F}$allyn's hand shook as she held the phone to her ear. Every cell in her body was cheering after Tony had worked his magic on her. Her blood pumped faster, her pulse dancing after the rush.

But all of that didn't matter as her bliss was cut short.

"Fallyn?" President Abraham Nicols spoke in her ear. "I'm glad I caught you."

Tony held her by the arm but Fallyn shooed him away. When speaking to a powerful man, you needed to exude self-confidence and competence. Lying on the couch enjoying a buzz from your latest earth-shattering orgasm wasn't going to get the job done.

Stand up, chest out, breathe deep. "Mr. President. So good to hear from you."

Tony finally moved out of her way and Fallyn got to her feet. Her legs were shaky and her damn heels were too high, throwing her off balance. One ankle gave out and she toppled back onto Tony's lap.

He chuckled while helping her upright once more, pinching her ass in the process. She slapped his hand away and marched a few steps out of his reach. In the mirror over the desk, she caught sight of her reflection.

Thank God, Nicols hadn't FaceTimed her. Her hair was a hot mess, and her blouse was half unbuttoned, revealing her lacy bra. Her skirt was in a puddle on the floor and she'd lost her underwear between the wall and the couch. Her stockings and garter were still in place, but by the look on Tony's face, they wouldn't be for long. He'd slouched back into the couch, throwing his arms out across the back and watching her like a hungry man eyeing a juicy steak.

The shiver of anticipation ran down her spine. "What can I help you with, sir?" she asked, trying to concentrate.

Nicols gave a tight sigh. "I know this is a difficult time for you, Fallyn, but we need to talk."

The tone of his voice reminded her of her father when he was disappointed with something she had done. She knew that tone well. Before she could check her response, she threw her shoulders back. *Exude confidence.* "Of course, sir. About what exactly?"

"I don't wish to get into it over the phone." Curt. Annoyed.

Hmm. "All right. I can swing by the White House first thing tomorrow morning."

"Now would be better."

Now? Fallyn bit her bottom lip. Telling the president *no* held appeal, but no one told the leader of the free world no. "I'm in a…a meeting. Just wrapping up, in fact." Tony grinned at her as she glanced at her watch and hustled over to pick up her skirt. She flipped him off while assessing the damage. The silk/linen skirt was too wrinkled to salvage. She would have to find an entirely new outfit. Plus traffic would be a bitch. "I can be there in, say, an hour?"

That was cutting it short and she was definitely feeling cheated out of spending the rest of the afternoon in bed with Tony. The night still held possibility though.

"That won't be necessary," the president said. "I'm downstairs."

Fallyn stopped mid-stride toward the bathroom. "I'm sorry. It sounded like you said you're downstairs."

That brought Tony to his feet. He made some gesture Fallyn didn't understand and she turned away from him. "Downstairs, as in the hotel lobby?" she reiterated.

"I'm in my car. I'm sending a Secret Service agent up to your room to escort you."

Fallyn nearly dropped the phone. She did drop the skirt. "Oh no. That won't be necessary, sir. Really. I'll be down in a...in a minute."

"Very good." The line went dead.

Fallyn whirled on Tony. "Holy shit. The president is downstairs and wants to talk."

"I gathered that." Tony hustled her toward the bathroom. "About what?"

"He wouldn't say." She closed the bathroom door and went to work cleaning herself up as best she could. She pulled on the skirt, regardless of the wrinkles, and ran a brush through her hair. "Do you think he's gotten wind of our little investigation?" she called through the door.

"Only if that rat, Blake, told him. Who else knows?" Tony said.

Carl and Jordan knew she was looking into the drugs in Heather's system, but they had no clue about what was going on with Senator Oren or Fallyn and Tony's theory about Ryan Nicols' possibly being involved.

Her cheeks were flushed, her lips slightly swollen from Tony's kisses. At least, she didn't need to fix her makeup. She buttoned her blouse and found clean underwear. Smoothed a few of the wrinkles out of her skirt. All in less than two minutes.

"How does he know you're staying here?" Tony asked as she opened the door.

"No idea." She marched past him, grabbed her trench coat, and tugged it on. The coat would cover her wrinkled clothes, thank God. She stuck her phone in the coat pocket and faced him. "How do I look?"

His face said, *like a woman I want to fuck*, but he kept that statement to himself. "Fine."

Fine? Really, that was the best he could do? Whatever. "I'll be back shortly."

He made his way to the door and opened it for her. "I'm going with you."

She sighed as she went past him, knowing that any argument she threw out would be vetoed. "Are you going to climb into the presidential limo with me as well?"

"If necessary." He closed the door behind them, then grabbed her hand and drew her close before she could walk away. "Make it quick, okay? I've got a woody that needs attention."

Leave it to him and his smart-ass mouth to make her laugh and release the tension between her shoulder blades. With her free hand, she reached down between them and gave him a little squeeze. "Believe me, I'd love nothing better than to stay in the suite with you and give you all the attention you want. In fact, the President of the United States is probably the only man alive at this moment who could keep me from ravaging your body."

Tony snickered. "Second fiddle to POTUS. Excellent."

"You're not playing second fiddle. I have no intention of fucking the president, so believe me when I say, your fiddle will be first and foremost in the spotlight when I'm done talking to him."

She gave him another little squeeze, winked, and headed for the elevator.

He didn't say anything, helping her inside, but once the doors shut, he backed her up against the wall and kissed her silly.

When she emerged from the elevator on the ground floor, she'd nearly forgotten the president and his order. That's what Tony and his damn kisses did to her. He made her forget everything else.

Which wasn't good. She needed to be on top of her game at the moment. Not sidetracked by a man who probably went through women like toothbrushes.

A Secret Service agent met them at the hotel lobby door. He was of medium height, medium coloring, and wore dark glasses to hide his eyes. "Gerard," the agent said, extending his hand. "Haven't seen you in ages. How you doin', man?"

"Emmett." Tony accepted the handshake. "Good to see you. You made it into the inner circle, huh?"

"Finally. Six years I've been at this Secret Service gig. The wife was threatening to leave me if I didn't get POTUS' private group."

They shared a chuckle and Emmett nodded at her. "Ms. Pasche," he said, motioning her across the sidewalk to where the motorcade was pulling up. How many times had they driven around the block waiting for her? "This way."

Tony followed behind them and Emmett didn't stop him. At least not until the agent hustled Fallyn into the back seat of The Beast quicker than she could say, "all hail to the Chief." Right before the door closed, she saw Tony's jaw tightened as Emmett backed him off and sealed her inside with the president.

"Fallyn." Abraham Nicols smiled from the seat opposite her, sincerity not quite reaching his eyes. "So lovely to see you. Again, I must extend my condolences once more on the loss of Heather. She was a great person and a savvy senator."

The spacious interior of the car was black leather and burled wood. The president sat alone, his brushed cashmere coat unbuttoned, legs crossed and fingers interlaced. The picture of relaxation, yet there was something in his eyes that told Fallyn he was anything but.

The president's expensive, if completely overpowering, cologne made her eyes water. Considering she probably still smelled like sex, it was probably a good thing he was so fragrant.

She covertly sniffed the air as he continued to speak about Heather, and yep, she caught a whiff of Tony's aftershave—that combo of musk and citrus—mixed with her own perfume and post-sex scent.

Great. Nothing like meeting with the president in close quarters while smelling like a porn star fresh from filming.

Nicols finished praising Heather and went on to say what a nice funeral it had been. Then he looked at Fallyn as though waiting for her to comment.

She worked with men on a daily basis who needed their egos stroked. Some powerful women as well. They often gave her the same look, as if because they strung a few words together, the heavens should part and adoration should rain down on them.

Work the case. Give him what he wants so you can get back to the fiddle and get what you want.

Working the case, in this instance, required she handle the president with kid gloves. "It meant the world to Dad and I that you took time from your busy schedule to honor Heather yesterday. So, please, tell me what I can do for you."

Nicols gave her that smile. The smile that said "good girl." He uncrossed his legs and leaned forward, putting his elbows on his knees. "The capitol police have brought it to my attention that there is an investigation going on into Heather's death. I'm told there may have been drugs involved?"

Oh boy. He was making it sound like Heather was into something illegal. Probably worried about a scandal that could harm his next presidential campaign. "The autopsy showed there was an elevated level of a prescription drug in Heather's system. A drug that could have caused her to have a heart attack and was not prescribed by any of her doctors. Detective Hollister from Metro is looking into it, along with the FBI. I received a call from Special Agent Bronco just a little while ago."

Her phone buzzed in her pocket, the vibration making her jump. It was probably Tony, wanting to know what was going on, and since pulling your phone out and checking it in front of the president was beyond rude, Fallyn ignored it.

Nicols frowned. "I see. I can't believe Heather would be so reckless as to take a drug that would knowingly cause a heart attack."

There it was again, that insinuation that Heather's death was something she'd done to herself. "Heather was never reckless, sir." Hadn't he just been singing her sister's praises? "You know that."

She wanted to add more, so much more, but she'd learned silence was often more effective at getting her point across. So she sat.

Waited. Saw the expression on the president's face that told her he didn't like the tone she'd just used on him.

Get used to it, buddy.

Her phone quit buzzing in her pocket. The president stared at her, waiting for her to elaborate. She didn't.

Abraham Nicols was good at tactical maneuvers too.

Finally, he broke the standoff. Sitting back, he fluffed his coat and crossed his legs again. "Along with the investigation into Heather and the drugs, I'm told you've been poking around the Foreign Relations committee about their conclusion in the CanAir disappearance. May I ask, why would you care about that?"

Bingo. That was what this little visit was all about.

Play your cards carefully, Fallyn. Her phone started going off again. Rudeness be damned, she needed to stall, so she pulled it out and saw it was the number from earlier, the FBI agent calling again. Apparently Special Agent Bronco had left a message, persistent little prick, but was bombing her with calls anyway.

Shutting the phone off, she jammed it back into her pocket. An idea came to her that wasn't far from the truth. "Heather was quite interested in that plane and what happened to it. You know how she hated flying over the ocean. That plane's disappearance unnerved her since she had that big Asia tour coming up."

"Her paranoia about flying over open water made you start poking around the committee?"

More than anything, Fallyn wanted to come out and ask why he ordered Senator Oren to drop any inquiries, if in fact, he had done that. Right now, all of it was speculation. Carefully crafted speculation. She'd prefer to be straightforward, get right to the heart of the matter.

In Washington, you never went right to the heart of anything without consequences, and being as how she was at the mercy of the president and his driver at that moment—with no real proof of anything—she decided not to tip her hand. "Heather left notes and questions she had about the whole thing in a...diary. I wondered if she had gotten answers to those questions, so I started asking around. That's all."

Nicols set forward again, pinning her with his stare. "This is highly classified stuff, Fallyn, not some tabloid rumor mill. That plane's disappearance is a tragedy but it was a terrorist act. Don't go digging around in it or you could be charged with a felony for impeding a federal investigation."

"I thought the investigation was over."

She nearly slapped a hand over her mouth. *Insubordination at its finest, folks.*

Like all men in power, the president didn't like being corrected or questioned. "If there were a continuing investigation, and I'm not saying there is, it would be top-secret and undisclosed in the name of national security. My top Foreign Relations committee members would be handling it in conjunction with the FBI and CIA. If someone were to stir things up again...well, you know, Fallyn."

He let the threat hang, twisting and blowing between them like a balloon that could pop at any moment.

Fallyn gritted her teeth and pasted on a fake smile. *Time to get the hell out of here before steam rolls out of my ears.* "Top secret. National Security." She gave him a thumbs up. "Got it, sir."

The *good girl* smile took over his face once more. He patted her knee. "I knew I could count on you. I haven't forgotten what you did for me last year. My son is the most important thing in the world to me. Anyone who helps him, I consider a friend."

She tried not to recoil from his touch. Tried and failed. Shifting in her seat to propel her knee away, she smiled. "I was happy to do it. Now, if that's all, Mr. President, I really need to get back to my meeting. I have a lot to wrap up with Heather's belongings and paperwork before I head back to New York."

"Of course, of course." He waved her off, now eager to get rid of her. "We'll talk again soon."

Sure they would. Fallyn reached for the door handle. The minute she touched it, it flew open, thanks to Emmett still standing guard. Behind him, leaning against the hotel wall, stood Tony. A wave of relief swept through her.

Silly really. It wasn't as if she'd given the president a hard time, he would have hauled her off and disposed of her body, right?

Emmett gave her a hand out and she brushed her coat down and thanked him, feet once more on the sidewalk. Tony boosted himself off the wall and headed her way.

"Tell your father hello from me," Nicols said, leaning forward to catch her eye. "Carl tells me his new restaurant downtown is all the rage. It would be a shame if anything happened to it."

And *bam*, another threat. This one at her father.

Rage, hot and slick, burned through Fallyn's veins. She took a couple of steps back, out of earshot of Emmett and the other Secret Service agents and murmured, "Did you seriously just go there?"

No one heard her, thank goodness. Casually throwing up a hand to wave goodbye, she called out, "Great seeing you, Mr. President. Have a good evening."

And then, seething, she turned on her heel, ready to hit something.

Or in this case, some*one*, as she came smack up against Tony.

"I take it that went well," he said looking down at her as he held her arms to keep her from falling. Sarcasm dripped from his voice. "You look like you're ready to go a couple of MMA rounds."

The presidential motorcade drove off and Fallyn ground a heel into the sidewalk, fighting the urge to flip off the entourage as it glided away. "The president warned me to steer clear of the CanAir disappearance and everything related to Heather's role on the subcommittee. He actually stooped to threatening not only me, but my father."

"So we're on to something," Tony said, staring after the disappearing cars with her.

"Damn straight we are, and we're not stopping this investigation. Nicols is hiding something and I want to know what."

"I'm sure he's hiding a lot of things."

"Something specific to that plane—it seems almost personal—and I'd bet money it has to do with Ryan. An Air Force pilot who works top-secret missions."

Tony gave her an incredulous look. "You think Ryan Nicols brought down that plane?"

"Either by accident or on orders."

"Digging into this could get dangerous."

She withdrew her phone and flipped it back on. Agent Bronco had left her two more messages. "Bring it on."

Tony smirked. "Do we have time to...finish up...before we take on the president of the United States?"

She wished, but she was so distracted by what had just happened, she wasn't sure she'd be able to focus in bed. "While I could use a good tumble to blow off steam, I have something to take care of first." She held up the phone log for Tony to see. "The FBI wants to talk to me, ASAP, regarding Heather's death. Apparently our good detective, Hollister, let everybody from the Capitol police to the FBI know he was investigating her suspicious drug interaction. Now their panties are all in a twist."

"Standard procedure, I'm afraid." He looked pissed. Or maybe sexually frustrated. She knew the feeling. "I suggest you wash off more...strategically...before we hit the FBI office."

Gah. She knew it. "I smell like sex, don't I?"

He held up his finger and thumb about a half an inch apart. "Just a little."

And then he laughed at her as she stomped upstairs to clean herself up.

Tony followed Special Agent Allan Bronco down a long bland-as-hell corridor with nicked white walls that needed a fresh coat of paint. Fallyn strode alongside him, easily keeping up as Bronco swung around a corner and waved them into an equally bland conference room. Nothing fancy here either.

"Have a seat," Bronco said.

The table sat ten and Fallyn grabbed the first chair on the left. Tony pushed her chair in, made brief eye contact, and hoped to hell her smart mouth didn't get her in trouble with the feds. He claimed the seat beside her and Agent Bronco took the head of the table.

Of course he did.

From the second they'd stepped into Bronco's space he'd had that shoulders-back, I'm-in-charge, stance about him that immediately rankled.

Feds. No wonder Grey and Mitch had bailed on the Agency.

Fallyn settled into her chair and folded her hands in her lap. "Special Agent, what can I do for you?"

"First, thanks for coming in."

She smiled. "Your rather ardent attempts to contact me indicated it was an emergency."

Fallyn. Total ball buster. Tony dipped his chin, rolled his bottom lip out to hide a grin and pretended to study a piece of lint on his pants.

"Well, we're investigating your sister's death and we assumed you could help us."

And, oh, boy. Tony didn't like his tone. The raw arrogance that was supposed to let all the little people know he'd do whatever the fuck he wanted.

Tony glanced at Fallyn, then at the agent who met his gaze, almost daring him to speak. Yeah, he'd speak.

Swiveling his chair, he leaned back a little. "Special Agent, I'm sure Ms. Pasche is happy to help in whatever way she can. She's already had calls from Metro and the Capitol Police."

"And," Fallyn added, "I just buried my sister. It would be extremely helpful if all the agencies could work together and not put me through this three times." She looked back at Tony, gave him a sarcastic smile. "But, that could just be me. What with the grieving and all."

Ha. Total ball buster.

Bronco focused on Tony. "Who are you again?"

"Close family friend," Fallyn said. "He's staying."

They both turned back to Bronco. His eyes bounced from Fallyn to Tony and back to Fallyn. If he were a smart man, he'd stand down. Between Tony and Fallyn, two people unafraid of conflict, Bronco had his hands full.

He cleared his throat and flipped open his file.

Smart man.

"I've received a copy of your sister's autopsy report."

That sucker traveled fast.

Silence extended into the awkward territory and Fallyn rolled one hand. "And?"

"I assume you've seen it?"

"I have."

"You've read it?"

"I have."

This poor bastard. He'd definitely drawn the short straw with her, a woman who made a living at molding information. She wouldn't give him anything she didn't want to. No need. She had Grey and his team on her side. This guy? His pay grade didn't give him access to the memo that explained the Justice Team had jurisdiction. That Grey and his crack team would find Heather's killer. Special Agent Bronco, much less the public, couldn't know that though. Not if Grey's super-secret Bat team was to stay covert.

Thus, Bronco. The figurehead. The trophy agent who thought he'd landed the case of the month. Only...nah...the brass had probably handed him Heather's case so it wouldn't look like the FBI was doing nothing about a dead senator while the Justice Team ran point.

Bronco sat back, flopped out a hand. "Okay. I see how this will go. Clearly, you don't appreciate being dragged down here—"

"That's not it at all, Special Agent. What I don't appreciate is the fact that my sister has died and three law enforcement agencies investigating her death expect to put me through the same battery of questions. What I don't appreciate is the fact that you boys, in your infinite wisdom, didn't think to coordinate with each other so we could have done all of this at once."

Atta, girl. But Bronco's head looked about to blow off. Ding, ding. Time to engage.

Tony leaned right, set his hand over Fallyn's. "I'm sure Agent Bronco will note your suggestion." He glared at Bronco. "Can we move on with this?"

Bronco nodded. "Absolutely. I apologize for the inconvenience. So, it seems you'd like to get right to it."

Ya think?

"Yes. Thank you."

"Were you aware your sister had a heart condition?"

"Before the autopsy, I was not."

"All right. Then I'm assuming you didn't know she was taking Perisoladol?"

"I did not."

Really, it was hard not to laugh. Tony did his best though. This woman was too damned much fun. He wished he could have eavesdropped on her meeting with the prez. Smart as whip and fearless, she might be his perfect match.

Assuming the two of them didn't get each other killed because they didn't know how to hit the brakes before charging forward. The two of them together?

Dangerous.

Agent Bronco flipped his file closed. "Ms. Pasche, does it concern you that you're sister had a heart condition, and yet, she was taking massive amounts of a drug that could cause her to go into cardiac arrest?"

Finally, Fallyn leaned forward, rested her hands on the table. "Of course it concerns me. But I was unaware of any of this. What is it you want from me?"

"I want you to give me something."

"Like what? I've turned over all of her medications already. Every vitamin bottle, every pill bottle. I've answered all the questions I can as honestly as I can. What else can I do?"

"Where were you the night your sister died?"

And, whoa, cowboy. What the fuck?

Tony's spine went rigid. "Hang on. Does she need a lawyer in here?"

Fallyn gasped. "You think *I* killed her? Are you insane?"

"Fallyn," Tony said, "shut up. Special Agent Bronco, does she need a lawyer? And, let me remind you, she hasn't been Mirandized."

Fallyn put her hands up. "I'll answer that question. I was in New York City where I reside and work. I had a client meeting in the afternoon and then a dinner. All of that can be verified. I hadn't spoken to my sister in more than a week. Check the phone logs."

"When did you hear of your sister's death?"

"Jordan—her assistant—called me. My sister didn't show up for a meeting and when Jordan couldn't reach her, she called my father."

"Your father found her?"

"No. Jordan didn't speak with him, so she left a message. When she didn't hear back after a few minutes, she went to Heather's to see what was happening. By that time, my father received Jordan's message and rushed to Heather's. He got there just as Heather's body was being loaded into an ambulance. They called me but, of course, it was already too late."

"And then what? You jumped on a plane?"

"Yes, Special Agent, I grabbed a commuter flight." Fallyn waved one hand. "You can check that as well."

"I will do that."

Bronco jotted a note and something in the way he moved, the four-second pause in the middle of it, sent Tony's shit-meter buzzing. He glanced at an unruffled Fallyn as she checked her nails, feigning —or maybe not—boredom. He went back to Bronco who watched her, his lips tight and...nope...not doing this.

Tony stood. Fallyn tipped her head back. "What's up?"

"In a second, it'll be you." He jerked his head to the door. "Get up. We're leaving."

"I'm not through," Bronco said.

Yeah, you are. Tony met Fallyn's gaze, held her stare.

Come on, sweetheart, work with me.

Something in this situation wasn't right. Whether the feds really suspected she had something to do with her sister's death or not, he didn't like this setup. Crazier shit than accusing a high-profile media whiz of killing her senator sister had happened in DC and Tony wasn't gonna let her hang herself by talking too much. Any other time, she'd probably have marched out already. Now? The big, bad spin-doctor was under a tremendous amount of emotional stress and she might not be tracking right.

Fallyn set her hands on the edge of the table and slowly pushed her chair back. "Sorry, Agent Bronco, I have things to tend to. If you have any further questions, we'll set up another time. Preferably with all involved law enforcement agencies."

Bronco didn't appreciate it. Not one bit, but he didn't make a fuss either. Unless he planned on arresting her, she was free to go wherever she'd like. In the hallway, Fallyn turned to Tony but he latched onto her elbow, ushered her toward the exit.

"Outside," he said. "Then we'll talk."

Shoving open the lobby door, he held it for Fallyn, then headed straight for his SUV, his steps devouring the pavement.

"Hey, big guy," Fallyn said, "what's going on?"

"I don't like him."

"Well, that makes two of us."

Tony dug his phone from his suit jacket, punched up Grey's number.

"Justice."

"It's Gerard."

"Where are you?"

"Just came from the J. Edgar Hoover Building. Loads of fun."

Silence. And how often did that happen with Justice Greystone? Something told him not a lot.

"Why?" Grey wanted to know.

"Fallyn got a call from Agent Allan Bronco. You know him?"

"Never heard of him."

"Well, he's got a monster bug up his ass. He hauled Fallyn in, wanting to know where she was the day Heather died." Tony stopped at the corner, grabbing Fallyn's arm before she high-tailed it into traffic. "Is she a suspect now or what? Because, gotta tell ya, I didn't like his tone. That fucker needs to stand down."

"Relax," Grey said.

As if that would even be possible? Considering he was on limited sleep, life as he'd known it had blown apart in the last month, and now he had a hot woman, a goddamned political spin doctor—*kill me, please*—he wanted to nail every time he looked at her.

Sure. Right. Relax.

The light changed and Tony stepped off the curb, bringing Fallyn with him. "All I'm saying is that guy isn't right. Give me ten minutes and I'll call you back from a secure line."

"Why?"

"Because our girl Fallyn, in addition to meeting with an asshole special agent, had an interesting visit this afternoon. From the president."

"Shit," Grey said.

"Bingo, brother. I'll holler back at you. But buckle up."

11

"The Feds think I killed my sister." Fallyn couldn't wrap her mind around it. The very idea made her sick to her stomach. "They think I fucking killed my twin."

"No they don't," Tony said. He'd just disconnected from a second phone call with Justice Greystone as they headed for Heather's townhouse. "That lobotomized fuckwit, Bronco, is fishing. Grey says this is Bronco's first investigation since a promotion landed him here in DC. He's out to make a name for himself."

Grey's fiancée, Sydney Banfield, was meeting them at the townhouse to pick up Heather's suits. Even with everything on her plate—Heather's murder, the president's threats, and now Special Agent Bronco's horrible insinuation—Fallyn had to take care of her sister's belongings. A part of her didn't want to give Heather's clothes away. It seemed so...final. She wished she could preserve Heather's home just the way her sister had left it.

But that wouldn't bring Heather back. Those suits, hanging unworn in her closet, could do some good for another woman down on her luck. Heather would have loved that.

No, Fallyn didn't have time to worry about suits. Yes, Jordan could have taken care of it. Yet, donating those suits to Sydney's shelter might help someone else, and although it was a small thing, it gave Fallyn something to focus on. Something good that could come from this tragedy.

She leaned her head back against the headrest and felt the anger at Bronco lessen slightly. Her pulse was elevated, her heart pounding. It had been one hell of a day so far, but she was up for it. Working the case was better than sitting in Heather's townhouse crying her eyes out, or worrying about the president's threats. "Anything back from Grey's lab on the vitamins and supplements?"

Tony pulled up to the townhouse. "They've analyzed about half of them. So far, everything is copacetic."

"And Teeg? Has he decoded anything else on Heather's tablet?"

"Not yet. There's one section that none of the codes you gave him have worked on. He's trying some different approaches."

Fallyn exited the car and headed for the steps. Anxiety pounded through her limbs. She needed to go for a run. Or maybe tackle Tony for a different kind of workout. "Ms. Banfield should be here any minute," she said as she unlocked the front door. "I'll grab the suits and bring them down."

Tony's cell phone was ringing again. "Wait," he said, following her inside as he answered the phone. "I need to check the place first."

Fallyn dumped her purse on the kitchen table, only half listening as Tony spoke to one of his sisters. The frustration in his voice let her know it was about his mother's birthday party again.

She smiled as she ignored his missive to wait and headed up the stairs. The sooner she got the suits to Sydney, the better. Then she could burn off some of this energy and think straight again. She wasn't going to quit digging, but how was she going to protect her father if the president decided to make good on his threats? And now, with the FBI looking into her, they could make her life hell. If they started digging into her clientele, asking *them* questions, annoying her employees, she was going to have to go into gladiator mode. The president and the FBI could ruin her business and her reputation in the blink of an eye.

No way in hell was she going to let them.

I will find out who did this to you, sis, and I will make them pay.

She was halfway into Heather's bedroom when she pulled up short. A man dressed all in black with a ski mask was coming out of Heather's closet.

Head down, he was putting a metal tool into a small black bag. He startled when he saw her.

Was this the man who had attacked her the other night? The man after the tablet?

Was this her sister's killer?

Fallyn opened her mouth and screamed, "Tony!" at the top of her lungs. She sneered at the man, anger pumping through her system like a steam engine as she bared her fingernails and lunged. "You son of a bitch!"

The window over the fire escape was open. As Fallyn went to rake her nails down his eyes, he smacked her in the shoulder with the tool, knocking her sideways. She fell, her upper body slamming into the end of the bed. The guy raised the tool again to bring it down on her head, but the sound of Tony's footsteps running up the stairs stopped him.

"Fallyn!" Tony yelled, his voice echoing into the bedroom.

The guy looked over his shoulder toward the door and Fallyn kicked out, slamming her heel into the guy's shin. He yelped and hobbled to the open window, half falling onto the fire escape.

She bolted up and lunged once more, grabbing onto his ankle. But her fingers slipped off his booted foot when he yanked himself the rest of the way through the window.

Tony burst into the room, saw her on the floor. "What the hell happened?"

Fallyn pointed at the open window. The guy had already disappeared from sight. "A man was in Heather's closet. He went down the fire escape."

Tony crossed the room to the window. "Are you okay?"

"Fine. Go after him."

He did as instructed and Fallyn pushed herself off the floor, watching out the window as Tony hauled ass down the fire escape, skipping huge sections of metal steps in an attempt to catch the man in black.

At the end of the alley he looked both ways. The man had disappeared. Fallyn watched as he went out into the street and then she lost sight of him.

When he returned, she met him at the front door.

"Bastard got away." His face was drawn, his voice filled with cold rage. He touched her cheek, then held her by the shoulders. "Are you sure you're alright?"

She forced herself not to flinch at the soreness in her shoulder where his fingers dug in. The same cold rage burned in her veins. "Whoever that is, he's got some balls. If I'd had my gun, I would have shot his ass."

This drew a brow quirk from Tony. "You have a gun?"

"In my handbag."

"Why does that not surprise me?"

From the light in his eyes, she could see that turned him on. Weirdo. "Our intruder opened the safe."

"What?" Both of Tony's eyebrows went up this time. He dropped his hands from her shoulders. "How?"

"He was a professional. It took me a minute to recognize the tool he was carrying." She rubbed her shoulder where a bruise was forming. "It was a small type of drill that safe crackers use."

"What did he take?"

"Nothing." She smiled at Tony's confusion. "I cleaned everything out the last time we were here."

"Damn, woman. Good job. Did you get a look at his face?"

"He was wearing a ski mask."

"Hmm."

At that moment, the doorbell went off. Tony checked the peephole. "It's Syd."

He opened the door, grabbed the pretty brunette on the doorstep by the arm, and ushered her inside before slamming the door shut again.

"Good to see you, too, Tony." Sydney Banfield said with a chuckle. "No need to be so hands-y, though."

Thank you, Fallyn thought, instantly liking her.

"Sorry," Tony said. "Security protocol. We just had an intruder, and I think there may be someone, or some*ones*, casing the place."

"Sounds like you're in a pickle. Is everyone okay?"

"Yeah. We're good."

Sydney turned to Fallyn and extended her hand. "Sydney Banfield. I run Fresh Start and Grey told me about your circumstances. I'm sorry about your sister. I appreciate you donating her suits to the shelter. Obviously this isn't a great time. I'm so sorry."

"These days, there's never a good time." Fallyn shook her hand. So this was the woman who had Justice Greystone wrapped around her pinky. "Heather was a strong women's advocate. She would be happy that her clothes could benefit your shelter."

Sydney smiled. "We run on a shoestring budget. Any donation is appreciated."

"After I clear things with my dad and find out what was in Heather's will, I may have more stuff that you're welcome too. Furniture, dishes, a bed."

Tony wandered off to the kitchen, punching buttons on his phone. Syd watched him go, then smiled again at Fallyn. "All of those things would be nice, but what I'd really like is some of your time, Ms. Pasche."

"Please call me Fallyn. My time?"

"You're a role model for women, as was your sister. A woman with a great deal of resources, power, and determination. You started your own business and turned it into a political and social machine. A game changer in this male-dominated world. I'd love to have you come and speak at our next career day. The women don't need a rah-rah speech, but they could use some real insight into building a successful career. Maybe you'd even consider looking at a few resumes, show them how to spin their skills into marketable assets."

Compliments followed by a call to action. Behind Syd's words, her meaning came through loud and clear: *with great power comes great responsibility.*

Fallyn had only just met the woman and already she was ready to sign on the dotted line. "I don't know how much of an inspiration I can be but I'm certainly willing to help the women fine-tune their resumes. When is this career day?"

"Monday from 1 to 8 p.m."

She had no plans to be in DC on Monday, but at this rate, it wasn't out of the question. She had to get to the bottom of Heather's death and wrap up things with the townhouse and possessions.

And then there was Tony.

She wanted to see him after this was over, but a future with him seemed like a pointless exercise. She lived in New York City. He lived here. While some of her clients were located here, and she routinely traveled to DC, they would still have a long distance relationship, and she didn't have time for that.

Maybe he wasn't interested in a relationship, anyway. She could swing by when she was in town and they could hook up, blow off some steam, and then she'd be on her merry way again.

"I'm not sure what my calendar looks like for Monday," Fallyn said, "but I *would* like to come by the shelter at some point and see your work there. Maybe I can chat with a few of the residents."

"How 'bout now?" Tony stood framed in the doorway. "Except you won't be chatting with the residents."

Fallyn and Syd both turned to look at him. "What are you talking about?" Fallyn asked.

"Syd, I have a big favor to ask."

"Okay." She eyed him cautiously. "You're part of the Justice Team family, now, Tony. What do you need?"

"A safe house."

"A safe house?" both Fallyn and Syd said in unison.

"Yeah." He pocketed his phone. "In the past few hours, the president of the United States showed up unexpectedly at Fallyn's hotel and threatened her, an FBI agent subtly accused her of murdering her sister, and an intruder was in this townhouse for the second time in the past few days. Someone is tracking your movements, Fallyn, and if Heather *was* murdered, which we're assuming she was, you could be in serious danger."

"Oh, boy," Syd said. "Sounds like a safe house is a good idea."

"I don't know." Fallyn shook her head. She wasn't worried her life was in danger, and she didn't like the idea of letting the president or anyone else know she was scared of them. "Isn't that a little extreme?"

Tony nodded. "I was just on the phone with Grey and he agrees we need to put you somewhere off the grid. Except the Justice Team doesn't have a safe house."

Syd shifted her weight, her right hip jutting out. "And you want to use my shelter?"

"Grey says there's a mother-in-law's suite over the garage out back that's empty."

Syd gave him a look that said he was crazy. "You want to hide Fallyn out there?"

"You hide women in there all the time, Sydney."

"And just how do you know...?" She caught herself and let out a sigh. "Grey told you. Of course. That information does not leave this room, you two."

Fallyn and Tony both made agreement nods, but Fallyn spoke up. "I don't want to impose on Sydney. We'll find somewhere else."

"The suite is not currently in use," Syd said, "but what kind of assurance do I have that hiding Fallyn there won't bring danger to my residents?"

"That's my job," Tony said. "She won't have interaction with anyone. We'll keep our comings and goings completely secret. You won't even know we're there. Plus, I'm gonna get some friends to help keep an eye on the place. Couple guys owe me a favor."

Syd tapped a foot and threw a thumb over her shoulder, pointing at the door. "How will you get her there without your watcher knowing?"

Tony gave Fallyn a devilish grin. "I got that covered."

Fallyn's ovaries did a cheer at that grin. Man, how she loved to see him smile like that, all full of himself. When he let that confidence loose—those rare times—she found it disarming and a total turn-on. "I'm not going to like this, am I?" she asked.

His smile widened but he didn't say a word.

Yep, definitely not going to like this.

Seeing that smile, though, was totally worth whatever was about to happen. "I'm in," she said, smiling back. "Let's do this."

"Here we go," Tony said shoving the dining room table off the Oriental rug.

Fallyn looked at him, perfect eyebrows drawn. "Here we go what? Be careful. My sister bought that rug overseas at a bazaar last year. She loves—loved—it."

He pointed at the rug. "Your chariot awaits."

Her gazed snapped to the rug and back. "I don't understand."

"We're gonna roll you up in it."

"Are you insane?"

"Probably. But if you want to get out of here with no one seeing, this is your chance. We roll you in the rug, I carry the rug out with the clothes and put everything in the van at the curb and it looks like what it is. That you're donating your sister's things. I'll come back inside, put on a few lights and the television, lock up and leave. If anyone is watching they'll think you're inside. By the time they figure out you're not—"

"I'm long gone."

He poked his finger at her. "Bingo." He turned to Syd. "Don't go straight to the shelter. Grey wants to make sure no one follows you. Loop around the city, then meet him at the bakery he said you guys get cupcakes from. Once he's sure no one followed you, he'll grab Fallyn and transport her to the shelter."

Fallyn faced Syd. "Are you sure you're comfortable with this? Whatever is going on, I don't want you or any of your residents to get hurt."

"As long as you're not coming in or out the front door, I'm okay with it." She glanced up at Tony, her lips spreading into a sultry smile and he suddenly understood Sydney's power. "And if the big man here is adding some free muscle, we're probably safer with you around."

"Working on it." Tony tapped his finger against his wrist. "Fallyn, tick-tock. We got shit to do. Grey is going to meet you and Syd at the cupcake place."

She let out a huff, added an eye roll to fully cement her frustration. "Oh, my God, you are so pushy."

But she dropped to the floor. Damn, he liked her. She might bitch a lot, but she knew when to give up the fight.

Stretched out on the rug, she folded her hands over her belly and Tony squatted next to her. "You good?"

"Yepper."

"You don't get claustrophobic do you?"

"Only around slimy politicians. Vocational hazard."

Syd snorted and Tony grinned down at Fallyn, took in her goofy smile and his chest seized. He leaned in, popped a quick kiss on her lips. Couldn't help it. The woman was fearless and it flipped every one of his buttons.

In one way or another.

He pulled back from the kiss and their eyes locked. "Thank you," Fallyn said. "We'll do more of that later."

"So," Syd clapped her hands together. "I'll just wait outside."

Tony pecked her lips again. "Honey, fair warning, when I get you into a bed, I'm gonna rock your world."

"Promises, promises."

She reached up, smacked her hand over the back of his neck and dragged him in for another soul-frying kiss that made his little brain salute.

Somehow, this thing just got a whole lot more complicated.

After loading Fallyn into Syd's Fresh Start van, an apparent donation from one of the local car dealers, Tony marched back into Heather's house, checked all the windows and doors, flipped on some lights and the television—CNN—and sat at the kitchen island to give Syd lead time.

He set his phone down on the cold granite and propped his chin in his hand. How much sleep had he'd gotten these last few days? Normally, he didn't require a lot. Five hours a night usually got him through. He might be averaging five over two days and now that he'd sat down, the lack of movement in the house, the lack of chaos lulled his body into thinking a nap might be imminent.

Not today. At least not now. Once he got Fallyn settled with his buddy Matt on lookout, he'd grab a combat nap.

And maybe, circumstances permitting, give Fallyn an orgasm or ten.

His tired and filthy mind drifted, formed a picture of Fallyn, stretched across a bed—a big bed—waiting for him. Bare-assed naked except for her shoes. What his obsession was with the shoes, he didn't know, but she had wicked sexy shoes and they would go nicely with her birthday suit.

The icemaker in the fridge flipped a fresh batch of cubes and the *thunk* brought him out of his mind travel.

He checked his phone again. Nothing from Grey yet. It had only been thirty minutes and with traffic, Syd could be stuck in a snarl while looping the city.

Sitting idle wasn't helping. Another walk-thru of the house wouldn't hurt. Just to be sure. He stood, shook out his legs, scooped up his phone and headed upstairs where the safe—that goddamned safe—in Heather's bedroom had been left ajar by the intruder. Another failed attempt to obtain the one thing he wanted.

Heather's tablet was proving mighty popular. Now all they had to do was figure out why.

Halfway up the stairs his phone rang. Grey. Finally.

He punched up the call. "What's up?"

"We got a tail. And I can't shake him."

12

One of Fallyn's clients, Gail Hanson, always said bad things happened in threes. Fallyn decided if that was true, she could relax. She'd met her day's quota. First the president, then Special Agent Bronco, then the intruder. In fact, after the past week, she was pretty sure she'd met the entire year's quota.

Justice Greystone's Dodge charger wound its way around a section of the city Fallyn had never seen before. She took another bite of cupcake and leaned her head against the headrest. "Syd was right. These are excellent peanut butter-chocolate cupcakes."

Grey glanced in his rearview. "They're her favorites."

Syd had driven around the city enough to make Fallyn's head spin; Grey was doing the same. It had taken Fallyn at least ten minutes to unroll herself from the rug in the back of Syd's van, Tony had wrapped her up so tight. She'd never been claustrophobic, but being wrapped up in that rug and not knowing where she was going made her a touch carsick. Once she was able to exit the rug and climb up to the seat to talk to Syd, her stomach settled. A few minutes later, and in a different vehicle driving through the DC twilight, she was ravenous.

Stress did that to her. The adrenaline and uncertainty of what came next. Not all stress was bad, but either way, it made her hungry. Her dad had never been big on doling out hugs, but he'd shoved more than a few plates of spaghetti in front of her during her teen years.

As she polished off another bite of cupcake, she wondered where Tony was and if he was okay.

Of course, he is. He's Tony Gerard, one-man army. He would have laughed at her for worrying about him.

Syd and Fallyn had met Grey at the cupcake shop, where the leader of the Justice Team had handed his fiancée a box of goodness. Syd had smiled, pecked him on the cheek, and dug out a cupcake for Fallyn. "You look like you could use this," she said. "Guaranteed to make you feel better."

"I like your girlfriend." Fallyn licked frosting from the top of the cupcake. The rich chocolate flavor mixed with the creamy peanut butter really was doing a world of good for her attitude. She no longer wanted to kill someone. "She's no nonsense like me."

"That she is." He checked his side view. "So who do you think is trailing us?"

Right. Back to reality. It sort of pissed her off that some freak behind them was ruining her moment. Sometimes a girl needed to enjoy her freaking cupcake without worrying about who might be after her. "Most likely, someone the president sent to make me nervous. Second guess? Special Agent Bronco."

She felt like adding that they both could go screw themselves, but that was unprofessional, and while Tony might appreciate her bluntness, she had the feeling Grey wouldn't. She wasn't worried about the person trailing them. If anything, this was a show of power from Nicols, following up on his earlier threats.

"Tony brought me up to speed on everything." Grey took a sharp right, running a red light without hesitation. They were on the outskirts of the city, passing endless row houses, interrupted here and there by a gas station or pizza place. "Do you think our tail is the same person who was in the townhouse earlier?"

"Could be, but I swear, Syd lost anybody who followed her. She was all over the city. And why would anyone follow her, anyway? Tony made it look like I was still at the townhouse with him, right? That was the plan."

Grey didn't verbally confirm, but he didn't need to. They both knew Tony was an expert at his job. "I didn't see this tail when I snagged you from Syd. We picked them up a mile after we left the cupcake shop. Who besides Tony would have a GPS tracker on you? Did the president or any of his men touch your clothing or handle your purse?"

Fallyn lifted an eyebrow at Grey. "Tony has a GPS tracker on me?"

"Three to be exact. Security precaution."

Security. Right. She still felt violated a teeny, tiny bit. Should probably insist Tony make it up to her later. "I understand the reason. I just don't understand why he didn't tell me."

Grey shrugged. "Did anyone handle your purse or coat besides Tony today?"

Fallyn thought it over. "No. I sat across from the president in his limo. He never touched me or my clothing, thank God. Neither did any of his Secret Service agents."

"I doubt Bronco would tag you either. Still might be a good idea to ditch the purse and coat."

Fallyn finished off the cupcake, brushed crumbs off her hands and shrugged out of her coat. "I left my purse back at the townhouse, so Tony has that. Where do you suggest I ditch the coat?"

Grey punched a button on his door. An electronic whirring noise came from her window as it slowly slid down and disappeared.

"You can't be serious," she said, hugging the coat to her. "This is a Burberry. It's my favorite."

Her exasperation didn't phase him. "Toss it," he said without so much as a glance her way.

Sighing heavily, she shoved it out the window as they drove over a tiny bridge. Cool air rushed in at her and she fought off a chill as the sun sank lower on the horizon.

All she wanted was a glass of wine, another one of those cupcakes and a hot soak in a big tub.

And maybe a little hot, bodyguard sex.

Yep, that would definitely be a bonus.

The window made its whirring noise as it closed. Grey took a left, cutting across a couple of lanes to drive by some large abandoned warehouses. "Let's talk about who had motive to kill your sister. I looked into the whackos who threatened her after the vote on the military pay raises and none seemed legit or capable of this type of thing. I agree with the FBI findings; there were no credible threats."

Mr. All Business. She tried not to grieve over her lost coat. "If the theory Tony and I are working on is correct, the president. If his son shot down that plane, he wouldn't want anyone to know about it. Plus, he has vast resources. Offing my sister would have been a piece of cake. He easily could have found out about her heart condition and had someone give her that dose of Perisoladol."

"True." Grey took another left. "But it's too sloppy to be the president. If he hired someone to kill your sister, the assassin would be a professional, someone who would know that a thirty-year-old senator dropping dead out of nowhere would have an autopsy performed. They would also know that Perisoladol would still be in Heather's system and call attention to the fact she wasn't prescribed that drug. A professional assassin would either make sure there was no trace of foul play or they would make sure it looked like a suicide."

She hadn't really thought about that. "So you don't think it's the president? It had to be someone who knew about her heart condition or found out about it *and* knew that she was looking into the CanAir fiasco. No one fits that profile besides him. Who else would care if she was looking into the plane's disappearance?"

"Maybe the sloppy murder setup was intentional. Anyone with a computer could figure out a drug that would negatively interact with Heather's heart condition. Someone had to know about it besides her doctors."

Headlights appeared in her side mirror. Whoever was following them wasn't even pretending to stay back anymore. "My sister didn't want to be seen as imperfect. She didn't tell anyone. Not me, my dad, or even Jordan, her assistant who was like her best friend, or Jordan's dad, Carl, who was like a second father to her. None of us knew."

"Or so everyone claims. Bronco is looking at you now. Is it possible someone is setting you up for this? That someone wants you out of the way so they're framing you for Heather's murder?"

She needed another cupcake. "You're saying the perpetrator made Heather's murder look like something that someone with more than average IQ would pull off, but not like a professional hit; in order to frame me?"

"Next of kin are always the top suspects in this type of investigation."

"And I'm her twin sister. Why wouldn't she tell me about the heart problem, right?"

"Exactly. Bronco thinks you're lying about not knowing about Heather's condition, and since he has no idea about the investigation she was looking into, he has no other solid lead."

"Even if he did, he's not going after the president."

"Probably not a good career move." Grey's jaw was jumping. He glanced in his rearview. "Your seatbelt's secure, right?"

"Yeah, why?"

"Hang on," he said and cranked the wheel.

Tires squealed, the car did a U-ey in the road. Before Fallyn could gulp a breath, Grey slammed his foot down on the accelerator and they shot off down another half-deserted street, street lamps here and there flickering to life.

The inertia flattened her back into the seat. She grabbed hold of the door and gritted her teeth. Buildings flew by on her right, the solarized street lights—at least the ones not broken in this part of town—zipped across the Charger's hood. The in-dash navigation system lit up with an incoming call. Caller ID read Tony's name.

Grey flew around a curve and used voice activation to answer. "Where the hell are you, Gerard?"

"A mile or so behind you." Fallyn's heart fluttered at the sound of his voice. "Closing in fast."

The car tailing them was gaining on them, the headlights shining high up and into their vehicle. It had to be a truck or SUV.

"What should I do?" she asked Grey.

Grey shook his head at her, spoke to Tony. "SOB's not hiding anymore. He wants us to know he's there."

"Whoever it is, he means business, then," Tony said. "We need to get you back into a safer part of town and take this guy out. I'll run interference as soon as I catch up to you."

The lights that had been in her side mirror disappeared, and the truck slid up Grey's side as it continued to gain on them. It was running on oversized tires and sporting a roll bar. Grey's speedometer was almost pegged.

"Shit's about to get serious, Fallyn." Grey shot her a quick glance. "Follow my instructions and don't ask questions, got it?"

He sounded just like Tony. She forced a smile to let him know she had complete confidence in him. Which she did.

But a small part of her wished it was Tony at the wheel. "Got it."

"Fallyn?" Tony's voice came from the speaker.

"Yes, Tony."

"Grey and I've got this. You just hold on, babe."

For the first time since she'd attacked the intruder, Fallyn felt a tickle of fear dancing in her veins. The cupcake made her stomach cramp. Bracing her feet, she wrapped her fingers around the door handle and slouched down into the seat. She didn't want Tony worried about her. Grey either. "I'm good. Holding on as instructed!"

The next few seconds were straight out of a Fast and Furious movie. She and Grey blew through stoplights, Grey weaving around cars like they were sitting still. There weren't many this time of evening in this part of town. At one point, he took a turn so fast, Fallyn was sure the Charger was up on two wheels.

Where was Tony? He'd disconnected the phone and she couldn't see him in her side mirror, blinded as she was by the truck's lights.

Grey kept cutting off the other guy, only to have him dodge and find a new hole to sneak up to them. Pretty soon, they were on a back-street filled with garbage and debris. One side was all woods, the other a construction site. The two-lane road was under construction, orange cones dotting the shoulder.

An onramp to the highway was a quarter mile ahead. Grey gunned the motor and swerved around a barricade. The truck, right on their tail, tapped the edge of their bumper.

The Charger fishtailed, Fallyn banging the side of her head against the passenger window. Grey clutched the wheel tighter, righting the car. He drove around another barricade, then a large dump truck parked on the edge of the road. The Charger kicked up gravel.

The truck loomed behind them again, the lights flooding the interior of the Charger. "Son of a bitch," Grey ground out.

Fallyn could see now that Tony had caught up to them. There was another vehicle trailing behind the truck, trying to get around it. With the road down to one lane due to the construction, the only way he was going around the truck was to bust through the barricades.

"Hit the nitrous oxide," Fallyn yelled, half-laughing. She couldn't help it. The adrenaline was too much. She was on a roller coaster ride, flying through the twilight with a man she barely knew while some asshole played bumper cars with them.

Her joke didn't garner so much as a change in breathing from Grey. They hit a pothole left by the construction workers and nearly went airborne.

Fallyn's heart was in her throat and another nervous laugh broke free. *Completely inappropriate*, some part of her brain still in logic-mode admonished.

But she realized, she really wasn't scared. With Grey and Tony handling the situation, she was just along for the ride. A hell of a ride, but everything would be okay.

And then, just as she was about to turn around and flip off the driver behind them, a deer came out of nowhere, flying up from the embankment. Grey cursed and jammed the wheel to the right.

At the same time, the truck bashed them in the rear.

The Charger went airborne. Just boom, and they left the road, Fallyn's stomach jumping up into her throat. One of Grey's arms flew out to stop her forward projection. Her breath caught as they went up, up, up and then the car realized it couldn't fly.

The front of the Charger fell forward and a scream tore from her throat as the ground rushed up to meet them.

The Charger hit hard, bouncing, once, twice, three times down the embankment. Airbags deployed. They were sliding sideways, Fallyn's head smacking back from the airbag hitting her in the face.

The car wasn't done dancing down the embankment, though. As she fought to catch a breath around the airbag, she saw mud and grass flying in all directions as the car continued to slide and spin. The sun was all but gone now, darkness closing in around them, their headlights skimming through the air as they spun around and around, sliding backward down the steep hill.

Just when she thought they were about to stop, the car hit something big and hard on her side. Next thing she knew, they were ass over tea-kettle.

How many times the Charger rolled she lost count. Her head smacked the passenger side window again, the airbag deflating in a cloud of powder. Her hands flew out, trying to find purchase, and one of her shoes flew past her head as the car did cartwheels. Glass broke, metal groaned. Grey stopped swearing. They bounced so hard once that Fallyn thought her spine would snap.

Finally, the car came to a stop. One of the headlights had broken out, the other trailed a beam at the ground. The dashboard was no longer lit up, shadows blanketing the interior.

Every bone in her body screamed in pain. Her vision was blurred, her ears ringing.

"Grey?" she said after a moment of gasping for breath. She blinked and tried to clear the pressure in her ears. "Are you okay?"

No answer.

"Grey?"

She felt weightless, as if she were hanging sideways. That's when her vision cleared enough for her to realize that she was indeed, hanging from her seatbelt. The car was up on its side.

Suspended halfway over a drop off.

Shit. Fallyn's breath came in gasps once more. *What the hell just happened?*

Alive. She was alive.

"Grey!" *Please be alive. Please be alive...*

He wasn't moving, didn't even seem to be breathing.

No, no, no. Not you too.

Dark, sticky blood streamed from his forehead. Fallyn tried to check for a pulse, her fingers sliding over his muscular neck and probing gently.

Where is it? Where is it?

There. A throbbing. Light but solid under her fingers.

"Grey, can you hear me? Can you open your eyes?"

No response. He was totally out.

Concussion? Probably. No telling if he had a spinal injury or was bleeding internally.

She had no purse, no cell. The car was still running. She poked at the navigation screen, straining against the seatbelt to reach it. "Come on, come on," she said at the dark screen. "On Star, where are you?"

Nothing.

Surely Tony had seen the accident. He had to be close. Fallyn yanked on the door handle and the car wobbled. The handle moved loosely in her hand. *Useless.* The door was jammed.

Duh. It was laying on the passenger side. There was no opening it, no way, no how.

Now what?

Her head pounded. What about the guy in the truck? What if he was out there sneaking up on them? Lying in wait for Tony?

She had to warn Tony. For half a second, she tugged at her seatbelt, trying to unlock it. The car rocked again, making her stop.

Breathe, she told herself. *Think.*

Somehow, she had to get herself and Grey out of this damn car. Without flipping it down the ravine and killing them.

"This isn't my area of expertise, Greystone, just so you know." Shifting her weight to the side, she slowly unbuckled her seatbelt and prayed. She reached behind her seat and grabbed the shoe that had flown off, shoved it on her foot. "But if you promise not to die on me, I'll give it my best damn shot."

The Fates, those fickle bitches, must have heard her, because at that exact moment, flames burst from the hood of the car.

Tony slid down the embankment, his dress shoes sliding on the moist grass and sending him to his ass. Ten feet in front of him, the hood of Grey's Charger ignited, the bright orange flames licking the air. The car had rolled to its side and somehow sat teetering at a ninety-degree angle on the two passenger side wheels.

Mother of God.

What the hell?

Dread marched up his body, swarming him, cutting off his air. Had they gotten out? Were they somewhere safe?

"Help!" Fallyn shrieked.

Alive. The second's worth of relief whipped inside him until the panic, that guttural roar in his head, drowned everything out. Her voice came from the direction of the car.

Inside the car.

He scrambled down the embankment, one hand skittering along the ground, keeping him half upright, half sliding. If he lost his footing he'd plummet into a burning wreck.

"Fallyn!"

Somewhere in that mess, he'd find her. But all he could see was the undercarriage of the car and the tips of the flames shooting into the air.

"Tony? Help us!"

His foot caught on something. Crap. Momentum carried him, his big body still moving past his snagged foot. His ankle tweaked and—shit—if that sucker snapped, they were all toast.

Literally.

He dropped to his ass, dug his fingers into the ground to slow his body's descent. His fingers ached from the pressure of holding two-hundred-thirty pounds of his weight—*hang on*—but he gripped harder, fighting against gravity. He halted and lifted his foot from what looked like an old tree root.

Scrambling, he got to his feet, ignoring the knifing pain in his bruised ankle to hustle down the embankment, one hand still close to the ground so he didn't go headfirst into the wreckage. "Fallyn! Where are you?"

"Front passenger side."

That was a problem. Considering the car sat wedged on that side. Something clicked in his brain and he surveyed the area, taking in the tiny details. Passenger side was out. *Driver's side.* He'd have to somehow climb onto the driver's side to free them.

And while he was doing so, pray that car didn't tip over on him.

Shit. As if on cue, the two suspended tires dipped, the car creaking with the movement and *no, no, no.*

"Fallyn, don't move!"

The flames grew higher and a fresh batch of heat blew back to him as he neared the wreck and that roar in his head wouldn't give. How the hell would he get them out?

"We're trapped!" Fallyn yelled. "Grey is unconscious! I think I can get to the backseat."

The car rocked again. If that kept up, this would be over quick. "Honey, please. Don't move!"

But, too late.

A loud groan like bending metal scraped the air and flames spit higher. *Do something.* His heart damn near shattered his chest wall and the tires, those goddamned tires dipped again.

No, no, no.

He took a step, but the car moved again and he lunged back. "Fallyn! Hang on, it's going over!"

The car collapsed, just clunked to the ground in front of him, bouncing as it landed and flames continued to pour from under the hood. Behind the wheel, Grey's upper body smacked forward, the seatbelt jerking his head.

Tony charged, his dress shoes refusing to cooperate and slipping. *Forget the shoes.* He drew a harsh breath, tasted foul air and—*fuck.*

Gas. Somewhere from this wreck, the car was losing gas and he smelled it now, that fresh, ripe smell of liquid that would blow them all to hell.

He reached Grey's door, wrenched it open just as Fallyn was climbing over the seat. "Help, Grey," she said. "I'll try to get out the back."

Before tending to Grey, he reached over, popped the handle on the back door and pulled. The door swung open. Finally, a break. Fallyn scrambled over the seat and pushed off with those spiked heels that made him insane.

She'd never make it up the hill in those. "Ditch your shoes and haul ass. I smell gas."

He reached in, unclipped Grey's seatbelt and the man's body slumped sideways over the console.

Wrong way, kid.

Sliding his arms around Grey, he locked his hands together, planted his feet and heaved. The first attempt got him halfway out and all that dead weight transferred to Tony, throwing him off balance on the steep incline.

Dammit.

"Let me help," Fallyn said from behind him.

As if she'd be able to carry a man that outweighed her by a hundred pounds. At least. And why the hell was she still standing there? "Jesus Christ, Fallyn. Go. Up that hill. Now!"

She let out a squeak and assuming she'd actually listened, he focused on Grey and freeing his lower body from the car.

Almost there.

Tony dug his feet in again, gritted his teeth and hoped to hell the moist dirt wouldn't give. *One, two, three.* Everything he had, every ounce of strength went into his task and he let out a grunt as his muscles strained and ripped and...*yes.*

Grey's body came loose, the car seeming to spit him out as momentum knocked Tony backward, right to his ass. He stayed down, grinding his feet into the earth, shoving back and dragging

Grey's dead weight with him as the flames, those nasty orange whips, engulfed the entire hood.

Get out.

Tony glanced down, took in Grey's face. The closed eyes. The slack cheeks and—*God*—not again. *Don't go there.*

Get out.

He got to his knees, stood and glanced up the hill where Fallyn crab-walked up the embankment, her feet skidding out from under her. The incline was steep and if she could barely get up by herself, how would he do it with Grey? They'd need a backboard and a towrope to pull this one off.

Another groan came from the car and that gas smell permeated the air, stinging Tony's nostrils. Flames spread, licking at the car's interior and he dropped his gaze. Even in the dark, he saw it. The trickle underneath the car. All that gas leaking free.

Grey moaned again and Tony noted the angry cut searing his forehead. No time to wait.

He squatted, hooked his arms under Grey's. "Listen up, friend. I'm gonna carry your ass up this hill. I'd appreciate some help."

And, upsie-daisy, he hoisted Grey over his shoulder into a fireman's hold. Hell on earth the guy was heavier than he looked.

Again, Tony glanced up the hill, saw Fallyn at the top—thank God for that at least—and wondered just how the fuck he'd carry two-hundred-plus pounds up a steep, wet embankment.

In dress shoes.

13

Tony's first step, with all of Grey's dead weight sinking into him, nearly leveled him. The ground gave, his foot slipped and panic ripped at him, pounding his mind as momentum pulled his body over. He put his free hand out, tightened his hold on Grey and caught himself before he face-planted. Grey's head snapped back and ricocheted forward again. If he had a spinal injury, forget it, game over. He'd be paralyzed.

You can't do it. Too steep. He shook his head, drew a long breath of air. The stench of smoke burned his throat and he swallowed, licked at the salty sweat from his upper lip.

Up the hill. *Get it done.*

Save this one.

"Come on!" Fallyn yelled.

At the top of the embankment, she waved both arms, urging him toward her. "Hurry! You can do it! Come on!"

You've got this.

If he didn't move, goddamn do something, the car might explode and send them all to an early grave.

And wouldn't that be the pisser of all pissers? More people dying on his watch.

No way.

He hoisted Grey higher on his shoulder, heard another groan and considered it a good thing.

"Move it."

Fallyn. Again offering her twisted brand of encouragement.

He took a step and kept his footing. One more step. That's all he had to do. One step at a time.

Until he got to the top of the embankment.

With each mud-entrenched step, Grey's weight shifted and Tony's back barked. Bone crushing pain laced straight down his spine. All those squats in the gym were coming in handy. He lifted his head, kept his focus on the top of that hill and a screaming Fallyn. Step, step, step. *That's all.*

Step.

Step.

Step.

"Keep going," Fallyn said.

Grey moaned again and Tony tightened his grip, tried not to jar Grey more than necessary. "Don't you fucking die on me, Greystone."

Don't you fucking die.

In the distance, sirens wailed and it hit him like a homing signal, drawing his body up that hill. He wrenched another backbreaking step, sucked in a hard breath and felt his knee wobble. Steadying himself, he looked up again, met Fallyn's eyes.

"You can do this, Tony," she said in that bitchy voice she used when she meant business. "Whatever you do, don't stop."

No stopping.

Two more steps and he was there. With her.

Safe.

One.

Breathe.

Step.

Two.

At the top, his quivering legs gave way and he dropped to his knees. Gently, he swung Grey to the pavement and collapsed next to him, flat on his back. An orange glow lit the darkness and he turned his head, the cold pavement shocking his system. Below, the car was completely engulfed and angry flames whipped in the light wind.

Gonna blow.

"Fallyn," he said, "run. Take cover."

"What?"

Did the woman ever listen? Not ask questions and just listen?

"Goddammit, run! Before that car—"

Boom!

The night exploded.

Tony heaved right, levered off the ground and threw himself on top of Grey, raising his hands to shield both their heads from flying debris.

Bits of car parts—plastic and metal and rubber—rained down. A hunk of the exterior crashed two feet away and Tony counted down the seconds until the air settled and the only sound was the siren drawing closer.

He raised his head, stared down at the burning carcass of Grey's car and his stomach pitched.

Fallyn.

Where was she? "Fallyn!"

"I'm okay," she called from somewhere by his car.

She was okay. He pushed off of Grey, rolled to his back where above him an array of stars winked.

Alive.

Everyone was alive.

Tony stood just outside the family waiting room in the hospital ER. Minutes ago a trauma surgeon had asked if Grey's family was present. Nada. Syd was on her way, but hadn't yet arrived. At which point, the surgeon informed them Grey needed immediate surgery. Implied consent, the doc had said. Which, by Tony's way of thinking, wasn't good since implied consent gave the hospital permission to perform emergency, lifesaving surgery.

At the scene, Tony had overheard the paramedics relaying something about Grey being hypotensive from possible intra-abdominal bleeding.

Internal injuries.

Fuck. The man was bleeding out from inside.

Don't you die on me, Greystone.

Hands in pockets, Tony kept his gaze locked on his shoes. Mud caked the edges and had splashed over the tops leaving a residue. He wiggled his toes, felt the rub against the soft leather and knew he'd be throwing these shoes away.

The fuckers were cursed.

These shoes, these goddamned black dress shoes he'd bought—on sale at the store he liked in Georgetown—had been on his feet the day Chief Justice Turner had been gunned down.

What were the chances—outside of supremely bad karma—he'd be wearing the same fucking shoes?

He let out a sigh and shook his head.

Yeah, blame the shoes.

He glanced up at Fallyn, leaning on the opposite wall, typing away on her phone. God knew what she was doing, but like him, she had to keep busy. On a primal level he understood that her high level activity was a coping mechanism. He knew it all too well.

Obviously sensing his attention, she stopped typing and raised her head. "You okay?"

She'd almost gotten killed and she was worried about him? Go figure.

"Fine," he said. "I think you should let them check you out."

"Outside of sore boobs, I'm all right. Really. Airbags are a wondrous invention. Besides, I don't want to leave you. Or Grey."

Tony reached up, dragged his hands through his hair. "Syd should be here soon." He jerked his thumb down the hallway where Grey had been rushed to surgery. "I don't know what to tell her."

Fallyn stowed her phone and closed the distance between them. She propped her shoulder against the wall and nudged him on the ankle with her bare foot. Somewhere on that hillside were her fancy designer shoes.

"We tell her what we know. That someone was following us and Grey swerved to avoid hitting a deer. It's not your fault, Tony. It was an accident."

"One that wouldn't have happened if you had been with me."

"Oh, please. You don't know that. Fate is a fickle bitch. If I'd been with you, maybe we'd be dead right now."

He gave her a look that he hoped would back her off.

She moved closer—apparently his scary look needed a tune-up—and elbowed him lightly.

"You don't scare me, Tony Gerard. And I don't care what you say, you saved both of our lives tonight. No matter what happens, you need to remember that. Without you, Grey would be in the morgue right now. Got it?"

An echo of clippety-claps came from the end of the hallway a few feet from him and—*she's here*. How he knew that was a mystery, but the sudden increased drumming of his pulse and his twisting stomach told him Sydney had arrived. She swung around the corner. Her previously neat hair was now a crumpled mess, tucked behind her ears and out of her face. A face that, opposed to ninety minutes ago, was now drawn and freakishly pale.

Last time he'd seen that look was the day his father dropped dead of a heart attack. Only that time, his mother wore it.

Syd met Tony's eyes and whatever she saw there stopped her.

She paused, searching for comfort, reassurance.

Hope.

None of which he could offer. Not with Grey lying helpless on a table, possibly hemorrhaging or perhaps worse.

Cold. Fallyn, ever the crisis negotiator, beelined for Syd and held her arms out, wrapping her in a hug. Fallyn the non-hugger hugging Sydney. Go figure.

Tony strode toward her, ready to plead his case, and stood behind Fallyn while the two women hung on. Syd held his gaze though, still trying to read him. What she couldn't know about him was his ability to isolate his grief. To compartmentalize.

To hide.

Finally, she broke eye contact and closed her eyes. "Is he dead?"

Not yet. Tony flinched. "No. Jesus, no."

Syd's hands fell away from Fallyn's back and hung at her sides, her body slumping into Fallyn as relief plowed through her. Fallyn held her tight, stroked the hair on the back of her head.

After a few seconds, Syd opened her eyes, backed away from Fallyn, and brought her chin up. "I took a cab over. I was afraid..."

She paused, shook her head.

"It's okay," Fallyn said. "That was smart."

Sure was. No explanation necessary. Not for Tony anyway. Syd didn't want to chance being behind the wheel in case the call shattering her life came in.

"How—" She cleared her throat, lifted her chin a little higher. "How is he?"

"There's no update since I called you. He's in surgery. He was in and out of consciousness once they got him here."

"Did he say anything?"

Tony shook his head. "Nothing that made sense. A lot of mumbling."

"What happened?"

Fallyn took that one, methodically giving Syd the edited version of the accident and how Tony *saved* them. Saved them. Fuck that.

A nurse who looked like she'd slept sometime last week approached and nodded at Syd, then Tony and Fallyn.

"Are you the family of Justice Greystone?" she asked.

And, oh shit. Tony's stomach dropped. Everything dropped. All of it, gone. Shit, shit, shit.

He's dead.

Syd raised her hand. "I'm his fiancé. I've called his father. He should be here soon. How is he?"

And, shit, shit, shit. Syd wasn't family. Not yet. And if anything went sideways and decisions had to be made, there was all kinds of red tape that had to be dealt with. Did Grey have a living will? Instructions for what should be done if he were to become impaired?

Jesus.

Tony swallowed, jammed his hands in his pockets again because —just...*fuck.*

"He's still in surgery," the nurse said. "There are some consent forms we'd like to have signed. And then, if you'd like, you can wait in the OR waiting room and we'll keep you updated."

The nurse broke free of them, moved on to the desk where another nurse handed her a clipboard.

"Syd," Tony finally said, "I'm so sorry."

Her eyes flashed, but it wasn't...anger. Wasn't the rage he'd expect from a woman blaming him for her future husband's life-threatening injuries.

She stepped closer, poked him in the chest. "You listen to me, Tony Gerard. This isn't your fault. Grey is a pain in the ass. He does what he wants. And if he didn't want to help Fallyn, he wouldn't have. My man wants to be a hero as much as the rest of you Justice Team maniacs. I swear, I don't know what makes you people tick, but what-ever went on in that car, he knew what he was doing. So don't you think you'll steal his thunder and take the blame because when he wakes up, he'll have a great story to tell."

"Amen," Fallyn said.

That wasn't helping. Tony shot her a look and she flipped him the bird. Right there in the corridor while their friend fought for his life. What the hell?

"Syd's right," Fallyn said. "I was in that car with him and he was a rock star. He's like us, Tony," she grabbed his hand. "He'd rather run into the fray than away from it."

"Ain't it the truth," Syd said. "If he survives, I'll kill him myself."

These people are nuts.

Syd shifted to her tiptoes, looped her arms around Tony and rested her forehead on his shoulder.

And, ah, dammit. One of the compartments in his brain, the one where he stored all that emotional shit he didn't let anyone see, busted open. He held his breath until his chest tightened, all that good healthy oxygen trapped there. *What the hell? What do I do?*

First his father, then the judge, and now this. And him, a guy who'd never figured out how to process grief. For him, it was easier to pack that shit away and ignore it.

He raised his hands, dropped them. Hell with it. He exhaled—hard—squeezed his eyes shut in case he did any pansy-assed crying and held onto Syd. Pussy that he was, he needed it as much as she did.

"Please," she said, "don't blame yourself. He wouldn't want that."

14

$\mathcal{T}$he apartment over the garage at Fresh Start was little more than a loft that at one time had probably been a workshop. Maybe a storage attic. Either way, Syd had appointed the place with soft yellow curtains, some comfortable chairs, a television, and a four-poster bed in the small bedroom. A picture of St. Agnes hung over the headboard.

Fallyn studied the picture of the patron saint of virgins as she unpacked a fresh blouse and some jeans from her overnight bag. She was no virgin, but she'd take help from any saint who would have her.

She was trashed, mentally, physically, and emotionally. She wouldn't let it show, though. Not to Tony. Not to anyone. The big lug was flagellating himself over Grey, and she shared that feeling. She hated herself at this moment for bringing any of them—all of them—into her warped, mixed up, and very dangerous world.

Caroline had shown up with her new husband, Mitch, in tow at the hospital. Fallyn loved Mitch from the moment he strode into the waiting room, all long legs and snarky attitude. He'd barely nodded at her, sizing up Tony's shutdown body language and pulling him aside.

As Caroline embraced Fallyn and then Syd, Fallyn had watched Tony draw even farther into himself as he told Mitch in hushed tones what had happened. Mitch wasn't hard to read; he was devastated. According to Tony, Grey was Mitch's best friend. They'd been partners together all the way back to their FBI days.

And like Syd and Fallyn, Mitch had recognized Tony's ridiculous self-blame game. He'd gripped Tony by the arm and told him to stop being stupid. "The Justice Team can only handle one idiot around here and that's me," Mitch had said. "Stop honing in on my territory, Gerard."

Caroline, Mitch, Fallyn, and Tony talked for a few minutes, then fell silent. What was there to say? While Grey was in surgery, Tony had drifted off to sit alone in a pale blue, plastic hospital chair. Fallyn followed, taking his hand and weaving her fingers through it. She didn't badger him anymore—the poor guy had been through enough. She simply sat with him as she turned her mental focus on herself.

She had to stop being so brash. Had to stop pretending she could handle the threats and the near misses. People were getting hurt.

Grey could die because of me.

She and Tony had sat that way for a long time. Hours probably, until an exhausted doctor emerged, letting them know the bleeding had been stopped and Grey was in recovery. He wasn't safe yet though. The next hours would be critical.

The hospital only allowed two people at a time in Intensive Care. Caroline had insisted on staying with Sydney; Mitch wasn't going anywhere either. So Fallyn and Tony had left, Tony silent and cold, his jaw hard as stone.

She'd seen him checking for tails, and she'd once again been on a tour of the city as he drove all over. He'd swung by the hotel and the doorman had brought her overnight bag to the truck. Once he was satisfied they weren't being tailed, Tony had parked in the garage downstairs, walked her up to the apartment, and then disappeared, saying he had to call Teeg and give him an update. He also had to follow-up with the police. Blah, blah, blah. Fallyn knew he was wrestling with his demons and needed time alone.

Being alone wouldn't ease the set of her shoulders, the sick feeling in her stomach. Fury burned a cutting edge through her veins, her bones, her bloodstream. She focused on it, keeping the fear creeping into her tight chest at bay. She would find whoever had done this and she would make them pay. For Grey, for Syd, for Tony.

Washing off in the bathroom, she ignored her bruised and battered body and put on the fresh clothes. She'd already alerted her team to what had happened, what *was* happening, and what she wanted them to do. Now, she needed to get Tony out of his personal pity party and thinking about something else.

Like me.

Except, he was gone. He'd come upstairs with her, cleared the rooms and disappeared. Feet bare, she padded across the floor to the door that led down to the garage. Her heels were gone. The only other pair she had were at the hotel. Whoever had packed up her stuff had missed them.

The old wooden stairs were cold and gritty. The garage smelled like oil and dirt. Tony's truck engine was still pinging as it cooled down.

As expected, she found him sitting stock-still behind the steering wheel, face drawn, eyes blank. Was he was reliving the accident?

When he finally registered her presence, his eyes snapped to hers and he bailed out of the truck, lickety-split. "Is everything okay?"

She crossed her arms and narrowed her eyes. "Not exactly."

"I told you to let the doctor have a look at you. Are you woozy? Sick to your stomach? He said you might have a concussion."

"I'm not concussed. I'm horny."

"Jesus, Fallyn." He let out a relieved breath. Or exasperated. She wasn't sure. "You almost died a couple hours ago."

"But I didn't. My near-death experience didn't turn off my desire for you. If anything, it made me want you even more."

"No."

Bitter. That one word full of self-loathing.

She took a step closer. "What, you don't believe that's possible?

That I watched you save Grey from going up in a ball of flames and it turned me on?"

"Stop it. You can't turn this around and make out like I'm a hero. I hate that fucking word and the pity behind what you're doing right now."

"Pity?" This man. She thought she'd jump out of her skin, he was so damn irritating. "I don't pity you, Tony Gerard, and the only reason I would is because you're too damn stupid to see the truth."

"If I'd gotten there faster or had you with me..." He shot a hand through his hair, making it stand up. "This wouldn't have happened."

She advanced on him, backing him up against the side of the truck. "If *I* hadn't pissed off the president, if *I* hadn't stirred the pot about Heather's death, if *I* had never called you two mornings ago and asked for help...if, if, if. The current situation is as much my fault as it is yours."

Reaching out, she tugged on a section of his hair that stood up like a soldier. "There are bad people out there. Evil people. They do terrible things. You can't stop them, Tony."

Her breath left her as he grabbed her by her upper arms, pulled in her close. "I *am* going to stop whoever did this. You gonna mother me to death or are you going to help me?"

Angry Tony. *This is better.* "Oh, I'm going to help you. Together we're going to bring the SOB down. We make one hell of an unstoppable team, you and me, but after today, we work smarter at figuring this out. No more putting others in danger. Agreed?"

Tony nodded, started to say something and stopped. Then, "Just you and me."

Fallyn went up on her toes to kiss him, realized she barely could reach his lips without the extra height of her heels. She wrapped her arms around his neck, brought his head down, and planted one on him.

The kiss was hot. Soul-scorching. He whirled her around, pinning her against the door of the truck. His hands found her breasts, a tiny gasp escaping from her mouth. Taking advantage of her parted lips, he swept his tongue inside, teasing her until she moaned.

Lord, the man could kiss.

His hands went to her jeans, fingers jerkily undoing the clasp and zipper, peeling the material down over her hips. She wiggled, helping him, and shivered when he ran his big hands up her bare legs. He tickled the insides of her knees, grazed her thighs, gaze locked on hers the whole time.

She was so ready for this. Ready to let him take her anywhere he wanted. Ready to help him release his worries and doubts, his frustration with himself. "I know you loved my stockings," she said, her voice sounding breathy, "but they were toast—literally—after the accident."

"I like you better naked." He took her mouth in a fierce kiss, touching her everywhere. She could feel his blatant erection through her panties.

Kissing him back, she arched into him and reached for his belt. He grabbed both her wrists and broke the kiss. "I'm going to make you moan. But first, you have to do something for me."

Panting, Fallyn nodded, her body on fire. Whatever he wanted her to do was just fine with her. "Anything."

He released her wrists and ripped open the front of her shirt. Buttons flew. The silky material slid off her shoulders and down her arms.

Tony's gaze locked on her breasts, her nipples pushing at the peach lace. "My God, you are beautiful."

She almost detonated when he reached out and brushed his knuckles across one taut nipple.

"Tony, please," she whispered.

And that's when she saw it. The self-confidence. The control. The power. His eyes flashed and it was all suddenly back.

He was back. "I like it when you say please, Fallyn."

The bastard was teasing her. "Well, then, let me say it again. Please, Tony. Is that clear enough for you? *Please* stop teasing me with your kisses and your fingers and tell me what you want."

He reached out and ran his fingers under the edge of her panties, grazing her skin. Next thing she knew, she heard fabric ripping. Her panties fell to the ground, shredded.

Tony caught her up, lifting her from the ground and carried her to the front of his truck. Boosting her up, he sat her on the shiny hood, still warm from the engine. The truck sat high, bringing her knees level with his chest.

"Spread your legs."

She obeyed, leaning back on her elbows and giving him the view he wanted, making her feel wanton and dangerous.

He trailed his fingers over her inner thighs, then slid them into her tight heat. She closed her eyes, quivering at the sensation. He brought them out, then sent those wicked fingers in deep again, his thumb finding her bud and circling it, building her desperate need to new heights.

Fallyn arched her back, enjoying the rhythm he built. Faster, deeper, taking her higher until she was begging him for release.

"Not yet," he said, pressing her legs farther apart. She looked up in time to see him lower his head.

She cried out at the feel of his lips, his tongue. Her arms wouldn't hold her any longer and she lay back, letting her thighs fall completely open.

"That's right, Fallyn." He held her legs down, his breath hot against her sensitive flesh. "Come for me."

His tongue dove into her, nearly pushing her into an orgasm. He withdrew it, ran it over her bud, then slipped it back inside.

Nonsense noises came from her throat. She couldn't help it, her mind blanked, her body existing only in this moment, only for him. A few more flicks of his tongue and she was gone. She swallowed a scream and dug her nails into the hood as a savage climax ripped through her.

The sweet bliss lasted forever, him milking her with his lips until the last shuddering spasm passed. Her legs were liquid, her body floating, weightless. When she could finally form words, she raised her head and looked at him through half-lidded eyes. "That was amazing."

His smile was as fierce as the kisses he'd laid on her earlier. He swept her off the truck and carried her to the stairs. "Good, 'cuz we're just getting started, sweetheart."

At the top of the stairs, Tony's hands were busy trying to unclasp Fallyn's bra so he kicked at the door leading into the apartment.

Nothing.

Tell me this door is locked. Wouldn't that be a craptastic interruption to what had started as an exceptional encounter.

Fallyn reached behind her, twisted the doorknob and—score—pushed the door open. A sliver of hazy moonlight illuminated the small kitchen and she gave him a wicked half-grin. "We are so good together."

Fuck her blind. That's what he'd do. Because Fallyn Pasche, on some primal level, understood him. Knew how to push his buttons just enough to motivate him rather than piss him off.

And right now? Highly motivated.

"Babe, you are going to howl before I'm finished with you."

"Aren't I the lucky girl?"

Getting his bearings, he hooked a left into the short hallway hoping to get to the bedroom before he exploded. Fallyn plastered herself against him, kissing the hell out of him, that amazing tongue making his mind race. *Fuck her blind, fuck her blind, fuck her blind.*

God, the woman would drive him to madness. No off switch. No brake pedal. Just go, go, go. Like him. Together? What a frickin' disaster.

A hot, adrenaline fueled disaster that made him want more. Always.

How far was the goddamn bedroom?"

Still kissing him, Fallyn laughed. "Where the hell is the bedroom?"

"Just wondering that myself. Ow! Shit!"

He hit something. Damned darkness. He unclamped one hand from Fallyn's ass and reached down. Sofa.

"Living room."

"Good enough." She grabbed onto his hair with both hands and tugged. "I want you inside me. Now."

"Lucky boy," he said, mimicking her voice. "We'll find the bedroom later."

Using one hand, he felt around, found the seat of the sofa and set her down. Immediately, like locked-on radar, she went for the waistband of his pants, looking up at him the whole time, smiling that wicked smile that made his already raging hard-on painful.

He slid his fingers along her jaw, stroking her smooth skin. "You're amazing."

And she was. Beautiful, smart, sassy. Gently, he ran his hands up her cheeks, through her hair, grabbed a fistful of it and tugged so she'd look up him. "I'm crazy about you."

"Ditto, handsome."

She jerked his fly down, sent his pants to his ankles and went to work on his boxers. "Come to mama, sweetheart."

At that he laughed. Had to. The woman was nuts. And all he had to decide was how to take her. Against the sofa, against the wall, bent over. What?

Something told him she liked it hard and fast. Like him. On the edge of rough because that's where things got crazy and hot and made the release a pure shot of insanity.

Boom and boom and boom.

That's what he wanted. That shattering release that would make his mind stop, just blow that bastard to bits and give him a few measly seconds of peace.

From his thoughts.

From his guilt.

That goddamn guilt that never gave up.

Fallyn wrapped her hand around him and his eyes rolled. Holy God, that felt good. He moved back, away from her and kicked out of his shoes, pants and the boxers.

Ready.

"So, what do you think?" he said. "Ready to scream?"

The measly moonlight shifted, threw shadows across her bare breasts and his heart damn near stopped, just froze right in his chest. He sucked in a breath and held it. So damned beautiful.

"Jesus, Fallyn."

"What?"

He slapped his hands over the top of his head. What the hell was wrong with him? By now, with any other woman giving him the go sign like she had, he'd be on her, the two of them body slamming each other into mind blowing orgasms.

Now? He shook his head. "I don't know," he said. "You...undo me."

She sat back, lifted one leg and rested her arm on her knee. "And that's a bad thing?"

"No. But my M.O. is bent."

"Thank goodness that's the only thing bent."

Shit. Totally irreverent this woman. He burst out laughing. Standing there in the middle of a strange living room, no lights, a hot woman naked and ready in front of him and he was laughing at jokes.

I'm losing it.

He sat down next to her, reached for her and kissed her. Long and slow. Savoring it because all of a sudden, he didn't want to rush. He wanted every second, every micro-second, drilled into his brain. For the first time, he didn't want to body slam his way through it.

With Fallyn, he wanted...different.

Still kissing him, she eased herself back, lying down and pulling him on top of her, dragging her warm fingers up and down his back, over his ass and he broke the kiss, buried his face in her hair and his mind slowed to...nothing.

Blank.

God, that was good. Better than good. Fantastic. Who knew? "Don't stop."

"It feels good?"

"Hell, yeah."

And it did. Slowly, she tickled her fingers over his back, the movement lighting up his nerve endings in a way he'd never experienced and he breathed in, let the silence take over.

While her magic fingers lulled him, she brought her legs around his waist and he was right there. *Right* there. All he had to do was ram himself home and rock her world the way he knew he could. Just pound away until they both screamed.

The way it had always been for him.

Pound. Pound. Pound.

Mind shatter.

Done.

Not this time.

He raised his head, looked down at her grinning up at him and kissed her. Softly. A gentle brush of lips as he sunk his weight into her, rested there for a second. Taking it all in. Absorbing the moment. For once.

Her hands stroked over his back. Up. Down. Up. Down. She pulled back, stared up at him, her green eyes, even in the dark, so focused. "You okay?"

Okay? Was he? He didn't know. If okay was this crazy calm feeling, yeah, he was definitely okay.

"I'm great," he said. "You ready for me?"

"You betcha, fella."

He slid into her and she arched up, gasping as she locked her legs around him and brought her hands to his cheeks. "Oh, that's perfect."

Perfect.

Forcing himself to move slowly, to not rush it—no pounding—he moved inside her, stayed there for a long second and buried his face in her hair again.

She nibbled his earlobe, then kissed it while her hands started another tour of his back. "I love being with you like this."

He moved again, rocking his hips—*slow, slow, slow*—taking his time, enjoying it. Not rushing to the finish line.

"Fallyn?"

"Yes?"

"You undo me and it's the best goddamn thing ever."

"Good. Because I have plans for you, mister."

Legs still locked around him, she arched up, urging him on and he lifted his head, stared down at her, kept his gaze glued to her as they moved together and something in his brain whipped at him, but no...he wanted it to last. To take his time.

"I'll fuck you blind next time," he blurted.

What an idiot.

"Isn't that what you're doing now?"

"No. I usually like it..." he shook his head.

"Rough?"

He kissed her again. "Fast. I like it fast. Not this time. This time, it's—"

"Perfect."

She ran her hands through his hair, brought his head down, hit him with another of those agonizing soft kisses and his body tensed. Not yet. No.

Here it comes. Too soon. Damn. He fought it, squeezed his eyes closed. *Not yet.*

"It's okay," she whispered. "Let go. I've got you. I'll always have you."

He opened his eyes, looked down at Fallyn. So beautiful. Perfect and flawed. He wanted her. Her and the explosion that would blow his mind.

Not yet.

Damn. He didn't know what he wanted.

He breathed in, rocked his hips and...pow. His mind and body exploded, a massive rush and he pumped his hips harder, praying the euphoria would last and last and last.

"Can't wait."

He threw his head back, pumped one last time, buried himself as deep as he could and let the release wash over him and settle.

"Tony?"

God, why was she talking right now? He opened his eyes, blinked and focused and—oh, yeah—she had that zoned out look and he grinned. He'd put that look on her face. "You're close, aren't you?" He kissed her. "You gonna come for me, Fallyn?"

He reached down, used his fingers to finish what the now resting little man couldn't.

Rocking her hips hard, she whipped her head sideways. "Don't stop. Please…"

She reared up, nearly whacked her head into his and grabbed his shoulders, digging her fingers in as she cried out and collapsed.

I did that.

He dipped his head again, ran kisses along her jawline. "You're beautiful, Fallyn. And you're mine."

"Damn, woman," Tony said, his big frame swinging in through the kitchen doorway. "That smells amazing."

Fallyn smiled, scooping a smidgen of spaghetti sauce from the pot, blowing on it softly to cool it before she held out the spoon. "I found pasta and tomato sauce in the pantry. My father would shoot me for making sauce from a jar, but it's the best I can do."

Tony slid over to taste it. Eyes widening, he licked his lips. "Tastes as good as it smells. I bet your dad couldn't tell the difference."

Tony was close, looming over her, touching her back. She liked it.

Oh, who am I fooling? I love it.

His touch, his kisses—all of it. She wanted him to keep touching her, keep invading her personal space. The sex was amazing, the best she'd ever had. She could talk to Tony about anything and he totally got her.

Not many people did.

In the past twenty-four hours, her phone and Tony's had been ringing nonstop—updates from Mitch and Caroline, the local police, Special Agent Pain-in-Her-Ass Bronco, Jordan, Carl, her dad, Dani and everyone back at Pasche & Associates—they all wanted to know what had happened with the accident. Still, she'd made time to touch Tony every time he touched her, to kiss him back. Any time she saw that self-incriminating doubt enter his eyes, even with Grey out of surgery and recovering, he still beat himself up. Maddening. The benefit was any time he grew quiet and moody, she'd brought him out of it with sex.

It was a tough job, but someone had to do it.

She'd prostituted herself to keep the man distracted and she didn't care. They'd christened every surface in the loft, St. Agnes looking on with her stoic face.

"Eric Pasche can smell jarred sauce from a mile away," Fallyn said, turning back to the stove. As she stirred, Tony put his arms around her and lowered his lips to her neck. Her concentration fled and the spoon slowed.

Closing her eyes, she sighed softly, enjoying the feel of his solid body pressing against hers. For once, she didn't want to *lean in* like all the women's magazines told her to do. She had a career and it was great, but right now, she was also strong enough to admit, she wanted a man in her life.

Instead of leaning in, she leaned back.

Against Tony's shoulder.

This. She sighed.

This was what she wanted.

What would it be like to come home to him every night? To cook for him?

"Luckily," she said, eyes closed, "I learned enough about cooking while working in dad's restaurant, that I can fake it with the best of them."

Steam rose from the boiling water in the second pot, the mist hovering in the air as the noodles cooked. When was the last time she'd stood over a stove and cooked for someone? She couldn't remember. Even though she knew how to make a variety of plates most people were impressed with, she usually ordered out. Too many years working at her father's restaurant had jaded her love of cooking.

Tony's hands slid around her hips to her backside where he cupped her ass cheeks. His lips nibbled at her ear. "How long before dinner's ready?"

"Not long." She knew where this was going. Despite what he'd said about preferring fast sex, Tony was not a quick, wham-bam lover.

He liked to take his time. The pasta would overcook if she let him have his way. "How much time do you need?"

"I bet I can make you come before the timer goes off."

She turned in his arms. *To hell with the pasta.* "Let's test that theory, shall we?"

He lifted her onto the counter with ease, the spoon in her hand falling to clang against the saucepot. He kissed and licked at the fine layer of perspiration on her collarbone, and she helped him unbutton her shirt. His lips moved down toward her left nipple.

She'd just unclasped his pants and he was sucking on that nipple through her lace bra when his phone went off.

Swearing, he fumbled the phone out of his back pocket. She saw him about to turn the whole thing off when he stilled. "It's Teeg," he said through gritted teeth. "I better take it."

Fallyn nodded, playing with his zipper anyway, slowly lowering it to slip her fingers inside. He sucked in a breath, caught her fingers and drew them away, giving her a warning look. She chuckled under her breath and licked her lips seductively.

"What?" Tony said by way of greeting to Teeg.

She couldn't make out Teeg's exact words, but Tony's brows crashed together and she stopped teasing him.

Tony put the phone on speaker and held it between them. "Say that again, Teeg."

The techie's voice sounded tired. "I unlocked a folder Heather had labeled personal email. Except it wasn't email. There was only a single jpeg in the file. A screenshot of a coded text."

Fallyn buttoned her shirt back up. "Who was it from?"

"Sending the screenshot to you now," Teeg said, "along with what I could decode. Doesn't make sense to me, but it may to you guys. Also, I haven't found anything credible—or consistent—with death threats. Anything related to her shooting down that bill was mostly one-time bitching. I'll let you know if I find anything else."

Tony's phone dinged with the incoming jpeg file. He brought it up as Fallyn slid off the countertop and stood next to him.

They read it at the same time, then exchanged a look. "I knew it," Fallyn said.

"You know what it means?" Teeg asked.

Fallyn scanned the words again.

D-Day, POTUS runt at MacDill.

Tony was staring at her, as if he, too, were waiting for her to enlighten him.

"MacDill," Fallyn said. "The air force base in Tampa? That's where Ryan Nicols' Special Operations team is stationed. MacDill hosts the Special Operations Command and twenty-something other mission partners. They patrol the Atlantic waters."

"D-Day," Tony recited. "Is it saying the day the CanAir flight disappeared, Ryan was at MacDill?"

"Exactly." Fallyn leaned her butt against the counter. "Who is the text from, Teeg? There's only a phone number associated with it and I don't recognize that number."

"It's a personal cell phone that isn't used much. A real dinosaur bought seven years ago." The click of keys filtered through the phone. "I managed to track down the name it's registered to."

Tony shifted his weight from one foot to the other. "And?"

"Carl Lomax."

"Carl?" Fallyn met Tony's eyes, a strong sense of betrayal sending sharp lightening strikes down her arms. She gripped the edge of the counter. "He was helping Heather look into this?"

"Looks that way," Tony said. "Heather must have figured out the Nicols angle and wanted to know where the kid was when the plane went down."

"He warned me off, told me not to dig into this." Fallyn shook her head in disgust. "He acted like I was a bitch for insisting Heather had been killed, and then he lied right to my face when I asked him if he knew Heather was investigating the plane's disappearance. He told me he didn't know anything about it."

Tony's fingers tightened on the phone. "Which means it's possible he lied about not knowing Heather had a heart condition as well."

Fallyn's stomach dropped. What was Tony suggesting?

Teeg's voice broke into their personal conversation. "What does Ryan Nicols have to do with the CanAir flight?"

Grey hadn't had a chance to tell anyone about Fallyn and Tony's theory.

Fallyn felt a new kind of heat rising in her body. The heat of treachery turning her blood to a rolling boil. "The president's son, a member of a secret Spec Ops group, was at MacDill the day the CanAir flight went missing. I think he shot that plane down on his father's orders. My sister was putting those links together and Carl knew about it. That rat bastard. He was helping her."

"Or he's the one who shut her down," Tony said. The timer on the stove went off and Tony met her gaze. "Carl just added himself to our suspect list."

15

*T*ony stopped on the walkway leading to Carl's stately colonial in one of the tonier neighborhoods in the DC area. For a guy who'd worked for the government most of his career, he had obviously cashed in working the private sector.

He scanned the fresh paint, the scrollwork on the oversized double front doors that had obviously been hand-carved. The doors alone were probably a year's worth of Tony's salary.

"Here's the deal," he faced Fallyn.

"Uh-oh. I don't like when people tell me what the deal is."

"I know. But hear me out on this one. I think you'll agree."

She pursed her lips, clearly prepping to argue before he'd even said anything. Tony had to laugh. Everything about this woman gave him a rush. The contrary attitude, the drive, the willingness to put herself in danger to find the truth, all of it tripped his 'she's-special' trigger.

He smiled. "What? No snappy comeback?"

"Oh, I have one. But you asked me to hear you out. Which I will do, considering the multiple, rib-shattering orgasms you gave me in the last twelve hours. Thank you, by the way for those. I want more."

Yeah, he might love her.

"Plenty more of that for you, babe. But first,"—he pointed to the fancy front door—"we talk to your buddy Carl. We show him the screenshot of his text to Heather and see what he has to say."

"Yes. That's the plan. We talked about this already."

Yep. Sure did. "This is the part that'll piss you off."

"Excellent."

"I think you're too close to this situation to question Carl. It's too personal and, as good as you are, I don't think you can distance your-self emotionally. That'll screw up the interview. Let me talk to him. You listen and see if anything clicks for you."

She tilted her head, nibbled her bottom lip and Tony's mind wandered back to the things she'd recently done to him with those lips and—crap—he was gone. Toast.

Without giving her a chance to respond—or argue—he started up the walkway. "It's a good plan," he said. "You can be the good cop."

Fallyn scooted up behind him, tugged on the back of his jacket. "Fine. But—"

"Ha. I knew that was too easy."

"But...if I have a question, I'm jumping in."

Tony poked the doorbell and heard the sing-song chime through the thick wood of the doors. "I'd expect nothing less."

"Charmer."

One of the giant doors swung open and Carl—what? No butler? —greeted them. He wore a perfectly pressed white dress shirt, no tie, black slacks and tasseled shoes. If this was his hanging around the house outfit, the guy needed to lighten up.

"Come in," he said waving them through.

Tony held his hand out to Fallyn then rested it on her lower back as she breezed by him. Somewhere in the last few days she'd stopped flinching every time he touched her. Welcome news since he consid-ered himself an affectionate guy who liked physical contact with the people he cared about. Hugs, pokes, tickles, whatever; he showed his love with his hands.

"I'm home alone," Carl said, "but let's go into the study."

The study. Sounded private. A place where they could talk openly. Possibly accuse a man of murder.

Fallyn led the way, chatting with Carl as they walked down a long hallway beside the curving staircase.

On an emotional level, this had to be difficult for her. These people were family friends and she'd probably visited their home hundreds of times for parties and holidays and dinners. But Fallyn? She was a beast. Nothing about her relaxed tone or the sassy swing of her hips indicated conflict.

Which was why she was so good at her job.

Fallyn, under all that cool, was a snake about to strike.

Damn, he could love her.

I'm toast.

At the end of the hallway, just before they reached the kitchen, Fallyn turned through another set of carved double doors. The *study*. The tall bookcases and dark green paint reminded Tony of something from an old movie. Old Carl was shooting for upscale and elegant, but what he got was tight and confined. Pretentious.

Carl sat behind the oversized desk and waved them to the guest chairs. *Power play.* The room, with the huge desk and wall of bookcases wasn't big enough for a seating area.

"Thank you for seeing us," Fallyn said.

"Of course. Anything for you. You know that. You said it was about Heather?"

Here we go..."Yes," Tony said.

Carl inched his head to Tony, gave him a puzzled why-are-you-speaking look.

Tony sat back, crossed his feet at his ankles and settled in. "Some things have come up about Heather."

"Like what?"

"Like that CanAir flight that crashed."

Carl met Fallyn's gaze then shifted back to Tony. "Again with this? She was on the Foreign Relations committee. They closed that investigation."

"No they didn't. And I think you know that." Tony grabbed his phone from his pocket, tapped on the screenshot of Carl's text and set the phone on the desk where Carl could see it. Take it in.

"We've uncovered this text."

Carl glanced down at the phone, but immediately brought his gaze up.

Tony held up his hand. "Before you say anything, you should know we've traced the text back to your phone. We know you sent Heather this message. We *know* Heather—at the request of Senator Oren—was covertly looking into that crash, even after Foreign Relations came up with that nonsense about closing the investigation. What we don't know is why you're involved."

"I'm not involved."

Liar, liar, pants on fire.

And, *hello*. Carl kept his eyes glued to Tony. In Tony's experience, if Carl wanted to launch a full-scale counterattack, he'd need reinforcements. Someone emotionally invested, someone he might try to manipulate based on their family history.

That someone, right now, was Fallyn.

And he couldn't look at her.

Guilt.

As much as Tony had anticipated that Fallyn's personal issues would impede this interview, it seemed he might be wrong. Tony had spent a lifetime dealing with guilt and defending against it. His mother and sisters were champs at guilt. If there were a Guilt Olympics, they'd take the gold. Every time.

Time to make Carl squirm.

Tony angled to Fallyn. "Tell him what you told me about the president's son."

For a second, Fallyn hesitated, searching his eyes, trying to figure out what the fuck he was doing after he'd instructed her to keep her trap shut. Yes, he'd gone off script. She could yell at him later.

But then, being the ace she was, she faced Carl. "Of course," she said, her voice light and agreeable and—yep—forcing Carl to look at her.

Atta, girl.

"I had a visit from President Nicols yesterday."

Carl's eyebrows hitched. "Really?"

"Imagine my surprise when he showed up at my hotel. Where I'm staying because someone keeps breaking into Heather's house trying to steal her tablet. Not to mention causing an accident yesterday that could have killed me."

"You said you were okay."

"Well, I'm not. My friend almost died last night because he's helping me with Heather's..." She drew a breath, shook her head. "He's helping me with Heather. A man almost died, Carl. I need to know what you know."

A long silence ensued. Carl stared at Fallyn. Fallyn stared back. Classic negotiating tactic. The first to speak would lose. Both of them knew it.

Right now, Tony was banking on Fallyn. She was too damned stubborn and motivated to lose.

Carl held his hands out. "You think *I* had something to do with it?"

"I think Heather confided in you about a lot of things. I know she sought your advice on political maneuvering."

"And," Tony said, "something this big? A junior senator doesn't take that on without knowing she can win."

Ignoring Tony, Carl leaned toward Fallyn, his arms resting on the desk, but stretched halfway to Fallyn. "You can't think I would hurt her."

"I don't want to think that."

"We're here," Tony said, "because Fallyn is loyal. *I* wanted to take this text straight to the FBI. She's got Metro Police and the feds all over her. And let's not forget the media hype. The pressure is insane. Something's gonna give and she'll be in the middle of it. Possibly facing obstruction charges. But, she's here. Now, are you gonna work with her or do we go to the feds?"

16

She was going to lose her shit. Just lose it. Any second now...

Fallyn gripped the arms of the chair she was sitting in across from Carl—Carl, her second father—and tried to breathe through the boa constrictor tightening its body around her lungs.

Betrayal burned like acid in her throat. First her mom, then her father's withdrawal, now Carl.

She'd reconciled herself on the way over that Carl could be the killer, yet it still seemed completely ridiculous. He'd loved Heather. Loved her as much as his own daughter. How could he possibly kill her?

Yet, her fingers had searched for the gun in her purse. Reassurance, in case she was about to come face-to-face with the person who had stolen her sister's life.

Fallyn had trained herself to read body language. Body language told her more than words. At that moment, Carl's body language suggested he was hiding something, but not a murder.

"Tell me the truth, Carl." Her own body language had to be screaming how upset she was, so she forced herself to ease up on her grip. "That's all I'm asking. You told me to back off, that you would look into what Heather was doing, but you already knew, didn't you?"

He sat back in his office chair and ran his hand over his face. Dark shadows clung to the bags under his eyes. In the past few days, he looked like he'd aged ten years. "This is dangerous stuff, Fallyn. You're digging yourself into a deep hole if you keep pursuing it."

"Are you threatening her?" Tony nearly came out of his seat.

Fallyn grabbed his wrist and gave it a squeeze. *Whoa, boy. Back down.*

Carl held up both hands in a gesture of surrender. "Of course not! It's not a threat, it's a warning. You've seen what happened." He focused his gaze on Fallyn. "I've already lost your sister. I don't want to lose you, too."

Her heart squeezed. She'd always loved Carl and looked up to him. She couldn't remember a time in her life when he wasn't there.

But emotional sentiment wasn't going to solve anything. *Work the case.* "You almost lost me yesterday by keeping me in the dark. Tell me what you know about the CanAir disappearance and Heather's investigation."

His gaze dropped to the blotter on his desk. His aged fingers worked at the leather-bound edge. "Heather asked me to look into where Ryan Nicols was on the day the plane disappeared. Yes, she confided in me that she was looking into it at Senator Oren's request, but asked me to keep quiet about it. She didn't want to ruffle feathers or have anyone catch wind that there was an ongoing investigation."

"Did she tell you she suspected the president's son shot down the plane?"

His chin moved in what seemed like a nod. "After I confirmed Ryan was in the area, she told me her theory."

"I say it's more than a theory at this point," Tony said. "Heather, and now Fallyn, have put two and two together."

Carl became animated again, looking up and scooting forward in his seat to tap the top of the desk with a finger. "I'm going to tell you the same thing I told her. Yes, I'm sure the president didn't cry over Nazari's death, but without the plane or an eyewitness, there's no way to prove the plane was shot down or that he had anything to do with that plane's disappearance."

"But we *do* have an eyewitness," Fallon said.

Carl's bushy brows crashed down. "Who?"

"Ryan Nicols."

Again, Carl's hands went up in the air, this time in frustration. "You can't be serious. Whoever gave the order to shoot down that plane believed Heather had enough information to prove it, and you and I both know who that person probably is. He killed your sister over it, right? Isn't that what you're saying? Now, you're in possession of that proof and you almost lost your life yesterday. Your friend is in serious condition. You go after the president's son, Fallyn, and the president will come after you."

"The alternative is that I sweep it under the carpet and pretend this never happened?" A dry, brittle laugh left her lips. "Sorry, no can do."

"You can't take on the most powerful man in the world."

"I can if my sister is dead because of him."

"The president is not untouchable," Tony said.

"If you believe that, son, you're either blind or stupid."

Tony stilled. Just *wham*. Pissed? Oh, yeah.

Time to end this. "Not long ago, President Nicols had me bury a news story about Ryan and his bachelor status," Fallyn said quietly. "Ryan is part of a Special Ops group and the president claimed his son's identity could be compromised, his undercover career destroyed by a bunch of publicity. Ryan was an adult and joined the Air Force before his dad became president, so he escaped a lot of the media attention First Kids often receive. I complied, making sure Ryan's covert life stayed exactly that—a secret, but now I wonder if it was more than that. The president ordered his son to shoot down that plane. He couldn't risk Ryan being in the spotlight for anything. Abraham Nicols used me to cover his ass, and now, he's had my sister killed." She rose and grabbed her purse. "I'm going after his son."

"He's not in the country anymore," Carl said. "I already checked. My source says Ryan's on a top secret mission in the Middle East."

"Then I'll find someone else who can verify he carried out those orders. There has to be someone. His teammates, someone higher up on the chain of command at the DOD. There must be a log of the mission somewhere. One way or another, I will find the proof I need."

She didn't wait for Tony to follow. She threw the study door open and nearly barreled into Jordan who was coming down the hall.

The woman had her coat half off, her cheeks pink from cool air outside. "Fallyn! What are you doing here? Is everything okay?"

Everything was *not* okay. She was still close to losing her shit.

Need to blow off steam. Fallyn whisked by the woman on her way to the front door. "You'll be happy to know, Jordan, I'm officially overwhelmed."

Tony caught up to her as she flew down the front steps toward his car. He didn't say anything, just opened the door for her and helped her up into the cab of the truck. They drove off and Tony headed for Fresh Start.

"Take me to the townhouse," Fallyn said, pulling out her phone.

"The townhouse?"

"I need to start boxing up Heather's stuff."

"You think that's a good idea after yesterday?"

"Good idea? No. We're doing it anyway."

"Yes, ma'am." He pressed the accelerator and they picked up speed. "On one condition."

For a second Fallyn's stomach dropped at the acceleration, the memory of her ride in Grey's Charger still fresh. By a battle of will, she shook off the memory. "Of course there's a condition. There's always a condition with you, Gerard."

He shot her a devious smile before pinning his eyes back on the road. "You need to extricate some demons. I get it. Just let me make sure the place is clear before you go inside. That's all I'm asking."

Reasonable. He usually was. "Deal. But next time you tell me not get emotional when we're interrogating someone, take a dose of your own medicine."

"What?"

"Back there with Carl. I thought you were going to go across the desk and strangle the old guy when you thought he was threatening me."

"I was."

"Good. I don't like being threatened. Nice to know someone else feels the same way."

He reached over and grabbed her hand. "I've got your back, Fal."

Fal. Heather had always called her that. Jesus, she missed her sister.

No time for this. If she gave into those thoughts, she'd lose it right here in the car. She reached for something lippy to say, to ease the tension building inside her. "You can have my front too. I insist. I'm an equal opportunity employer."

Another grin. He let go of her hand and she tackled the first order of business on her Do Not Go Insane work list.

Call Metro PD.

When Detective Hollister came on the line, Fallyn didn't bother with greetings. "Have the results come back on the pills I gave you?"

There was a slight pause on his end, but he caught on quick. "Ms. Pasche. Good to hear from you. I was just speaking with Special Agent Bronco, and—"

"The pills, detective. Did the lab results come back?"

She felt more than heard his sigh. "No, ma'am. Like everything else around here, the lab is overworked and has a backlog of requests. They'll get to those medications as soon as they can."

"Uh huh. Why don't you have them ship the pills over to Agent Bronco at the FBI and ask him to get them analyzed? I'm sure he'll be happy to cooperate."

Plus, it would keep the good agent busy for a while. Anything to get him out of her hair.

Before Hollister could argue or start asking her questions she didn't want to answer, she cut him off. "Let me know if anything new in your investigation breaks, K?"

She hung up. *Next.*

Her second call to Special Agent Bronco went to his voice mail. *Good.* She didn't want to talk to him anyway. "Detective Hollister is sending you the pills from my sister's medicine cabinet for your FBI lab to analyze. Also, you should know I'm compiling a file on an investigation Heather was looking into and how it may play into her death. I'm not ready to share details yet, but if something happens to me like it almost did yesterday, I'm instructing my team, and specifically Tony Gerard, to give you access to that file so you can open an official investigation. Believe me, Agent Bronco, it will make your career."

Or get you killed.

But seriously, how many people could the president kill off before someone exposed him? Bronco was probably safe.

Her dad was next. Their conversation was about the weather, a new dish he was offering at the restaurant for the next month in Heather's honor.

His bunions.

Kill me now.

On the heels of that thought came another. *Be careful what you wish for.*

They talked a little longer and Fallyn realized her father was getting old. Like Carl, he'd aged just in the past few days. She needed to spend more time with him.

They shared a few more minutes of genial conversation. She hung up with her dad, took a deep breath, and dialed her office in New York.

It was Saturday afternoon, and she didn't expect anyone to answer, but they'd all been working overtime with her absence, so she wasn't too surprised when her office manager answered on the first ring. "Pasche & Associates."

"Hey, Katrina. It's me. Has the press deluge settled down at all?"

"Sixty-one calls today, but hey, who's counting?"

Katrina had a wicked sense of humor and fit in perfectly with the rest of the crew. "Only sixty-one, huh?"

"You're old news already. Fifteen minutes of fame and all that."

The sensationalism of Heather's death had given way to an earthquake in California, but Fallyn's accident with Grey had attracted a lot of local attention. She'd just lost her twin sister and now she'd nearly lost another person close to her. Everyone wanted to know who the mysterious driver was who'd ended up in an undisclosed hospital. Was he her boyfriend? A hook-up? A new client?

Respecting Grey and Syd's privacy, Fallyn had kept mum, her official statement describing him as a friend. That, of course, only made the media vultures speculate even more.

Let 'em spin it however they wanted. Until Syd—or Grey—told her to come forth with the truth, she was sticking to her friend story.

"Anything else important I should know?"

"There was a package in the mail today."

Nothing unusual about that. "And?"

The woman hesitated. "There was no return address, but the handwriting is familiar."

Something about Katrina's tone made Fallyn's stomach drop. "Who's it from?"

Two beats of her heart went by. "I think Heather," the woman finally said.

Her belly clenched. Her hand holding the phone shook. "Open it."

Tony glanced her way. She avoided his eyes, setting her attention on the scenery passing by.

Fallyn heard the ripping of an envelope in the background. "It's a USB drive," Katrina said.

That boa constrictor was back, squeezing until Fallyn had to lean over to catch a breath. "Is there a note?"

"No. Sorry. Do you want me to see what's on the drive?"

Tony's hand caressed her back. "You okay?" he said softly.

"Yes," she said to him, sitting up. The word worked for Katrina too. "Go ahead while I'm on the phone with you."

The familiar neighborhood leading to Heather's townhouse came into view while Katrina plugged in the thumb drive to her computer. "Hmm. Looks like video files but their encrypted. I can't open any of them."

Encrypted videos. Holy shit. Had Heather gotten some kind of confession on tape? From who? Ryan? Someone else? "Get Dani on it. ASAP."

"You got it, boss."

They disconnected and Fallyn sat looking at her phone. She couldn't breathe, couldn't think. For some stupid reason, a memory of her mother shooting videos of them one summer flashed across her brain. She and Heather had been six or seven, splashing in a plastic pool one summer day. Their mother had a new video camera, one that sat on her shoulder as she filmed. "Look at momma, girls!" she called. Fallyn and Heather had made faces at her, splashed water on each other, laughed and giggled, and finally started splashing their mother when she got too close.

"Fallyn?"

Tony's voice brought her out of her reverie. She shoved her phone in her bag and cleared her throat. Her eyes burned with unshed tears. "Heather sent me a USB with encrypted videos on it," she said as they pulled up in front of the townhouse.

"Videos? Any idea what those could be?"

"Your guess is as good as mine. My tech person is going to work on them."

"All right. Sit tight until I check on the house. Is your gun loaded?"

"Yes, sir."

"Get it out. Anyone approaches, shoot their ass."

It was good to be back in the present. With Tony. Solid, grounded Tony. "Shoot first, ask questions later?"

He winked at her. "Works for me."

She waited for him to bail out before grabbing the gun, not wanting him to see her hands were shaking. Waiting was not her forte, but she forced herself to do as he'd asked. The second hand on her watch seemed unusually noisy as it *tick, tick, ticked* off the seconds.

Two minutes passed, then five. Fallyn scanned the front of the townhouse, watched the windows looking for Tony's shadow.

Nothing.

Come on, Tony. Where are you?

Had someone been inside? Had they jumped him?

She was about to go storming in with gun raised when he appeared in the doorway. As he approached the truck, she tucked the gun away and sucked in a relieved breath.

A moment later, he escorted her inside. "Place is clear. Everything appears exactly how I left it yesterday."

"Good." She dropped her bag and her coat on the couch. She'd held it together until now, but the impending meltdown hovered just under her skin. "Whatever you see and hear for the next couple of moments, go with it, okay?"

One of Tony's brows rose. "Dare I ask what you're about to do?"

She grabbed a vase off the nearest display cabinet, an ugly thing Heather had no doubt brought back from some third-world country. "Nope," she said and promptly flung it to the floor.

Crash! The vase smashed into a thousand pieces. Fallyn grabbed another knick-knack—an artsy porcelain cat statue—and fast-pitched it at the nearest wall.

Boom! Bits of porcelain rained down, joining the glass.

She took out the books and DVDs Jordan had so carefully put back into place, clearing a shelf with wild abandon before attacking the next. She beat her fists into the couch cushions and tore a picture from the wall so she could smash the glass against her knee.

When she was done, the living room looked worse than it had after the initial break-in and Fallyn sat, chest heaving, on the floor.

Her ears rang and her pulse raced. If she didn't know better, she'd think she was having a panic attack.

Heather. Mother.

Gone.

The word was so final. One dead. The other dead to Fallyn, if not physically buried.

Carl. Dad.

Gone in a different way. One never there for her emotionally. The other there when she was growing up, but now he'd lied to her, betrayed her, as well.

The crunch of class echoed in her ear. In her peripheral vision, a man's leg came into view.

Tony. He had to think she was crazy.

She glanced up, saw a crooked smile on his face. One big, strong hand reached down. "Shall we do the kitchen next?"

The following morning, while standing in the kitchen dumping the last batch of broken glass after Fallyn completely trashed her sister's house, Tony's phone beeped. He had no doubt this was one of four people.

People being his sisters.

Today was Mom's party and they'd dogged him with reminders about getting candles, and—oh—they needed an extra disposable tablecloth for something or other. Hell if he knew. All he needed was a list. King of the List. That was him. With a list, he could get shit done. Fast.

He set the dustpan on top of the garbage can and retrieved the text that had just come in. Shannon. With an update to the list. An extra corkscrew. Sure. Why not? After the last few days with Fallyn and this nightmare scenario, the simplicity of checking off a list was a vacation.

Fallyn.

Shit. He dragged a hand down his face. With Grey in the hospital and Monroe hanging with Syd, who the hell would stay with Fallyn while he went to his mother's party? Because, there was no way—no way—he could miss that party. Not only did he want to be there, but the abuse he'd take from Team Estrogen would be epic if he wasn't.

He dipped his head back, stared at the ceiling where just above him footsteps creaked a floorboard. Twelve hours ago, after a much-deserved freak-out, Fallyn crashed hard, landing on top of her sister's bed and passing out.

The woman was flat-out exhausted so he'd snagged her phone and let her sleep while he repaired the damage she'd done.

He'd even managed a catnap while playing bodyguard. He'd activated the alarm, pushed one of the living room chairs right up to the base of the stairs and slept. If anyone tried to get up those stairs, they'd have had to get through him.

Multitasker and King of the List. *Atta, boy.*

He tracked Fallyn's footsteps, walking along with her. At the staircase, he looked up, spotted her at the top, still in yesterday's clothes, her hair a rat's nest and—wow—his body responded. In a big way.

The woman was a mess and yet, he wanted her. All day long.

"Good morning," she croaked. "Did you steal my phone?"

"I did. You needed rest and that thing goes off constantly. I think the world did okay without you for a few hours."

She came down the stairs, her eyes on him, and with the crazy hair she looked...demented. Straight out of a B-grade horror flick. If she wanted to yell at him about the phone, so be it. He'd do it again in a nanosecond.

Plus, he wasn't afraid of her. When she got mad, it turned him on. *Warped.*

Totally unhealthy. Had to be. The two together might land them a slot on one of those prime time crime shows after they killed each other. *Breaking news folks, a Supreme Court police officer and a political spin-doctor fucked each other to death after an argument.*

He laughed. Couldn't help it.

Fallyn stopped on the first step and stood eye to eye with him. "What's funny? Certainly not you confiscating my phone."

"Certainly not. I was thinking about the insane hair you're sporting and"—he waggled a finger at her—"the mean look in your eye, and I must be nuts because—guess what, babe?—it's off-the-charts hot. I mean, how sick is that?"

She kissed him. Just bam, an immediate assault that included use of her tongue darting into his mouth and poking at his. *Damned hot.* Fallyn, no matter what, threw herself into a situation. Every time. No matter what.

This kiss? This lip scorching, soul-shattering monster that got him so hard he might explode, was no exception. He pulled her in, clamped his hands over her ass and gave her as good as he got while she and her tongue rocked his world.

Oh-kay! Good way to start off, considering he'd just insulted her. A good twenty seconds in, she ground her hips against him and— holy shit—they'd light this place up.

Afraid he'd humiliate himself and erupt on the steps, he backed away from the kiss, dropped little pecks along her jaw and moved to her ear. "I guess you're not mad at me."

"Keep that up and I won't be."

Oh, he'd keep it up. But they had business to tend to before he did. "Not to kill the mood, but we need to talk about the schedule today. How do you feel about birthdays? My mother's specifically."

She stiffened and—whoopsie—not a good sign. Yeah, he'd killed the mood. He faced her again, let go of her ass and set his hands on her shoulders in case she tried any diversionary tactics. Like running up the stairs screaming.

"I'm sorry," he said. "My mom's party is today. I have to go."

"Yes, you do. I'd be upset if you didn't."

"And Grey and Monroe aren't...available."

"To babysit me."

"We're not babysitting you. We're helping. Big difference. So, I was thinking, while we wait on the reports from the medications and whatever that thumb drive was, we pop in at my mom's party. Eat some good food and cake and chill for a couple of hours."

"You want me to meet your mother."

So, okay. Already she was freaking out. "Sure. Why not? But, I can see your wheels spinning and let's not get crazy here. If you want, I'll tell them I'm working your security and didn't want to leave you alone. Personally, I don't care what they know about us." He leaned in, tugged on the ends of her hair and his knuckles skimmed the rise of her breast. "I'll tell the world. That's how crazy I am about you."

Something in her eyes flashed—heat mixed with a lightness he hadn't seen much of since he'd met her. He'd seen it the other night though. Right when he pushed inside her.

She slid her hands up his arms and the feel of her, the warmth of her skin against his mixed with his wicked thoughts, made his blood race.

"You're crazy about me?"

"I sure am. Thought I proved that with all the body slamming the other night. In fact, you're lucky I let you get any sleep at all last night."

"Mmm. I see. Well, you know, since we have this party to go to, I'll need to get showered. Maybe put something nice on." She stopped that slow slide of her hands and let them rest on his biceps. "I'm feeling pretty grimy right now. I mean, really," she moved closer, "really, dirty."

Damn, he loved this woman. Intense one minute, playful the next. Just like him.

"Un-huh," he said. "You'll definitely need a shower then."

"A long one. *Hot* one."

Man, oh, man, he was so doing her before his mother's party. And if his translation skills were still intact, it sounded like it might happen in the shower.

"I'll...uh...need a shower too, you know."

"We should save time. And water. Is that what you're saying? Shower together? There are efficiencies there."

At that he laughed. A good laugh. A laugh that, before Fallyn, he hadn't had in weeks. She made him...happy. There. Admitted it to himself. Sure he was a fuckup sometimes, but somehow, crazy Fallyn Pasche made him happy.

"I'm all for efficiencies." He spun her around, smacked her on the ass. "Now get upstairs, woman and let me make you scream."

17

$\mathcal{F}$allyn had new shoes. Sure they were from a local box store and had cost all of fifteen bucks, but hey, a new pair of heels could do wonders for your outlook, regardless of the lack of a designer name.

Tony drove. The tangle of DC streets gave way to the interstate. A few miles past that, suburbia. His eyes kept cutting over to her feet.

"What?" she finally asked.

"Those shoes. They're so…"

"Call Girl Special? It's the latest fashion for political fixers."

"Sparkly was the word I was going for, and God strike me down, I can't believe I just said 'sparkly.' There's just no other word for them. They look like the princess shoes my nieces wear when they play dress up."

That pulled a laugh from her. She gave him an exaggerated thumbs-up. "Your mother will think I'm a tramp, but I'll be in good with the five-year-old segment."

He grabbed her hand in mid-air and pulled it to his lips. "My mother will love you," he said against her knuckles, brushing a kiss over them.

And, oh boy, didn't that make her ovaries do that now familiar dance. *I want to have your baby.*

Hold the phone. That was so wrong. She didn't want kids, didn't have time for a husband. God knew, she didn't know thing one about being a mother after her own had lit out.

What is wrong with me?

She'd spewed all her stress on the walls and floor at Heather's townhouse last night. Gotten all the bottled up shit out. Then she'd slept like a baby for twelve solid, blissful hours. She'd showered, eaten, had sex with her boy toy, showered again. Her makeup was on, her hair was decent, and she had shoes on her feet.

Life was good. Or at least manageable once more.

So what excuse did she have for her current thought process? Tony and babies. Ayiyi. "You did tell your mother why I was tagging along, right? She didn't have a problem with it, did she?"

"Stop being nervous. I didn't share specifics, but yes, I gave her the gist of the situation. She's used to keeping mum about my work. I had to tell her enough to prep her and my sisters. It's not like they won't recognize you. Your face has been all over the news."

"I still feel like I'm crashing the party."

"Believe me. Team Estrogen will love having you show up."

"Team Estrogen?"

"Growing up in a house with four women is amazing, but daunting. I had to grow big balls or I would've been wearing shoes like those everyday. I love them, but they gang up on me constantly. Hence, I often refer to them as Team E."

She laughed and it felt good. No wonder he oozed testosterone like a wild stallion. "I promise to behave myself and stay in the background as much as possible."

"That sounds boring, and there's no way my sisters will allow that. I apologize ahead of time, but you're about to experience the Spanish Inquisition."

Great. She could hardly wait. Good thing she had on her sparkly princess shoes because with the level of emotional fatigue currently invading her body, she needed all the sparkle she could muster.

Teeg had found nothing else buried in the tablet. He'd made a clone of the tablet's hard drive so Tony and Fallyn would pick it up after the party. Dani had texted to say she was almost done decrypting the USB video. Fallyn should have it within the hour. The really good news for the day was that Grey was recovering from his surgery, although he continued to go in and out of consciousness. Still, optimism for a full recovery reigned and Fallyn said a silent thanks for guardian angels.

She'd called and checked on her dad again. He was back to work at the restaurant, which was a good sign, so she left a message with his office gal. She'd heard nothing further from Hollister or Bronco and hoped they were playing nice together, along with the Capitol Police.

A half-hour after they left the city, Tony took a couple of turns and they ended up at a long paved road with white fencing running the length of it. Balloons and a happy birthday sign hung at the entrance. As Tony pulled up the lane, Fallyn saw immaculate barns in the distance and a big, old rambling plantation house at the end of the lane. Horses grazed in the green pasture to her right.

"This is beautiful," she said. "Did you grow up here?"

"I did. Actually, my mom grew up here. When my grandparents died, she inherited the property. She's done a lot to it over the years. It used to be a lot smaller. A ranch. After my dad died, Mom needed a distraction and renovating the house was it."

"She turned a ranch into this?"

"Yep. Added the second story plus some."

"Wow. Did you love having all that extra room?"

Tony looped around the curved drive, parked and stared up at the house for a second.

"I should have loved it."

"But you didn't?"

He looked at her, his eyes a little sad. "Not without my Dad. We would do stuff together all the time. Fishing, dealing with the horses, throwing a ball. Whatever. It was manly time in a house full of women and sometimes we both needed a break. Then he was gone."

Gone? Just like that? "Stop it."

"Honest to God. I was outside playing. Shooting hoops. I kept thinking it was the best day ever. The sun was out, we'd been out on the boat fishing that morning and I was loving life."

Fishing. Boat. Sun.

"Your tattoo. It's for your Dad, isn't it?"

He looked over at her and grinned. "Very perceptive, Ms. Pasche." He smacked at his arm. "The compass is a copy of the one he carried whenever we went on the boat. The sun is for that perfect sunny day and the roses are from his funeral. Anyway, I was shooting hoops and came inside for a drink and there he was on the kitchen floor. Massive heart attack. Boom. Gone."

"Oh, Tony. I'm so sorry."

He lifted one shoulder. "Eh. I adjusted. My uncle—Dad's brother—helped. I'd have been screwed without him." He laughed softly, the sound filled with sadness. "I'd have drowned in estrogen without him. Thus, the Team Estrogen line. My uncle gave me that one."

A gaggle of kids emerged from the front door and ran down to greet them. "Tony! Uncle Tony!" they yelled, squealing and laughing as he picked up each girl and boy in turn and flew them up into the air.

One of the little girls—maybe four or five years old—stood off to the side, chewing on a nail and eyeing Fallyn.

She'd handled diplomats, actors, and leaders of first world countries, but she wasn't sure what to say to a small human.

She stuck out a hand. "I'm Fallyn. What's your name?"

"Esme." The girl stopped chewing her nail and glanced down at Fallyn's shoes. "It's short for Esmeralda. I'm a princess. Where are your wings?"

"My wings?"

The girl pointed at Fallyn's shoes. "You're wearing fairy godmother shoes."

Of course. She'd take fairy godmother over princess any day. "I left them at home. They needed cleaning."

The girl nodded solemnly as if this were a serious, but common occurrence. "Oh."

Tony had finished greeting his nieces and nephews and took her by the elbow, scruffing Esme's hair. "Ready for the next wave?" he said to Fallyn under his breath.

Not really, but what the hell? All she had to do was play the part of his client, not his lover. Besides, she wanted to know more about him and what better way than to be immersed in his family's world? "Lead the way."

The house was as impressive on the inside as the exterior. A tall, circular staircase met them in the generous entryway. Dark wood floors, ivory walls, plenty of family portraits and antique furniture met her gaze everywhere Fallyn looked.

The birthday decorations were fun but elegant. As Tony led her through the throngs of people, she spotted a dining room where music flowed and kids ran around the table, sneaking cookies. A large three-tiered cake sat in the center, surrounded by gifts.

Someone pressed a cup of punch into her hand as they passed through a den where a group of men gathered around a college playoff game on the big screen TV.

Fallyn had always been good at remembering names. By the time they'd gotten through the main living areas, however, she'd begun to lose track of the multitude Tony had thrown at her. He was like a magnet, drawing everyone to him. Kids, teens, adults.

He'd make a great father, her ovaries insisted.

The sisters came at Tony all at once, emerging from what Fallyn guessed was the kitchen. He had to bend over to hug each of them, all four much shorter than him.

Amber had hair the color of her name. She threw her arms out and gathered Fallyn in a hug when Tony introduced her. Fallyn tried not to flinch at the sudden and uninvited intimacy, but instead found it rather nice. She gave Amber a smile once she could breathe again.

Rachel was quiet and shook Fallyn's hand like a normal adult, her dark eyes a match for Tony's. "We're sorry about your sister."

"Thank you," Fallyn said.

"It must be terrible to lose your sister." Faith was the youngest and pregnant. Her hair was braided and she held a sleeping toddler in her arms.

"I can't imagine it." Amber touched Faith and Rachel on their arms. The fourth sister, Tony introduced her as Shannon, closed ranks with them and nodded.

Sadness welled in Fallyn's chest. She pushed it down and changed the subject. "The house is beautifully decorated for the party. I hope I'm not imposing."

"Don't you worry about that," Amber said. "We've got enough food to feed the whole county and you've made our day by being seen with our brother."

Shannon had a quick smile and gave Fallyn a wink. "We're telling everyone you're his girlfriend. I hope you don't mind. It's just...well, he's a bit of an embarrassment after the Kimberly fiasco."

Fallyn arched a brow at Tony. "Kimberly?"

Three sets of hands clamped onto her, pulling her toward the kitchen. "We'll fill you in about Kimberly," Shannon said, "after you meet Momma."

"No, no, no." Tony followed, getting shut out by the four women propelling Fallyn forward. "We're not filling her in on a girlfriend I had in 8th grade!"

Fallyn laughed as she was shuttled into the kitchen. A short woman with beautiful platinum hair leaned against a counter with a glass of wine in her hand, laughing at something a friend was saying.

"Momma," Amber called. "Tony's here with his *girlfriend.*"

Fallyn waited for Tony to raise his voice and argue. He didn't.

"Oh, I'm not..." Fallyn started but then stopped as Jacqueline Gerard's friend moved out of the way and the woman regarded Fallyn with a cool stare.

Her gaze dropped from Fallyn's face to her shoes, back up to her face.

Ho, boy. Look out. Mamma Gerard didn't like Fallyn being called Tony's girlfriend one bit.

Pulse jumping, Fallyn flashed her a big smile. "Mrs. Gerard, it's lovely to meet you." Why hadn't she bought a gift at that box store? *Damn it.* "Happy birthday."

The stare moved to a point over Fallyn's head and off to the left. A smile that warmed those cool eyes broke over the woman's face.

"Tony." Jacqueline ignored Fallyn and went to hug her son. "I was getting worried. Was traffic bad?"

Tony wrapped his mother in a bear hug. "Happy birthday, Mom. Sorry we're late. Had to make a pit stop."

For shoes. Her shoes. Why didn't I pick something more conservative?

Gads, this could be a nightmare, but then, why did she care what Tony's mom and sisters thought of her? It wasn't like this was a permanent thing between her and Tony.

Although, that thought wasn't exactly horrible. The man loved his mother and was good with kids. He was supportive, he understood her insanity, and he was good in bed. What more could she ask for?

"I waited to cut the cake," Jacqueline said to Tony.

"You didn't have to do that, Mom."

The love between them was obvious and jealousy sparked in Fallyn's chest. Where was her mother, especially now when she needed her?

Water under the bridge.

"Tony's her favorite," Shannon whispered in Fallyn's ear. "But I'm next."

Amber swatted Shannon on the butt with a dishtowel. "No you're not! I am."

"I'm her favorite," Faith yelled, laughing.

Jacqueline blushed and waved all of them off. "Stop it. You're all my favorites and you know it. Now, let's cut that cake. The natives are restless."

The cake was a big ole' monstrosity that could feed a lot of guests. Good thing since there were at least fifty people there. After everyone sang, she blew out the candles, cut the cake, and the sisters began passing out pieces.

Tony was constantly engaged with friends and family and Fallyn found herself shuffled between the sisters until the cake was gone and people started filtering out.

Needing a break, she was on the floor, shoes off, playing with Esmeralda in the kids' room on the second floor when Jacqueline found her. "Ms. Pasche, would you help me clean up, dear?"

"But we're playing Cinderella, Grammy," Esme said.

Jacqueline picked up the girl and kissed her cheeks. "I only need her for a moment. She can come back when we're done."

Cleaning up was not what the woman really wanted, but Fallyn was game. Where were the sisters? Surely they hadn't left the mess for their mother. "It's your birthday, Mrs. Gerard. You should sit down and relax. I'm happy to clean up after you were so gracious in letting Tony bring me."

"I'll relax later. Come."

Right.

Jacqueline led her downstairs and Fallyn followed her into the dining room, quiet and deserted now. They began gathering plates and wiping up frosting.

"I have three questions for you," Jacqueline said.

Fallyn stacked a couple of plates and kept her eyes down. What was this, *The Walking Dead* and Rick's three questions? If she didn't answer them correctly, Jacqueline would leave her to fight off the zombies on her own?

You've handled rabid journalists, angry girlfriends, and overbearing presidents handing out veiled threats. You've got this. "Okay, shoot."

"Tony speaks highly of you." Jacqueline smiled, her voice sugary smooth. "What is your relationship to my son?"

Hadn't Tony already explained this? "He's my bodyguard."

"You and I know there's more to it than that."

Step carefully.

At that moment, Amber swung in. "There you are, Momma. Go sit down. We are not letting you clean up after your own birthday party."

"I'm sixty years old, not helpless." Jacqueline shooed a hand at her daughter. "Ms. Pasche and I are having a talk."

Amber gave Fallyn a knowing look. "*Oooh.* Well, excuse me. I'll just be in the kitchen."

Once the room was clear again, Jacqueline put a hand on one of the ornate dining room chairs. "What are your intentions for my son?"

To kill him. But then she wouldn't be having great sex tonight, and he *had* warned her this might happen. Only she'd been expecting it from his sisters, not his mother. Team Estrogen's quarterback was a pro. "I'm sorry. Intentions?"

"Ms. Pasche, he is my only son."

"Please call me Fallyn."

Jacqueline went on as if she hadn't heard. "He's a good man. One who's always tried to do the right thing. He's been struggling lately and I won't stand by and see him get hurt. He needs a strong woman like you by his side, but not if you're going to break his heart in the end."

She was not going to pull one over on Jacqueline Gerard. No siree. *Do what you're good at. Spin the situation.*

But when she started to spin it in order to get out from under the woman's interrogation, she found she didn't want to. "Tony means a great deal to me, Mrs. Gerard. I have no intention of hurting him."

"Honesty. How refreshing." She flashed a smile, a real one this time, and Fallyn saw where Shannon got hers. "He's happier today than I've seen him in a long time."

Was there a question in there? "He makes me happy, too."

"Even after all you've been through in the past few days—that says a lot."

"Yes, ma'am, it does."

Jacqueline went back to cleaning the table. Fallyn did as well, waiting. Biding her time.

Waiting some more.

Finally, Fallyn couldn't stand it. "Ma'am, by my count, that was only two questions."

"Don't be impertinent, dear. I haven't forgotten how to count."

Fallyn laughed softly under her breath. Yep, Tony got his straightforwardness from his mother. "No, ma'am. I wasn't implying you did, I'm just curious. *Is* there a third question?"

Jacqueline, hands full, slid up beside Fallyn and looked down at her shoes. "Promise you won't tell anyone," she said sotto voce.

"Tell them what?"

"I have a pair of shoes just like those, but I'm afraid to wear them anywhere. They're cheap and gaudy, and I'm a bit old to be so flashy. Right?"

This was the third question? Not something more along the lines of *do you want to marry my son and have his babies?*

"Mrs. Gerard, I'm a firm believer that shoes only make the woman if the woman hasn't already made herself. You've certainly made a wonderful life here and have an awesome family. I don't think there's anything wrong with your wearing flashy, sparkly, cheap-ass shoes if you love them. Life is short. You should wear whatever the hell you want."

For a moment, Jacqueline was silent, looking slightly shocked.

Was it her language? Her boldness?

Then a big smile, like the one she'd given Tony earlier, raised the corners of her mouth. "I like you, Ms. Pasche."

"Fallyn."

"Fallyn, you may call me Jackie."

Progress! "Yes, ma'am."

Jackie winked and walked out.

Fallyn took a deep breath. First name basis. *No fending off zombies tonight.*

Did it matter that she'd passed Tony's mom's test?

Deep down, it did. She wanted all of them to like her. She wanted Tony to be proud of her for impressing his hard-to-impress mother.

Tony slid up behind her, startling her, and she nearly dropped the plates in her hands. "Hey, lady. Where've you been?"

"Being interrogated by your mother. You owe me."

He nibbled her ear. "I'll make it up to you tonight."

"Damn straight, you will. Here." She offloaded the dishes into his hands. "Go help your mother."

"Where are you going?"

"To check my phone. I've been so caught up in the party, I need to see if Dani decoded that USB."

Her phone was in her bag lying on a bed in the guest room with her coat. She dug it out and found she did, indeed, have a message from Dani with an attachment.

She clicked on the link and held her breath.

Heather's face appeared on the phone's screen. "Hi, Fal. It's me. I know you're probably wondering what this is about. I have a couple things to tell you. What I'm about to say will sound crazy, but I swear to you, I've done my due diligence on this. It's real and it's...scary."

Heather looked over her shoulder. The scene appeared to have been shot in her office at the Capitol. "First," her focus came back to the camera and she lowered her voice. "I want you to know, I love you, Fal. I know we've had our differences, and I get it if you don't want to help me after you watch this video, but I need you, sis. I'm in a mess here and I need you."

The sound of her voice, the sight of her face on Fallyn's screen, was too much. Her knees went weak and she slumped on the floor. Her shoes went askew and she kicked them off.

Touching the screen, she froze the picture of her sister in place. The burn of grief roiled just under her skin. "Oh, Heather. I love you too."

For a long moment, she sat there, tears running down her face. Esme wandered in and patted her back. "Are you sick?" the little girl asked, slipping her too small feet into Fallyn's shoes.

Fallyn pulled herself together and smiled at the child. "Nope. Allergies," she lied, scooping tissues from a box on the nightstand. "I'm fine."

"Can I wear your shoes, Fairy Godmother?"

Fallyn nodded and Esme tromped out of the room in the too-big heels.

Fallyn watched the rest of the video, dry-eyed, her grief turning into shock and then white-hot anger. As Heather spilled her confession on screen, she had to stop once when Jordan interrupted her without knocking on her office door first.

Off screen, Jordan said, "Here's your pharmacy pickup. They had your prescription, the magnesium, the fish oil, and your multivitamins, but they were out of your favorite brand of protein powder. A new shipment is coming in tomorrow. I'll pick it up on my lunch hour."

Heather had quickly lowered the phone and from the angle of the camera, Fallyn couldn't see anything but the edge of a white bag being plopped down on the desk.

"Thank you," Heather said.

The door creaked shut in the background and suddenly Heather was back.

For the next three minutes and twenty-seven seconds, Fallyn was glued to the screen. At the end of the video, Heather once again pleaded for Fallyn's help. "I don't know who to talk to," she said. Her face was strained. "I hope you can give me some advice. I'm in love with him, Fal, and he didn't know what he was doing. If anyone can help us, I know it's you."

Heather and Ryan. Lovers.

Fallyn couldn't wrap her mind around it.

"Fallyn?" Tony crowded into the doorway, Esme leading him. "Are you alright?"

Esme dropped Fallyn's shoes on the ground next to her feet and leaned over to kiss Fallyn's cheek. Fallyn patted the girl's arm and Esme took off. "It's Heather."

Her dry eyes didn't last long. Just saying her sister's name brought a fresh wave of tears. She held out the phone so Tony could see it.

He grabbed the whole box of tissues and tore a few out, handing them to her. "What did she say?"

A lot. One bomb after another.

Have to find the man who knows what went down.

She had a name, thanks to Heather's video. The man who was the key to connecting all the dots. Who this guy was, exactly, Fallyn had to find out.

Fallyn blew her nose, wiped her eyes, and reached deep for that rage she'd felt a minute ago. "I know where to get the proof that the president's son shot down CanAir Flight 702."

18

$\mathcal{T}$ony woke up to the sound of Fallyn's voice. Something, he decided, he could get used to.

Easily.

He rolled over in the creaky bed, forgot it was only a queen and nearly face-planted off the side. Sometime this month, he needed his own damned bed where his giant feet didn't hang off the end.

The digital clock glowed 6:30. They'd slept, what...three hours? Fallyn had been on a tear all night trying to track down this Donald Fox, whoever the hell he was, because he had some serious inside information on Heather and her personal life. Why he had that information, they didn't yet know. But Heather had talked about him in her video.

Peeling his gritty eyes open again, Tony rested his head against the pillow and blinked up at the ceiling. When this was over, he'd sleep for a week.

Hopefully with Fallyn beside him. But he wouldn't get too far ahead of this thing. Right now, she was vulnerable and probably latching on because the sex was good and it gave her a distraction from her personal shit storm.

Did he really believe that? With the way they were together?

"No," Fallyn said from the other room. "I need to talk to this guy *today*. This morning. ASAP."

The tiny garage apartment was only so big and from the clarity of her voice, she had to be in the living room. Near that couch they'd done wicked things on. *Don't tell Syd.* Just thinking about the steam they'd blown off on that couch made his morning erection damned near wave a white flag.

But the way she was talking on the phone, he figured his chances of luring her back to bed were zero.

Who the hell could she be talking to at six in the morning? When he was hoping to get laid.

He swung his legs over the side of the bed, reached for the shorts he'd tossed on the floor last night. Sure, he could walk out bare-assed, but with his luck she wouldn't be on the phone and his mighty chubby would make its debut in front of Fallyn's guest.

Nuts as she was, she couldn't be crazy enough to bring someone here.

Could she?

"His name is Donald Fox," Fallyn said. "Yes...Fox...That's all I know."

On the phone. Definitely. He marched into the tiny living room where she sat curled under the red blanket that'd been draped across the back of the couch. One long leg poked out, her creamy skin seriously begging him to reach out and touch.

What exactly did she have on under that blanket?

Still holding the phone to her ear, she glanced up, waved with her free hand and patted the spot next to her.

"Okay, Dani, I have to go. As soon as you find this guy, call me... Right. Thank you."

She punched off the call, adjusted the blanket—pity, that—and shifted to face him. "That was my office. They're on this Donald Fox."

She flapped one arm and the blanket slid down her shoulder. More skin. Please let her be naked under there. Call him twisted, but her conducting business while naked? Hot, hot, hot.

"I mean, how did I not know my sister was screwing the president's son?"

Speaking of screwing...with the Donald Fox revelation on the video, came Heather's admission that she and Ryan Nicols were *involved*. His eyes wandered to her leg again where the blanket separated just below her crotch. They needed that blanket gone. He met her gaze again. "If she didn't tell you, how could you know?"

"Exactly my point. I *should* have known that."

"Why?"

Her mouth dropped open. "What's that supposed to mean?"

"You're sisters. You don't live inside each other's skin. You met my sisters yesterday. They're up my ass all the time. From the time we left that party last night, my phone was blowing up."

"I heard it."

"That was them. Texting me. *Group* texting. About you. Because that's what they do. One of them asks a question and then the other three chime in. Twelve texts happen before I even get a word in. So, as you can imagine, I don't tell them seventy-five percent of what goes on in my life. Doesn't mean I don't love them. Doesn't mean I wouldn't step in front of a truck for them. It means it's my life and when there's something to report, I'll report it. Otherwise, they need to stay the fuck out."

On cue, his phone rang. He hopped off the couch. "Swear to God, if this is one of them, I'm blasting her." On his way to the bedroom, he looked back at Fallyn. "Please tell me you're naked under that blanket and you'll let me give you ten orgasms after I take this call."

In response, she ditched the blanket.

Hello, nipples.

Hallelujah.

He scooped the phone off the nightstand and—whoa. Syd's number. He poked the screen. "Hello?"

"Gerard," Grey said, "where the fuck are you?"

Tony's stomach dropped. Splat. Right to his feet as relief swarmed. He'd known Grey was recovering. Recovering, but not completely stable. That not-stable part ate away at him, burrowed deep inside, but thanks to Fallyn, he'd been trying to convince himself he hadn't screwed up. That he'd pulled Grey from the wreckage. He'd gotten there in time. Still. *Not stable.* Those two little words rang in his ears, reminding him if he'd gotten there a little bit sooner...

He spun around, lowered himself to the bed and slapped his free hand over his eyes. *Jesus, Jesus, Jesus.* Grey was on the phone. Talking to him. *Talking.*

Not dead.

Very much alive.

"Grey, holy shit."

"Yeah. What? You thought I'd die? From a car wreck? If I'm going out, it'll be better than a fucking car accident. Shit, Syd will probably talk me to death."

Alive.

Tony laughed, shook his head a little. Thankful for this moment. For Grey talking to him. "Damn, it's good to hear your voice."

"I gotta get out of this hospital. All night long they bug you. If you want rest, don't come to the hospital."

Crabby. But hell, crabby was better than nothing any day.

"Listen," Grey said, "I got a call from the lab."

"Dude, are you kidding me? You almost died and you're taking calls?"

"Not with Warden Sydney here. Man, she's tough. She took my phone away."

"Maybe because she loves you?"

"Whaa, whaa. Shut up a second because she just went for coffee and I don't have a lot of time. Before she confiscated my phone, I checked my messages. There's a call from the lab. The results on the senator's meds are in. You need to call them back. They have your name so it shouldn't be a problem. I'd do it, but Syd'll kill me."

Lab results. Tony straightened up. "I'm on it. What's the number?"

Grey read off the number and his contact's name. "She's back. I gotta go. Call me later."

The big, bad Justice Greystone was afraid of his fiancée. Tony would hang on to that bit of info candy. "I'll holler back at ya when I have something."

"Good. And, Tony?"

"Yeah, boss?"

"Thanks for saving my life. I owe you."

In the background, Syd's voice came through the line. "Hang up," she said. "Right now. You're barely alive and you're on the phone? What is *wrong* with you?"

The line went dead, leaving Tony sitting on the bed in the quiet room, where the whirring of the heat through the vent circled in his mind. Grey had just thanked him. For saving his life. *That one you got right.*

He let his shoulders sag, rolled his neck where tension had locked it tight. Brutal few days. But he'd saved a man's life.

A man who was probably getting his ass chewed out at that very second. Those two were a couple of hardasses. But they made it work.

He stared out the door to the hallway that led to Fallyn. Another hardass. Just like him.

If Grey and Syd could...

"What's up?"

Fallyn, amazingly naked, leaned against the doorframe, one hand on her hip and that beautiful body there for him to visually—and hopefully more—feast on.

"That," he said, "was Grey."

"Stop it."

He laughed. "Yeah. Spitting mad because he can't get any rest and Syd won't let him use his phone."

"And yet, he called you."

He nodded, but kept his eyes on her, moving up and down her long legs, over her belly to her breasts. Yeah, he wanted her. Always.

"Fallyn?"

"Yes?"

"It hurts."

"What?"

"How much I want you. All the time. It's a physical ache in my chest. You're so damned beautiful and ornery and..." he jammed the heels of his hands into his eye sockets. Damned fatigue. "We're a train wreck together. We're all *go, go, go* when we should be *stop, stop, stop.* But I don't care. I want it all. I want...you. All of you."

She walked toward him, that amazing body tearing him up in all kinds of ways. She straddled him, settled her weight on him. This couldn't be bad? No way. She rocked her hips against him, held his cheeks in her hands and kissed him. Long and slow and sweeping that wicked tongue across his lips.

Sex with them was epic. Every time. They both knew it. But he wanted more. For the first time in way too long, he wanted this woman in his life.

Every day. For the big stuff. The little stuff. Dinners, breakfast, a movie, whatever. As long as she was with him.

He backed away from the kiss. "I don't want a fuck buddy. None of this flying in from New York when you need to get laid. You get that, right?"

She shoved him back on the bed, stretched across him. "Please. I've never had a fuck buddy and I'm not about to start now. Of course, I've also never had a man I cared about like this so early in. If we're in this, we're in it. Can you live with that?"

Clamping his hand over her ass, he lifted her higher so he could get his damned shorts off. But...the lab. Goddammit. The lab. He set his hands on her hips, gave her a pat. "Grey said the lab results are in. I need to call them."

She cocked an eyebrow. Hesitated a second. "You'd rather call the lab than have me?"

Ha. That'd be the day. "*You* wanna wait on the lab?"

She levered up to straddle him again, rocked her hips one more time making him groan. "What I want is you. Then we'll call the lab and we'll find Donald Fox. We'll do that because we're good together. In many ways. But, right now, for once, what I want comes first."

. . .

Sydney was giving her that look—the one that said she knew how the world worked, how shit happened every minute of every day, and yet, she didn't really give a damn at the moment. She had her own shit to deal with. "I know you have a lot on your plate," Syd said, "but I need a favor."

Tony and Fallyn had helped Sydney bring Grey home from the hospital. Tony hadn't even had a chance to check in with the lab yet to find out the results of the tests. Syd had called, which happened to be the minute Fallyn was having her second morning orgasm, and announced that one Justice Greystone had thrown a hissy and checked himself out of the hospital. Against his doctor's orders.

The drugs had to be messing with him. Had to be.

Tony and Fallyn had dropped everything mid-sex to go to the hospital.

Two orgasms down, eight on rain check.

Grey was far from being back to his old self physically. His personality, however, was just fine. He was, at that moment, giving Tony a hard time. "Stop acting like my goddamn nursemaid." His voice echoed in the garage where Tony helped Grey out of Syd's car. "I'm not helpless."

"Never said you were, boss," Tony shot back. "Stop acting like a bratty toddler and lean on me or I'll be forced to carry your worthless ass up the stairs to your bedroom fireman style. I'll have Fallyn take a picture and send it to Monroe. He'll have a t-shirt made out it before you can call me an SOB."

Mitch and Caroline were at the office working on an emergency case. A National Intelligence agent had gone missing under suspicious circumstances that involved a former FBI agent. Grey had insisted going into the office to handle it himself and Syd had been frantic. The only way they'd talked him out of it was putting Mitch and Caroline in charge of the investigation. They were former FBI, too, and had connections that might help lead to finding both men.

Fallyn and Syd watched Tony and Grey argue from the safety of the kitchen door. Fallyn's phone had dinged with a text from Dani as they followed Syd in Tony's truck. The Pasche & Associates techie had located Donald Fox. His address, phone, employer, family members, his elementary school grades...the whole bloody works.

Her fingers itched to dial the man up and get some answers. To take a drive, show up on his doorstep, and find out what the hell was going on.

Right now, though, she had to figure out what Syd wanted.

There were genuine reasons when you couldn't do something for someone and then there were simply excuses you used to get out of doing it. Fallyn had genuine reasons for begging off on helping Sydney, but Syd needed her. Enough said.

So instead of begging off, she found herself saying, "Anything, Sydney. What can I do?"

She thought it would be something simple; a run to the grocery store or to pick up Grey's meds at the pharmacy. Easy, peasy. She and Tony could get the errand done and head for Mr. Fox's address in an hour or so.

Or maybe all Sydney needed was a bottle of wine and some more of those wicked good cupcakes she'd introduced Fallyn to. It wasn't every day you saw the man you loved nearly dead and if Syd needed sugar and liquor at nine in the morning, so be it.

Syd's dark eyes watched Grey reluctantly accept a hand from Tony when he lost his balance. "The Fresh Start Career Day is this afternoon."

Uh oh. Fallyn sensed she'd just stepped in quicksand. "And you need to be here with Grey."

"Exactly."

"I'm sure they'll understand if you have to postpone," Fallyn said. "Your fiancé nearly died."

Syd shook her head. "Too much time and energy has gone into this to postpone it. The women have worked their backsides off for weeks to prepare for it and they've invested a lot of emotional energy as well. This could be a jumping off point for many of them to get their lives back on track. They need this. Desperately. I can't take that away. We have several national speakers lined up as well as recruiters from a temp service and the local community college to see if they can match any of the women up to jobs and/or continuing education services. I can't postpone it."

Tony got Grey up the two short steps into the main house from the garage and Syd and Fallyn parted to let the two of them pass.

"I can make it from here," Grey said, pushing Tony's hands off of his arms.

Tony caught Fallyn's and Syd's eyes behind Grey's back and shook his head. Grey was half hunched over and sweat beaded on his forehead.

"Sure, man," Tony said, staying right behind Grey as he held onto the kitchen countertop and snail-walked his way toward the living room. Grey couldn't see him, but Tony kept his hands out to grab him in case he lost his balance and went down.

Just like with me. He's always there.

Syd's jaw was clenched. Fallyn felt for her. Torn between her fiancé and her job—a job where she was responsible for the safety and well-being of several dozen women.

Sydney was a mother to them all.

Fallyn wrestled with the guilt inching up on her. She wanted to help, she did. Throwing herself into the middle of career day with no prep and no team to help her wasn't ideal. She always gave a hundred and ten percent. Hard to do when you had no clue what was needed. "Do you have an assistant or someone who can take your place? I have no experience with something like this, Syd, but I could help if your assistant simply needs a warm body to answer phones or make sure there's water and coffee."

Syd clutched Fallyn's arm. "I'm a one-woman show at the shelter. A few of my long-term gals assist me with new clients and day-to-day operations, but none of them have the confidence to take over something this big. I need someone who's familiar with organizing large groups, greeting speakers, and making sure everyone sticks to the itinerary. I need someone who can schmooze with the best of them and make everyone, especially the Fresh Start women, feel comfortable. They don't like new and they lack confidence. They don't like stepping out of their comfort zones."

Grey made it to the couch. Tony helped him sit and prop his feet on the coffee table.

Syd filled a glass with water and pointed at a teakettle on the stove. "Heat some water for tea, would you?"

Fallyn nodded and filled the kettle while Syd took the water to Grey.

"Where's my whiskey?" she heard him grumble. "Water ain't going to cut it."

Fallyn set the kettle on the burner and peeked around the corner. Syd hovered over Grey, sliding a pillow behind his head and covering his legs with a blanket. "No whiskey for you, Fed Boy. Your organs have been through enough in the past forty-eight plus hours and you're on medications that don't play well with alcohol. Fallyn's making you tea."

Fallyn went in search of a mug.

"Tea?" Grey barked. "I'm not drinking that namby-pamby shithouse tea of yours."

"Mint," Syd called to Fallyn. "Top cupboard to your left."

What a hoot these two were. It was like they were already married. Fallyn smiled, snagging the box of mint tea and prepping a teabag for the mug.

Grey's voice was ominous. "I don't drink tea, Syd, and you know it."

"Shut up, Greystone," Tony chimed in, making his way into the kitchen. He slid up behind Fallyn at the counter and ran his hands up and down her hips, pinning her between the counter and his body. He nibbled the sensitive skin under her ear. The man was insatiable. "You're getting tea," he called back over his shoulder. "Stop your bellyaching."

"He's right," Syd added. Fallyn heard the TV click on.

There was more arguing from the patient but Fallyn tuned it out as Tony's hands did naughty things to her.

Syd put a clamp on Grey's grumblings and came back into the kitchen. Tony stopped molesting Fallyn and leaned against the counter as she poured the hot water into the mug.

"That man," Syd said, rubbing her fingers over her temples and down her neck, "could drive me to drink. Thanks for helping get him settled."

"No problem." Tony lowered his voice. "Fal and I need to run a few errands. You need anything?"

Syd looked at Fallyn. "Can you help me this afternoon?"

At that moment, Grey called from his perch. "Tony, did you talk to Teeg yet about that lab report?"

"No working," Syd yelled back.

Tony gave her a wry smile and went off to talk to Grey again.

"I know you're supposed to be laying low," Syd said to Fallyn. "And putting on a career day at Fresh Start isn't exactly staying under the radar, but with Caroline tied up, I need someone I can rely on."

She didn't say trust. No, not Syd. She didn't know Fallyn well enough to trust her, but she knew a kindred spirit when it came to getting a job done. She saw Fallyn as someone tough and indestructible like her.

And didn't that play right into Fallyn's get-shit-done personality? Not to mention the fact Syd guessed Fallyn would help for the sole reason she felt so damn guilty about Grey. *Yes, folks, we have a winner.* "I'll handle it," Fallyn said.

Syd gave her arm a squeeze. "I knew I could count on you."

She looked so wrung out, so relieved, Fallyn felt the urge to hug her.

So she did. "Everything is going to be okay, Syd," she said, drawing the woman into a sisterly hug. It felt weirdly right. Kind of like it had at the hospital.

Like it had with Tony's sisters by the end of the party yesterday. There had been lots of hugging before she and Tony had finally made it out. Even Tony's mother had given Fallyn a hard squeeze and thanked Fallyn for making her son happy.

There were tears in Sydney's eyes when they broke apart. She dashed the back of her hands across them and blew out a sigh. "Thank you."

The weight of the world had been riding on her shoulders. She couldn't let anyone down. Fallyn understood that. "No thanks necessary. I'll need your files on everything—the speakers, the schedule, the caterer, you name it."

"There's no caterer." Sydney looked oddly amused. "Fresh Start doesn't have funds for that and I couldn't sweet talk any of the locals into donating their food and services. I was going to make sandwiches and a fruit salad but then this happened with Grey and I didn't have a chance to shop. I can call Brice and Hope. Maybe they can get the fixings for me."

Fallyn loved a good challenge and she knew who to go to for help. Jordan. The woman knew everybody and could sweet talk a mule into climbing Mt. Everest. She'd have a caterer lined up in nothing flat. "I've got it covered. You just take care of Grey and get some rest. Tony and I will handle the career day."

"We will?" Tony strolled into the room. "You mean that thing I saw the posters about at Fresh Start?"

He looked like he was about to run the other way. Fallyn grabbed him by the coat sleeve. "I have a plan, don't worry. You just keeping being your charming bodyguard self."

His grin was pure cockiness. Why did she find that so damn sexy? "That should be easy," he said. "But you can't put yourself out there like that. No way. And what about Donald Fox? I thought we needed to find him."

"We do." She gave Syd's hand a squeeze. "But first I have a career day to handle. And as charming as you are, Tony Gerard, you're not talking me out of it."

19

ony sat on the windowsill in Syd's office while Fallyn and Jordan did their thing. Watching these two ladies work was like watching a military operation. One that Fallyn shouldn't be anywhere near. He got that Syd needed help, but this? For Fallyn? Crazy.

The more he tried to keep her out of danger, the more she fought him.

Lessons to be learned here because Fallyn's *go, go, go* attitude might get her killed.

Jordan stood to Fallyn's right, looking over her shoulder at a file Syd had said contained the schedule for the day. Fallyn tapped her pen against the desk. "What about the human resources lady? Is she here yet? She's supposed to help some of the women with their resumes."

"She hasn't checked in with me yet. I'll double check with Anita. She's playing receptionist and signing everyone in."

"Okay. Good. How'd you do on the food?"

"I called the caterer Heather liked and begged. The best I could do on such short notice was sandwiches, cold salads, and a simple dessert tray with cookies and brownies. The sandwiches will be good though. No white bread with deli meat. We're talking fresh ham and turkey on artisan bread. They have a turkey and brie sandwich that's to die for. It'll be good, I promise."

Sure sounded good. Particularly when Tony hadn't eaten since breakfast. Maybe he'd get Jordan to snag him one of those babies.

And a brownie.

"Thank you," Fallyn said. "I knew you'd pull this off."

"No sweat. It's fun. Let me get out there and see what's happening. Call me if you need me."

Jordan left and Tony folded his arms. "I don't like this. Any of it."

Fallyn waved him off. "Of course you don't. Relax. I'm fine."

"How much does she know about you hiding in Syd's office?"

"Not a lot. I told her you were a freak and thought someone was following me and wanted me to stay out of sight."

Tony rolled his eyes. "Because I'm afraid the shelter residents will rat you out? There's no way she bought that."

Fallyn let out the mother of all sighs. "Hey, I improvised. I was talking so fast I didn't give her a chance to question it. Did the lab call back yet?"

That damned lab. He'd tried twice so far, but the woman he needed to speak with was behind closed doors. All damned morning. Women everywhere were rebelling today. "Not yet. Got a couple of calls in though. I'll try again in a few."

His phone rang and he dug it out of his suit pocket. *Maybe.* Fallyn swiveled the chair toward him, her gaze focused on the phone.

"Relax," he said. "It's Syd."

"Shoot."

"Hey, Syd, what's up?"

"Oh my God." Her voice had a blade-against-glass shriek to it and Tony stood. "He fell."

"Grey?"

"I didn't fall!" Justice yelled from somewhere on the other end.

"Fine," Syd said. "He didn't *fall*, but he somehow landed on the floor, and now, guess what? I can't get his giant rear back to the couch."

Shit. "He's on the *floor*?"

"Yep. Yep, yep, yep."

Fallyn stood, walked over to him, touched his arm. "Everything okay?"

He held his finger up. "Syd, is he hurt? Bleeding? Anything?"

"His pride is hurt, and I think he may have torn a stitch. And I might kill him, but aside from that, he appears intact."

"He's got to go back to the hospital. This is nuts. He's not ready to be home and you can't take care of him. He needs a few more days."

"I keep telling him that. Tony, I'm sorry, but I need help and he won't let me call 911."

"Let me talk to him."

She handed the phone off to Grey. "She's not calling 911," Grey said. "This isn't an emergency. I don't want to tie up an ambulance. I don't need it. I just need to catch my breath."

"From the floor."

"*Fuck* you."

"Listen to me," Tony said. "I'm coming over there and we're gonna haul your ass off that floor and into my truck. Then we're taking you back to the hospital where you will check yourself in again. You almost died once on me. If something happens to you, I'm not living with that. Man, I get it. You don't want people up your ass all the time. I'd be the same way, but what you're doing isn't fair to Syd. She's worried about you and as strong as she is, she's not equipped for you right now."

"I hate that goddamned hospital."

"Well, yeah. But there's no getting around it. You need a couple more days. Please."

The line went quiet. Did that fucker hang up on him?

"Hello?"

Syd's voice.

Tony wrapped his hand around his forehead and squeezed. The damned tension might give him an aneurism. "Hey. I thought he hung up on me."

"No. He just handed me the phone. What's going on?"

"I'm coming over there and we're taking him back to the hospital."

"Thank God."

"Give me twenty minutes."

He hung up and shook his head. Rebelling. The whole friggin' universe was rebelling against him today. "This is one fucker of a day."

He jammed his phone back into his pocket.

"Go," Fallyn said. "Take care of him."

"I'm not leaving you here. You gotta come with me."

"No. I promised Syd I'd take care of this."

Ha! As if. Tony cocked his head back, stared up at the ceiling and closed his eyes. He needed a second here. Maybe two. To think. Work a plan. Fallyn alone, Grey ripping stitches. Total cluster. One that wouldn't have happened if he'd had control of this fucking situation in the first place.

"You are out of your mind if you think I'm leaving you here. Jordan can handle this."

"Yes, but we're winging this. I can't dump it on her after Syd asked me to do it." She waved him off, went back to the desk. "I'll be fine. You said yourself, it's not like the residents are going to rat me out. I'll stay in the office out of sight. Besides, I'm still trying to connect with this Don Fox guy. I don't want to risk missing that call because of bad cell service in the hospital. Not doing it."

He didn't like it. Not at all. He folded his arms, dipped his chin to his chest and starting doing the math. Drive time from the shelter to Grey's to the hospital and back would be an hour. Tops. But as slow as Justice was moving, it could take another hour to get him in and out of the car.

Can't risk it. He lifted his head. "I'm gonna call someone over here. Someone I trust."

Fallyn gave him the mother of all eye rolls. "You are so damned stubborn. I told you, I can handle it."

"I'm stubborn? Are you kidding me?"

She rubbed her temples. "Tony, I just want to get through this and go find Fox. Grey and Syd need you, and I'll be fine. No one knows I'm here. Stop being overprotective and go help your friend."

"Overprotective? You were in that car with Grey. Someone was tailing you. Before that, you had two close calls with intruders at Heather's place."

"No one tried to kill me. The intruder roughed me up, but that's all. If he'd wanted to kill me, he could have. Yes, we were being tailed in the car, but the accident happened because of a deer."

"You really have no clue of the danger you're in, do you?"

She returned to the chair and eyeballed him. "Please. Just...stop."

Stop? "I won't stop. You don't get it, Fallyn. And I'm not going to wind up with you in a hospital, or worse because you *don't get it.*"

"Oh, snap. You just knock it off with the attitude. Don't put this on me. This is about you and a boatload of transference on your part than actual danger."

"Transference?"

"You're afraid to leave me, to not control me and my surroundings because of what happened with your dad and the judge. You're afraid if you turn your back on me for a second, I'll end up dead. You need some perspective, here, Tony."

Did she just go there? Seriously? "This has nothing to do with my father or the judge. Someone killed your sister over the same information you're digging into, and you've had three near misses *and* a threat from the president. Who needs perspective, here, Fallyn?"

"I'm in a shelter with two dozen women, Jordan, and a host of guest speakers. Jordan is the only person who knows I'm here, but if anyone were to come after me, I'd have plenty of people to help me out. I'll go get my gun. All in all, I think I'm pretty damn safe. Meanwhile, your boss and friend is sitting on his ass waiting for you. He's the one in trouble."

Maddening woman. All he needed right now was a little cooperation. From someone. Anyone. The damned lab, Grey, *Fallyn.* But, no. She had an agenda and screw everyone else. "This is nuts. You're being reckless."

She smacked a hand on the desk. "I'm being logical. And you're overreacting! No one is going to bother me! Will you please get the hell out of here and go help Grey?"

"Not unless you're going with me."

He saw it. The hardening of her eyes. "I'm not going with you, Tony. Stop trying to control everything. I gave Syd my word I would handle this and I don't go back on my word."

"She'll understand."

"You think?" She shook her head and started shuffling papers, refusing to look at him. "Tony Gerard, you're fired."

"I'm what?"

"I said, you're fired. I don't want you as my bodyguard anymore. Get out of here. Go help Grey."

"You can't be serious."

The look she shot him was pure defiance. "Oh, I'm serious. As of this moment, we're done. Finished. Your friend, who's actually in trouble and needs you far more than I do, is waiting for you. I suggest you get to him."

He stood, anger boiling in his veins. "I'll get someone out front until I can get back here. I'll call you with his number. Anything goes wrong, you call him and he'll bust in here."

Hopefully, Matt was available. If not, Tony was screwed.

"That's not necessary," Fallyn said, once more staring at the papers in front of her.

"Sure as hell is. We're not done here, Fal. When I get back, we're finishing this discussion."

20

_M_att Stevens was the man. Tony's former police academy buddy, now a private security contractor, had come through for him and agreed to keep an eye on the shelter for a couple of hours while Tony dragged one Justice Greystone back to the hospital.

That blowout with Fallyn didn't help. Unbelievable. The two of them pushed each other's hot buttons in every way. They'd either have to figure out how to avoid doing that or they'd kill each other one day.

And Tony would definitely have a heart attack along the way. Just like his father. Boom. Gone.

"For the record," Grey said. "I thought I was ready to go home."

Finally. Someone giving him a fucking break. Tony came to a stop at a light and glanced over at Grey in the passenger's seat. "Yeah. I got that part. But seriously, hospitals are usually tossing people out. When the doc is telling you to stay, it generally means stay. But, forget it. We'll get you back there, and in a couple days, you'll be good to go."

Grey looked in the sideview mirror. "Syd's still back there."

"Did you think she wouldn't be?"

"After this morning, I wondered."

Now that was funny. "She loves you. And something tells me she doesn't scare off easily."

A loud blinging erupted via the Bluetooth and Tony hit the button. "Gerard."

"Mr. Gerard, this is Emily Latham."

The lab. Another break. Things were looking up. "Hi," he said. "You're timing is good. I have Justice Greystone in the car with me."

"Oh, excellent. I'm emailing him a full report, but wanted to let you know we detected Perisoladol in the protein powder sample you gave us."

The protein powder. For whatever reason, he hadn't seen that one coming. "All the other supplements were clean?"

"Yes, sir. Only the protein powder. It was pure drug. Only slight traces of protein powder, which was probably residue from the bottle."

Grey sat a little straighter. "Someone replaced the powder?"

"Yes. It's all in my report. Just wanted to give you a heads up."

Tony punched off the call and tapped his fingers against the steering wheel. "The protein powder. We need to figure out who had access to it."

In the back of Tony's mind, something niggled at him. He worked through it, ticking away at the events of the past week. Helping Fallyn collect the supplement bottles, searching Heather's office. The protein powder, he was sure, had come from the townhouse. Hadn't it? When they were in Heather's office, Fallyn had handed him bottles, but they'd been vitamins. No powders.

The light changed and he hit the gas, moving along with the traffic while he backtracked over the last week. *What is it? What is it? What is it?*

"Talk to me," Grey said.

"Thinking about where we collected all the bottles. Nothing is popping though. I think the protein powder must have been at the house. If it had been in her office, I'd start with Jordan. See if she knew where the powder came from."

Jordan.

The video.

Heather's video. Jordan's interruption.

"Oh, shit."

Tony pulled to the side of the road. "I have to call Fallyn."

21

The speakers were done, the residents of Fresh Start were in the kitchen enjoying a late dinner of leftover sandwiches. A handful of them had landed jobs, half a dozen more were going back to school or exploring internships that would refine their marketable skills. All in all, the day had been a success.

While the residents were busy feeding their faces, Fallyn and Jordan worked on cleaning up the downstairs area that had been converted into a meeting space for the day's events. Jordan had told her to stay in the office, but Fallyn couldn't stand it any longer. She had to do something to help that involved physical movement. If any of the women saw her, she'd spin the situation like she always did and disappear up to the loft.

Fallyn shoved dirty coffee cups into the garbage can and tossed some papers into the yellow plastic recycle bin next to it. Even that, with the stresses running her life lately, seemed a major accomplishment.

Staying busy kept her mind off the hollow feeling in the pit of her stomach. She shouldn't have yelled at Tony. Should never, ever had used his father and the judge against him.

It had been the only way to get him to go to Grey. That and firing him.

He's coming back. We'll work it out.

So why wouldn't the sick feeling in her stomach go away?

Beside her, Anita worked on taking down the overhead screen while Jordan folded up the chairs and stored them away.

"You made a real difference here today," Anita said, releasing the screen and sending it whooshing up into its holder near the ceiling. "Thank you for everything."

"*We* made a difference," Fallyn corrected her, tying up the garbage. *Stay busy. Don't think.* "I'm glad I could help."

"Sydney was a fan of your sister's because Heather was one of our biggest advocates. We all hoped she'd run for president someday."

"I hoped that, too." The hollow sensation moved from her belly to her chest. She missed Heather. Right now, she missed Tony as well. He'd filled the void Heather's death had left and given her a fresh perspective on what was important in her life. "Working with the women today was great. I wish I could have had more face time with them, but I plan to come back when I can work with them individually."

Anita smiled and shook Fallyn's hand. "That would be wonderful. We could use someone with your public presence to keep a spotlight on what we're doing here."

Continuing Heather's work—that's what Fallyn wanted to do. Not easy when she lived in NYC, but maybe it was time to expand Pasche & Associates. A satellite office in DC would increase revenues significantly—there were plenty of political messes that needed fixing—and provide an excuse to work with Syd, rebuild a relationship with her father, and see Tony.

If Tony still wanted to see her.

How much she'd changed since he'd come into her life a few days ago. She felt unbalanced without him by her side.

Jordan returned from putting the chairs away and sagged against a table. "I'll clean up the kitchen once the gals are done in there."

Fallyn's phone rang. She snatched it out of her pocket, hoping it was Tony with an update on Grey. It wasn't. She almost didn't recognize the number and started to ignore the call. That's when it hit her.

Don Fox. *Finally.*

"I'm sorry, I need to take this," she said, heading out of the room. She couldn't take the call inside Fresh Start. Too many ears possibly overhearing the conversation. "Jordan, I'll come back in a few minutes and help with the kitchen duty."

Jordan waved her off as she started helping Anita take down the tables.

In the front hallway, Tony's friend Matt, her *bodyguard,* abandoned his post and followed her to the back door. Fallyn answered the phone on the third ring. "Hello?"

The connection was terrible. Static filled her ear. "Miss Pasche?"

Placing a hand over her ear, she headed through the night toward the loft. "Yes, this is Fallyn Pasche. Thank you for returning my call, Mr. Fox."

"I don't know..." Static. The man's voice sounded far away, like he was in a tunnel. "...can't help you."

Why was the connection so bad?

Fallyn took the stairs from the garage up to the apartment. Behind her, Matt stayed put at the base of the stairwell.

"Mr. Fox, I understand where you're coming from. Please, I need to speak to you in person. My sister told me some things I need verified."

Silence met her ears. Complete silence. Not even a hint of static. Fallyn banged the phone into her palm out of frustration. The screen said they'd been disconnected. Had he hung up or had the connection simply been too weak?

Letting herself into the apartment, she flipped on a light and hit redial. The phone on the other end rang three times and went to voicemail.

Dammit. She had to talk to this guy. She dialed again. Voicemail. *One more try.*

Come on, come on.

"So this is where you've been hiding," a familiar voice said from behind her.

Fallyn whirled. "Jeez, Jordan. You're always sneaking up on me. I thought you were working on the tables."

Jordan moseyed through the door and closed it behind her. Her gaze swept around the room to the sofa and then to the small kitchen off to the side. She sunk her hands into the pockets of her trench coat. "When's Mr. Gerard coming back? Although, his friend Matt is kinda cute. I passed him at the bottom of the stairs."

"Tony? I'm not sure. Why?"

She shrugged one shoulder and ran a hand over the back of a chair as she walked around, continuing to eye the place. "He seems very protective of you."

"That's sort of his job right now."

"Right. After the break-ins and the car accident."

She'd made it to the kitchen doorway and was leaning into the kitchen so far, Fallyn finally asked. "Would you like a drink or something? There's tea."

"No, I have to get back soon." Jordan swung out of the doorway and smiled. "Dad's expecting me tonight. We have our standard Monday night game of chess, you know."

Fallyn didn't know, but it sounded nice. She'd never shared anything more with her father than conversation over a plate of meatballs.

But that was okay. So they'd never played chess or went to a play together like Carl and Jordan were always doing. Her dad had taught her how to make a mean primavera and run her own business. Food service wasn't all that different from being a fixer. You found out what people wanted and gave it to them.

"Why don't you head out, then, and enjoy your evening with Carl?" Fallyn said. "I can handle the rest of the cleanup with Anita."

Jordan sat in the chair and crossed her legs. "Have the cops figured out how that drug ended up in Heather's system? I know Daddy will ask me tonight."

For someone who said she had to leave, Jordan seemed to want to talk instead. Fallyn sunk onto the sofa and rubbed her temples where tension thrummed. "Nothing that I know of. I think we may have a lead from an independent lab we sent the supplements to, but I haven't seen the results of the tests yet."

"Is that so?" Jordan huffed out a sigh. "What a shame about all of this."

It *was* a shame. Heather had been trying to do the right thing and had been caught in the crossfire. *If only I'd known sooner that she needed help. I could have fixed this. Protected her and Ryan.* "Did you know Heather was seeing someone?"

"No way." Jordan chuckled. "Are you serious?"

Fallyn nodded, but it didn't seem like Jordan was all that surprised. She was studying the window across the room. "It's okay if you knew. Heather told you lots of things she never shared with me."

"Honestly, I sort of did." Jordan met her gaze head-on. "I wanted to tell you, but I didn't know for sure that it was anything serious, and I had no idea who it was, so I kept it to myself. Don't hate me?"

Actually it was kind of a relief that Heather hadn't confessed her relationship to Jordan. "Of course not."

Jordan waggled her brows. "Who was it? Was he hot?"

They shared a laugh. Like old times. Before jealousy had crawled under Fallyn's skin. "He's very attractive, yes. And powerful. At least his dad is."

"Good for her. I'm glad she had someone, you know...before the end."

Maybe it was time to put all that old jealousy to rest. "Me too. I just can't help feeling that this is all tied together. I have a source"— she held up her phone—"whom I believe knows exactly what happened, but I can't pin him down."

"A source?"

"Sounds like his boss was doing unscrupulous things to get his hands on information Heather had secured during an investigation. He might have even been bribing or blackmailing someone in your office. He's reluctant to talk though. Can't say I blame him."

A subtle cloud passed over Jordan's face. "Someone in our office? You're kidding. Who?"

A fission of worry spider-walked across the nape of Fallyn's neck. She'd shared more than she should have.

Setting the phone on the coffee table, she propped her feet up on it. "I don't know yet, and you can't say anything, Jordan. Not until I get this figured out and can take it to Feds or the Justice Department, okay?"

A heartbeat of silence passed. "What did you do with that tablet of Heather's?"

"What?"

"The one you found in her safe."

There *was* only one, wasn't there? "What about it?"

"You said it had encoded files on it. Did you get them decoded?"

The fission of worry morphed into a warning. What was this?

Jordan must have seen the expression on Fallyn's face. "Isn't that why someone broke into the townhouse? That's what you claimed they were after. I just wondered if you figured out why."

"Of course. Right." She *had* mentioned the encryption. But she'd already shared too much. "There was nothing but receipts and notes on a couple of subcommittee meetings."

"Interesting." Jordan slid out of the chair and walked to the window, looking out at the night sky. "Why would someone break into the townhouse for that?"

"I must have been wrong about its importance," Fallyn lied.

Jordan turned from the window and gave Fallyn a knowing look. She scanned the room again, her gaze landing on Fallyn's purse hanging on a hook by the door. "But you have the tablet, right?"

Her attention came back to Fallyn, a malicious gleam in her eyes. Demanding. Challenging.

Fallyn felt her insides grow cold. The headache's thrum in her temples pulsed harder.

Her voice sounded strange, even to her own ears. "Why do you care about that tablet?"

Jordan smiled. Easy, breezy, as if Fallyn was being difficult. "Because it's worth five million dollars, Fal."

"Five million—" Fallyn's phone buzzed from the coffee table, interrupting her. *Tony.*

She started to reach for it, found herself staring at the hollow end of a very black handgun.

"Uhn, uhn, uhn," Jordan said. "Don't touch that phone. Tony can't help you now."

Her hand hovered above the phone, pulse ticking wildly as understanding dawned. Jordan was the insider. She was the one who wanted the tablet. "You."

"Yep, me." The grin that lit her face was nervous. "It wasn't supposed to go down like this, I swear, but you were so damn nosy. If you'd just stayed out of it, I'd have gotten that tablet and been out of your hair."

Betrayal swarmed her like a nest of angry bees. *Stupid, Fallyn.* "I never did like you."

"I know. I never liked you either."

Would Jordan really shoot her?

Did it matter?

She had maybe one chance to get this right. If she could get to her purse...

Why hadn't she snagged that damn gun from her purse like she'd told Tony she would do after he left? Fallyn raised her hands in a show of surrender. "I don't have the tablet."

Jordan cocked the gun, the awful sound echoing in the high-ceilinged room. "I don't believe you."

Fallyn rose to standing, making sure to move slowly. "Okay, okay. Don't shoot. I'll get it for you."

She started to step toward the purse on the hook.

"Stop!" Jordan moved around in front of her. "Sit down. I'll get it."

Shit. If Jordan dug in her purse, she'd find Fallyn's weapon. Game over.

The woman grabbed the bag.

Panic clawed at her chest. "I lied," Fallyn said, waving her hands. "I don't have it. It's not in there."

Jordan dropped the purse on the coffee table. "Then you're going to get it for me. I know it has information from Heather's investigation. I have a buyer for that information and I'm on a deadline. If I don't get the information, I may as well shoot myself because I'll be as good as dead."

"What does your buyer want with it?"

"To ruin the president before the next election. You and I both know who shot down that plane, don't we? How do you think that will play out in the press? Across the globe? My guy exposes that and President Nicols and his baby boy are going down in a blaze of corruption and murder, that not even you, the great fixer, can spin into something noble."

Like she would do that. "And in turn, your guy will be a hero to the American public."

She winked. "You got it. He probably won't even need to go on the campaign trail. He'll be elected to president without so much as breaking a sweat."

The purse. Get the purse. Fallyn dropped her raised arms. "Have you considered what the president might pay to keep that information under wraps? It's priceless to him. You could make a lot more than five mil."

"Yeah, but I don't like Nicols." She grinned as if this were a schoolyard game. "My guy is rich and famous. An actor who wants to run the world. I'm going to be by his side. I'm *his* fixer, Fallyn. Only I won't waste my time with peons like you do. I'm going straight to the top."

Jesus, the gall of this woman.

She had to get her gun and lure Jordan away from Fresh Start. She couldn't endanger the women there. "I'll take you to get the tablet. It's not here. It's at Tony's workplace."

Adrenaline firing her blood, she started to reach for her purse.

Jordan yanked it off the coffee table. "Why don't I believe you?"

Fallyn's phone buzzed again. She glanced down.

Tony.

He would freak if she wasn't answering her phone. Knowing him, he was already flying through traffic to get back to her. If she kept Jordan talking, kept her distracted...

The muzzle of the gun was pointed at her face. Looking into it, Fallyn felt something inside her snap. If Jordan would point a gun at her, what else was she capable of?

"Were you the one who broke into the townhouse and attacked me?"

"Not me. A guy I hired. He's a former spook. Got his ass booted for insubordination. He hires out."

"He was the guy who trailed Grey and I too."

"He's been watching the townhouse for me. We planned to grab the tablet from the safe before you arrived, but he got arrested for DUI and had to spend the night in jail. By the time he was out, you were already here."

Her voice came out low, rough. "Did you kill her?"

"I didn't mean to." Jordan's face was rueful. "Honestly, I didn't. I just wanted her out of my hair long enough to find that damn tablet. I thought if she had one of her heart episodes and ended up in the hospital, I'd have time to sneak into the townhouse and snag the tablet."

"You knew about her heart condition?"

"She told me everything." She gave another one-shoulder shrug. "For what it's worth, I'm sorry. I loved Heather. I didn't want to hurt her."

The words sunk in, slowly at first, then with the weight of an elephant. They suffocated her, making Fallyn's chest seize. "You bitch. You goddamn, worthless piece of shit."

She went over the coffee table, jumping Jordan and taking her to the floor. The gun went off, the sound exploding near Fallyn's head as Jordan rolled her over. Plaster from the ceiling rained down on them, Fallyn grabbing for the gun.

Another roll and she regained the top position. Jordan swung the gun at her head and Fallyn blocked it. She felt the whiz of a second bullet speed past her head above her ear, raising her hair.

Jordan kneed her in the kidney, making her grunt. She knocked the woman's wrist against the edge of the coffee table. The gun fell free.

Rage and panic warring inside her chest, Fallyn dove for it.

Jordan did the same, using their combined momentum to knock Fallyn off balance. Her chin narrowly missed the corner of the table, her hand tangling in the purse straps.

Jordan's fingers brushed the gunstock and Fallyn kicked out, nailing her in the hip with the heel of her shoe. The woman flinched, and that was all Fallyn needed. Wrapping her hand in the purse straps, she hauled the hard-sided designer bag back and whacked Jordan upside the head.

Jordan's head snapped back, an angry cry parting her lips. But before Fallyn could turn loose of the purse, she scrambled over onto her stomach and lunged for the gun.

Fallyn was half a second ahead of her, dropping her knees down on Jordan's back and forcing the air from her lungs. Grabbing a chunk of Jordan's hair, she yanked hard, jerking her head up and keeping her from reaching the weapon.

Jordan bucked under her, sending her sprawling forward, sailing over the gun and slamming into the sofa.

When Fallyn looked up, she was looking at the menacing end of that black barrel again.

Someone banged on the door. *Matt.* "Ms. Pasche! Open up."

"Tell him you're fine. Where's the tablet?" Jordan's chest heaved like she'd run a mile. Her makeup was smeared, her hair a tangled mess.

Fallyn swallowed hard. *Stall her. Distract her. Do something!* "It's in the bedroom."

A chin cock. "Get up. Show me. Tell him or you're dead! Your father too."

"Matt, I'm okay."

"Yes," Jordan called. "She's fine. Now go away. Or she won't be fine."

To emphasize the point, Jordan blasted off another shot.

"All right," Fallyn said. "Just, please. Stop shooting. Matt! Please, don't come in here."

Slowly, Fallyn dragged herself to her feet. Somehow her ankle had gotten twisted. When she put weight on it, a ragged, knifing pain shot into her foot and up her calf. She kicked off her shoes, willing her erratic heartbeat to slow.

Hobbling, she inched her way to the bedroom. *No one will get here in time.*

It was up to her. To save herself. To get justice for Heather.

Weapon. Her eyes scanned the bedroom as she led Jordan inside. *What can I use for a weapon?*

St. Agnes gazed down on her from above the bed. The bed where Tony had loved her back to life.

The end of the muzzle jabbed into her back. "Where is it?" Jordan demanded.

Fallyn pointed. "Nightstand."

"Get it."

The only things in the nightstand were her e-reader and a Bible. St. Agnes wasn't going to be much help, but maybe King James could lend a hand.

From the drawer, Fallyn withdrew the e-reader with one hand, the Bible under it with the other. "Here," she said, and tossed the hard, plastic tablet-sized e-reader in the air.

Instinct made Jordan reach for it just like Fallyn had hoped. She raised the Bible with both hands and swung.

The gun went off one more time, nailing poor St. Agnes. The picture fell from the wall as Jordan went down to one knee from the impact of the hardbound Bible. Fallyn lifted the heavy book again and hit her once more, Jordan's head smacking into the spindle on the footboard. She fell to the floor, motionless, the gun dropping from her hand.

"Fallyn!"

Tony's muffled voice cut through the roar between her ears, bringing her head up. For good measure, she grabbed the picture off the bed and whacked Jordan over the head with it, once, twice, three times. Glass sprayed, the picture ripped. Fallyn dropped the frame on Jordan's back.

"Fallyn!"

He's here.

She tried to answer him, found she had no voice. Her ankle burned as she made her way into the living room. Sirens came from far away.

Across the room, the doorknob twisted, jerked.

Tony screamed her name again. Fallyn tried to pick up speed, but her ankle, her whole leg, wouldn't cooperate.

She felt lightheaded, her knees weak. The door seemed so far away and she had to grab onto the back of the chair for support.

Boom! The door burst open in a hail of splinters and metal. Tony raced into the room, gun drawn and Matt hot on his heels. Tony's eyes took her in. "Jesus, God."

Fallyn pushed upright, using the chair for balance. She tried to smile. "I'm okay."

Something moved in her peripheral vision. Tony's gaze snapped right and so did his gun. "No!" he yelled.

A gun went off. Then another.

White-hot pain exploded between her shoulder blades, the force arching her back. Her fingers lost their grip on the chair. She was falling, pitching forward...

But she wasn't.

Tony caught her, one arm circling her waist and pulling her against him.

He fired again, *bambambam*, and Fallyn wanted to throw her hands up over her ears, but she couldn't make them move. Tony screamed her name as he lowered her to the floor.

Her mouth was dry, her tongue thick. Were the sirens getting closer or was the ringing in her ears getting louder? Agony in her back, her chest. "Tony?"

He brushed hair back from her face with his free hand. "I thought I'd lost you," she heard him say over the hissing in her ears.

She turned her face up to his and smiled past the pain. "You'll never lose me. I'm yours."

That's when she saw the blood print, like a flower blooming on his shirt. Her blood.

The bullet had torn straight through her.

"I...love...you..." The words were hard to form. She couldn't get enough air. But she needed to get them out. "Tony, I love...you."

His hands were on her, pressing something into her chest. He stared down into her eyes, anguish on his face, in his voice. "Fallyn, don't you dare. Swear to God, don't you dare die on me."

This man. He was like no other. She loved him to her very core. He'd made her feel whole again, like she belonged after a lifetime of always feeling like the odd man out. Rejected by her mother, neglected by her father. "...not...dying..." she managed to whisper.

But she felt incredibly cold, the light around Tony's face dimming. "...just...need...sleep."

"No." He shook her. His voice broke as he spoke. "Keep your eyes open, Fallyn. For me. Please, honey, keep your eyes open."

She wanted to, but the darkness seemed to want her more. Her lids were heavy, her body a lead brick. She couldn't move her fingers, couldn't feel her feet. Another man's face swam into view above Tony's. Matt.

His face was screwed up in an *oh, shit* look and Fallyn knew exactly what that meant.

She closed her eyes.

Tony shook her again. "Fallyn, fight it."

She blinked open her eyes. There he was. Her man. The love of her life.

Not enough time. Don't close your eyes. Every second with him counts.

But then people in blue uniforms came in behind Tony and Matt, pushing them aside and hovering over her. She knew they were touching her but she couldn't feel it.

Fighting the sensation, she forced her eyes to stay open, but she couldn't help it. Without Tony to pin her gaze on, she drifted away.

22

*F*allyn was half dead.

Tony stood in the hospital hallway outside the surgical waiting area, his back against the wall, his shoulders back, his body tall in his typical *all's fine here* stance. Anyone walking by wouldn't blink at him. Just an average guy waiting.

That's what they'd see. That's what he wanted them to see.

Inside?

Fucking train wreck.

Another one. He'd left her and now... *Jesus.*

Matt stepped out of the waiting room, swung his head left then right, his gaze landing on Tony. So much for wanting to be by himself after an hour of questioning by the PD. Plus, staring at Fallyn's father wasn't helping.

Escape.

That's all Tony could think because the man's broken expression, the sunken eyes and hollowed cheeks, only reinforced the misery.

Total failure.

Matt met his eyes and started toward him. "Tony, holy Christ, I feel like an asshole. She walked right by me. I thought she was clear."

They all thought that. That's what Tony had told him. She's good, he'd said. A pain in the ass, but safe.

Tony looked away, focused on the bland white wall across from him and a picture flashed of Fallyn, on the floor, her long hair fanned out around her, her face dangerously pale.

Bleeding out.

Something in his brain broke loose, snapped at him. Just like the judge, she'd bled out in front of him.

Almost.

"Not your fault, Matt. This one's on me."

Gaze fixed on the wall, his heart slamming hard enough to break a few ribs, he inhaled, sucking enough stale air to make him gag.

He ran both hands over his head, the full weight of what he'd done landing on him.

Fallyn nearly dead.

And he'd shot Jordan.

An off-duty Supreme Court police officer had just shot a woman. The first time he'd discharged his weapon in an emergency and he'd hit her center mass.

Matt propped an elbow against the wall. "Any updates?"

"No. Both still in surgery. Jordan's father is here." Tony jerked his head. "He's in the waiting room."

His phone rang. Grey. Who was down in the ER getting checked out and waiting for a bed. What a fucking cluster.

"What's up?"

"Don Fox. He's in DC."

Tony boosted off the wall. "Seriously?"

"Yeah. Teeg is texting you his address. We need to turn that video over to Agent Bronco. Then, my guess is Bronco will haul ass to Fox's. I'm kinda busy here in the hospital. Can't get to a phone to call Teeg and tell him to send that video. You get what I'm saying here?"

He got it. "You'll give me a head start?"

"At least an hour."

Ha. Had to love Grey.

"Any word on Fallyn?"

"Not yet."

"You want to stay here?"

He should. He should stay right here and wait for Fallyn. Wait for her to come out of surgery.

Dead or alive.

He should be here.

But...what?

She'd want him figuring out why her sister had to die. And Grey was giving him a one hour free pass at the man who could tell him.

Standing around like this? Fallyn would hate that. Like him, she wanted action, result-oriented action. Constantly.

"No. Send me that address."

He hung up and turned to Matt. "You wanna run shotgun on something? Help me question a witness before the feds get to him."

"If it'll help you, yeah. Let's do it. Whatever you need."

A doctor pushed through the double doors, made eye contact and turned into the waiting area. "Pasche?"

Fallyn's doctor. "Give me a sec and we'll roll."

He hustled over to the doorway leaving Matt still leaning on the wall. Fallyn's father jumped from his seat and the doctor strode up to him, pulled him to the side. Tony took two steps. Wait.

Not my business.

Family matter. Who the hell was he in this? Busting into the middle of it wouldn't score him any points with the old man. Particularly since he'd let his daughter get shot.

He'd wait. Give them privacy and hopefully Mr. Pasche would update him. If for no other reason than he'd stayed. After calling Mr. Pasche from Fallyn's phone, upon his arrival at the hospital, Tony had introduced himself, given her father a decidedly scaled down version of what had happened and helped the man to a chair.

Where he'd asked to be alone. Tony couldn't blame him. The recent days, after losing Heather had been enough of a blow. Now coupled with Fallyn?

The man was wrecked. Flat-out destroyed. First Heather and then Fallyn.

Now he stood, taking in whatever the doctor was saying and—oh, shit—his shoulders dropped and Tony's stomach squeezed.

Shit, shit, shit.

He couldn't hear. Even in the agonizing silence of the room. Not a damned thing. So he watched, studied Mr. Pasche's body language. The partially open mouth, how he rubbed one hand over his forehead. What did it mean?

Horror?

Or relief?

He said something to the doctor who spun away angling around Tony and nodding, his expression lacking any telltale.

Another one he couldn't read. Terrific.

Mr. Pasche looked over at him and Tony waited. But, dammit, he needed some answers. Inappropriate or not, he needed to know.

He closed the distance between them, stopped a foot in front of Fallyn's father and squared his shoulders. "Mr. Pasche how is she?"

"She's...alive. Thank God."

Alive. Tony looked down at his feet, closed his eyes a second, let relief—finally—squeak a victory. Alive. Good. That was good. He huffed out a breath, met Mr. Pasche's gaze. "She's in recovery?"

"Yes. The doctor said she'll be out for a while. Hours probably. He said I should go home. Get some rest and come back in the morning."

Go home. Ha.

The man rubbed his hands over his face, then plucked at his stained shirt. "I was at work. I stink like garlic." He laughed. "My Fallyn hates that. I'll go home and shower. Get cleaned up and come back."

Tony nodded. "Do you need a ride?"

"No, son. Thank you."

Son. Wow. That knocked him a little sideways. Hundreds of men had called him son. Somehow, this time, coming from Fallyn's father, it meant...something.

"Sir," Tony said, "I want you to know, I care for Fallyn. Very much. She's...special."

The side of Mr. Pasche's mouth quirked. "I figured that out. I didn't expect a business associate to stay here." He waved at the chair behind him. "I've been sitting here wondering just what my daughter means to you."

What she meant to him? Good question. "A lot," he said. "Beyond that, I don't want to comment. You're her father and she and I have things to talk about. If I'm going to tell someone how I feel about her, she should hear it first."

Because, damn, he'd blown it. His only job had been to keep her safe and he'd fucked that up good. And then that blowout they'd had didn't help. How would she ever trust him again?

Mr. Pasche clapped a hand on his shoulder. "Go home. Get some rest."

Rest?

Forget that. What he needed was to find Don Fox and pin a murder on Jordan. That scheming, deceitful, traitorous bitch.

If she survived, by the time Tony got done with her, she was gonna wished she'd died.

Tony strode up the walkway to Don Fox's door with Matt in tow. The interior of the home, a cushy brownstone in one of the finest neighborhoods in DC was dark. Not a surprise at nearly midnight but the man was about to be woken up.

"I'm gonna badge this guy. Get him to open the door."

Matt shrugged. "Works for me."

Tony pressed the doorbell. Inside, a chime rang out. "Fancy."

Under the glare of the streetlight, Matt nodded. Tony waited another few seconds and gave the door a couple of solid raps.

"Coming!" a man yelled from inside. "Who is it?"

Tony held his badge to the pane of glass next to the door. "Police, sir. We need to speak with Don Fox."

After a few seconds, enough time for Fox to study Tony's badge and decide, yes, this might be important, the door whooshed open. A skinny guy in his thirties, short reddish hair, nodded at them. "I'm Don Fox."

Tony didn't wait to be invited and walked right in. "I'm Officer Tony Gerard."

He didn't bother to introduce Matt.

"Come inside."

A brunette—maybe mid thirties, maybe younger—wearing a fluffy pink bathrobe appeared at the top of the curving staircase. "Donnie, what is it?"

"Business, hon. Go back to bed."

"Now?"

"Yes," he said. "Now. Go back to bed."

Fox led them toward the back of the house, through the kitchen to a family room and waved them both to chairs.

"What's this about?"

"Heather Pasche," Tony said.

Fox's shoulders tensed, the movement so slight Tony had almost missed it. *Nice try, Ace.*

"Sorry," Fox said. "Can't help you."

Oh, what the fuck? Tony sat forward, rested his elbows on his knees and clasped his hands together. "You don't know what we're going to ask. Or do you?"

He had Fallyn laying in a hospital bed because he couldn't protect her and he wasn't about to let this asshole skate. Fox knew something and with any luck, he could tie Jordan to Heather's death.

"Mr. Fox," Tony said, "are you familiar with a woman named Jordan Lomax?"

Fox shifted his gaze to Matt, then back to Tony. "Again, what is this about?"

Tony sighed just as Matt's phone chirped. He checked the screen, grunted and stood. "I gotta take this." He pointed to the back door just off the adjoining kitchen. "Can I go out this door?"

Fox nodded then rested his head back, closing his eyes for a second. *Yeah, buddy, the shit's hitting the fan.*

Tony dove right in. "Look," he said, "I work for Fallyn Pasche. Who, as we speak, has just gotten out of surgery due to a bullet that shredded her back. After she started poking around about her sister's death and"—he held his hands out—"guess what? Found you."

Still with his eyes closed, Fox rolled his head from side to side.

Okay. If this guy wasn't going to pony up, Tony would help him along. "Dude, don't be stupid. We got one hell of a mess here and I can help you. Fallyn can help you. But you need to be straight with us."

Fox opened his eyes, met Tony's gaze. "What do you know?"

Now they were getting somewhere. "You contacted Heather Pasche regarding the cover up of the disappearance of that CanAir flight. In about twenty minutes, the feds will know it too. Heather Pasche outlined it all in a video that's on its way to FBI headquarters. If Fallyn Pasche dies, you'll be implicated in two murders. And one of them was a United States Senator. If you're straight with me, I might be able to help you. Fallyn, if she survives, will be able to help you."

Fox sat forward, dug his fingers into his scalp and gripped hard enough to make the veins in his hands pop. This guy had some serious guilt. And Tony was an expert on that. "Now is the time to talk. You talk now, you might have a shot at staying out of prison."

The back door came open again and in stepped Matt. "I had someone from my office at the hospital. Jordan Lomax is dead. She died on the operating table."

Fox lowered his hands, focused on Tony with dark eyes more than a little spooked.

"Now we got two people dead."

And Tony had killed one of them. Shit.

Matt reclaimed his seat, shot Tony a look and Tony raised his eyebrows. The we're-almost-there-don't-fuck-this-up look.

"I didn't think it would go this far," Fox said. "It was just information being passed along."

Come on, come on.

"What information?"

"My boss. Barnard Shaw. He's aiming for a White House run. He wanted me to find him someone who could dig up damning information on the president. He wanted the skeletons. I hired a political operative. The guy has major contacts at State and in Congress."

"Name?"

Fox shook his head. "If I have to give up the name, I will, but I'm not doing it yet."

Tony nodded. "Okay. Fair enough."

"The operative stumbled into some interesting coincidences."

"Like what?"

"Like the president's son flying out of MacDill hours before the CanAir flight was shot down. Like, a maintenance guy taking a photo of the president's son climbing into the cockpit of his plane that same night. Our operative pieced it together with the CanAir disaster and ran with it. He assumed the President ordered the mission. The cherry on top was his son firing the missile that took the plane down. He didn't have proof though. Not rock solid."

"How does the senator play into this?"

"My boss needed proof and our operative couldn't get it. We needed someone inside Foreign Relations and he'd made hefty donations to her campaign."

"Foreign Relations? Because they were doing the investigation into the crash?"

"Yeah. My boss figured if he could buy off a senator, he'd be privy to whatever they had."

If all this legwork led to them finding out Heather Pasche was on the take, Fallyn would be devastated. The best spin-doctor in the world couldn't manipulate into something usable.

But he had to know. Had to. "He bought off Senator Pasche?"

"He tried. She wouldn't bite."

Jordan.

"But her assistant did."

Fox shrugged. "I don't know who. My boss never said. It was someone in her office though. I couldn't stand the whole setup. Hiring an operative to investigate was one thing, nothing illegal about that. But this whole CanAir thing involved the deaths of hundreds of innocent people. The collateral damage was off the charts. There were Americans on that flight. All to get one terrorist? No way. I didn't like it. Any of it. I resigned and called Senator Pasche to let her know she had a mole. I also gave her copies of the reports and the photos the operative had given to us. I felt it was my duty. She was on Foreign Relations. I figured she'd know how to deal with it all. She assured me she'd protect me. That was the day before she died."

Tony sat back, somehow not believing that Heather Pasche was handed evidence that her boyfriend had shot down a plane filled with Americans.

23

ne day later

Fallyn ran a comb through her hair and tried to get her thoughts together. Her team was due at the hospital any minute. She'd told them not to come, but they wouldn't listen, insisting on driving down from New York City.

She hated them seeing her like this, in a hospital bed, barely able to move. Her compact mirror showed her skin was vampire white accentuating the dark circles under her eyes. One jaw sported a bruise from her tussle with Jordan.

But as long as her team was coming to see her, she planned to put them to work.

"Ms. Pasche? Fallyn?"

Fallyn snapped her head up. A tall, handsome man with light blue eyes and a military buzz cut stood at attention just inside the door, a cap in his hands.

"Ryan." Lowering her compact, she motioned at him. "Please come in."

He rolled the cap in his hands. "I'd like to speak to you about a couple of things, but if this is a bad time…"

The hair, the eyes, the ramrod straight posture. The bachelor article she'd buried for the president had it right. Ryan was a catch. *Oh, Heather. No wonder you fell for him.*

Fallyn set her compact and comb aside. "Pull up a chair, Lieutenant."

He did as instructed. "I'm not supposed to be here. With you. I'm in the hot seat right now, even though it hasn't leaked to the press yet. My lawyer told me to stay away from you, because I…"

"I know all about it," Fallyn reassured him. "Heather left me a video about you and what happened with CanAir 702."

"Oh." He looked worried. "You know about what I did?"

"I know it was under orders from your commander-in-chief, who happens to be your father. I would imagine that could be awkward on a good day. Throw in the target your father ordered you to shoot down and I imagine you're having a hard time living with yourself."

Two large hands worried the cap in his lap. "I never meant for any of this to happen. Heather's dead because of what I did."

Oh, these men and their guilt trips. "My sister is dead because a woman whom my entire family trusted was a money-hungry bitch. That's not on you, Ryan."

"Heather was so fond of Jordan. I can't believe Jordan did that."

"Jordan's father can't believe it either. Carl visited me and he's devastated. She was his everything."

He was silent for a long moment, his voice subdued when he did speak. "We talked about getting married, you know. Heather and I. Right before all of this happened. I was in town before she died and I had planned to propose to her. We drove to Virginia, to a bed and breakfast there, for a few days. We wore disguises so no one would recognize us, but I couldn't do it."

The receipts. The ones Heather had saved on her tablet. "Why not?"

"I was afraid. We couldn't keep a lid on CanAir, it was so, so wrong." He glanced up at the ceiling, drawing a deep breath. "My father was... He shouldn't have done what he did. That day, when I got the orders, I didn't know why I was going out or who was on that plane. I just did what I was told."

That's what good soldiers did. "It's not your fault."

Seemed like she was saying that a lot right now.

"We had to tell someone, but we didn't know who. She suggested you. I had to think about it. Then I tried to end things with her. I knew she'd be flayed by the media once it all came to light, and I didn't want that for her. She had this bright, shining career ahead of her and there was no way I could ruin that. So I told her I would go public with the information and we had to break up. She refused to let me."

Fallyn smiled. "Bullheadedness runs in our family."

Ryan's eyes shone with tears. "I hate to ask you this, but I need your help."

Of course he did. He needed a fixer the size of King Kong. "My sister loved you, Ryan. I'll make sure you get a copy of her video, so you get to hear her gush about what an incredible man you are. You were a hero in her eyes for wanting to do the right thing, and I agree. Going up against your father, testifying to what he ordered you to do, will be the hardest thing you've ever done in your life, and even though it's the right thing to do, you'll never forgive yourself, so you need to be prepared to live with that. He may have committed a terrible act, but he's still your father."

"I have to do this." His face contorted with anguish. "For Heather."

She had to do this for Heather too. "I know someone at Justice who can help you, and I'm friends with one of the best JAG lawyers in the Northern Hemisphere. You're done with the old one. Don't talk to him any more today. Give me and my team until tomorrow morning and we'll have a game plan for you, okay?"

Ryan Nicols stood and stretched out a hand. "Thank you."

Fallyn eyed his hand for a second before shaking it. "Thank you for loving my sister. She was happy, Ryan. Even with this horrendous situation the two of you were dealing with, she was happy. She loved you so much, and I can understand why."

A brief smile passed over his lips. "She loved you, too, you know. Talked about you nonstop. She was pretty proud of you."

Fallyn's heart clenched. Her father had said the same thing to her earlier that morning. Their relationship seemed to be morphing, growing. Fallyn realized she might not have been the easiest child to handle and maybe—awful thought—she had reminded him of his wife. There was still space between them, but the gap was closing. "I appreciate you telling me that."

He released her hand and returned the chair to its original place. "I'll talk to you tomorrow, then?"

She nodded. As he left, her team started piling in.

"Was that...?" Maureen said, pointing over her shoulder as the door closed silently.

"Yep. Lieutenant Ryan Nicols. First Son. He's our new client."

"We come to see you, and what do you have us doing?" Dani slouched in a chair and set her laptop on her knees. Her hair was shocking pink today and the multitude of rings on her fingers clinked against each other as she typed. It looked like she had a new tattoo on her left wrist. "Working."

"I agree," Maureen said, eyeing Fallyn over her reading glasses as she brought out her notepad and pen. "You almost died. This is a bit extreme, even for you."

Fallyn sat up in bed—as upright as she could stand, anyway, thanks to her sore chest and back—and ignored their complaints. Work was all she had right now. Work and a steady supply of pain pills.

Neither of which was keeping the pain away. Her body ached all over, her chest was still taped, and she was fucking sick of the anti-septic smell in the air.

Maureen, Tabitha, and Niles hovered around the bed while Dani played on her laptop. Katrina was still in New York, handling the office.

Tabitha held up a gold box with a red ribbon in her hands.

"Tell me you brought chocolates," Fallyn said.

Tabitha opened the box from Fallyn's favorite shop on 5th Avenue and handed it to her. Fallyn dug in.

The first bite of chocolate nearly made her pass out, it was so good. She closed her eyes and leaned her head back. "Chocolate. Better than painkillers."

The box made the rounds so everyone could take a piece. "Do you have the lease agreement for the new office?" she asked Maureen.

Their client load had expanded exponentially after the press got wind of the fact Heather had been murdered and Fallyn had been shot by the killer.

If it hadn't been for Tony, I'd be dead too.

The thought of Tony sent a spike of pain through her chest. She gritted her teeth and ignored it.

"Just came in," Dani said. "I'll sign it electronically for you if you want."

"Are you sure about this?" Niles asked. "A second office here in DC? Moving?"

He wasn't worried about her moving back to Washington. He was worried about taking over the New York office. "We need a presence here." She finished chewing her chocolate and swallowed. "No more constant commuting for me, and you're more than capable of taking over the New York office. Need I remind you, you have an excellent staff."

The ladies all smiled at him and Niles rolled his eyes.

"Go ahead and sign for me," she told Dani.

Maureen wrote something on her notepad. "Will you be moving in with your dad?"

"I'm keeping Heather's townhouse for now. It's an easy commute to my father's and I need..."

What *did* she need? Time to process everything. Time to mourn. Time to work out things with that bullheaded lug who hadn't been to see her yet. "I feel close to Heather there," she admitted. *The memories of Tony aren't bad either.*

Tony, Tony, Tony. Her damn brain wouldn't let up on him. Where was the bastard anyway? He'd told her he loved her, then disappeared to work the case.

Don Fox had been questioned and given up the information needed to arrest Barnard Shaw, a billionaire businessman with a boner for the West Wing. He'd bribed Jordan to find dirt on Ryan's dad once he'd found out Heather and Ryan were meeting in secret. Grey, who was in a matching room down the hall, had told her all about it. So Barnard was toast and Fox was free. Metro had turned everything over to the FBI since they now knew the whole thing involved the murder of a senator and the FBI had taken over slogging through the details of Heather's death while working with Justice on how to sort it all out. What did Tony possibly have to do?

Of course, he'd killed Jordan, who'd tried to finish what she'd started and had shot Fallyn in the back. Granted, it was self-defense, but still. He might be tied up with the police.

He's not coming back.

Just like Mom.

Everyone was always leaving her.

Or maybe, I just keep driving them away.

Beep, beep, beep. Her heart monitor sped up, echoing in the room and drawing everyone's attention. Fallyn's eyes seemed too tight, tears threatening.

"You okay, Fallyn?" Tabitha asked. "Maybe you should pass on the chocolates."

Work the case. If Tony could do it, so could she. "I'm lying in fucking hospital bed, so no I'm not okay, but I will be." *I just need time.* "Don't touch anymore of my chocolates."

She reached for a salted caramel mocha truffle. Tabitha didn't seem upset at Fallyn's outburst—her team was used to her brusque, get-it-done attitude—and helped herself to a dark chocolate anyway.

"Okay, moving on. Ryan Nicols. Hire Tim Plantar as his lawyer and let's do a full court press on media before they even get their talons out. We also need to contact Aledo Walton at Justice."

"What the hell is going on here?" a deep male voice interrupted.

Fallyn looked up, and yep, her world, her heart, exploded.

Tony stood behind Niles, looking over the guy's shoulder with a mean expression on his face as he sized up Fallyn in bed.

He looked completely strung out. Three days' worth of beard growth, eyes bloodshot, a permanent crease in his forehead...

Still looks good to me.

He met her gaze head on, crossing his arms over his enormous chest.

Touch me. Please come over here and touch me.

Then she would know it was alright. *They* were alright.

Yes, she'd pissed him off and sent him away right before everything went south, but she'd had to. He never would have left her to help Grey if she hadn't acted pissed off and told him to get out.

Later, in his arms, she'd told him she loved him. She'd been woozy on the floor after Jordan had shot her, and she wasn't sure about a few of the details, but dammit, she remembered telling him she loved him.

Niles backed out of the way and the rest of the group skirted to the opposite side of the bed, putting Fallyn in between them and Tony, who was doing a damn good impression of Mad Max from Justice-dome.

Fallyn couldn't blame them. A pissed Tony Gerard past his expiration date was nothing to mess with.

He didn't make a move toward the bed. Didn't act like he wanted to look at her, much less touch her.

Ouch.

"Leave," he said to her team, and, in unison, they all looked at her.

"We're done here for now," she told them with an *it will be alright* smile. "Update me on your progress before this evening."

"Are you sure about this?" Niles said under his breath as he leaned over and air-kissed her forehead.

"Yes," she said, seeing the look of anger Tony shot him. "I'll catch up with all of you later."

Dani closed her laptop and stood as the others filed out ahead of her. She grabbed Fallyn's cell phone off the bedside table and handed it to her. "I'm going to work here for awhile in the waiting room down the hall. You need anything, you text me."

How did I get so lucky to have such devoted employees? "Thank you," she said, accepting the phone. "Now, get to work."

Dani—all five foot three inches of her—walked past Tony slowly, glaring at him with her chest puffed out and holding the laptop like she'd like to use it on him. Tony met her glare and returned it with a sneer, the two of them like dogs, circling each other until Dani finally walked out the door.

Silence filled the room. Tony didn't look at her. At least not at her face. He stared at her feet, encased in her favorite pink polk-a-dot socks.

Fallyn waited, biting her bottom lip to keep from bursting out and saying something she knew she'd regret. Tony obviously had something on his mind. She needed to let him talk. To get it all out.

Knowing Tony like she did, she figured he needed to tell her what he'd found out and update her on his situation with the Jordan shooting.

He'd killed a woman to save her. She owed him everything. Yet... she sensed he didn't see it that way.

So much guilt.

How could a man live like that?

Her chest felt like it was a balloon filled with too much helium. The sensation pulsated all the way up to her throat. She had to break this god-awful silence before it choked her. "I'm glad you're here. I've missed you."

A muscle jumped in his jaw. "I've been at FBI headquarters since early this morning. Don Fox has agreed to testify against Barnard Shaw. The FBI found emails between him and Jordan proving she was willing to sell him the information once she obtained it from Heather."

"So what happens now to Ryan and the president?"

He still didn't look at her, her voice unemotional, dry. "Agent Bronco took it to Justice an hour ago. They'll open a formal investigation today."

"It'll take months to sort out, won't it?"

"At least."

The straight line of his broad shoulders told her he was holding himself rigid. *Why won't he look at me?*

"Tony, I'm sorry about what I said that night at the shelter. Before...you know."

His gazed bounced to his shoes, back to her socks, then away. "You were under a lot of stress."

"That was no excuse. So were you. You shouldn't have been put in the situation of choosing whether to stay with me or help Grey. All I was doing was trying to make your choice easier."

"And look what happened."

"What happened is I didn't take my situation seriously enough, even after everything that had happened. You were right, and that's on me. You did the right thing going to help Grey. Even if you had stayed, Jordan would have gotten to me sooner or later. So knock it off with the guilt train. You saved my life busting into the apartment when you did and..."

"Stop it, Fallyn." He rocked back on his heels, his face grim as a tank. "Stop making excuses for me."

"I'm not making excuses for anyone. I'm stating facts. I owe you my life, Tony Gerard. So does Grey."

He let go of a derisive snort and headed for the door.

"Where are you going?" Fallyn said.

"Grey's being released. I'm going to take him home."

"Are you coming back, then, after that?"

He looked at her—finally looked at her—over his shoulder as he opened the door part way. "For what? That fight was inevitable, Fallyn. We've talked about this. We're both too aggressive. Always pushing. Eventually, it'll do us in. I think it's better this way. Before we get too deep into this."

All the air went out of her lungs. He was leaving. As in *never coming back* leaving.

Her throat constricted. "You're human, Tony. You can't protect everyone all the time. We're good together. Damn good."

Another snort and he shook his head.

"I love you, Tony. I'll always love you. So when you're done beating yourself up, I'll be here, waiting."

Nothing changed for a moment. He glanced down at the floor, his knuckles white from the grip he had on the door handle.

And then she saw the slight drop of his shoulders. It wasn't much, only a fraction, but it was there.

If only he would come back. Turn around and come back to the bed. Touch her, kiss her, hold her.

She thought, in that moment, he might. He might give up that tight string of control and let the guilt go.

Come on, big guy. Do it.

But he didn't. Without a word, he swung the door open the rest of the way and left her lying there.

The pressure in her lungs detonated, bringing with it a torrent of tears. She cried in silence, letting the grief take her. Grief for the life she wanted with Tony that would never be. The sisterhood she'd fantasized about with Heather that also would never be.

She'd spent her whole adult life going after what she wanted. For the first time since she'd left home to go out on her own, she'd failed.

Miserably.

The coming days and weeks stretched out in front of her. The new office would keep her busy for awhile. All the new clients beating a path to her door as well.

Her dad. Lot of fences to mend there.

None of it mattered without Tony.

She thought about Ryan and Heather and how much they had lost. How stupid would it be for her and Tony to let their relationship fall apart over guilt and a lousy argument? They could have everything Ryan and Heather missed out on.

If only...

Picking up her cell phone, she texted Dani.

．　．　．

"Why are we doing this?" Dani asked as she pushed Fallyn into the hallway. "I mean, I get that this guy trips your lust-o-meter. He trips mine too and I'm a total lesbo, but seriously, Fallyn, he's demented. You said yourself two days ago that he has issues. You hate guys with issues."

Which might be why she was single. Fallyn took short breaths to keep the pressure off her lungs. They burned from the all the shifting to get up and into this damn wheelchair, but she couldn't let Tony get away. "This one is different."

"Oh, God, you're not going to try and fix him, are you?"

That's what she'd wanted in the beginning. She saw the wild drive in Tony. The pain that made him stay in fourth gear all the time like she did, trying to outrun it. The past couple of days—hell, the couple of minutes she'd spent with Ryan—had made her realize no one could outrun their demons.

Tony didn't see that. He wanted to walk away from his failure with her, probably because he saw himself as a failure and didn't want to burden her with that.

What utter bullshit.

So she was going to dog him. Be his demon come to life in order to make him face what had to be faced.

"He has to fix himself," she said. "No one can do it for him. Not even me."

She was not leaving him alone until he got over himself. He was not carrying the guilt over Jordan shooting her to his grave. All that other nonsense about them pushing each other too hard. Well, they'd have to figure out how to adjust. Couples did it all the time.

"First time I've ever heard that out of your mouth," Dani said.

"Can't this thing go any faster?"

Dani grumbled under her breath. "It's a wheelchair, Fallyn. Not an Indy car."

"The room is down there at the end of the hall."

"You already told me that."

"Just stop and let me get out. I can shuffle faster than you can push this thing."

"Will you stop? I've got this. I promise I won't let Terrible Tony get away before you bitch-slap him."

They were almost to the door when it cracked open.

"I knew it. He's about to leave." Fallyn smacked the arm of the wheelchair. "Hurry."

Dani complied and the wheelchair picked up the tiniest amount of speed.

But it wasn't Tony that popped his head out and looked both ways. It was Sydney.

"Fallyn?" she said when her gaze landed on her and Dani. "I was just looking for Grey's nurse with his discharge papers. Is everything okay?"

"No. I need to see Tony. Is he still here?"

Syd backed up and cocked her head toward the inside of the room. "In here."

Dani pushed her through and nearly ran into Tony who was heading right for them.

"What's wrong?" he said, concern etched on his face.

Dani pulled up short, all that forward momentum coming to a screeching halt. "What's wrong?" Fallyn said. "What the hell do you think is wrong?"

Grey, sitting on the edge of the bed, raised his brows.

He was looking better, the ashen color gone from his face and his demeanor back to *don't mess with me*. "Jeez, Gerard. What the fuck did you do now?"

"Me?" Tony whirled on the man.

"Yeah, you," Syd chimed in. "What did you do to upset Fallyn this time?"

Tony's head bobbed back and forth, eyes wide in disbelief. "I...I..."

"Shut up," Fallyn said. "You're going to listen to me, whether you want to or not."

Tony gritted his teeth and stared straight ahead. He'd known that was too easy. No way Fallyn would let him walk away without a fight.

Regardless of how she felt about him, it wasn't in her nature to give up.

But this wasn't happening. Together, they were an impending train wreck. That fight at the shelter? That was child's play. The closer they grew they'd become more volatile. Passion did that to people.

Made them insane.

And he was already halfway there.

He squared his shoulders, readied for the war. "Fallyn, there's nothing else to say."

"I disagree."

"Of course you do."

A weird noise came from Grey. "Can you wait until I'm discharged for this so I can get the hell out of here?"

This time it was Syd who said, "shut up" as she looked pointedly at Grey. "They need to work this out."

"Not with me in here!"

Syd closed the door and walked over to sit on the edge of the bed with Grey. "Go on, Fallyn."

Fallyn drew a deep breath and Tony knew, knew, he wasn't getting out in one piece.

"This thing about us not being good together is bull. Why don't you want to be with me?"

Tony threw her a scathing look. "What?"

"You heard me. Is it because every time you look at me, you're reminded that you failed to protect me from Jordan?"

He didn't answer, screwing up his lips as that muscle in his jaw jumped again.

Grey threw up his hands and looked at the ceiling. "Why me?" he muttered. "Why do I always get stuck in these things?"

Syd pinched him on the leg.

"Ouch." He swore and gave her a look that would send most people cowering.

Syd swatted his arm and Grey slouched on the bed, looking like a three-year-old who had to sit in the corner.

Fallyn grabbed the arms of the wheelchair and put her feet on the ground. She pushed herself up to standing, wobbling for a moment and Tony made a move toward her. Dani reached out as if to assist, but she gently knocked the girl's hands away.

Of course. Because that was Fallyn. Always pushing ahead on her own.

"Look at me," she said to Tony.

Why was she pushing herself right now? He should just pick her up, toss her back in her bed and strap her down. They could talk about this later. In private. When she was better. Now? It wouldn't do anyone any good.

He met her gaze and held it.

"If I fall right now, are you going to reach out and keep me from hitting the ground?"

What the hell kind of end-run was this now? "Stop it."

"Just answer it, Gerard," Sydney said.

He sighed, continued to hold Fallyn's gaze. "If you fell, of course I would keep you from hitting the ground."

"Why?"

"*Why?*"

"Give the poor man a break," Grey said.

"Shut up," Fallyn and Syd told him in unison.

"Because," Tony said without further prompting, "I don't want to see you get hurt."

"Exactly." She took a step toward him. "That's who you are, Tony. It's not a mantle you wear and take off at the end of the day. You're a protector. The problem is, you can't protect everyone you love every minute of the day. No one can do that. The control freak in you hates that, but that's life. You can't control everything. Believe me, I get that. We're alike in that way. Always wanting to control the spin."

He looked away, that mental wall trying to shut her out. She'd said it herself, they were too much alike. But, damn, it was hard to let her go.

"You're here for Grey," she stated.

"So?"

"You blamed yourself for his accident, yet you didn't abandon him after it all went down, like you're doing with me."

"That's different." He raised his eyes to hers. "Grey is... well...Grey."

"Damn, right," Grey muttered.

And...*swat*. Syd smacked his arm, looked at Tony like she was going to swat his as well.

"He's alive because of you, Tony," Fallyn said. Her voice was low, controlled, but there was a rawness to it that made his chest ache. "*I'm* alive because of you. You didn't *fail* this past week. You succeeded beyond measure. You saved the lives of *two* people. You helped solve a murder and expose corruption at the highest level of our government. Yeah, some stuff got out of your control, but your overachieving ass outdid itself once again."

"She's right," Syd said from the bed. "I might be making funeral arrangements right now if it weren't for you."

"I was a camp counselor once," Fallyn said. "Heather and I went to the same camp every summer and our third summer there, we were both counselors. Each of us was in charge of a house with younger campers. My best friend's little sister, Suzie, was in my group of twenty-four kids. We went for our usual morning hike one day and Suzie wandered off without me knowing about it. We got back to the cabins and Suzie was gone."

Just...hell.

"Oh, my God," Syd said. "That must have been horrible."

"It was my fault."

Fallyn's legs trembled harder now. He could see it and stepped closer, anticipating her going down. He extended his hands and she grabbed on. "Sit. Please," he said.

But she didn't move. Stood there, looking up into his eyes.

"My best friend blamed me for her sister's disappearance. She wouldn't talk to me, wouldn't have anything to do with me. I was sent home early from camp. Many of the parents came and picked up their kids when they heard. No one wanted their kids around me."

Grey had tuned in to her story. "Did they find the girl?"

"Yeah, actually they did three weeks later. She hadn't wandered off, she'd been abducted by a neighbor who snuck into the woods that day and waited for her. He was a serial pedophile and had been watching Suzie for months, I guess."

"It wasn't your fault," Tony said. "She knew the guy, thought she could trust him."

"But I should have kept a closer eye on her. All twenty-four of those kids were depending on me, a fifteen-year-old girl. My best friend was depending on me to keep her little sister safe."

"You couldn't have known that bastard was after her."

"Just like you couldn't have known Jordan was after me."

He stared at her.

She stared back.

"That was different." And, damn, he was losing this battle. Score one for the pushy spin-doctor. "I knew you were in danger."

"But you didn't know from whom. Neither of us did. You called in Matt. You did everything you could do to keep me safe."

"Tony, if we use your method of splitting hairs," Syd said, "I'm as responsible as you are for Fallyn being shot."

Tony glanced at Grey as if begging for help, then slid his attention to Syd. "How so?"

"I asked her to help me out and take over for career day. She wouldn't have been there otherwise."

"And I decoded the fucking video," Dani said. "Which led her to Don Fox and Jordan knew that was going to backfire on her so maybe I'm responsible for her being shot."

Who the hell is this woman anyway? Syd offering up an opinion was one thing, but the kid with pink hair? He didn't even know her.

"Wait," Fallyn said. "I've got it. Heather knew there was someone in her office that was selling out the president, so maybe we should blame her. It's all my dead sister's fault when you get right down to it."

Tony held up a hand. "All right, all right. I get what you're doing, and I even halfway appreciate your enlightening, if completely illogical, way of spreading the blame around."

"I hear a 'but' coming," Fallyn said.

Tony frowned at her. "You don't understand."

"I do, actually, because I'm a control freak, too, but this obsession of yours isn't healthy. We all agree. So I'm not letting you out of this hospital room until you give it up. And until you admit we're good together. Yes, there will be some rocky moments. Everyone has those. We're alphas. Both of us. We'll work through it."

"Fuck that. This is not an intervention."

"Call it whatever you want, but you're not going anywhere until we work this out."

Finally Tony took a step toward her. "Why won't you leave me be?"

"Because, you idiot, I love you."

"Jesus Christ," Grey said. "We're going to be here all fucking night."

Syd patted his leg. "Looks like it. And I didn't bring popcorn."

Fallyn squeezed his hands and he felt the tremble. "Don't make me throw myself across the door to keep you here."

Tony looked all around the room. Grey, Syd, Dani and Fallyn. When had he entered this alternate reality and why couldn't he get back to *his* world. The one before Fallyn. "I..."

"You what?"

He let out the mother of all sighs. "Fine. Whatever. You want the truth? Here it is. I thought I was going to lose you. You took ten years off my life when you were lying there bleeding out."

"Let me get this straight," Fallyn's assistant—he guessed this was Dani—said. "You thought you were going to lose Fallyn and it wrecked you so hard, that now that she's alive and pouring out her heart to you, it's easier to walk away? That's screwed up, man."

Tony opened his mouth to say something, shut it. *Wait.* He couldn't be pissed. Couldn't be. "I actually followed that logic."

"That's not logic," Syd put in. "It's an observation. What Dani is trying to say so nicely is, you're being stupid."

The floor rippled under his feet. His universe shifted again. Fallyn wobbled a little, tipped slightly sideways, then forward.

Tony caught her, wrapped his arms around her. Steadied her. "Now will you please sit down?"

She clung to him, letting him gently guide her back into the wheelchair. "Syd's right. Stop being stupid. I need you."

He shook his head, touched her face, his fingers gliding along her jaw. He cupped her chin in his hand. "Are you doing this on purpose? Pretending to be this weak?"

"I wish. I should be in bed, but I have an idiot boyfriend who's making me do an intervention. And by golly, I may pass out, but I will not go back to bed willingly unless he carries me there himself and promises to stay with me."

"You are the most stubborn woman I know."

"Really?" Fallyn glanced over Tony's shoulder at Syd who gave her a thumbs up. "You know some pretty stubborn women."

The door burst open and Caroline and Mitch rushed in, stopping short when they found Dani, Fallyn, and Tony blocking their way.

"Hey," Caroline said, looking around at everybody. "What's going on?"

"Thank God." Grey pushed off the bed. "Gerard, take your woman back to her bed. Monroe, get me the hell out of here. These people are warped."

"You don't look so good," Mitch said to Fallyn. "What are you doing to her, Tony?"

"I'm not doing anything to her!" He stared into her eyes and shook his head in frustration. "But I'm about to."

"Just kiss her already," Grey said. "Then get the hell out of the way."

Tony smiled. "This is so fucked up."

"Should we maybe..." Caroline thumbed at the door behind her. "Come back?"

"No," everyone said.

"You're crazy, Fallyn Pasche," Tony said, "if you want me hanging around."

Her eyelids drooped, but she fought to open her eyes again. His girl. Always battling.

"I'm your brand of crazy, Tony Gerard, and you know it. You'll never be happy with normal anyway."

"I don't want normal. I want you. I just..."

"No qualifiers. Stop where you are. Quit while you're ahead and all that. Besides, it's about time you admitted that. You're a little slow on the uptake, you know that?"

"Yeah, but something tells me you'll help me with that."

Everyone laughed.

"Let's get you back to bed," Tony said. "You have a lot of healing to do before you conquer the world."

"Especially if you're taking Ryan Nicols on as a client," Dani chimed in.

"You're taking on the president's son as a client?" Grey barked.

Tony squeezed her arm. "Of course she is. That kid is going to need the best political fixer in the business to salvage his reputation as an ace airman after the press gets done with him and his father."

Fallyn grinned at him. "He might need a protection detail, too, and not the Secret Service guys. They're loyal to his dad. He won't feel comfortable with them."

Grey straightened to his full height and glared at Fallyn. Yep, definitely feeling better. "Are you poaching my employee?"

"Technically, I haven't signed up for anything long term with the Justice Team," Tony said. "I'm still an employee of the Court."

"You're not going back to the Supreme Court." Grey sounded pretty sure of himself. "We'll iron out the details of your employment with the Justice Team first thing tomorrow morning."

"Don't sign anything until you read my offer first," Fallyn said, sending Grey her best *don't mess with me* face, which was fairly comical considering she was having trouble standing.

"Seriously?" Grey said.

"Damn straight," Fallyn answered. "I'm tired of contracting out for security services for clients who need it. Tony's top notch, just the type of guy I can use on my staff here in my new DC office, and I can offer him three times the salary you can."

Mitch whistled under his breath. "You got any openings for former FBI agents? I can work security."

Caroline slapped his arm.

Tony reached down and oh, so carefully, scooped Fallyn up into his arms. No doubt, this woman would kill him. "Okay, badass, let's call it a day and get you back to bed."

She curled into him and his chest got tight. He inhaled and the flood of warm air shattered the tension.

They could do this. Even if it got crazy once in a while, they were both too stubborn to give up. What he had now? Hope. And wasn't that an interesting development.

With her, he was home. They'd both lost a lot in their lifetimes, but now they had each other.

He skirted past Mitch and Caroline and carried her down the hall. Nurses smiled, Dani walked beside them.

"You can go, now, Dani." Fallyn yawned into Tony's shoulder. "I'm in good hands."

Dani glared up at Tony. "You sure about that, boss?"

Tony rolled his eyes.

"I'm sure," Fallyn said.

Dani sighed, then waved and took off.

Inside her room, Tony laid her down carefully in the bed. "A DC office, huh?"

"I need to stay close to you. Seems like a good idea."

"You're opening a satellite office here in DC so you can stay close to me?"

"Of course, you big dummy. I have plenty of clients here and I want to keep an eye on Dad, but the real reason I'm expanding my business is to be close to you."

He brushed hair from her face and sat on the edge of the bed, leaning over her. "You're a force, you know that?"

"I actually have no idea how much Grey will offer to pay you, but you should join his team. They need you more than I do. I just wanted to make sure he appreciated your worth."

Tony chuckled. "I'm supposed to be looking out for you, remember?"

"How about we look out for each other?"

He leaned down and kissed her, slow and gentle. "I'm game if you are."

"I've been game since the first morning you entered my life."

"Good, cuz if you're taking on Ryan Nicols as a client, you're going to need as much protection as he is when the shit hits the fan."

She pulled Tony down into the bed next to her and scooted over to make room for him. "You're right. Why didn't I think of that? I'll definitely need 24/7 security."

"Yep, all day and all night." He fumbled at putting an arm around her, trying to find a safe place with all her bandages. Finally, he gave up and simply nuzzled her earlobe. "Think you can handle me?"

She nestled into him.

Home.

"I can't tell you how much I'm looking forward to it. I feel safer already. I love you, Tony."

"I love you, too, Fallyn. You believe I saved you, but honey, you saved me. Believe it. You're stuck now. I'm never leaving your side." He kissed her forehead. "Get some sleep. We have a big day tomorrow and a whole lifetime of craziness ahead of us. You're going to need your energy."

Fallyn closed her eyes and smiled. Following her lead, Tony rested his head back and closed his eyes. Sleep. Finally. It wasn't his bed, but with Fallyn next to him, it was where he belonged.

Keep the adventure going!

Thank you for reading *Protecting Justice*. If you'd like more of the Justice Team Series, check out *Missing Justice*.

A rising star at the FBI, Taylor Sinclair has a perfect close rate on cold cases. When the bones of a senator's murdered wife turn up seven years after her kidnapping, the case lands on Taylor's desk, putting her in the

crosshairs of the media—and the killer. Success will solidify her career at the Bureau, but a provocative one-night stand with cocky PI Matt "Mad Dog" Stephens could ruin it.

Matt's on the hunt for the killer as well, along with the senator's still-missing child, and believes joining forces with Taylor will get them both the answers they need. He's determined to get the sexy agent to work with him—in and out of the bedroom—but Taylor is convinced the senator is a murderer. Matt is just as certain he's innocent.

With a child's life on the line, Matt and Taylor must plunge into the world of undercover ops as they battle a dangerous attraction that could prove fatal to them both.

Click here to download *Missing Justice*.

READY FOR YOUR NEXT JT ADVENTURE?

o undercover with Matt and Taylor in *Missing Justice*

Chapter 1

Cold case investigators really should stay away from karaoke machines and alcohol. The combo was criminal.

Especially when fellow investigators from the FBI, AISOCC, and dozens of experts from cold case units around the country were gathered together in the same bar listening.

Taylor Sinclair scanned the room as she swished the two fingers of scotch around in her glass. The country's top minds in forensics, law, behavioral science, and medicine had gathered together this weekend in DC to share the latest in solving cold cases, and yet, a handful of them were now killing off brain cells and possible career advancement opportunities while belting out Prince songs in the wrong key.

The woman on stage singing *I Wanna Be Your Lover* with a bright orange drink in one hand and the microphone in the other hit a high note—flat, of course—and Taylor flinched.

Her bar buddy didn't seem to notice as he jabbered on beside her, nursing a light beer. A journalist who'd applied to the American Investigative Society of Cold Cases but had been rejected, Tom—or was it Ted?—explained his lifelong obsession with missing persons. She understood the passion; it was hers too.

But she also knew why AISOCC had turned him down for their Academia Committee. They only accepted people with the credentials and motives to fulfill their mission of assisting law enforcement professionals with solving cold cases. Tom/Ted might have the passion, but he didn't have the experience, even though he was boasting about his professional skills in the hopes of wooing her to his room upstairs.

He was sort of handsome in that academic way—wire-rimmed glasses, bow tie, and a large vocabulary—but she'd sworn off sex, and alcohol, for the weekend.

At least she hadn't failed on both counts. The scotch had been a prop to help overcome her social awkwardness. To make her seem friendly and normal. Approachable.

Like that's ever going to happen. Who was she kidding? Put her to work on a case and she was a rock star, but in a social situation where she had to make small talk and pretend interest in drunk people's lives? Failure with a capital F.

It was enough to make her drink.

Which she was, thank you very much.

Sex, though, no way. Out of the question. The last thing she needed was to hook up with some random conference attendee and risk the fallout from that. Being the best of the best required keeping her nose clean in public—Meredith's orders. Her boss ran a tight ship and had no patience for agents who let their personal affairs interfere with their careers.

No problem there. Taylor had no personal life.

Even if she did need alcohol to numb herself to the stares and advice from all the experts dying to 'help' her find Isabel.

Like Leo.

Cutting her eyes to the huddle of three men at the bar on her right, she could practically feel the power oozing off Leo Wellington. The FBI profiler was six feet of confidence, nerve, and a close record that made Taylor green with envy. Only last month, he'd helped her and her cold case team nail the Coffin serial killer, a man who had victims he'd buried alive stretching back thirty years. She had to admit, working with Leo had been no hardship. The man profiled killers and other high-profile criminals with the ease and accuracy Taylor's one-time mentor had until he'd gotten himself fired from the FBI.

She missed Grey. A lot. She'd learned so much from him in the few short months they'd worked together. Before he'd shredded his career.

Now she had Leo. Amazingly proficient and incredibly sexy. Listening to him on the Offender Profiles and Crime Scene Assessment panel at the conference that afternoon, Taylor had toyed with the idea of making Leo Wellington her next *un*official case. One that involved one-on-one, in-depth investigation...and a lot fewer clothes.

He was her perfect match—smart, driven, successful. Sex with Leo and a bottle of scotch—the perfect cocktail to kill the anxiety humming under her skin over this conference.

Leo had his back to her, casually leaning on the bar and close enough for her to touch. He smelled like a warm day at the beach all sun and water. He smelled like power.

Taylor looked away, shaking her head to rid it of the thoughts tumbling around in her brain. She wasn't about to shred her career like Grey, and Leo, *the shark*, wasn't about to play nice. He'd use her, like he did everyone else, and take her team away from her if she wasn't careful.

No way in hell. No one was worth that.

Her cold case team had gained national media attention with their success rate. Nothing played on the nightly news as sweetly as missing kids being found alive and reunited with their families. Taylor and her team had returned three this year alone. *Three kids still alive*, and by God, she intended to find more.

The statistics were daunting, but she wouldn't stop until she found every kid who'd disappeared, dead or alive, and gave their families closure.

She owed it to Isabel. If only Isabel were still alive.

Maybe she is. Maybe she's still out there, waiting for me to find her.

Taylor knocked back the last of the liquid in her glass along with the familiar twinge of guilt over Isabel.

"Agent Sinclair." Leo turned, suddenly at her elbow. "Nice to see you. My friends and I were just discussing your case."

Agent Sinclair? She'd thought they were on a first-name basis after working so closely together only last month. "Enjoyed your panel today, Leo. Your insights on the Yvonne Coleman case were fascinating." Leo's friends eyed her with equal parts eagerness and smugness. She recognized both of them from the same panel. "Exactly which case of mine were you reviewing?"

He looked bemused. "Why, your sister's case, of course. Today is the anniversary of—"

Another screech echoed through the bar, courtesy of the Prince wanna-be, and Taylor set her glass on the bar a little too hard. Everybody was a flippin' expert. Everybody had heard about poor Taylor Sinclair and the hunt for her missing sister. Everyone had a goddamn theory and a profile on the abductor.

As if the Bureau's lead cold case investigator hadn't gone over every possible aspect of the case a million times already, eviscerating her heart each and every time.

"Of course. Silly me." Taylor pasted on a fake smile and used her equally fake cheery voice. "Why don't you grab those two agents from Vermont? They're over there at that table. You all can have fun discussing your meaningless theories while I go gag myself."

Tom/Ted raised his brows as Leo sputtered something she didn't hear.

Unfortunately, the Bureau hadn't sprung for any of her teammates to accompany her to the conference. She needed a wingman— or another drink—but there was no one else in the vicinity she was remotely interested in talking to, and even liquor couldn't dull the ice in her chest. She should just call it a night. Try to sleep.

As if.

"I used to like that song," a deep male voice said from behind her.

One distraction coming up.

"Me, too," she said, hoping the man matched the voice as she pivoted to take a peek.

And, *ho-boy*, he was as sexy as that deep voice, but dammit, why did it have to be *him*?

Even in her heels, she had to look up. There she saw blue eyes so vivid in the subpar lighting they nearly blinded her. The smile wasn't bad either. A little crooked, with a couple days worth of beard growth on the jawline, but it matched the messy hair and made his eyes crinkle good-naturedly in the corners.

"Matt Stephens," she said. "What a surprise." *Not.*

Matt "Mad Dog" Stephens looked pleased that she remembered his name. Hard not to when he'd stolen a case out from under her a year ago. Hard not to remember those intense, sky-blue eyes and that crooked smile that irritated the crap out of her.

"Special Agent Taylor Sinclair." The way he rolled her name off his tongue made it sound like he was sucking on a piece of sweet candy. "I didn't take you for a Prince fan."

The karaoke had mercifully stopped and someone hit the juke-box, a Rhianna song kicking in.

Taylor was about to blow Matt off even though he was cute and kind of charming, because no way was she cavorting with the enemy. But then, from the corner of her eye, she noticed Leo and his friends staring at her with *that* look. The one people used for *poor Taylor Sinclair*, sister of an abducted girl and from a broken family.

Show them you're fine. Better than fine.

She gave Matt a flirty smile and playfully punched his arm like they were buddies. *Hello, new wingman.* "Why wouldn't I be a Prince fan? That's practically sacrilegious or unpatriotic, or something, isn't it?"

"I've been trying to talk to you all day," he said, flashing that infectious, quirky smile again.

She fought to keep her lips from mirroring his. "Why?"

"Duh. You're the brainiest chick here. Your close rate makes me a huge fanboy. Plus, I'm not one to ignore beautiful women. Why wouldn't I want to talk to you?"

Damn, he was cute. A liar, but a cute one. "Yeah, so you can steal my cases."

His eyes grew serious. "Look, I know you think I stole the Riley Miller case, but the FBI was limited in what it could do. I have more..."—he shrugged—"resources."

Illegal ones. "So you're feeling guilty. That's good. You can buy me a fresh drink."

He grinned and took her hand, stroking his thumb over her palm. "How about a dance instead?"

She should pull her hand back. "Oh, hell, no. I don't dance with the enemy."

He grabbed her hand again, tickled the palm. "But you'd drink with him?"

Her turn to grin, the ice in her chest melting a smidgen. "Depends on whether he provides top-shelf sustenance."

They stared at each other for a long moment and something changed between them. Something hot and sexy that warmed Taylor's blood even more than the scotch she'd consumed listening to Tom/Ted.

What was she doing flirting with Mad Dog Stephens?

Down girl. She glanced away, toward the bar.

Leo and friends were still watching, still talking. She could tell by the way they kept sizing her up that they were discussing Isabel.

God! Enough. Like she wasn't already struggling to not let pain control every moment of her life without everyone always trying to fix her. If she believed that any or all of the experts here tonight could actually find Isabel, she would have been the first one to huddle up with them and explore their theories. But she'd heard them all, tried all the angles, got her hopes up with every new expert who came along and wanted to analyze the case. She would never give up looking for her sister, that was a given. If only hoping for something made it real.

Mad Dog Stephens tugged on her hand. "Taylor?"

She sighed, giving him her attention again and saw a touch of concern behind his smoldering eyes. Men like Stephens—unpredictable and mouthy—were generally a handful, but she liked a challenge on occasion, and it had been one hell of a dry spell. Plus, he wasn't FBI. He couldn't screw up her career or take her team away from her.

Your odds are looking up, wingman. At least he was an alternative to the scotch for now.

She withdrew her hand from his gentle grip and took a step closer to him, invading his personal space. Would he run when she moved in for the kill or stand his ground?

"Why are you here at the conference, Matt?" She ran a hand over his tie. "Are you looking to steal another of my cases? Why did you leave the police department? Who are you working for now, or did you go out on your own?"

"Jeez, Sinclair." He frowned, but didn't back away. Undaunted by her provocation, he moved closer, his chest grazing her nipples. His eyes searched hers and his voice lowered a notch. "What is this, an interrogation? If so, why don't we take it somewhere more...private?"

Hot damn. He wasn't running. She stood her ground, not letting him intimidate her. She liked—no, *loved*—his cockiness. "I don't trust you, Mad Dog."

"Dance with me and I'll answer all of your questions." He ran a finger over his left chest area. "Cross my heart."

A negotiator. Even better. She could get what she wanted and leave him happy too.

Challenge danced in those blue peepers and she sighed. Men came onto her all the time, but few gave her pause.

Funny, this one did.

Her phone buzzed, the ringtone she knew all too well and avoided skillfully.

"Do you need to take that?" Matt asked.

"Nah, it's nothing." *Just my mother.* And wasn't that exactly what she needed on top of everything else tonight? Her mother calling to sob about Isabel. Perfect.

Pain pinched her heart. *Sorry, Mom. I just can't tonight.* She had enough demons for both of them.

I may need that bottle of scotch after all.

But then she looked into Matt's eyes. He might be the only numbing agent she needed tonight in order to forget about the significance of today.

With all the old shit the conference had brought up, the one thing she didn't want was to be alone with the memories of Isabel. No way she could face that cold, sterile hotel room tonight.

She tapped her foot for a moment. "One dance," she agreed.

The challenge in Matt's eyes morphed into self-assured confidence. If possible, his smile grew even wider. "You won't be sorry."

"*You* will be," she said, as she let him lead her to the floor. "I have two left feet."

The song was pop with a fast tempo and Taylor had no rhythm on a good day. Luckily, her new wingman was a skilled dancer and she had enough alcohol in her system to make her limbs loose. Matt twirled her out, brought her in close, guided her through a sexy bump and grind. She grew dizzy trying to keep up with him, but the light graze of his fingers on her shoulders, hips, and lower back, kept her moving in time with the beat and loving it. At one point, she laughed just because it felt so damn good.

Meanwhile, Leo watched, a subtle tick under his left eye.

Eat your heart out, Wellington. I am not discussing Isabel's case with you.

Not tonight. Not ever.

As Matt spun her across the floor again, a bubbling sensation rose up from her chest into her throat.

My God, I'm having fun.

Fun wasn't in her vocabulary. Not since *that* night.

Damn. She needed a good weekend fling. To burn off the stress of her day job. To refocus her energies on her caseload. *Might not be a bad idea to make sure all the parts down there still work after this latest dry spell.*

But mostly, she needed to forget for a few minutes about the ice in her chest.

Because tonight was the anniversary of her little sister's kidnapping.

She'd hoped the conference could make her forget, but that was stupid. She'd known better, and yet had hoped she could drown herself in work. Now...

The song ended, and out of breath, Taylor clung to Matt. Another song started—this one slow and sexy—and he raised a single brow.

An invitation to stay on the dance floor.

In the middle of the other couples now gluing their bodies to each other, Taylor held his gaze. "Who are you working for, Matt?"

"Schock Investigations," he said, and then pulled her close and started rocking her body to the slow tune.

"Private investigations, huh?" She liked the way he felt against her. Solid, strong. Competent. "I've heard of them. They work a lot of cold cases, don't they?"

"It's our specialty."

"That's why you're here."

His eyes danced with humor. "You were worried I was only here to stalk you?"

He wanted information on some missing persons case, no doubt, but she gave him credit for trying to seduce her first. "Anyone who stalks me is going to get more than he bargained for."

She believed in giving fair warning.

"Sounds like fun." One of his hands went to her lower back and rubbed a thumb through her silk blouse over the sensitive flesh there. Leaning forward, he sang softly in her ear, *"I wanna be your stalker,"* to the Prince tune.

And damn, if he didn't hit the notes perfectly.

A man who could sing and dance.

My lucky night.

Three dances later, Leo and the other experts in the room were a distant memory as Matt pressed her up against the door of her hotel room while she tried to get the keycard into the lock. His lips nibbled at her earlobe as his hands cupped her ass.

"Will you stop for a second and let me unlock the door?" Taylor chided, but she was laughing. She didn't really want him to stop, but letting him molest her in the very public hallway wasn't professional.

"Here, let me do it." He snatched the card from her hand.

In. Out. Boom. The stupid button went green, Matt hit the door handle, and they practically fell into the room.

"I'm not used to sleeping with the enemy," she told him, flipping on a light as he went to work stripping off her white, button-down shirt.

"I returned Riley Miller to her mother but I'm a bad guy in your book?" He unzipped her pencil skirt, not looking the least bit chastised. "Something about that seems wrong, Agent Sinclair."

The image of the eleven-year-old girl reuniting with her mom after six years of being held captive by her estranged, drug-dealing father filled Taylor's memory. It had been her first case with the FBI's missing persons unit and they'd never been able to solve it. Six years later, Taylor had had the file in her desk drawer, one of the cases she'd still been trying to close when Matt Stephens had come along and done it for her.

He was a hero and the press loved his boy-next-door looks and cavalier attitude. She could only imagine the number of women who had thrown themselves at him after that.

But those women weren't here and she was. *Good for me!*

Having a weekend fling with him wasn't the best idea, but it wasn't the worst either. He was a playboy and playboys didn't want commitment—that worked for her. Her job was everything.

"I think you owe me some mind-blowing sex in order to make it up to me," Taylor said, kicking off her shoes.

Matt let her skirt drop and then he shoved her unbuttoned shirt off her shoulders. For a moment, he stood still, his eyes raking over her from head to toe.

Taylor sucked in a breath, pulling in her abdomen at the same time. Total vanity, but she couldn't help the reaction. She wanted the man in front of her to continue thinking she was the brainiest, sexiest woman in the place.

He reached out and touched the satin of her bra, brushing his knuckles against her tight nipples and whistling softly. "You are stunning, Agent Sinclair."

Taylor sat on the bed and reached for the zipper of his slacks. "Bring it on, Mad Dog."

Ringing phone.

Matt opened his eyes to a ray of light slipping through the curtains. He stared at the back of a very attractive blonde head, but focused on the sound of a ringing cell phone.

Not his.

Good. Because his extremely engorged dick had plans that didn't include phones.

He might do some talking, but it wouldn't be on the phone.

He locked one leg over Taylor and tightened his arm around her waist. Jesus. They'd slept like this? All wrapped up? When it came to getting a solid night's rest, being a decent sized guy, he needed space. A lot of it. Particularly in crappy hotel beds.

Taylor's arm shot out, her hand blindly searching for the still-ringing phone on the bedside table. The glare of the digital clock announced the time to be 6:43.

"Ignore it," he croaked.

"Can't. Boss's ringtone."

"Then I'd definitely ignore it."

He bit the back of her shoulder, nudged closer, bringing that badass erection flush against the curve of her ass, leaving no doubt what he—and it—had on their minds.

"That's a healthy beast you're sporting there, Mad Dog. Now shut up while I talk to my boss."

At that, he laughed. This woman. From the first day he'd met her, back when he'd supposedly *stolen* her case, he'd had a thing for her.

An undefinable yearning that left him wanting to...possess. And that was also unusual. Women weren't objects to own. He'd lectured his buddies on this fact for years, but at thirty-three, he'd suddenly found a woman who challenged, cajoled, and rattled him enough that he'd fantasized about pinning her to a mattress and bringing a smile to her face.

Which he'd done three times last night. *Here's hoping for a fourth.*

She cleared her throat and poked at the phone. "Good morning, Mer."

Matt busied himself by pulling her closer and nibbling on the back of her shoulder blade. Was he being an idiot? Sure. But Taylor getting a call before seven a.m. meant something was cooking and being the dedicated civil servant she was, she'd look to hightail it from this bed before he had the chance to put that fourth smile on her face.

The nibbling? Hopefully she'd see it as the prelude to what could be a fantastic morning.

"Yes," she said. "I understand. I'll be there."

Matt stopped nibbling. Dammit.

She tossed the phone on the nightstand. "I have to go."

"Okay."

But he didn't loosen his hold. He did abandon his nibbling campaign, opting for a full attack of licking.

She let out a soft moan and his hard-on became painful. How many times had she moaned like that last night? When he was so deep inside her and still wanted more.

"Matt, I can't. I have to—"

"Shh," he said, sliding his hand up and cupping her breast. "We should start the day off right."

She arched her back, pressing her nipple into his palm. "You are so evil."

"I know. If you want, we can make this a quick one. Or," he swirled his tongue over her shoulder again. "We can go slow. Really slow. Your call, Sinclair."

All he knew was he wanted her. Again. Wanted her under him,

with the morning sun cracking through that curtain so he could see her hair fanning across the pillow, see her eyes go wild when he made her moan.

"I...can't," she said. "I caught a case."

A case. A shot of envy whipped him. The woman was a machine when it came to solving cold cases, especially those involving missing children, and lately her team had been racking up some serious close rates. What drove her, he couldn't be completely sure, but suspected. Make no mistake, you didn't get that good at your job without some serious motivation. He understood that on an emotional level most couldn't.

And he wanted to know what this case was. He'd find out. After last night, he intended on seeing a whole lot more of Taylor.

All he had to do was get her to agree.

Starting right now. He nudged even closer, this time licking that spot on her neck he'd accidentally discovered during round two.

"I want you," he said.

She reached back, wrapped her hand around his dick and squeezed, making his eyes nearly explode from his head. "I know," she said.

Closing his eyes, he dropped his head back and his body started to hum. The motion of her hand made his limbs go slack and oh, boy, she was gonna get it.

The mattress shifted. Hopefully she was getting onto her back where he'd do incredible things to her. His mind roared and just as he opened his eyes, ready to pounce, she let go, ripped the sheet off and jumped from the bed.

What the fuck?

She bit her lip, hiding a smug smile and—damn—he should have seen that coming. The scheming witch. She'd duped him. Made him think they'd have some nice, hot, goodbye-sex so he'd loosen his hold on her. And then she slipped away.

She stood beside the bed, staring down at his chest—she liked it. She'd told him so a hundred times last night.

"Taylor," he said, "that wasn't nice." He held one hand out. "Come back to bed. Let me make you scream."

Her eyes flashed, but she shook her head. "No, but I'll take a raincheck."

Freaking career girls. A raincheck. He wanted more than one, no doubt about it. "Seriously? You're going to leave me like this? I'm hard as a brick."

She laughed as she tied her hair into a messy knot on top of her head. The movement made her tits bounce and his eyes followed the motion of those perfect breasts he'd damn near devoured all night. She leaned over him, kissed him quick and leapt back before he could pull her on top of him.

"This is an important case, Mad Dog. Otherwise I'd happily fuck you all morning and maybe into the afternoon."

Damn, that mouth. She'd been talking filth all night. He didn't care one way or the other. Some women used it as a tool to amp up the sex. He never minded, but he also didn't need it. Her? All that hot nastiness coming from a pulled-together woman who wore traditional suits and a pair of diamond earrings that probably cost more than his entire college career? Total turn-on.

"Now you're just making it worse," he said. "How about I hop in the shower with you?"

She gathered up a bra and what looked like a red thong—*Jesus, help me*—from her suitcase and set it on the bed.

"No," she said. "You're too much of a distraction."

"That's good."

"Not when I have a case to work." She went to the closet, pulled one of her FBI-wear pantsuits out. "I'd love to do this again with you, but we'll have to set some boundaries. Mainly you not stealing my cases."

And here we go. "Once again, I did *not* steal your case. I beat you to solving it. That's all."

Because that's what good investigators did. They solved cases. No matter who it supposedly belonged to. And he didn't allow himself to be lured from the PD homicide squad into the private sector to not solve them.

"Right," she said. "Whatever. But if you want a replay of last night, we need to come to an agreement. No sharing information about cases. No crossing lines. No work talk, period."

"Boy," he said, "you sure know how to kill a mood."

She met his gaze, then let it slide down his body. "You are a tempting man, Matt, but my job is my life. This?" She waggled a finger between them. "This could have serious complications."

As if he wanted to screw up his own career? Plus, he didn't like what she was implying about his work ethic. "Complications. Sure. Got it."

He sat up, put his feet on the floor and snagged his boxers from the lampshade. The lampshade? Whatever.

She cocked her head as he jammed his legs into his shorts. "Oh, so now you're mad?"

"Mad? No. I'm absorbing the rules you've set. Taking it all in." He pulled on his pants, shrugged into his shirt, walked to her, and kissed her hard with plenty of tongue. "Thanks for clarifying, Special Agent Sinclair. Call me when you need to get *fucked* again."

Was he being pissy? Damned straight. They'd had a great night and suddenly she was accusing him of...what? Some kind of investigator espionage? Like he'd deliberately try to steal her cases.

Well, fuck that.

"Matt, come on."

He held up a hand. "It's all good. You've outlined the parameters of what you feel our relationship should be. Got it. Maybe you could have consulted with me first, but hey, why should we have to talk, right? I'll just come on by, toss you on the bed and bang away. Works for me."

"That's not what I meant."

Her phone rang again. Same ringtone. Matt shook his head. "Get your phone, Taylor. It's your boss again. If you want a replay, you know where to find me."

Grab your copy of *Missing Justice*.

WANT MORE OF SEXY THRILLERS?

The Justice Team Series

Stealing Justice

Cheating Justice

Holiday Justice

Exposing Justice

Undercover Justice

Protecting Justice

Missing Justice

Defending Justice

SCHOCK SISTERS MYSTERY SERIES

1st Shock

2nd Strike

3rd Tango

MORE BY ADRIENNE GIORDANO

DEEP COVER SERIES

Crossing Lines

PRIVATE PROTECTORS SERIES

Risking Trust

Man Law

Negotiating Point

A Just Deception

Relentless Pursuit

Opposing Forces

THE LUCIE RIZZO MYSTERY SERIES

Dog Collar Crime

Knocked Off

Limbo (novella)

Boosted

Whacked

Cooked

Incognito

The Lucie Rizzo Mystery Series Box Set 1

The Lucie Rizzo Mystery Series Box Set 2

The Lucie Rizzo Mystery Series Box Set 3

THE ROSE TRUDEAU MYSTERY SERIES

Into The Fire

HARLEQUIN INTRIGUES

The Prosecutor

The Defender

The Marshal

The Detective

The Rebel

JUSTIFIABLE CAUSE SERIES

The Chase

The Evasion

The Capture

CASINO FORTUNA SERIES

Deadly Odds

JUSTICE SERIES w/MISTY EVANS

Stealing Justice

Cheating Justice

Holiday Justice

Exposing Justice

Undercover Justice

Protecting Justice

Missing Justice

Defending Justice

SCHOCK SISTERS MYSTERY SERIES w/MISTY EVANS

1st Shock

2nd Strike

3rd Tango

MORE BY MISTY EVANS

SEALs of Shadow Force Series

Fatal Truth

Fatal Honor

Fatal Courage

Fatal Love

Fatal Vision

Fatal Thrill

Risk

SEALS of Shadow Force Series: Spy Division

Man Hunt

Man Killer

Man Down

The SCVC Taskforce Series

Deadly Pursuit

Deadly Deception

Deadly Force

Deadly Intent

Deadly Affair, A SCVC Taskforce novella

Deadly Attraction

Deadly Secrets

Deadly Holiday, A SCVC Taskforce novella

Deadly Target

Deadly Rescue

Deadly Bounty

Deadly Betrayal

Deadly Threat

The Super Agent Series

Operation Sheba

Operation Paris

Operation Proof of Life

Operation Lost Princess

Operation Ambush

Operation Christmas Contraband

Operation Sleeping With the Enemy

The Justice Team Series (with Adrienne Giordano)

Stealing Justice

Cheating Justice

Holiday Justice

Exposing Justice

Undercover Justice

Protecting Justice

Missing Justice

Defending Justice

ACKNOWLEDGMENTS

Adrienne and Misty would like to thank all of our Justice Team fans for being so loyal! We have an absolute blast writing these books and pushing the literary limits with our characters. It's nice to know you love our crazy characters as much as we do!

For this story in particular, we'd like to extend our gratitude to Karen Overbey-Gallegos for helping with Tony's tattoo design and Brandi Knight-Prazak for the medical advice on Grey's injuries.

A special shout-out to our amazing fan, Heather Machel, for allowing us to name a character after her!

If you'd like to have a future Justice Team character named after you, and participate in Adrienne's and Misty's street teams, be sure to check out the About the Authors at the end of the book.

ABOUT ADRIENNE

 **Adrienne Giordano is a *USA Today* best-selling author** of over forty romantic suspense and mystery novels. She is a Jersey girl at heart, but now lives in the Midwest with her ultimate supporter of a husband, sports-obsessed son and Elliot, a snuggle-happy rescue. Having grown up near the ocean, Adrienne enjoys paddleboarding, a nice float in a kayak and lounging on the beach with a good book.

For more information on Adrienne's books, please visit www.AdrienneGiordano.com. Adrienne can also be found on Facebook at http://www.facebook.com/AdrienneGiordanoAuthor, Twitter at http://twitter.com/AdriennGiordano and Goodreads at http://www.goodreads.com/AdrienneGiordano.

Don't miss a new release! Sign up for Adrienne's new release newsletter!

ABOUT MISTY

USA TODAY Bestselling Author Misty Evans has published over seventy-five novels and writes romantic suspense, urban fantasy, and paranormal romance. Under her pen name, Nyx Halliwell, she also writes cozy mysteries.

When not reading or writing, she embraces her inner gypsy and loves music, movies, and hanging out with her husband, twin sons, and three spoiled puppies. She's a crafter at heart and has far too many projects to finish.

Don't want to miss a single adventure? Visit www.mistyevansbooks.com to find out ALL the news!

Check out her humorous pen name Nyx Halliwell for magical mysteries https://www.nyxhalliwell.com .

www.ingramcontent.com/pod-product-compliance
Lightning Source LLC
Chambersburg PA
CBHW060404260626
47160CB00006B/2428